The Atlantic Street Murder

The Atlantic Street Murder

Detective Watters Mysteries Book 2

Malcolm Archibald

FOR CATHY

Prelude

'March, march, march and die of thirst.' Private Costello flapped a hand in a futile attempt to clear some of the dust that clouded around the column of British infantry. 'I didn't join the army to wear my feet out.'

'Then, why did you join?' Private Williams asked.

'Because I was bloody starving,' Costello said.

'Well, then,' Williams stumbled, swore, and recovered, 'you're not starving now, so stop grousing.'

'Aye, stop grousing, you bastard.' Private Doyle shifted his Brown Bess musket to ease the pressure on his shoulder. 'You should thank Her Majesty for sending you to sunny India, away from sodden Donegal, where even the ducks hide from the rain.'

'If we had found ducks, we would have eaten them, you Connaught bugger,' Costello said, 'feathers, beaks, and all.'

'Ducks have bills, not beaks,' Williams said. 'You Paddies can't even speak the Queen's English.'

'No?' Costello's attempt to spit failed. 'I bet her bloody Majesty doesn't know a single word of Irish. Not even the first one we all learn.'

'What would that be?' Williams asked.

'Starvation,' Costello said.

'That's an English word,' Williams said.

1

'Is it, indeed?' Doyle did not hide the bitterness from his voice. 'In Ireland, we've learned the true meaning.'

'You're not in Ireland now,' Williams said. 'And the past is gone.'

'The past is with us always,' Costello said. 'It makes us what we are.'

'Bugger that,' Williams said. 'The past is done, and soldiers might not have a future. Live for the present, boys, look for a drink and hope for a willing woman.'

Private Gallagher, one file behind, laughed. 'That's the way, Williams! Drink and women are the only things that make life worth living.'

The men of the 113th Foot marched through heat that poured from a brassy sun to pound the Punjab plain. Footsore after three days of constant marching, the British infantry sweated and swore and scratched at the itch of hot dust and insect bites.

'How many Sikhs are there?' Costello swatted at the flies that tormented him.

'Too many,' Gallagher grunted.

'One Sikh is too bloody many,' Williams said.

'I heard there were thirty-five thousand,' Doyle swore as his foot caught on an exposed root, 'all nice and cosy behind their artillery.'

'Three to one in their favour, then,' Costello hitched up his trousers. 'Exactly the odds Paddy Gough likes.'

They marched on with the straps of their packs cutting grooves in their shoulders and the vultures circling far above, waiting for the fresh meat that armies always provided.

'Drink and women?' Doyle swore again. 'By Jesus, I'd settle for five minutes of Connaught rain and a sniff of a widow's shift.'

'There's a bloody jungle ahead,' Costello said. 'I'd wager a snyde farthing to a gold watch that the Sikh devils are inside, watching us right now.'

'We'll halt soon,' Gallagher said, 'old Gough won't have us advance into jungle-country with Johnny Sikh waiting for us.'

Costello hawked and spat on the ground. 'Gough? He's a bloody butcher. He's finishing England's job of killing off as many Irishmen as possible.'

Williams snorted. 'Don't talk nonsense. He's as bloody Irish as you can get, is old Paddy Gough.'

'He's working for England,' Kelly spoke from two files in the rear, 'like all the bloody officers.'

Williams blinked the sweat from his eyes. 'There's a village ahead, on this side of the jungle,' he tried to stop the incessant grousing, 'and there's a dirty great river as well. I can smell the water.'

'Water,' Costello sighed. 'Back in Donegal, I used to curse the rain. Now I would live under a storm and smile.'

'Listen, men!' Riding in front of the company, Major Snodgrass wheeled his white horse to face them. 'The Sikhs are entrenched in the village of Chillianwalla, beside the Jhelum River. They have a picket on that mound right ahead. You can't see them, but they are there, and we are going to destroy them.'

Gallagher grunted. 'We are going to destroy them.' He copied Snodgrass's voice, and the others laughed.

'You should have been an officer,' Costello said. 'You sound just like them.'

'Aye, or a circus clown, Mimic.' Doyle dodged Gallagher's halfhearted punch.

'My name is Gallagher!'

'Mimic suits you better.' Williams watched as the British artillery lined up behind them. 'Here we go, lads. There's no rest for the wicked.'

'For what Johnny Sikh is about to receive, make his God make him truly thankful,' Costello said. 'And there go the cavalry.'

The British guns barked in unison, arcing their fire high above the cavalry that advanced on the mound. The Sikh artillery replied, with smoke rising and the orange flare of the muzzle flashes obscenely pretty against the jungle. Bugles sounded clear and bright, followed by the twinkle of sunlight on a hundred sabres.

'They're going in for the charge!' Private Kelly, recently turned seventeen, sounded excited.

'That's the way, boys,' Williams approved as the Sikh artillery ceased fire and hurriedly withdrew when the British cavalry closed.

'If every battle was as easy as that I'd be a happy man,' Costello said.

'Johnny Sikh doesn't give up that easily,' Williams said. 'He's tough stuff.'

'Here's old Paddy now,' Kelly said. 'Raise a cheer for the General, boys!'

Distinctive in his white fighting coat, General Gough rode through the smoke and scattered bodies to the top of the mound. He raised his arms and pointed ahead.

'He's seen something,' Doyle said, 'look at him jumping around.'

'Maybe he saw that.' Costello pointed to the flank where a troop of Sikh horse artillery trotted from a patch of light scrub jungle. With hardly a pause they unlimbered and opened a stinging fire on the British skirmish line.

'Here we go then.' Costello ducked as a cannonball screamed overhead, to raise a fountain of dirt fifty yards away. 'Let's die for England's glory.'

'Queen and country,' Gallagher adopted the refined accent of an officer. 'Let's fight for the flag, my boys.' He stamped his boots on the hard ground and returned to the accent of his native Munster. 'Queen and country? Bugger them both.'

British and Sikhs exchanged artillery fire with cannonballs thumping and rolling among the British lines and screaming through the trees toward the Sikhs. After a quarter of an hour, it became apparent that the Sikhs far outgunned the British, and Gough gave smart orders to his officers. The words drifted along the line of scarlet uniformed soldiers passed down from generals to more junior officers to NCOs and eventually to the men.

'We're going in with the bayonet,' Costello said, 'bayonets against three times our number of the best soldiers in India, dug in behind heavy artillery. As I said, the general is finishing what England has started, killing off all the Irish.'

'He's killing off the English, too,' somebody shouted.

'And the Welsh,' Williams reminded.

With Sikh roundshot bouncing among their ranks, the British formed their battle lines. Brigadier Pope's cavalry was on the extreme right, then Gilbert's division, at the side of the 25th Native Infantry, the Queen's 24th Foot, then the 45th Native infantry, and finally Colin Campbell's infantry and Brigadier White's cavalry. In reserve marched the 113th Foot, so far untried in war.

'It's bloody suicide for these boys in front.' Costello slid free his bayonet and clicked it in place. 'Please, God, they don't expect us to do anything heroic.'

'We also serve who only stand and watch,' Gallagher said.

'I want to fight them!' Kelly was shaking with anticipation.

'Stand still you young fool,' Williams said. 'And keep your position.'

The sun was halfway down the western sky when Gough ordered the advance. Brigadier Mountain led the centre, with the 24th Foot the pivot around which the entire British line poised and the 113th still in support, fifty yards behind the main fighting line.

'We're marching right into the jungle,' Doyle said. He hitched up his belt, spat on his hands and hefted his musket. 'Come on you turbaned bastards; let's see how good you are.'

'I'd prefer to be fighting the bloody English,' Costello said.

'Maybe the next war.' Williams gave a lopsided grin.

'I'll start that one myself.' Costello ducked as a roundshot howled overhead.

Scrub jungle slowed the 113th as they advanced, with the colours unfurled before them, the symbol of regimental pride. The men struggled through the undergrowth, with sections losing formation and halting to re-form before they advanced, as roundshot screamed through their ranks or plunged from above. Men cursed their luck, their fate, their God, their lives and bloody John Company, the Honourable East India Company, whose expansionist ambition sent them here.

Eventually, disorganised, dismayed, and ragged, the 113th Foot emerged from the jungle onto a wide *maidan,* a large clearing, with the Sikh gunners directly opposite, half-seen through a curtain of white powder smoke.

'It's a bloody killing ground,' Costello said. 'They can't miss us.'

'Let's get the buggers.' Doyle reached for his ammunition pouch. 'Our turn now, you yellow turbaned bastards!'

As the British line reformed, the Sikh guns changed from round shot to grapeshot that scythed down the scarlet ranks. Men fell in pairs and groups, the lucky killed outright, the less fortunate mutilated, eviscerated, shorn of legs or arms to lie in screaming, writhing reminders of the obscenity of war.

'No firing!' the order came along the line, 'only use the bayonet!'

'Bloody told you,' Costello said. 'We're just targets. The officers are trying to kill the Irish off!'

'Charge them, 113th!'

Obeying the orders to only use the bayonet, the 113th advanced, taking horrendous casualties, falling in scores, cursing, grumbling, but never faltering and not considering a retreat. They might be Irish, Welsh, Scots or English but they were British infantry, damn you.

'Where's the supports?' Doyle looked to left and right. 'Where's the bloody sepoys?'

The order to charge had only reached the 113th. The native infantry on either flank remained in the jungle fringe watching as the Queen's infantry advanced alone.

'Vanished, that's where' Costello said. 'The bloody English have withdrawn them, so we get wiped out.'

'Charge!'

The 113th lowered their bayonets and ran right into the blazing, smoking muzzles of the Sikh guns. As the survivors closed ranks, the Sikh gunners drew their tulwars and met the British blade to blade.

Blinded by smoke, shocked by the carnage, Costello lunged forward. He saw Lieutenant Lloyd fight in fury until he fell before myriad cuts, while young Kelly bayoneted a gunner, grunting as he twisted the blade in the man's chest. Costello ducked under the swing of a ramrod, hacked upward with his bayonet and spitted the Sikh clean. He swore, gasped, and looked around.

'We've done it,' Costello shouted, 'We've breached their lines.'

The 113th triumph was short-lived. The Sikh artillery on either flank wheeled around and hammered the 113th with a vicious crossfire that felled more men.

'Withdraw,' somebody ordered, and the 113th, sullen, fighting, snarling, fell back in good order across the bodies of their dead and the screaming wounded.

'We'll be back for you boys,' Kelly promised. These were the last words he uttered as a twelve-pound cannonball hit him clean on the head. Costello thought it sounded like an explosion in a box of feathers, except it was brains and blood and shards of bone that sprayed his colleagues.

As the Sikhs perfected their aim, the retreat of the 113th became a rout; they ran back, ignoring the officers and sheltered in the jungle, licking their wounds as the Sikh army, still vastly outnumbering the British, fled the battlefield. Only when they were clear of the jungle did the 113th halt to lick their wounds and count their dead.

'Are we still alive?' Doyle tied a bloody bandage around his arm and drained the contents of his water bottle.

'You and I are,' Costello said. 'A cannonball took Kelly's head off. He was a fine Cork man too.'

Doyle swore. 'I've had enough of fighting England's bloody battles for them.'

'Me too,' Costello said quietly. 'The Sikhs will welcome two British soldiers, and then off we go.'

'Make that three,' Gallagher said. 'I'm coming too.'

'Where to?' Doyle asked, 'where will we go off to?'

'California,' Costello said. 'Where the gold is.'

Doyle slid his bayonet into its scabbard. 'We'll leave when it's dark,' he said.

Chapter One

London, December 1854

Whatever time of day and however many people crowded on board, London omnibuses always smelled of damp wool mingled with stale beer and sweat. Watters sat back in the uncomfortable seat, tipped his tall hat forward to conceal his eyes, tapped his cane on the floor, and surveyed the other passengers.

A fussy looking businessman hid behind his newspaper as if scared of meeting the eyes of the woman sitting opposite. She was an erect schoolmistress with a mouth like a closed gin-trap. There was a young clerk with a gilt-topped cane and a hole in his shoes; a shifty-looking woman whose face was a stranger to soap and water and whose hair sadly wanted brushing, and a strikingly handsome woman who looked out of place on the bus. Watters swivelled his eyes to watch the latter. He did not like enigmas. This woman dressed and sat like a gentlewoman yet lacked a gentlewoman's calm assurance. She had excellent eyes, Watters noticed absently, startlingly blue. Perhaps she merely had domestic worries. He shifted his gaze to the back of the bus where Detective Silver sat beside the stairs with a curl of dark hair escaping from his cloth cap and smoke trickling from the bowl of his pipe. The omnibus cad leaned out of the open back to check for potential passengers.

The omnibus eased to a stop. The businessman and shifty woman stepped off. A young woman in a grey cape stepped on, followed by a scarlet-coated sergeant, and then another young woman carrying a basket. The cad followed the soldier as he headed to the cheaper seats upstairs, while the two women entered the lower deck. Watters caught Silver's eye and gave a tiny nod.

The caped woman glanced around the bus with eyes as bright and predatory as any eagle, and then slid beside the gentlewoman, while the woman with the basket sat opposite, gave a broad smile, and began to talk.

'I'm sure I know your face. You and I have met before, haven't we?'

The gentlewoman shook her head as if she did not understand. When the first woman shifted slightly, the bottom of her cape slipped, seemingly accidentally, over the gentlewoman's lap. Watters caught Silver's eye again and touched the brim of his hat with two fingers. Silver removed his cap and tried to flatten his dark curls. The cad ran down the stairs and requested the fares as the bus rolled on.

'Well pet, you are so like a gal I know. I am sure we rode on this shillibeer together only last week.'

The gentlewoman smiled and shook her head. 'I have not ridden one before.' Her accent was foreign; French perhaps, Watters guessed. With this blasted Russian war bringing so many foreigners to London there was no telling what the woman was.

Watters barely saw the furtive movement, but he knew that the caped woman's hands were busy searching for loot. He knew the system: a pair of pickpockets boarded the bus and selected their victim, their gull. While one woman engaged the victim in conversation, the other slid her hand into his or her pocket to gather whatever she could. Watters allowed the caped woman a few moments to incriminate herself with substantial evidence before he moved in. He sighed; he had been sent to stop the spate of pickpocketing on the omnibuses, and after three days of travelling through the streets of London, he had the culprits or, more accurately, two of the culprits. In London this winter of 1854, there would be many more.

The woman with the basket leaned forward, holding the attention of the gentlewoman with her bright smile. 'Well pet, you are so like a gal I know, are you certain we have not met?'

'I am quite certain thank you.' The gentlewoman's attempt to shrink away was unsuccessful with the caped woman on one side and the impoverished clerk on the other.

'What the devil!' the driver shouted as the bus jerked to a sudden stop, ramming the passengers against each other. The cad staggered, swore, and put a hand on Silver for balance. Silver's pipe clattered to the floor and slithered along the centre of the bus until it came to a halt at the caped woman's left boot.

Watters glanced out the window and saw a group of laughing street Arabs cartwheeling across the road in front of the traffic as the smallest and most ragged held out a cap, more in hope than expectation.

'Come on sirs, we are starving, and it's nearly Christmas.' The young voice was clear above the muted curses of the driver.

The cad leaned outside and gave the urchins a mouthful of invective that bounced off their slum-hardened ears like hail from a plate glass window. One paused to stick out his tongue while the beggar tried again.

'Spare a penny for starving boys?' His voice was midway between a whine and a threat. A ragged man on the pavement plucked a farthing from his pocket and tossed it into the boy's cap.

'Get up there!' The driver flicked his reins, so his horses began to pull again, hauling the omnibus on its strictly timed route.

The caped woman stood up and straightened her clothing, 'I do apologise. I was thrown all over the place by that wretched driver.' She patted herself down.

Watters caught Silver's eye and nodded. Silver retrieved his pipe, tapped the glowing embers onto the floor and casually stood on them.

The caped woman began to move toward the exit at the rear of the bus, to find Silver blocking her path. 'Excuse me please, sir; I have to get off at the next stop.'

'We'll come with you,' Watters put his left hand on her shoulder, 'and your companion in theft will be accompanying us.'

The caped woman tried to shake herself free from Watters's grasp. 'I'm sure I don't know what you mean, sir.' Her voice had a similar mixed tone of whine and threat to that the juvenile beggars used. 'Who do you think you are to manhandle me?'

'I am Sergeant George Watters of Scotland Yard, and this is Detective William Silver.' Watters rapped his cane on the pickpocket's arm. 'Come along now.'

Immediately Silver took hold of the basket-woman, the omnibus again jerked to a stop. There was a loud curse from above, and the army sergeant tumbled down the stairs. As Silver moved instinctively to catch him, the caped woman suddenly pushed Watters and leapt off the bus.

'Here! Stop that woman!' Watters looked around. Oxford Street was a shifting mass of people, easy for the pickpocket to hide in. Swearing, Watters staggered as the omnibus pulled sharply into the flow of traffic. A hansom cab braked suddenly, and the driver of a brougham cracked his whip in frustration as the 'bus crossed his path. Watters saw a brief swirl of a grey cloak disappearing behind a woman with a large crinoline.

'You secure the other one, Silver,' he shouted, 'and get the victim's details.'

Without waiting for a response, he leapt from the omnibus and followed the grey cloak. 'Police! Stop that woman!'

A multitude of faces confronted him. Faces smiling, faces laughing, faces pinched with the cold, well-fed middle-class faces, unconcerned faces, red faces, plump faces, bespectacled faces, faced festooned with ribbons, faces gaunt with hardship but no faces that tried to help. Watters pushed a stout man aside and plunged on, grabbed at the fold of a grey cloak, missed, staggered as a large matron banged against him, and shouted again.

'Police! Stop thief!'

For a moment, Watters lost the grey-cloaked woman in the press of bodies, and then he saw her reflection in one of the windows. The plate-glass superimposed her image upon an array of silks and satins such as she would never be able to afford in her lifetime, and he felt an impromptu twist of sorrow that poverty should coexist with useless indulgence. However, the woman was a thief, and he had his duty to perform. Lunging forward, Watters swore as a nanny pushed a perambulator into his path; she threw him a look that should have killed him where he stood and rammed the clumsy machine over his left foot.

Watters winced, roared 'Stop, thief!' and pointed to the cloaked woman.

One man in a light-coloured top hat looked around at the fleeing woman and then averted his eyes and walked on, ignoring Watters as if he was not there.

The pickpocket did not turn around. Instead, she dashed across the road, jinking through the traffic to disappear behind a corpulent man carrying a parcel. Watters followed, swore as a passing brougham sprayed him with mud, and barged into the crowd.

A woman in a long coat squealed and dropped a pile of gaily wrapped parcels. Watters hesitated for only a second, grabbed hold of his hat that threatened to go the way of the packages and pushed on. The woman in the grey cloak had pulled ahead and now broke into a run, knocked down a child, and kept moving. The street Arabs were following, screeching with excitement until the woman turned around.

'That man there!' She pointed to Watters. 'He's a peeler come to lock you up. Stop him!'

'Stop, thief!' Watters yelled.

'Stop peeler!' one of the urchins parodied his words, with the rest echoing his words.

'Stop peeler! Stop peeler!'

They formed a solid mass in his path, dodging this way and that to slow him down. Watters roared at them to get out of the way, staggered as the tallest one tripped him, jumped over another attempted trip, swiped his cane at an imprudent backside, grunted with satisfaction at the resulting squeal, lengthened his stride and powered through the crowd.

Watters was so intent on following the pickpocket that he did not take notice of his surroundings until he realised he had passed through Holborn, Chancery Lane, and Fleet Street and was inside the rookery of Seven Dials. He was out of the brightly lit streets of prosperous London and running along a lane of crumbling brick houses with sagging roofs and blank-eyed windows that accused the world of bitter cruelty. The buildings on both sides of the passageway inclined forward so women leaning out of the windows could nearly shake hands with those opposite, while gaunt-faced girls with the eyes of old women pulled shawls over their heads and stared at Watters as he pounded past.

'It's a bloody peeler.' A woman stopped knitting to point wooden needles at him. 'I know that smell.'

Somebody from an upper window dropped a stoneware jar that shattered into a hundred pieces a yard behind Watters. He looked up and saw only a flapping washing line with patched linens side by side with stained woollen underwear.

'Stop that woman!' he shouted again, knowing that in this location, nobody would come to his aid.

'Murder!' The pickpocket gave a high-pitched scream. 'Help!'

In such a street, most of the inhabitants would watch a crime with either no concern or a professional interest in the criminal's technique. However, with the words following so close after the revelation that there was a peeler present, people rushed to block Watters from his quarry.

'Where are you going, bluebottle bastard?' The speaker was short, stout, and cocky with the shoulders of a stevedore.

'Police. Get out of my way.' Watters's attempt to push him aside was like blowing on a granite mountain.

'That's him, Joey. Kill him!' The pickpocket had stopped running and pushed to the front of the crowd that was forming around Watters. She smiled to him, 'not so brave now, are you, peeler?'

As Joey stepped closer and spread his arms, Watters feinted at his eyes and kicked evilly upward into his groin. When Joey crumpled in agony, Watters smashed a fist into his jaw.

'I am Sergeant Watters of the Yard,' he shouted, 'and you,' he grabbed at the pickpocket, 'are under arrest.'

The crowd which she had whistled up now proved the pickpocket's undoing as she could not run through the press. Watters's hand closed on the collar of her cloak. 'Come on you.'

'Don't let him take me!' the pickpocket screamed. 'Murder!'

Watters jerked back his head as her nails raked the air quarter of an inch from his eyes. He dragged her away, pushing through the mob.

'Let her be, peeler!' A tall female pushed to the front of the crowd. 'Go on, boys, get him!' Her accent was pure Cockney, but her face and hair would not have been out of place in Connacht.

Angry faces glared at him, men shouting threats, waving fists or cudgels. A woman thrust a poker at Watters's groin, and a gang of bare-foot boys screeched their hatred of the police.

'Move aside there!' Watters hauled his prisoner onward, swinging his cane to try and clear a path.

'Yes, let her be, you blue-devil bastard.' A group of men pushed in front of him. The yellow patch on the left elbow of the tallest contrasted with the stained brown flannel jacket while the knees of his burly companion showed through ragged tears. The third carried a flat-iron as a weapon and wore a battered billycock hat with a broken seagull feather in the band. Despite the cudgel that swung from the hand of the fourth, Watters knew that Billycock was the most dangerous.

'I am Sergeant Watters of Scotland Yard!' Watters swore as the pickpocket twisted in his grip and tried to bite his arm. 'Keep still you!' he growled and reversed his cane, so the lead-weighted handle hung down from his left hand.

Billycock shook his head. 'We don't care a damn for the police, blue-bottle bastard.' He glanced at Watters's cane and gave a gap-toothed grin. 'That don't scare me neither, Sergeant, I'm handy enough with my mauleys not to need a twig like that.'

'Save me, boys! Kill the peeler!' The pickpocket's heels caught Watters on the shin. He gasped and slackened his grip. She slipped to the ground at his feet. 'Let me go, peeler, please, sir. I ain't done nothing wrong!'

Stooping, Watters hauled her to her feet by her hair. 'Come on you!' He stepped forward, dragging her behind him and swinging his cane in a hissing arc. 'Clear out of my way!'

The man with the cudgel leered and swung wildly. Watters sidestepped, thrust the end of his cane into the man's throat and crashed the lead-weighted end onto the side of his head, sending him staggering. The cudgel clattered to the cobbles.

Billycock lifted his flat iron and gave a sudden kick; Watters swung his prisoner round, so Billycock's boot thudded into her leg. She shrieked, 'leave it out,' as Billycock assumed a prize fighter's crouch.

'Come on then, Peeler.'

Without hesitation, Watters shoved the pickpocket toward Billycock, yanked her back the second they came in contact and swung his cane to the side of the man's jaw. The pickpocket squealed, but her flurry of skirts and waving arms distracted Billycock long enough for Watters to land a second blow on his left hand. The crack of breaking knuckles was audible even above the pickpocket's high-pitched screams.

As Billycock winced and doubled up to cradle his injured hand, Watters saw a slight gap in the circle of spectators and barged in, dragging the pickpocket by her hair and slashing left and right with the supple end of his cane.

'Move aside there! Make way for Scotland Yard!'

People cringed or pulled aside from the cane as Watters pushed on, dragging the struggling pickpocket behind him. Bottles and broken bricks battered down from the upper windows, endangering the crowd as much as Watters.

'Out of my way!' Watters slashed at the arms of a thin-faced virago, twisted his hand tighter in the pickpocket's hair, flinched as a woman's sharp-toed boot thudded into the side of his leg, and hauled onward until the volley of missiles ended. The five men who blocked his path were broader, taller, and better dressed than their compatriots. One wore a broadcloth suit, with his stovepipe hat tipped back on his head. They were smiling as they waited, with Broadcloth at the rear and the largest in front.

Watters knew that the odds against him had lengthened; these were professional bullies rather than gutter scruffs wasted by drink and weakened by poverty. He tightened his grip on the pickpocket's hair and balanced his cane.

'Right, you bracket-faced bugger,' the largest said and moved smoothly forward, with two others coming at Watters from the side. Watters swung the pickpocket around in a screaming flurry of skirts and kicking legs and staggered as a round-house punch landed on his shoulder.

Reversing his cane again, he cracked it onto one of his attacker's heads, saw the immediate spurt of bright blood and kicked out, missing as the man rolled away.

'You bloody bastard,' the pickpocket screamed and thrust her nails into the back of the hand that held her hair. 'You let me go! Please, sir, I ain't done wrong, sir.'

Another boot thudded onto Watters's leg, and then a brick knocked off his hat. He stooped to retrieve it with the hand that held his cane, swiped sideways at the legs of his attackers, and dragged his prisoner another few steps toward the more respectable parts of London. The crowd surged around him, screaming their hatred.

'Now we'll slate you, peeler!' The pickpocket kicked out at him, clawed with hooked fingers. 'You're a dead man!'

'I doubt that,' Watters said. 'Listen!'

As the sound of the police rattle echoed harshly above the renewed clamour, Broadcloth gave a loud whistle, and his bruisers withdrew.

'This way, boys!' Silver dropped his truncheon from up his sleeve and cracked it across the head of one of the retreating bullies. Half a dozen uniformed constables charged into the street, swinging their truncheons with callous unconcern whether the blows landed on male or female, old or young. In the back slums of London, the police regarded everybody as actual or potential criminals.

Watters ignored the screams of vituperation. 'Right, my girl,' he transferred his grip from the pickpocket's hair to her arm as he fastened handcuffs onto her wrists, 'let's see what you have managed to steal and find a nice snug cell for you. Keep you out of the winter chill, shall we?'

Chapter Two

A rising wind spattered rain against the panes and rattled the frame of the tiny window with its view of Whitehall. Watters slammed a hand on the pile of papers on his desk as the draught threatened to skiff them onto the floor.

'Blasted wind!' Running his gaze over the desk, he lifted a bottle of ink and placed it on the papers. 'We'll have to get a better office.' Lifting a candle, he applied the flame to the tobacco in the bowl of his pipe, puffing until it glowed red. 'When the world is glum,' he said, 'the only consolation is a good smoke.' He looked up, 'you remember that William when that woman of yours starts giving you trouble.'

'Angela will never give me trouble,' Silver said. 'She's a trump.'

'Wait until you're married to her.' Watters shielded the guttering candle from the draught. 'Experience brings knowledge if not wisdom, so I've heard. Now, let's see what we have here.' He spread the contents of his search of the pickpocket over his desk. 'Two purses, one pocketbook and a watch. Good takings for a spree, I would say.'

Silver took out his notebook to record their catch. 'Yes, Sergeant.'

'You got that gentlewoman's name and address, I hope?'

'No, Sergeant. By the time I had managed to secure the accomplice, she had hooked it.'

'Hooked it?' Watters raised his eyebrows, 'what do you mean, hooked it?'

'I mean she ran off, Sergeant. She left the bus and ran as if the devil was thrusting a red-hot pitchfork into her ar … she ran away, Sergeant.'

'She ran off without giving her name?' Watters shook her head. 'Some people deserve to lose their possessions. I hope we can find out about her here.' He lifted the first purse and peered inside. 'There is one shilling and sixpence here, Silver.'

'Yes, Sergeant.' Silver duly noted the figure down.

'This feels more like it.' Lifting the larger and heavier of the two purses, Watters tipped out the contents. A golden cascade of sovereigns rattled onto the desk, only marginally dulled by a few silver crowns and half-crowns. 'This will be the purse our girl took from that gentlewoman,' Watters said. 'She did not want for money anyway, not with all these golden boys.' Watters inserted his fingers into the purse and extracted a sheaf of folded documents. He had a quick look. 'I thought she was foreign,' he said. 'Some of these are in French.'

'I know a little French, Sergeant. May I?' Silver held out his hand.

Watters passed them over, silently ashamed of his lack of formal education.

'That's not French, Sergeant,' Silver said at once, 'I don't know what it is, but it's not French.'

'Well, it's some blasted foreign language anyway,' Watters snapped, 'I don't care what type of foreign it is.' He pushed the purse aside and lifted the pocketbook. 'There's not a penny in here, only more papers.' He shoved some across the desk. 'Is there anything interesting, Silver?'

Silver sifted quickly through the papers. 'They are mostly simple accounts, Sergeant, receipts from shops, that sort of thing. There is no name or address.'

Watters sighed. 'Go to the shops involved and see if they can match up the receipts. They might have a record of her name. Tell them she was foreign. French or something.' He looked up, expecting Silver to repeat that the language was not French and prepared to pull rank. Silver merely nodded. 'This should have been a simple arrest of a pickpocket, Silver. We don't have time to chase up every fool woman who absconds.'

'No, Sergeant,' Silver agreed.

'Are you humouring me?' Watters rammed the pipe between his teeth.

'Yes, Sergeant.' Silver looked up. 'Why the fussing? It's all part of the job.'

'Because big things are happening in the world, William, and we are chasing silly little girls stealing purses from passengers on a blasted omnibus.'

'We're doing our job, George.' Silver stopped when he saw the expression in Watters's eyes. He stood up. 'I'll get on with it,' he said.

'Before you go, this may mean something to you.' Watters lifted the final piece of paper, a much-folded scrap with a scribbled message written in a cramped hand. 'This means nothing to me either, but at least it's in English. It says, 'the flying duck' with a scribble beside it.' He looked closer. 'No it's not a scribble; it's one of these fancy foreign sevens with a stroke through it. Why can't foreigners write a seven like the rest of us? Why must they add a stroke?'

'I'm sure I don't know, Sergeant,' Silver said tactfully.

'No wonder there are so many blasted wars when we can't even understand each other's figures. Do you have any idea what that means? Flying duck?'

'It sounds like the name of a public,' Silver said, 'but not one that I am aware of.'

'I thought you were an expert on London publics,' Watters said sourly. 'You spend enough time in them. Well, Angela will cure you of that, mark my words.' He glowered at the paper again as if his bad mood would be sufficient to unravel the words. 'Oh never mind, that is just something else to waste our time searching for.'

'I'll ask around when I am going to the shops,' Silver began and looked up when somebody squeezed through the packed room.

'You're Detective William Silver?' The newcomer was burly and efficient looking, with an impressive set of side-whiskers and a visible air of authority that the white scar on his forehead only enhanced.

'Yes, sir.'

'I am Inspector Larkin, A Division, taking temporary charge while your usual inspector is sick.' He glanced at Watters, 'and you are Watters, I presume.'

'Sergeant Watters.'

'Quite so. Well, Watters, I am taking your detective officer away from you. I need him to chase a ghost.'

'He's deeply involved in another case with me,' Watters said quickly.

'There have been reports of a ghost on top of house roofs in Hesse Square.' Larkin turned his back on Watters. 'I want you to see what it's all about.'

'Yes, sir,' Silver glanced helplessly at Watters, 'but we are in the middle of an investigation.'

'Do both then,' Larkin said, 'but make the ghost your priority.' He handed over a small file and walked away.

'Sorry, Sergeant,' Silver shook his head.

'Orders are orders, William.' Watters pulled all the papers toward him and sucked smoke into his lungs. 'I don't understand this. We have a foreign gentlewoman, travelling on an omnibus, and for the first time, judging by her naivety. She gets her purse stolen with a great deal of money in it, but rather than wait to tell the police her name and address, she runs away. Why?'

'I am sure I don't know.' Silver opened the file Larkin had given him. 'Oh, this is a lot of nonsense!'

Watters looked up. 'Of course, it's nonsense. Ghosts indeed! It will be a blackguard up to some dodge or other. What does the file say?'

'It says that residents have seen a ghost on rooftops, a figure dressed all in white.'

'Oh, for God's sake!' Watters sighed. 'It'll be some apprentice lad larking about in a sheet. He'll fall and break his fool neck, like as not. You had better catch the scoundrel quickly, William, and then get onto something more important.' He counted the money on the table. 'There is over twenty pounds here!'

Silver consulted his notebook. 'Three and twenty pounds, five shillings, and threepence.'

'That's about four year's wages for a maidservant,' Watters ignored his accuracy, 'or five months for a skilled man. That's a lot of money to abandon.' He looked up, 'the inspector has given you a job to do, so you'd better get along now.'

'I wish old Field had not retired,' Silver said.

'And I wish I had been born a belted earl,' Watters told him. 'Now get about your business.' He returned to his perusal of the scribbled paper, shaking his head.

* * *

A heavy sky pressed smoke from ten thousand chimneys onto the streets, cutting visibility to a hundred yards and ensuring that every breath tasted of soot. Watters stood at the stall and sipped at the hot sweet coffee.

'How is business, Peggy?'

Grey hair bounced beneath her shawl when the coffee vendor shook her head. 'Oh, it's queer, Sergeant Watters, bad as bad ever was.' She swept her hand over her stall, a spring barrow with a trestle table on which stood three cans of coffee and a selection of simple food. Hard-boiled eggs nestled beside slices of cake and hot baked potatoes as the charcoal-burner glowed red against the murk of early evening. 'You see how much food I have left. I still have to pay for all this whether others buy it or not?' She gave a long sigh. 'It's not been the same since the tatty rot, Mr Watters. It's not just the Irish who suffered.'

Watters sipped at his coffee. 'Your coffee is better since then, Peggy.'

'You don't call around as often as you used to, Mr Watters.' Peggy turned away to talk to a bald, nondescript man as Watters watched a hansom cab whirr past, the driver huddled against the chill and the horse high stepping across the cobbles.

'You have been here for a long time, Peggy,' Watters said.

'I have been here two and thirty years, Mr Watters, girl and woman. I am fifty years old now and don't feel a day over ninety.' Her laugh cracked around the street. The bald man dutifully joined in until she pushed at him.

'You look fine, Peg. I had no idea you were that young. You know everything that goes on, don't you?'

'I keep my ears open,' Peggy's smile was as broad as her eyes were shrewd, 'and my pockets deep.'

Watters sighed. 'I remember that you drive a hard bargain, Peg.'

'A woman has to live, Mr Watters, particularly in these hard times.'

'I have a question for you, Peg.'

'Ask me. I might have an answer; I might not.' Peggy took a small bottle from within her voluminous clothing, pulled out the cork and sipped, then offered it to Watters.

He shook his head.

She shrugged, took another sip, slapped away the hopeful hand of the bald man and returned the cork. 'Suit yourself, Sergeant Watters, it's the best London gin.'

'Have you heard of a place called the Flying Duck? It may be a public.'

'I know it,' Peggy re-opened her bottle and smiled to him across the neck, 'but it will cost you.'

'I knew it would,' Watters parodied her words. 'How much?'

'Half a sov?'

Watters forced a laugh. 'Now Peggy, I am only an underpaid police-man, not the Queen's kept man.'

'Mr Watters!' Peggy feigned shock. 'That's not the way you should talk about Prince Albert!'

'I might go as far as a shilling,' Watters mused, 'and that's a day's pay for the redcoats that are risking their lives out East to keep you safe in your bed.'

'A shilling?' Peggy's eyes gleamed momentarily and then she shaded them again. 'And who says I am safe in my bed? A good-looking woman like me? I keep my door locked and a big stick beside me.' She glowered at the bald man as he laughed again. 'We'll have none of your lip if you please. Not you, Mr Watters; I was a-talking to this queer cove here. If you make it a crown, I may agree, Mr Watters.'

'A shilling,' Watters said. 'No more. Other people need my custom in these hard times.'

'All right Mr Watters, a shilling.' She took the coin in hands covered in fingerless gloves, inspected it minutely, and secreted it away in some hidden corner of her clothing. 'The Flying Duck. That's not its name Mr Watters, it's only what some people call it. It is the Wild Geese.'

'The Wild Geese in the Ratcliffe Highway' Watters nodded. 'I know it, although I haven't heard it called the Flying Duck before.'

Peggy's laugh was at him rather than with him. 'You're not as dab a cove as you thought are you, Mr Watters?'

'I never thought I was clever, Peggy,' Watters told her. 'I have another question you may help with.'

'Then I will need another shilling.' Peggy held out her hand.

'Information first,' Watters said. 'I am looking for a foreign lady.' He put his hand in his pocket to find a coin.

'And I considered you a respectable man!' Fifty years of London fogs had roughened Peggy's laugh.

Watters removed his hand from his pocket. 'She is fairly tall, and we don't think she is French, but we don't know what nationality she could be.' He frowned as he remembered the woman. 'She had bright blue eyes and had her pocket picked.' *She had wonderfully clear eyes,* Watters thought but kept that memory to himself.

Peggy shook her head. 'Does this blue-eyed foreign woman have a name?' When Watters shook his head, she shrugged. 'Half the foreign women in London could have blue eyes Mr Watters, and probably had their pocket picked as well. You will have to give me more than that.'

Watters nodded. 'I thought it was a bit steep expecting you to know her. Thank you for the information, Peggy,' Watters fished another shilling coin from his pocket and pressed it into her hand, 'and thank you for the coffee.' He drained the mug and placed it on the table. 'If you do hear anything ...'

'I will get word to you.' This time she was not laughing. 'Who is this woman?'

'I don't know, Peggy, my dear, I don't know.'

'I'll keep our eyes and ears open.' Peggy nudged the bald man. 'Won't we?

Watters nodded, touched a finger to the brim of his hat and strolled away, twirling his cane, and stopping to swing it like a golf club. He had found out where the Flying Duck was, while Peggy would put out the word about that foreign woman; that was a little progress.

* * *

'Did you hear that Admiral Dundas is coming to London in a few weeks?' Silver hardly looked up from his newspaper as he scribbled in his notebook.

'Is that so?' Watters sunk onto his chair. 'I hope the weather keeps fine for him. And what has that to do with this case?'

Silver put his finger on the paper to mark his place. 'Nothing at all, Sergeant. I just thought it interesting that the papers should tell us the movements of the commander in chief. It says that he is coming to see our newest ship, HMS *Royal Albert*, with some foreign navy officers and diplomats and so on here to admire us.'

'Oh well, if he is here, then he can't do any harm elsewhere,' Watters said. 'Old Peg told me that the Flying Duck is what people call the Wild Geese.'

'The Wild Geese?' Silver nodded. 'That's one of the largest Academies in London. It's pretty quiet, though. The proprietor keeps a firm hand on the place and employs some extremely muscular porters to make sure there is no trouble, but a brothel all the same. It's not quite Kate Hamilton's although I have heard rumours that some of the well-to-do know it well. What the devil would a gentlewoman want with a place like that?'

'That's one more thing I would like to know,' Watters said. He tapped his fingers on the desk. 'This woman is an enigma. One, she fled the scene leaving a great deal of money behind and two, she has some association with that house of infamy.' He lifted the documents he had taken from the woman's purse. 'I wonder what these say.' He shook his head. 'That is the third thing I would like to know: what these papers say. I rather think that they may be the key to this blasted woman.'

'Why concern yourself so much, Sergeant?' Silver asked. 'She is just one of many. There were probably fifty people had their pockets picked yesterday.'

'I am not sure; not sure at all.' Watters contemplated the papers on his desk. 'There is something not right here.' He looked up sharply. 'Something feels queer, William.'

Silver shrugged. 'She is only some foreign dupe who had her pocket dipped.'

Watters raised his eyebrows. 'Maybe you're right, William.' He glanced again at the documents and tried to forget the clarity of her eyes. 'You concentrate on laying your ghost while I try and find this woman. One more day on this case and then,' he waved his hand at the pile of files on his desk, 'I will start to work through that; petty theft, shoplifting, and other minor offences.'

Silver frowned. 'There have been two murders that I know of, Sergeant.' He closed his mouth at the expression in Watters's eyes.

'Inspector Larkin prefers that others take more serious crime. You and I get the dross.' Lifting his hat and coat, Watters forced a smile as he stepped toward the door. He stopped and looked over his shoulder. 'Inspector Larkin has no patience with me, William, nor I with him, so you would be better not associating with me. Ask to be appointed to another sergeant if you wish a more interesting life than chasing non-existent ghosts.'

He left before Silver could reply.

* * *

Thames side was busy as always, with river barges in mid-channel and ocean-going vessels coming in with cargoes from all quarters of the globe. Watters watched a battered brig push upstream under light sail with the master standing at the helm, shouting orders to four men aloft.

'I'm too old to go to sea,' Watters said to himself, 'and I would not want to, now.' He watched the seamen scramble and run at the bellowing of the master, nodded at his memories, and turned his attention elsewhere. A rowing boat drifted down the river with half a dozen men on board, all eyes watching the ships passing. 'River pirates.' Watters recognised the type at once. He watched them for a few minutes, wondering what undiscovered crimes they were guilty of before he turned away. He had not been assigned to prevent river theft. His job was to stop pickpockets on the omnibus routes and hand back the takings, for God's sake, like he was some young uniformed constable on his first week on the job.

The noise alerted him to the mudlarks on the bank as they waded into the bitter cold river. Barefoot and bare-legged, their clothes spattered with Thames-side mud, they would suffer chilblains and the risk of a severe foot injury as they searched for fragments of coal or anything else they could salvage and sell. Watters watched them for a moment, remembering his childhood in Edinburgh's Cowgate when Burke and Hare were on the rampage, murdering people and selling their bodies to Knox, the anatomist.

'Halloa!' He shouted the word through instinct rather than desire.

The nearest of the mudlarks looked up, wiped a streaming nose with a filthy hand, ran his other equally black hand through a rank tangle of hair and shouted back.

'Halloa yourself.'

'Any luck there, boys?' Watters remembered the persistent itch of vermin crawling in his hair lice on his body. Pauperism was hell on earth.

'Not much.' There was natural suspicion in the boy's voice.

'Here,' Watters produced a handful of copper and tossed them to the boy, 'that's to keep you out of trouble.'

'Thanks, mister!' The boy's suspicion fell away. 'Don't tell the bloody peelers!'

'I am the bloody peelers!' Watters said. He watched the boys back away, into the Thames. 'I am looking for a foreign woman,' he said, 'she is tall and elegant, a gentlewoman.'

The boy shook his head solemnly and looked around at the muddy wasteland where he worked. 'I ain't seen no gentlewomen round here, mister,' he said.

'No, not round here,' Watters agreed. He understood the world of these boys; mud and cold, poverty and hopelessness. It was only by sheer luck and perseverance that he had scrabbled clear of the gutters; what chance had these rascals?

None, Watters thought, which was about the same chance as he would have if he ever left the force. He would be back on the streets, an ex-policeman with no trade and no skills. He straightened his shoulders and looked over the London skyline. Larkin? Who was he? A temporary blemish on a career he was forging out of nothing. Watters turned away quickly and swished his cane through the air. There was no use looking to the past or complaining about the present: he had a job to do.

Chapter Three

Ratcliffe Highway was hectic, with crowds of seamen just off the ships, at least one prostitute for every two men. Standing out among the majority, a few respectable families who had taken the wrong turning searched for a quick escape before the locals contaminated them by touch or association. Watters had exchanged his high hat for a low-crowned affair that was less distinctive and tried to adopt a slouch as he shouldered his way through the crowds.

As he walked, he took mental notes of the places he passed to remind him what sort of place the Highway was. He fingered his cane: it was only two months since an American seaman stabbed Constable Ambridge exactly where he stood. Across the road was the Hope and Anchor where two friends fell out over the immoral earnings of one of them, and close by was the coffee shop of Mr Jones, the bigamist.

At the far corner was where an escaped American slave called himself Eliza Scott had picked up sundry seamen until they discovered he was a man and nearly made his deception permanent. On the farther corner, Watters looked at the building where John Stevens had appointed himself as a medical man and sold all manner of poison until one of his patients died, and he was taken up for manslaughter. Crime and unpleasant characters filled this street, and Watters knew the Wild Geese would be no different.

Watters swung his cane as a drunken Dutch mariner came too close. The man squared up to him, decided discretion was better than a poke in the throat and fell into the gutter instead. Watters left him to the tender ministrations of an over-dressed prostitute who would undoubtedly pick his pocket.

He walked on, remembering the casual violence that made the Highway so dangerous. There was the corner of Fortunate Place where four men recently pounced on Constable Thomas Jones and kicked him half to death. Watters saw the Cock and Neptune, outside which the German seaman Frederick Pratt stabbed his shipmate before a mob chased him down Virginia Lane and took summary vengeance, handing what remained to the police. Then there was Ryan's coffee shop, kept by a man whose nose was bitten off by George Barry, the so-called cannibal, much to the delight of the prostitutes who lived in the shop.

What a locality, Watters muttered to himself, rapped a well-known pickpocket across the knuckles with his cane and jerked his head in the direction he wished the man to go. This street was no place for a gentlewoman to come, and undoubtedly not a place for a lady with beautiful eyes.

At the corner of Atlantic Street, the Wild Geese proclaimed its identity in garish green and white under a swinging sign that showed a flight of three geese flying into an impossibly red horizon. A screen inside the windows blocked all inquisitive policemen from spying on the interior, although music and laughter told its own story. Watters straightened his hat, tapped his cane from the pavement, pushed open the door and walked into a different world.

He was not sure what he had expected: if anything a typical seaman's public with a dark bar and a dozen cheap dollymops clinging to the arms of drunken men. Instead, the large brass-framed mirrors reflected the light that sparkled from a brace of chandeliers while a four-piece orchestra played lively music to an establishment that would put the term gin-palace to shame. The seats were of padded leather, the bar of pure mahogany with fittings of brass with a polish that would not look out of place on a Royal Naval flagship and the barmen were uniformed, polite and attentive when Watters ordered a half-and-half. In one corner of the room, sitting on a capacious leather armchair on a raised dais, a tall woman held a pewter tankard in one hand and surveyed everything that happened. Her eyes rested on Watters for a second, roamed around the room and stopped at a young, unaccompanied woman, whereupon the tall woman motioned with her thumb in Watters's direction. Two large men lounged nearby; one black, one white and both ugly as the devil's promise. Watters knew they were the porters, the muscle men who would ensure there was no trouble in the establishment.

'Certainly, sir.' The barman smiled as he produced Watters's drink. 'What ship, sir?'

'No ship,' Watters said.

'Ah, Army officer, are you?' The barman took Watters's money with professional skill and returned far more change than Watters had expected. 'We don't serve civilians here, sir, and you're certainly not a swaddie. If you were a civilian, sir, I would ask you to drink up and leave.' He looked towards the porters.

'I'm certainly not a swaddie.' Watters used the colloquial term for a private soldier and wondered why this establishment was so particular; the Highway was anything but exclusive. 'I am looking for a woman,' he began, and the barman smiled.

'Then you have come to the right place, sir. Women come to the best public in the Highway and one of the best in London.' He leaned closer and lowered his voice. 'We have all sorts here, sir, suitable for every taste and, eh, requirement.'

'I am looking for a particular woman,' Watters said. 'She is foreign, tall and—' He stopped as the barman shook his glossy head.

'About half the girls here are foreign,' he said, 'German, Dutch, Jewish, Irish; add the odd black or Chinee for spice.' His grin covered a multiple of sins. 'They say God made the Chinee different: sideways.'

'They're not,' Watters said solemnly. 'They are the same as every other woman.' He decided to follow a military tack. 'I served in Hong Kong with the Royal Marines.'

'Ah,' the barman began to polish a glass. 'The famous Royal Marines. Your unit serves all over the world, by land and sea.'

'We do,' Watters agreed without a word of a lie.

'Hong Kong is a long way from the Highway.' The barman's initial suspicion gave way to that same broad smile. 'I understand! You are waiting for a transfer to one of the vessels that are out East.'

'You are a clever man,' Watters said. 'So you have not seen my woman then?'

'Sorry.' The barman placed the now highly polished glass on the counter. 'I have seen so many.' He adopted the air of a man of the world.

Watters nodded. 'Thank you anyway.'

The barman selected another glass. 'She must have been something special if you are looking for her.'

'I have something of hers I wish to return,' Watters said.

The barman laughed. 'Normally, it is the man who has left the girl a little bundle, and she looks for him! What's her name?'

'I wish I knew,' Watters said truthfully.

'Well I wish you the best of luck, but I am sure you will find a woman her equal in the Geese.' The barman moved on to another customer as Watters settled into one of the chairs and surveyed the room.

The barman had been correct: most of the clientele in the Wild Geese were bluejackets or scarlet-coated soldiers, with one civilian lounging in the corner. Although the man had a bowler hat covering his face, Watters noticed that his eyes were always mobile, watching everything that was happening. Moving among the redcoats and blue jackets were gaudy, befeathered women who chatted as they paired off with their choice of customer. Or rather, Watters noted, with the customer that the woman on the raised chair selected for them. As soon as a man entered the pub, the tall woman on the chair caught the attention of one of the parading women and nodded in the newcomer's direction. He wondered when his girl would arrive.

Watters shifted his gaze from woman to woman, trying to picture the bright-eyed gentlewoman from the omnibus in the feathers and ribbons of these fluttering birds-of-prey.

No; Watters shook his head. *That woman was no prostitute.* He was sure of that. He had met a great many prostitutes and other denizens of the shaded area between crime and poverty, and that woman would not fit in. She was a gentlewoman, of that there was no doubt.

'Are you talking to yourself, sir?' The woman was of middle height, with a bonnet complete with the ubiquitous array of feathers slated across her forehead. Her green eyes sparkled with mischief or perhaps gin, Watters was not sure which.

'I am.' Watters made space for her beside him and tried to force a smile.

'They call me Lily.' She slid beside him with a practised movement that pressed her hips against his.

'I am George,' Watters told her. When he looked up, the barman was already waiting for him to order Lily a drink. The price was again more moderate than he had expected. Watters glanced at his change. 'That was very inexpensive.'

'Mother Flannery has reduced her prices for military and naval gentlemen,' the barman explained. 'It's her way of helping defeat the Russians.'

'And of increasing her customer levels,' Watters said.

'Only Tommy Atkins and Tarry Jack are welcome,' the barman said. He nodded to the two large men who were closing on a semi-sober civilian who had crashed through the door. 'You can see what the porters do to those that don't fit the bill.'

One of the hefty porters lifted the drunk by his collar while the other cleared a path to the exit. Watters watched unmoved as the porter threw the unwanted customer outside. The two porters returned to their positions beside the woman on the dais.

'Ben tells me that you are an army officer.' When Lily pressed herself closer to him, Watters was glad he had not brought a pocketbook with him and had distributed his money in a variety of places in his clothing.

'Is that what Ben said?' Watters glanced at the barman, who immediately nodded agreement. 'Well, if Ben says that, then I am sure I cannot disagree, although he is not quite correct.'

Lily tasted her drink and smiled. 'You are very generous,' she said. 'I've never been with an officer before.'

'Oh, officers are just like other men,' Watters told her.

'Except better.' Lily looked up at him with wide green eyes. 'I have heard what officers like.' She slowly walked the fingers of her right hand up the length of his thigh. 'They are gentlemen and like their pleasures.' Her finger continued its journey, slanting across Watters's trousers.

'And do other men not like similar things?' Watters did not halt the progress of the fingers. He tried to work out her accent, London overlays but with a background to it.

'All men are after the same thing, but some take different routes to get there.' Lily's fingers reached their ultimate destination and halted, accompanied by a quizzical smile. 'What regiment are you with, sir?'

Watters thought Lily had to slightly force out the 'sir.' 'No regiment,' he said at once. 'I am a Royal Marine.'

'Royal Marine?' Lily raised her eyebrows. 'By land and sea.'

'You know us then.' Watters did not have to pretend surprise. Prostitutes would have extensive experience of garrison troops but would hardly be expected to know the mottos and function of individual units.

'Yes, everybody knows of the Royal Marines.' Lily's fingers were doing interesting things to him.

'And so they should.' Watters put his hand on top of hers. 'I am in transit between North America and the Crimea.' He placed her hand firmly in her lap. Lily looked more scared than disappointed. Her glance at the woman on the dais told its own story.

'Please sir.' Lily's hand crept back to its previous position.

Watters raised his eyes to the mirrors. The woman on the dais was looking directly at them, her long, weathered face as amiable as the muzzle of a loaded cannon. He nodded. 'You seem a very companionable girl,' he said slowly, 'have you worked here long?'

Lily's smile was composed more of relief than pleasure. 'Since Mother Flannery took over,' she said.

Watters jerked his head backwards slightly. 'The lady on the raised seat being Mother Flannery I take it?'

'Yes,' Lily said quietly.

Watters sipped at his drink and looked around again. 'I am not used to this kind of establishment,' he said. 'What happens now, Lily?'

'Now we go upstairs.' She stood up with as much grace as a hunting cat and put out her hand. 'Come, George, and we will get to know each other better.'

Watters had a last look around the room. 'Give me one moment,' he said and stepped toward Mother Flannery.

'George.' Lily grabbed hold of his sleeve and dropped her voice. 'Be careful.'

The two large men stepped forward as Watters approached, but Mother Flannery waved them away with a flick of her fingers. They stepped back; the black man had one hand in his inside pocket while the white pushed something back up his sleeve. Watters twirled his cane and held it ready to thrust, slash or swing.

'Good evening, Mother Flannery.' Watters ensured he was out of reach of the fists and blackjacks of the two bodyguards. He touched his cane to the brim of his hat.

Mother Flannery inclined her head slightly. Close to, she looked even taller, with intelligent eyes beneath a high forehead. 'Good evening to you, sir.'

'May I ask you a question?' Watters tried to emulate the refined tones combined with the lazy drawl that the officers of the Marines had used. He spun the cane around his fingers, acutely aware of the two porters only a few feet away.

'You may if you wish.' The accent was from Ireland, educated, intelligent, not a product of the bog-poverty of Connaught or Donegal. Mother Flannery might hail from Dublin.

'I was told to come here by a very charming foreign lady,' Watters said. 'I had hoped she would be here as I have something of hers to return.'

Mother Flannery held Watters's eyes, saying nothing. She raised her eyebrows.

'I know it is unlikely, Mother, but I wondered if one of your ladies had reported missing something.'

'What?' That one word sounded like a threat.

Watters felt the two men move toward him. He braced himself. 'Her purse.' He gave his best impression of a smile. 'It was not empty.'

'My ladies work only for me.' Mother Flannery's voice cut like a bayonet. 'If I ever find they have been working without my permission, I will ensure that they are unable to show their face anywhere again.'

Watters touched his hat again. 'I must have been misinformed. My apologies for disturbing you, Mother.' He turned to Lily and proffered his arm. 'Come my pretty, take me to your boudoir.'

Watters allowed Lily to take him to the back of the room and up a flight of well-carpeted stairs. 'Your Mother Flannery keeps some style in the Geese,' he said.

'It wasn't always like this,' Lily said, 'it used to be like any other house. Only the last few months it's got better.'

'Mother Flannery must be a good businesswoman,' Watters said. *If so,* he thought, *it was not because of the prices of the drink.* There was a mystery here, and in Watters's world, mysteries usually indicated a crime.

The pub's upper floor had been extended to take in the properties on either side and divided into small cubicles, each with a separate door. Lily stopped outside a cubicle near the centre and pointed to the brass nameplate that had been screwed on. 'Lily' she said proudly. 'That's me. I got my own name here.'

'Very nice.' Watters checked the length of the corridor. It was not unknown for men to be bludgeoned unconscious in Ratcliffe Highway brothels, and to wake up naked and bloody in some filthy back slum, or not wake up at all. This corridor was empty and serene.

Lily's door opened into a small, but surprisingly comfortable room complete with a bed, dressing table with large mirror, and a simple chest of drawers. The perfume that assailed Watters was more delicate than he was familiar with from soldiers' prostitutes and the small notepad complete with inkbottle and pen was surprising. On one wall was a garish print of the Madonna and child, while opposite it was an equally colourful picture of a swordsman in a long green cloak, both hung comfortably against a wall of green-painted wood. Everything was neat and astonishingly clean.

'It's an honour to have an officer here.' Lily sat on the bed and patted the coverlet beside her. 'Come on, George, don't be shy.' She loosened the top of her dress, so her cleavage gleamed in a tempting invitation. 'After all, you are an officer and a gentleman.' She pulled him onto the bed. 'You are shy, aren't you?' She patted his thigh. 'There's no need, you know. You've nothing I haven't seen bigger and better,' her smile lightened her eyes, 'or smaller and worse come to think of it.'

Lily bounced on the bed. 'It's all right, George; we can just talk first if you like. Do you like to speak about things first? I do. I like to get to know my gentlemen. It makes it all,' she screwed her face up, 'less formal if you see what I mean, less business and more personal sort of.' When she removed her feathered bonnet and shook her head, auburn curls cascaded to her shoulders. 'There now, that's better. Here, let me.' She unfastened the buttons of his coat and eased it from his shoulders. 'How's that?'

'Much better, thank you.' Watters decided he had better act the part of a nervous British officer.

'Let's talk first.' Lily put a small hand on his arm. 'Tell me about yourself, George. You must be a captain at least, maybe even a major in the Marines?'

'Only a captain.' Watters remembered his days in the Marines when rankers such as he had treated even a lieutenant like a god while a captain was such a high rank he lived in a different world.

'Did they let you away for a holiday?' Lily slowly removed her upper clothing and pulled back her shoulders to allow him the full glory of her breasts.

'I'm waiting for orders,' Watters said. 'I'm waiting to get out East.'

'I heard that many men are sick there.' Lily began to unbutton his shirt, keeping her mouth close to his ear. Her breath was sweet. 'That must make them very unhappy.'

'Very,' Watters agreed. He remembered the sickness that ravaged the ships and garrison in Hong Kong. 'It is worse than battle casualties.'

'Oh, poor, Captain George.' Lily leaned forward, so her breasts swung toward him. 'Does that help?'

Watters smiled. 'I would prefer just to talk,' he said. 'Do you have any foreign ladies that visit here?'

'Are you still interested in that other woman?' Lily sat back on the bed, arched her back to present her breasts to the best advantage and pouted to him. 'Am I not good enough for you?'

'You could not be better, but you are a pleasure,' he said, 'while this other woman is only business.' He described her as Lily tried to look attentive.

'Oh I don't know,' she said at last. 'There are too many different girls here. Mother Flannery only wants the best, you know. Maybe this other woman did not measure up?' She started to wriggle free of her skirt, 'help me with this, could you, George? I am sure you know what to do, a man with all your experience of the world. Then we can talk about you and not about other women! Are you keen to get to the trenches outside Sevastopol?'

'That's the idea.' Watters knew there was something wrong; his experience in arresting prostitutes told him that Lily was not acting as she should. She showed no concern for money and asked all the wrong questions. This room was queer too; it was too ornate for a soldier's prostitute. Too comfortable, too well-appointed.

'There must be a lot of desertions with the horrible cold weather and the sickness.' Lily gently squeezed his thigh. 'My poor Marine boy.'

'What is it you want from me, Lily?' Watters asked suddenly. 'You're not acting like any other of your profession that I've ever met.'

For a second Lily looked taken aback but rallied quickly. 'Why, George, I like you, you can see that.' Her hand began to stroke his thigh.

Watters took hold of her hand. 'Mother Flannery told you to like me,' he reminded. 'Now, Lily, you know as well as I, that soldiers are good to walk with, but they don't pay for your work cause they ain't got no money.' Watters adopted the London vernacular to try and make Lily feel comfortable. 'And you've not asked me for a penny since we got here, so what is it you want from me?'

Lily shook her head, 'Nothing, George.' She tried to draw her hand free, but Watters held her tight. 'I do assure you, sir, I just want what we both want, or you would not come in here.'

'That could be more truthful than you realise,' Watters said dryly. 'You've been pumping me for information since you sat beside me, and I want to know why.'

'Oh George, I like you.' Again Lily tried to pull her hand free, and again Watters held her tight. 'It's a plucky thing to hurt a woman,' she said.

'And a foolish ploy to argue with an officer of Her Majesty,' Watters told her. 'Now, Lily, tell me what this is all about.' He released her and stood back.

Lily looked up through tear-bright eyes. 'To tell you the blessed truth I don't know and that's a fact.'

'Now I do believe that,' Watters said, 'but tell me what you do know.' He looked around the room again, unhooked the picture of the Madonna and examined it. 'Are you a Roman Catholic?'

'No, sir,' Lily shook her head solemnly, 'I never put the pictures up, sir, that was Mother Flannery.'

'I wager there is a reason for that,' Watters said, 'but I'm damned if I know what it might be.' He tried to lift down the picture of the man in the green cloak, but it was firmly attached to the wall. 'What the devil is he supposed to be anyway?'

'I'm sure I don't know, sir.' Lily looked away. Watters saw a single tear fall to the bed.

Watters squinted closer at the picture, read the name below without any comprehension and frowned when he saw the spyhole neatly bored and camouflaged. 'I see,' he said. 'Voyeurism as well. It takes all sorts I suppose. Have you always followed this profession, Lily? Always had scarlet fever? Always liked a soldier's embrace?'

'I always liked to be noticed by the sojers,' Lily spoke quietly, 'but you may take your dying oath that I never thought it would take me to a house like this.' She sighed. 'I found out that sojers is cowards that think nothing of sticking a woman when they're drunk, or they'll take off their belts and wallop us.'

'I know what redcoats are like,' Watters said, 'and how people treat them.'

'You've never been a woman in their company.' Lily's smile faded as the real woman surfaced from the professional facade. 'It's enough to drive a woman wild to think she's given up a nice home and children for a lot of sweating, panting red-coated men.' She looked up at him. 'What you asking such a heap of questions for?'

'I am curious.' Watters lifted the notepad beside the bed. 'You write as well, I see.' He held the pad to the light in an attempt to make out any indentations from previous writings before ripping off the top sheet. 'You don't mind, do you?' He folded it neatly and placed it in his pocket.

'Here, Mother Flannery won't like that!' Lily sounded indignant.

'Well, don't tell her then, unless she already knows.' Watters nodded to the spyhole.

'I hope not,' Lily said. 'She'll have my hide for a blanket.'

'Do you work all day and all night, Lily?' Watters asked as an idea came to him. 'Or does Mother Flannery allow you some time off to recover?'

'Yes, sir. Mother Flannery says we should go to the Church on a Sunday, so we stop at midnight on a Saturday.'

Watters nodded. For an instant, he had a mental image Mother Flannery leading a long crocodile of demure-seeming prostitutes into a church with a bemused priest inviting them one by one into the Confessional. The poor man would have hours of blushing education, or perhaps not. The Roman Catholic priests that Watters had met were full of wisdom and knowledge. 'Do you attend church?'

Lily shook her head. 'No, sir. I told you that I'm not even a Catholic.'

Watters smiled and lifted his coat, 'Well, Lily, it's time I was getting along.'

'We haven't done anything yet.' Lily sounded suddenly scared. 'Mother Flannery won't like that.'

'How will she know unless you tell her?' Watters dug into his pocket and produced a crown piece. 'Here you are Lily.'

'Well, I never did.' Lily stared at the coin. 'Is it a smasher?'

'No, it's real enough, and so is this advice.' Watters stopped at the door. 'Leave here the first chance you get, Lily, run fast and don't ever come back. Don't even look back. I think you are a brick, Lily, and there is something here that is most decidedly queer.'

'Are you going to preachify now Captain George like some canting dodger?'

'No I am not.' Watters lifted his hat and cane. 'You heed what I said Lily and take care of yourself.'

Lily lifted her chin stubbornly. 'Well, George, this feeds me and clothes me. I've never troubled the parish for help and I never will.'

Watters nodded and stepped away. When he turned at the door, Lily was writing in her notebook.

* * *

Inspector Larkin leaned back in the seat that Inspector Field had occupied for so long.

'Something wrong, Watters?'

'It's Sergeant Watters, sir, and I think there is.' Watters stood in front of the desk. 'I am trying to trace the gentlewoman who had her pocket picked on the omnibus, sir, and the trail led to the Wild Geese public house in the Ratcliffe Highway.'

'I know it,' Larkin said at once. 'It's a seaman's pub, blackguardly, ruffianly, and full of low characters.'

'According to Silver, sir, it used to be like that, but I was there last night, and I would not recognise that description.'

Larkin sighed, pulled a sheet of foolscap toward him, and began to write. 'I hardly think that merits the attention of a criminal officer, Watters.'

'Sergeant Watters, sir.' Watters did not alter his tone. 'The whole establishment is wrong, sir. The prices are too low, the barman too attentive, and the customers too well selected and—'

'All of which is of no interest to Scotland Yard, however fascinating you seem to find it, Watters.'

'Sergeant Watters, sir. The ladies who work there...'

'Prostitutes, troopers, sluts, trolls, baggages, bobtails, flashtails, picking-up-molls, chicksters, ladybirds, even academians they may be, Watters, but never ladies.'

'Quite so, sir, and it's Sergeant Watters. The ladies who work there seem less concerned with taking money from their customers than in questioning them about their military experiences.'

'That's hardly our concern.'

'And they take notes, sir.' Watters produced the top sheet from Lily's notebook. 'I extracted this from her and dusted it with soot to get the impression of earlier writings.'

'The scribblings of a prostitute are of no concern of ours.' Larkin did not look up.

'Perhaps not, sir, but Lily's notes seem to be about regimental movements and morale.'

'Which may be of interest to a prostitute,' Larkin said, 'but not to Scotland Yard. Good day to you, Watters.'

'Sergeant Watters, sir. I am very interested in how the Wild Geese makes its money. It is certainly not across the counter, not at the prices they charge, and the girls don't seem to hurry, which is unusual in such places.'

Larkin looked up briefly, 'I presume you have a great deal of experience of brothels?'

'I have been in a few, sir, in the course of my duty.'

Larkin dropped his gaze again.

'I wonder if the public is only a front to a gambling house, sir, except the management did not invite me to a table.'

'That is enough speculation. I am sure you have better things to do than waste my time. Good day to you, Watters.'

'Good day to you, Larkin.'

Larkin looked up at last. 'You call me sir, Watters.'

'And you call me Sergeant Watters.' Watters held his gaze.

Larkin returned to his papers.

Chapter Four

Clouds had threatened London all day, but it was the night that dragged down torrents of rain that still failed to cleanse the sin from filthy streets. Watters stood at his living room window and sucked at his pipe, allowing the aromatic smoke to drift around his face and head.

'Christmas Eve,' he muttered as he surveyed the length of Easter Street below. 'It should be snowing.' He remembered the scene in Dicken's *Christmas Carol* when Scrooge sat at his fireside on this very day and gave a short laugh. 'Bah, humbug,' he said.

People stood in the street below. He saw a family of three standing arm-in-arm, with the father laughing while the mother adjusted her daughter's cape against the rain. A young gentleman hurried past them, with rain dripping from the brim of his tall hat and gold gleaming from the knob-handle of his cane. A sweep encouraged his climbing boy with hard pushes as he balanced his bundle of brushes over his shoulder and two stout matrons surveyed the sweep and the world through jaundiced eyes.

Young and old stepped away from the edge of the road as a carriage rushed past with the coachman huddled into his greatcoat as he cracked his whip to make his pair pull faster. A constant curtain of mud and water rose from the wheels to fall in a dirty patter onto the pavement, splashing the smart trousers of the businessman who marched past, unsmiling, and intent on the commercial realities that filled his world. Nobody spared a glance for the ragged woman who tried to keep warm within a shawl that was more holes than wool.

All human life passed his flat in Easter Street, Watters thought as he pressed tobacco to the bowl of his pipe and closed the shutters. He looked into the room with the tiny fire that barely raised a reflection from the brass coal-scuttle, the single chair at the battered table, the forlorn picture on the wall, the old leather chair beside the fire, and the bare floorboards that he swept daily. 'I might well be Scrooge,' he said, and again pulled on his pipe. 'Everybody has somebody. Even William has his intended, God help her.' He gave a sour grin. 'I am happy alone; I can think better that way.' On an impulse, he lifted *Christmas Carol* from his small bookshelf and leafed through the pages, shook his head, and put it down on the table. Instead, he spread out the foreign woman's documents.

'Let's have another look then.' Watters sat down and spread the papers in front of him, hoping that he could work something out. As he puzzled over the strange words, he bit into the bread-and-cheese he had made for himself and sipped at the mug of tea.

Although he had picked up a few words of various foreign languages in his time at sea and in the army, he had never had to read them. The words on the documents meant nothing to him; they were merely a succession of letters arranged in straight lines with incomprehensible meanings. After an hour, he sighed in frustration and stood up to pace the room in an attempt to create a systematic pattern of thought.

'So what do we have: a foreign woman who does not remain to claim twenty sovereigns, foreign words, and a scribbled mention of a brothel with fancy rooms and low prices where the girls questioned their military customers and wrote down what they said. He looked again at the impressions on Lily's paper. Despite the jumble of overlaid words, he could make out regimental numbers and the names of army barracks. Why would any prostitute have an interest in such things? And why was Mother Flannery collecting the information? That woman would bear further investigation.

Watters lifted the kettle to make more tea, swore when he realised it was empty, and picked up the tub he used for water. The trip to the well outside might clear his head. Pulling on his boots, he clattered down the stairs, opened the door, and nearly fell over the woman who huddled in his doorway.

'What the devil!' he gasped as he twisted his ankle, tested it by gingerly pressing it on the ground and grunted. Painful but bearable. He recognised the woman with the threadbare shawl. 'Do you realise the police will move you on the second they set eyes on you?'

The woman wrapped the shawl closer to her thin body. She sat on the stone step with her face surprisingly clean for a beggar. 'I'm not doing any harm, sir.' She had an Irish accent, soft and smooth.

'You're breaking the law,' Watters growled. Stepping over the woman, he limped to the well and worked the pump handle. When water lapped to the lip of the tub, he began the journey back, cursing as he slipped on the rain-slicked cobblestones.

The woman still cowered under the meagre shelter of his doorway, trying to keep out of his way.

'Have you nowhere better to go?'

'No, sir. If I had, I would go there.' She looked at him through narrow eyes.

Watters grunted and stepped back inside the house. It was not warm but a relief after only that few moments in the chilling rain. He carried the water tub into the tiny kitchen, filled the kettle, placed it on the glowing embers of the small range and swore.

I don't want company, he told himself. *I avoid company. I am happy being alone.* He swore again, moved to the window, opened the shutters, and looked outside. The woman had squeezed into the least wet corner of his doorway as the pelting rain bounced from ever-increasing puddles and wept from the eaves of the surrounding houses. Watters looked around his bare, bleak but secure room and swore again, loudly. He stomped down the stairs and flung open the door.

'Are you still here?'

The woman turned big eyes to him and inched as far away as the limited space allowed. 'It's the driest place.'

Watters grunted. 'It's drier in the house.' He stepped aside and jerked his head in brusque invitation. 'Christmas Eve is not the night to spend outside. Come in out of the rain.'

The woman looked up with her eyes wider than ever. The rain had plastered her hair close to her head and dripped from her nose and chin. 'I've no money to pay lodgings,' she said.

'I'm not asking for money.' Watters heard the growl in his voice. 'Come in out of the rain for God's sake.'

'I've nothing else for you.' He saw her instinctively pressing her legs together. 'I'm not that sort of woman.'

'And I'm not that sort of man,' Watters told her. 'Are you coming in or are you determined to catch your death of cold? Come in! I'm not a patient man.' He saw the woman's internal struggle between suspicion at his motives and the natural desire to seek shelter and warmth.

Avoiding his gaze as if ashamed, the woman struggled to her feet. She was taller than Watters had imagined, about five feet four inches in height, and with her scanty clothes clinging to her she looked half-starved, which she probably was.

'You're safe with me.' Watters knew his voice was brusquer than he intended. 'Come on. It's drier inside.' He knew his words sounded foolish, but he could think of nothing more reassuring.

The woman staggered as she negotiated the stairs and Watters instinctively put his hand on her arm. 'You're all right,' he said. 'When did you last eat?'

She shook her head, wordless.

After the dull chillness of the night outside, even Watters's stark room seemed welcoming. He guided the woman to his chair, added a few more lumps of coal to the fire and poked it to reluctant life. 'You're sodden wet.' Watters touched her arm. 'Wait here a second.'

Watters's bedroom was as stark as the living room, with one bed and two chests. He lifted the lid of the larger, where his clothes were on one side, with blankets on the other. Touching the clothes, Watters shook his head and instead removed two blankets. He added a towel from the kitchen and stepped back into the living room. The woman was huddled over the fire, trying to dry her hair on the hem of the shawl.

'Take your clothes off.' Again he heard the harshness in his voice. 'Here's a blanket – put it around you. It's dry and will keep you warmer. And here's a towel. It's a bit threadbare but better than nothing.'

She looked up, suspicion mingling with gratitude in her face. 'But—'

'I'll be in the next room. Call me when you're decent.' He poked more life into the fire, added another lump of coal, glanced at her, and piled the fire higher than it had been all winter. He hated wasting fuel. 'You're safe here. Have you eaten recently?'

'No, sir,' she spoke quietly. 'Sir, I've no money to pay you.'

'If you had I'd have ordered you to a lodging house,' Watters told her. He pushed the blankets into her arms. 'They're clean,' he said, 'but maybe a bit musty; they've been in the chest for some time.'

She held the blanket close to her face. 'Thank you, sir.'

Watters withdrew into the bedroom when he saw the moisture in her eyes. *I've no patience with weeping women,* he told himself. *That's my night's peace ruined now, damn my soft heart.*

He stared into the open chest for a long moment before forcibly closing the lid. Sighing, he tapped on the living room door. 'Are you decent?'

'Wait a minute.' Her voice was strained, near panicky. Watters stepped back.

'Don't rush,' he said.

He glanced at the chest once more as she said 'ready' in a soft, small voice.

The blanket covered her like a tent, with her bare feet sticking out below and her hair a tousled mess above. 'Are you sure you don't mind?' The Biblical association suddenly hit Watters.

'There's room at this inn,' he said, 'but there's neither a wise man nor a shepherd.' He grunted. 'There's no baby either.'

The woman said nothing as she watched him, rather like a rabbit watching a stoat.

'You must be hungry.' Watters decided for her. He left for the kitchen and brought back the bread and cheese. 'I'm afraid it's not the most festive of foods but better than nothing.' He watched as the woman put forward a tentative hand before grabbing the bread as if scared Watters would whisk it away.

'Thank you.'

'A mug of tea?' Watters hesitated, 'I've nothing stronger, I'm afraid.' *Damn; why am I putting myself out for some woman? London is full of waifs and strays.*

'Thank you.' Her eyes peered from a cocoon of blankets. She opened her mouth to say more but could only repeat, 'thank you' in a broken voice.

She held the blankets close, cringing in her chair before gently biting at the bread-and-cheese. Watters half-filled the kettle and put it on the fire to boil.

'The tea will be ready in a minute.' He spooned tea leaves into his two cups, selected the least battered for the woman, waited for the water to boil, and poured it in, adding milk to both.

'Here.' Watters held out a chipped mug. 'It's real milk,' he assured her, 'not diluted with chalk or anything else.' He watched as the woman put the cup to her mouth. She was still shivering, but whether from fear or cold he could not tell. She drank slowly with her gaze fixed on him, gave a brief smile, and drank again. He saw the warmth in her eyes and looked away. *I don't want a woman in my life.*

'Thank you.' The woman's voice broke as she fought tears.

Watters picked up her wet clothes and shook his head as she put out a protesting hand. 'It's all right,' he said gently, 'I'm not taking them away from you. I'm going to squeeze them out the window and hang them up to dry.' Water gushed from her meagre clothes as he leaned out of the window, and then he lowered the pulley and draped them across the wooden spars to dry. It was the first time that female clothes had dripped water down the back of his neck, and probably the last, he told himself. The woman had worn nothing but a single skirt, linen top, and a shawl.

'I am George, by the way,' Watters said, but the woman had fallen asleep, gripping her mug of tea as if it was a magic talisman. Watters sighed, heated a poker in the embers and carried it through to light the fire in the bedroom.

Taking a deep breath, he returned. 'Happy Christmas,' he whispered. Wondering at his foolishness, Watters lifted the woman within her swathe of blankets. She stirred, murmured something, and returned to sleep as Watters laid her on his bed. He sighed, watched her for a moment, then left the room, closed the door quietly, and settled into the chair beside the fire, ready for an uncomfortable night's sleep.

* * *

The fire had died to a group of black embers and rain continued to patter on the windowpanes. Watters looked up as the woman slipped silently around the room. She had dressed, and her clothes clung, still damp, to her thin body.

'I hope it's all right,' she said, 'but I put the kettle on the fire.' Her eyes were hazel, Watters noticed, and sunk deeply behind dark shadows.

'Of course.' He rose and stretched, easing cramped limbs. 'How did you sleep?'

'Very well, thank you.' She bobbed in an unexpected little curtsey.

'Let's find some breakfast,' Watters said.

'You've already been too kind,' the woman said. 'I'll get out of your way now.'

'You'll stay for breakfast, dammit!' Watters growled. 'Food,' he said, and walked into the kitchen. There was only enough space for one in the minuscule room, so Watters grabbed what he could and passed it to her shaking hands. 'There's nothing festive,' he apologised. 'I was not expecting guests.'

Her smile was a mixture of shame and gratitude. 'I should leave you in peace,' she said.

I wish you would, Watters thought. *I don't know how to talk to women.* 'You'll stay for breakfast,' he said. 'I am George.' He waited for the response the woman did not make. 'You must have a name too.'

'I am …' She hesitated. 'I am Rowena, although I don't like the name,' she said at once. 'I prefer my middle name.'

'Rowena is a fine name,' Watters said. 'How do you do, Rowena.' He held out his hand. 'I am still George.'

Rowena hesitated again; her hand was cold and delicate within his. 'Thank you.' She withdrew quickly. 'I won't bother you long. I'll be on my way soon.'

'It's Christmas Day.' Again Watters thought of Dickens' *Christmas Carol*: had the three spirits visited him without him knowing? God, how he hated company, yet he could not send a vulnerable young woman out in the sleeting rain. He temporised by saying, 'where do you normally spend your time. Do you have a job?'

Rowena looked away. 'I live by picking up crusts in the streets, put out on the steps by the mistresses of the house, or whatever people discard.'

'That will be poor picking sometimes. Yet you were not always poor,' Watters pointed out. He looked at his bread and cheese. 'Not much variety, I am afraid. I live simply.' He looked up, 'it must be hard being homeless.'

'It is,' Rowena said. She looked around the room, allowing her eyes to rest on the golf clubs that leaned against the small bookcase, Watters's only luxuries. 'You play golf, I see.'

'Not often,' Watters said. 'It's a game I picked up years ago. If ever I move back home to Scotland, I'll take it up again.'

Rowena was quiet for a few seconds. 'You keep a neat house.'

'It does me.' Watters found he was on the defensive and changed the subject. 'Do you wish more bread? You must be hungry.'

'I can't stay to eat.' Rowena shook her head; there was near panic in her eyes. 'You've already been too kind.'

'It's Christmas,' Watters said, 'you don't want to be walking the streets on Christmas Day.'

Rowena glanced outside where rain smeared the windows and wept from the roof above. 'Are you sure you don't mind?'

'I'm glad of the company,' Watters told her. 'I don't like to be alone at this time of year.' Why had he told her that blatant lie? *For God's sake,* he said to himself, *don't show weakness; you might be arresting her for vagrancy in a day or two.*

'I can understand that' Rowena said quietly. 'Christmas should be a happy time, but when one is alone, it can be the bleakest of all days.'

When one is alone? That is very educated from a woman walking the streets. There is more to our Rowena than meets the eye.

'It can.' Watters turned to the food. 'I'm not the best of cooks,' he apologised.

'After stale crusts and what I could find outside the market stalls, it's better than a feast,' Rowena said. She lifted *A Christmas Carol.* 'I haven't held a book for a long time.'

Watters had to stop himself from snatching it back. 'That's one of my favourites.'

'I'm sorry.' Rowena replaced the book carefully on the table.

'It's all right.' Watters had no wish to destroy her fragile confidence. 'Is there a Mr Rowena? A husband?'

'He died. Joe was an engineer on the railways. The boiler burst and killed him.'

It was Watters's turn to offer sympathy and support. It was not hard to put his hand on her shoulder. When she pulled gently away, he did not follow.

The sudden knocking took him by surprise. 'What the devil ...'

'There's somebody at the door,' Rowena said.

'Nobody comes to my door.' Watters looked out the window.

'It's the police!' Rowena looked at him. 'What have you done ... who are you?' She pulled her clothes closer and stepped back in sudden alarm.

'It's all right.' Watters held up both hands. 'I *am* the police. I am Sergeant George Watters of Scotland Yard. 'He ran down the stairs to open the door.

The two uniformed constables thundered up the stairs. 'Sorry to disturb you on Christmas Day, Sergeant.' He took off his hat. 'Sorry to bother you, Mrs Watters.'

'I'm not Mrs Watters—' Rowena began, but the constable had already returned his attention to Watters.

'There's trouble at the Portman Street barracks, Sergeant, and the inspector wants you there.'

Watters lifted his hat and coat before the constable finished speaking. He was not sure if he felt more relief or sorrow. 'My apologies, Rowena but I must go. Stay as long as you wish and eat what you like.' He was on the street before he realised that he had left his pocketbook on the kitchen table. He swore softly. *I've lost that then;* he thought and bent his head to face the rain.

Chapter Five

The religious filled the streets, summoned to worship by a hundred church bells that clattered joyfully in defiance of the teeming rain. Larkin stood on a raised step outside the barrack door with a circle of police officers around him, the uniformed men huddled into their greatcoats and the plain-clothes detectives disgruntled at being called out on a wet Christmas Day. 'And here's Watters now,' he said, 'at last.'

'I was off duty, sir,' Watters excused himself.

'A good officer is never off duty, Watters.' Larkin gave him a reproving look. He raised his voice. 'Now we can finally start. 'There has been a murder here and an attempted murder.' He paused to survey his audience.

'He's making sure we all know how important he is,' Silver said softly.

'Did you say something, Silver?' Larkin asked.

'I said this is very important, sir.'

Larkin's look contained as much scepticism as dislike. He stood erect despite the rain.

'Both the victims were soldiers.' Larkin said the word as if it were poisonous. 'You know what sort of men soldiers are; the type that consort with the lowest of star-gazing doxies in the worst back-slums.' He looked at the assembled men. 'You were a soldier, were you not, Watters?'

'It's Sergeant Watters, sir, and I wore Her Majesty's uniform but as a Royal Marine, not a soldier.'

'Very well, then you are the best man for this somewhat tiresome case.' The insult was obvious. 'Drop whatever you are working on for a day or two and look into it.' Larkin gave a contemptuous snort. 'It was probably some drunken row over a ladybird.'

'I'll find out, sir.' Watters heard the heat in his voice. 'These lads have a bad enough life serving the Queen for a brown without being murdered at home. Portman Barracks holds the Guards, men who fought at Alma and Inkerman.' He stopped before his anger carried him to words he knew he would later regret. He looked around. Larkin had already walked away, and most of the police had followed. Only Silver, a young detective named Baltimore, and a tall army officer had remained.

'Larkin has them all scared of him.' Silver tried to excuse his colleagues.

'You were a soldier, I understand.' The Guards captain was tall, slender, and immaculate. The rain did not seem to affect the cheroot he puffed.

'I was a Royal Marine, sir.' Watters fought the instinct to snap to attention.

'Did you see any action, Sergeant ... Walters, isn't it?'

'Sergeant Watters, sir, and I saw a little.'

'I am Captain Fletcher, Coldstream Guards.' Only when they got close did Watters see the pallor on Fletcher's face and the empty sleeve of his left arm. 'That was my man who somebody murdered, and my man who somebody injured. They were due to ship out East next week, and we need all the good men we can get.'

'I will do my utmost to find the murderers, sir. May I see the dead man?'

'We carried them both inside. Follow me please.' Fletcher led the way.

The exterior of the Georgian building looked impressive, but the accommodation was as cramped as any barracks in which Watters had ever lived. The Guardsmen lived, slept, and ate in rooms with less space than allowed for convicts, and breathed stale air laced with the stench of inadequate sewage. Silver was coughing long before they reached the makeshift morgue.

'Is this your first time in an army barracks?' Watters asked.

Silver nodded, unable to speak.

'They are not the healthiest of places,' Watters said and stepped aside as a brass-lunged sergeant hectored a file of young recruits past. 'But some seem to thrive here.' He grunted. 'Army sergeants are a breed apart.'

The body lay on a bare mattress in a makeshift morgue. Dried blood covered the face and head, and dark stains spread across what remained of the uniform. Both the Guardsman's eyes were black and very swollen, while one of his fingers was missing.

'It looks as if a pack of wild dogs attacked him,' Silver said. 'Somebody made a good job of it.'

'Close the door,' Watters said. 'Has the police doctor examined him yet?'

'Your Inspector said there was no need.' Fletcher looked at the body.

'Send for him, please, Silver,' Watters ordered. 'How about your own doctor, Captain Fletcher?'

'Our man proclaimed him dead on arrival and said there was nothing we could do for the poor fellow.'

'Except maybe find his killers.' Watters heard the edge in his voice. 'I will wait until the police doctor examines him. In the meantime ...' Ignoring Silver's look of distaste, he eased his hands into the man's pockets and pulled out his possessions. There was not much: four dirty pennies, a cheap cotton handkerchief, a penknife and a metal watch. 'He was not robbed. Take me to the other chap, please.'

'Guardsman Elwood is here, Sergeant.'

Guardsman Elwood lay on a cot in the hospital, with what was visible of him through the bandages, bruised and battered. His eyes, swollen and black, were closed in unconsciousness.

'He's in a bad way.' The doctor was younger than Watters expected, with worried eyes.

'Will he pull through?' Watters asked.

'I can't say.' The doctor shook his head. 'He was pretty badly knocked about. He has one finger missing, three broken ribs, fractured skull and cheekbones, some teeth broken, with many bruises and other injuries. But he's a strong lad, and he might make it.'

Watters reached for the small notepad he kept in his pocketbook, grunted when he remembered he had left it in his flat, and nodded as Silver came into the room. 'Detective Silver will write out my name and how to contact me. I wish to be notified as soon as Guardsmen Elwood regains consciousness. In the meantime, I wish you to inspect the deceased ...'

'Guardsman Nixon.'

'... Guardsman Nixon and tell me what killed him.'

'Somebody beat him to death,' the doctor replied at once. 'Multiple wounds and blows to the head, face and body.'

'By one person or more than one?'

'There were two tall guardsmen together, somebody killed one and very badly injured the other. I would say more than one somebody, and probably more than two.'

'Excuse me.' Guardsman Elwood's uniform was beside the bed, bloodstained and torn. Watters searched the pockets. 'He was not robbed, either. These men were not attacked for gain.' He bent closer to the injured man, 'I can smell alcohol on his breath.'

'They had been drinking in the Highway,' Fletcher said.

Watters grunted. 'That is not surprising. Do you know where?'

'The Old Cock, I think.'

'The Cock and Neptune,' Silver translated quietly. 'Do you know if there were any witnesses?'

Fletcher looked blank.

'Detective Silver and I will ask locally,' Watters said. 'In the meantime, please let me know when Elwood wakes or if you hear anything.'

Knocking on doors on Christmas Day did not prove rewarding. Watters was always greeted with a smiling face as the householder expected a friend or relative calling around for Christmas, but the mood altered as soon as he introduced himself. The smile changed to withdrawn suspicion and the open welcome to a half-closed door as if to shield whatever was happening inside the house.

'Did you notice anything happening in this street earlier today?'

'Nothing.' In this part of London, a negative answer was the inevitable response, even before the question was complete. That would be followed by: 'we heard nothing neither, Sergeant,' with sometimes a look over a shoulder for confirmation from a husband or wife. The hasty closing of the door followed and then an outburst of renewed merriment as the Christmas festivities continued.

'Nothing, Sergeant,' Silver reported.

'Nothing from me either,' Watters said. He checked his watch. 'With the injuries these two guardsmen got, the attackers must have been at least splashed with blood.' He looked down at the ground, 'this rain will wash away any bloodstains, but their clothes will still be splattered.'

'Some publics are still open,' Silver pointed out. 'The Old Cock is closed.'

'It was never open,' Watters said. 'Captain Fletcher got the wrong pub.' He looked over to the Wild Geese, across the road. 'I am going to try the Duck next.' He emptied rainwater from the brim of his hat. 'This is not your case. Did you find that ghost yet?'

'Not yet.'

'He'll keep.' Watters jammed his hat back on and turned up the collar of his coat. 'It's afternoon now. You'd better cut along back to that girl of yours.'

'Thank you, Sergeant. She'll be wondering what's happened.'

Watters watched Silver march away, sighed, and walked to the door of the Wild Geese. It was closed, with green painted shutters on the outside of each window and a massive padlocked bolt across the door. Nobody answered his knock. A window across the narrow street lit up, and somebody peered out, his dark figure silhouetted against yellow candlelight. A group of women reeled past, hooting and screeching in drunken revelry, one approached Watters.

'Police,' he said quietly, 'keep moving.'

'He's a bloody peeler,' the woman shouted to the world, 'he'll lock us all up!'

Still shrieking, the women staggered on, to pile into the doorway of a house further up the street. There was an outbreak of shouting, the ugly crash of breaking glass, and a few moments' silence before another burst of raucous laughter echoed between the houses followed by somebody singing a Gaelic song, the nasal music somehow out of place in this narrow, festering street.

Moving away from the Wild Geese, Watters knocked on the adjacent door, and the next, with no reply from either. Some instinct made him look up, to see a shadowy figure watching him from a window next door to the pub.

He focussed on the face. Mother Flannery stared directly at him without expression. When Watters pointed to the door of the pub and shouted that he wished to see her, she remained static.

'Police,' he yelled, with the word echoing up the length of the street. He heard doors open behind him as Mother Flannery raised her hand.

Three men emerged, dark shapes in a dark doorway. They stood in a line against the brick wall of the street, tall, broad, and unsmiling. They stared at him, wordless.

'I am Sergeant George Watters of Scotland Yard,' Watters said quietly. 'I am enquiring about a murder in this area.'

The men remained silent.

Watters heard the snick of a lock and looked up the street; another door had opened, with two more men standing by their door, watching him. He reversed his cane, so the weighted end pointed downward.

'Did any of you men notice anything untoward earlier today? There was an attack on two soldiers. One of the soldiers subsequently died, and the other is seriously injured.' He did not expect a reply.

'Mother Flannery?' Watters raised his voice to a shout. 'I act with the authority of Scotland Yard. Open the door and allow me in.'

Mother Flannery moved her head to one side, and all the men withdrew inside their homes. The doors shut. Within a minute, the street was deserted.

Watters felt the relief slide over him as he rapped his cane on the door of the Wild Geese. 'I'll come back later,' he shouted to the empty street, 'and I expect answers.' The echo of his words mocked their futility.

* * *

Watters was not prepared to find Rowena in his flat when he returned, and he was stunned that she had swept the floors and had laid the fire.

'I brought in water from the well and coal from the cellar,' Rowena said, 'I hope that is all right?'

'You've washed the dishes as well.' Watters noticed. He glanced at the table.

'It's in the drawer.' Rowena anticipated Watters's question. 'You are looking for your pocketbook.'

Watters nodded. 'I was,' he admitted.

She produced it at once. 'I did not look inside,' she said.

He held it, glanced at Rowena, and then put the pocketbook back in the drawer. 'That as good a place as any to keep it,' he said.

'Thank you,' Rowena said.

'For what?'

'For not checking to see if I stole anything.'

Watters nodded, knowing he would look later when she was not present.

'I'll get away now,' Rowena said. 'Thank you for letting me shelter last night.' Her smile was hesitant but welcome. 'It was very kind of you, and the warmth was good.'

'Oh, for goodness sake!' Watters snapped, 'you better get something to eat before you go. It is Christmas Day.' He struggled between his desire to be alone and his sympathy for this woman. 'Wait here!' Jamming his hat on his head, Watters grabbed his pocketbook and left the house. He returned within half an hour.

'Can you cook?' he asked as he placed a small goose on the table.

'It will take time,' she said. 'But—'

'No buts,' Watters said. 'It's Christmas, and we should celebrate.' He wondered if he would ever get any peace. He needed peace to gather his thoughts together and valued his privacy ever since he escaped the confines of barrack and shipboard life with the Royal Marines.

'It's late now,' Rowena pointed out quietly. 'You will want me out of your house. A goose will take hours to cook.'

'Do what you have to do,' Watters told her. He opened the box that contained his purchases. 'These might not fit.' He put a selection of women's clothes on the table. 'There's a coat against the rain. And a skirt and things.' He could not bring himself to name the items he had purchased. 'And here's some fruit, apples and oranges for Christmas.'

'Oh...' Rowena put her hand to her face, 'oh...'

Watters turned away from her tears. 'It's not much,' he said gruffly. 'You need some better clothes. Excuse me. I have work to do.'

He sat at the table, once again puzzling over the papers he had retrieved from the foreign woman's purse. He heard Rowena slip into the bedroom that had never known a female before and sighed.

'They fit,' Rowena interrupted his perusal. 'Thank you.'

Even Watters could see that the clothes were too large for Rowena's food-deprived body. He nodded. 'Are they warm enough?'

'Yes.' Rowena was close to tears again.

'I'm glad.' Watters made the required noises of admiration before he collected his scattered thoughts and looked back at the papers.

'So, you are a peeler?' Rowena had changed back to her old clothes and knelt to put more coal on the fire.

'I am a policeman,' Watters confirmed.

'I've never met a policeman before,' Rowena said, 'except when they move me on from sleeping in doorways.'

Watters sighed and pushed the papers away. It was apparent that he would get no peace with this woman in the house. 'You have never been in trouble with the police then?'

'No,' Rowena shook her head. She tilted her head sideways in a less-than-subtle attempt to read the documents. 'Do you know Gaelic?'

'Gaelic?' For a second Watters was surprised. 'No, I don't know Gaelic.'

'You're reading it,' Rowena pointed out.

'I knew it wasn't French,' Watters said. 'Can you read this?'

'Yes,' Rowena put her hand out, 'I've been wondering what you were reading. Is it very important?'

'Frankly, I have no idea what it is,' Watters said.

Maria scanned it. 'It's from the Ulster Cycle,' she said, and read out loud: "*Now whilst Cuchulain was in the Land of the Shadows it chanced that Skatha made war on the people of the Princess Aifa, who was the fiercest and strongest of the woman-warriors of the world—*"

'Enough,' Watters held up a hand, 'what sort of nonsense is that?'

When Rowena smiled, her eyes took on a life of their own. 'It's part of the cycle of stories about a great Irish warrior named Cuchulain, thousands of years ago.'

Watters raised his eyebrows. 'What was that name?'

'Cuchulain – here.' Rowena pointed it out in the handwritten script.

'I've seen that name before,' Watters said, 'under the picture of a man in the Wild Geese public in Ratcliffe Highway.'

'Cuchulain was a great man,' Rowena said. 'One of the Irish heroes.'

'Are all these documents about him?'

Rowena lifted another sheet of paper. 'No, this one is about the Morrigan.'

'The what?'

'The Morrigan. She was a sort of goddess who fell in love with Cuchulain, listen "*and the Morrigan came in the form of a great crow where Cuchulain sat with the women, and croaked of war and slaughter.*" '

'Stuff and nonsense,' Watters decided. 'I thought these papers might help me find their owner and instead I've been wasting my time over children's stories.'

'They're not for children,' Rowena said. 'They are a major part of Irish culture.'

'Maybe so,' Watters did not hide his disappointment, 'but I had hoped for something else, perhaps the name and address of a woman I'm searching for.' He realised that once more he was saying too much to Rowena, so he clamped shut his mouth. *Why would some foreign woman carry Irish folklore with her, and why was she in the Wild Geese?* He remembered that picture of the warrior in the green cloak with the name Cuchulain beneath; that was a tenuous connection but the only one he had. Watters frowned; this small mystery intrigued him, but he had to push it aside and concentrate on the guardsman's murder.

'Are you all right?' Rowena asked, 'you don't look very happy.'

'There was a man murdered this morning,' Watters said. 'Sorry; I did not mean to spoil your Christmas.'

Rowena looked at the fire and then at her new clothes over Watters's bed. 'You didn't spoil anything,' she said. 'It's years since anybody was so kind to me.'

Watters realised he had not eaten since early that morning. 'How long will that goose take to cook?'

'Hours and hours,' Rowena told him. 'Are you hungry? You only have bread and cheese in the kitchen …' her voice trailed away as if she wished she had not made the admission that she had looked.

'That sounds fine.' Watters moved toward the kitchen at the same time as Rowena, so they collided in the doorway and recoiled together. 'I do apologise,' he said.

'It was my fault,' Rowena spoke simultaneously.

They looked at each other, both hiding a tentative smile.

'It's your house.' They spoke together and laughed in unison.

'You first,' Watters said. He watched Rowena step in front of him. Evidently of good quality, her clothes were now worn, and neatly patched around elbows and hips. A gust of wind battered rain against the window and pushed smoke and a dribble of soot down the chimney.

'You're not going out in that tonight,' Watters said suddenly. He felt her unspoken relief. 'Stay another night. You can sleep in the bedroom, and I'll throw up something in the box room.'

'I can't deprive you of your bed for another night.'

'I'll be fine.' Watters dismissed her protests. 'I insist.'

'You'll lose your reputation for respectability,' Rowena said, 'having a woman stay overnight.'

'You're staying,' Watters said. 'It's a lot better than being in the streets or some lodging crib, and anyway, I might need more of your help with the Gaelic words.'

He saw her shoulders shaking and knew she was crying. He turned away and closed the kitchen door.

Chapter Six

The bald man stood aside as Peggy passed over the mug of coffee. 'You'll be asking about that murder in Atlantic Street, Sergeant.'

'I will be, Peggy.' He sipped the coffee. Piping hot, it seemed to seep inside every corner of him, giving comfort on this cold day. He had spent the last four hours touring pawn shops, searching for bloodstained clothing in the hope that the murder of one of his companions had been less than careful. He had found nothing.

'Well, I never heard much.' She leaned closer, frowning as a street urchin came too close. 'You clear off, see? Not you Mr Watters, it's that young vagabond I'm shouting at.'

Watters glanced downward. 'What are you after, youngster?'

'You're a bluebottle bastard,' the boy shouted and ran away before Watters could react.

'Young rogue,' Peggy shouted. 'I'll tan your backside if I catch you!' She lowered her voice. 'Poor lad lost his mother six months ago. She just ran and left him on the streets.'

Watters nodded. 'I see. Anything about the murder would be helpful. Any snippet.'

'I heard only one thing,' Peggy said, 'and that might not be any use. I heard that there's to be a prize fight in the Heath soon. That's all I heard.'

'What has that to do with the murder?' Watters asked.

'A prize fight, in the Heath,' Peggy repeated. 'Is that worth a sixpence?'

Watters checked his watch. Quarter to ten. He had an hour and a half in which to get ready. 'When?'

'New Year's Day.'

Watters dropped sixpence into her outstretched hand. 'Thank you, Peggy.'

Peggy's hand closed tight. 'It's Ireland against England,' she said, 'and all the smart money is on the land of the Paddies.'

Watters nodded. 'These blasted Irish are everywhere this season.' He rechecked his watch. 'Thank you, Peg.'

'Walk warily, Mr Watters, I don't want to lose any more custom this season, what with the sojers all being out East and business being depressed.'

'Do you expect there to be trouble Peg?' Watters tucked his watch away.

'I heard that there's a storm coming,' Peggy said. 'I don't know what it meant, but that's what I heard.'

'A storm is coming. Thanks, Peg.' Watters touched his cane to the brim of his hat and walked briskly away. He had little time in which to change into his borrowed suit, and he had something else to consider. Peggy was a useful whiddler, but she did like to talk in riddles.

* * *

Watters must have passed the wedding cake spire of St Brides in Fleet Street a hundred times, but now he was inside the church and had seldom seen anything more beautiful. An array of potted plants in every corner enhanced the soaring roof and bright stained-glass windows of the church. Yet despite the glories of the interior, Watters was far more interested in the events that were unfolding around him.

'Bride or groom, sir?' The usher wore a white ribbon favour as he asked the quiet question.

'Me? No, I'm only a guest … oh, I see, sorry.' With his mind still preoccupied with the murder, Watters had to focus on the matter at hand. 'Groom, please.'

'This way, sir, if you please.' The usher showed Watters to his position and moved on to the next guest.

With his back against the wall, Watters watched the father of the bride walk her to where Silver stood, fidgeting nervously, in front of the altar.

'Keep calm, William,' Watters whispered to himself. 'Angela is as decent a girl as ever walked the earth. She'll take care of you.'

'Are you bride or groom?' the dark-haired lady at his side asked in a hoarse whisper.

'Groom.' Watters tried to keep his voice low, although the soaring music of the organ would have covered all except a full chorus from the Brigade of Guards.

'Isn't Mr Silver handsome?' the lady said. 'I would marry him myself if he was not already spoken for.' She nudged Watters in the ribs. 'I shall tell him that if it turns out to be a misalliance, I shall be here to retrieve his situation.'

Watters thought that a brief nod was the best answer to that. He had never considered William Silver as handsome. He was just William Silver, cynical, dependable, methodical, and utterly reliable. There would be no misalliance as far as William was concerned.

'They say that all wedding cakes copy the tiered spire of this church' the lady was persistent. 'I am Elizabeth Tealing. That's Miss Elizabeth Tealing.'

'George Watters.'

'Are you a married man, Mr Watters?'

'I am not,' Watters replied. 'Here comes the bride now.' He followed the lead of the man in front by standing as the music reached a crescendo. Every female eye in the church followed the bride's progress up the aisle. Following the example set by Queen Victoria, she wore a flowing white dress, while a bandeau of brilliants encircled her hair.

'Isn't she lovely,' Miss Tealing's hand rested on the crook of Watters's elbow, 'quite the catch if just a leetle too slender for my taste.'

The bride glided past the assembled congregation with her back as erect as any guardsman. Her father stopped three paces short of the groom, and she completed the distance alone, to stand beside Silver, man- and wife-to-be in front of the altar.

'You're a trump, William,' Watters muttered to himself, 'though God alone knows how you managed to snare such a peach as Angela.'

Miss Tealing's hand squeezed slightly. 'The best man is quite handsome too, I declare, but not as much as William. I do like older men, and William's brother is just a leetle too young.'

Adam Silver, shorter, stockier and more self-assured, stood beside William. The music continued, filling the church, appealing to God to bless this union. Watters closed his eyes. He did not have the heart to remove Miss Tealing's hand from his arm.

The congregation gave a collective sigh and sat back as the priest began his address. The solemn words that bound Silver to Angela droned above the rustling of women's clothing and the deep breathing of men who remembered when they were in such a situation. Miss Tealing's grip tightened on Watters's sleeve.

'Do you, William Silver, take this woman, Angela Joyce ... '

Watters watched as the couple made their vows. He saw Silver face Angela, and then the best man produced the ring, the single thin gold ring that Silver had paid to have engraved with both their initials and the date. And then Silver dropped it.

Instinctively Watters jerked forward as if to pick it up, but Miss Tealing stopped him.

'It's all right! That is meant to happen. It shakes away all the evil spirits!'

Watters nodded his thanks. *Evil spirits, indeed! The year was 1854, not 1254! What with ghosts and superstitions he may as well be in Hispaniola or darkest Africa.* He looked up to see the ring safely ensconced on Angela's finger and the congregation watching in silent enjoyment.

The door of the church opened with a loud bang, and a uniformed constable thundered in, his boots clumping up the sacred aisle. He stopped momentarily as the vicar continued with his discourse.

'Ah there you are, Sergeant!' the constable's voice sounded plainly above the priest. 'I couldn't see you in the crowd!'

Half the congregation looked round to see what the disturbance was. The women continued to watch the wedding ceremony.

'For God's sake, man!' Watters hissed at the constable. 'You're in a church! A holy place!'

'Oh, yes, Sergeant.' The constable removed his tall hat and stood awkwardly for a moment.

'I've got a message for you from some army officer cove.' The constable did not lower his voice. He produced his notebook and read slowly with his mouth forming the shape of every word. 'Guardsman Elwood has awakened and would Sergeant Watters care to come to the barracks.'

Watters reached for his hat. 'Thank you, constable. You may leave the church and for God's sake, do it quietly.'

'Yes, Sergeant.' The constable's attempt at silence was if anything, even noisier than his earlier entrance.

Watters rose. 'Please give my apologies to the bride and groom,' he whispered to Miss Tealing.

'Oh, yes indeed, Sergeant Watters.' Her eyes were bright. 'How thrilling that was!' She patted his arm. 'You're a sergeant.'

Silver was kissing his bride; he did not look round as Watters left the church.

* * *

Elwood lay at attention in his narrow cot, with one bruised eye barely visible amidst the bandages that covered the rest of his face. He tried to move a broken arm as Captain Fletcher brought Watters to his bedside.

'This is Sergeant Watters of Scotland Yard,' Fletcher announced. 'He is here to ask you questions. You will answer them promptly, accurately, and with respect.'

'Yes, sir.' Elwood's voice was little more than a muffled croak.

'You were pretty badly beaten,' Watters said, 'and your colleague, Guardsman Nixon, was killed, so we are determined to find who attacked you.'

'Yes, sir.' Elwood tried to move his head but subsided onto the pillow.

'Did you see your attackers, Guardsman?' Watters asked.

'Yes, sir.'

'Please tell me all you can remember. Try and leave nothing out.'

'Yes, sir.' Elwood's voice cracked, and Watters held a cup of water to his lips. 'Guardsman Nixon and me had been on the ran-dan sir. Somebody told us that there was a couple of publics on the Highway that was offering cheap beer for soldiers, so we went there.'

'Do you remember their names, Elwood?'

'The Cock and the Duck, sir. Sorry, I mean the Cock and Neptune and the Wild Geese. They are across the road from each other in the Highway, sir.'

'I know them,' Watters said.

'We went into the Cock, sir, but the landlord closed early, so we crossed to the Duck.' Elwood's voice cracked again, so Watters eased it with water.

'We went inside, and there was beer at a penny a pint, so we drunk some and then the woman of the house said the place was shutting.'

'The woman of the house? Was she tall and sat on a raised chair?'

'Yes, sir.'

'Mother Flannery.'

'Could be sir, I never was there before. When we left the public, there was a group of men following us. Connaught men by the sound of them.'

'You're from Ulster, I think?'

'Yes, sir, me and Nixon both, sir.'

'So they attacked you?'

'Not at first, sir. They just followed and taunted us, sir. Old Nick – that's Nixon, sir, sorry, he turned and faced them a couple of times, challenged them to fight, but they backed off.'

Watters could imagine the scene with the half-starved mob gathering, yapping at the heels of the two tall Guardsmen. The crowd would encourage each other by throwing insults at the soldiers, who, alcohol-fuelled, would also be looking for trouble and hoping for an excuse to retaliate.

'Then it blew up, Elwood?'

'Not quite, sir. There was one man who caused it. He was a nothing, a wee leprechaun of a creature with a soft voice but he stirred them up telling them that we were traitors to old Ireland and slaves of the English and other things.'

'Because you joined the army?'

'That and other things, sir.'

'Other things? What other things, Elwood?' Watters leaned closer to catch the words.

There was silence until Captain Fletcher took Watters aside. 'Elwood and Nixon were both members of the Freemasons, Sergeant. That seems to have been significant.'

'You are both Masons?' Watters asked Elwood. 'How would they have known that?'

'We wore rings, sir, with the Mason's symbol on them.' Elwood's eye swivelled toward Fletcher. 'We only wore them off duty, sir.'

'Pope Clement XII banned Catholics from joining the Masons in 1738,' Fletcher said quietly, 'because Freemasonry has its own oaths and dogma.'

Watters nodded. 'Thank you for the information, sir.'

'We fought back, sir, and I let go at one and gave him a beauty in the eye.'

'Good man, Elwood,' Fletcher approved.

'We were holding our own, sir; these Connaught men are nothing to good Ulstermen, and that woman from the Duck was watching the whole thing.' Elwood's eye swivelled toward Fletcher again. It was red-rimmed, with blood around the pupil. 'Then another woman comes up, she wore a saffron shawl, sir, and threw a black powder in Nick's face, and he roared and held his face. I went to help him, and the same woman threw the powder in my face. I could not see anything, and the pain was something dreadful.'

Watters glanced at Fletcher, who took him aside again.

'The doctor says he may lose the sight of one eye.'

Watters nodded. 'So you were attacked because of your Masonic rings then, Elwood.'

'Maybe sir, and maybe not. They never mentioned them, but they took our rings away. They bit off Nixon's finger, sir, bit it off like a dog with a bone.'

Watters disguised his thrill of horror. He had seen and heard a lot worse, but every case presented him with some new depth of human depravity.

'Do you remember how your attackers looked? Could you give me a description of any of them?'

There was silence for a moment, and then Elwood spoke again. 'The woman who threw the powder was small, sir, with a saffron shawl and hair as black as the Earl of Hell's waistcoat. Once the attack started, I never saw the leprechaun man again. He done his stuff and vanished. There was a lot of men and women, don't know how many. I saw a man with red side-whiskers, and a big man, near as tall as we were, with a cudgel, but most were—' He stopped and coughed up bright blood.

'Take your time.' Watters gave him another drink.

'Thank you, sir. You are too kind. Most were just ordinary men and women, poor-like folk.'

Watters nodded. He could see it all in his head; he could imagine the leprechaun man whispering his hate. He could see bitter men using the Masonic ring as an excuse for violence, the initial rush repelled by the soldiers. He envisioned the woman throwing some black powder in the Guardsmen's eyes and then the mob surging over the reeling victims, fists and boots pounding.

'You have done well, Elwood. Now get better soon.' Watters rose and spoke to Fletcher. 'If he remembers anything else, sir, I would be obliged if you contact me.'

Captain Fletcher nodded. 'I will do that, Sergeant.'

Despite his years as a police officer, Watters had to fight the cold anger that engulfed him as he left the barracks. He had seen much worse injuries during his time in the Marines, but the sheer pointlessness of one good man badly hurt and another killed purely because of their membership of some society affected him.

'It's a damned shame.'

* * *

'Where's the inspector?' he asked as he walked into Larkin's office to make his report.

'Inspector Larkin is not in the office,' an officious sergeant told him. 'I believe he is at home with his family.'

'I need some uniformed men,' Watters said. 'Who is in charge in Larkin's absence?'

'I am.' The sergeant smirked. 'Don't you know it's Boxing Day? You won't get any men today.'

Watters felt the anger rising within him. 'I don't give a two penny damn if it's Boxing Day or Judgement Day. I need some uniforms to help with a murder case.'

The sergeant leaned back and folded his arms, 'You won't get any,' he said. 'You'll have to do your own work, like the rest of us.'

Watters took a deep breath. This man was his equal in rank and to judge by his age, probably his superior in length of service. He could neither browbeat him nor pull rank. That left him with two choices: either he left his investigations for another day and joined Water's post-wedding celebrations, which was very appealing, or he walked alone. Watters hefted his cane. He would follow the line of duty, as always.

'Thank you for your help, Sergeant,' he said. 'I would be obliged if you could note in your Day Book that I made the request.'

'Of course.' Now that he had won the argument, the uniformed sergeant was eager to prove he was friendly. 'I can find you some men for tomorrow,' he suggested, but Watters had already stomped away.

'Do you sell cold water?' he asked Peggy at the coffee stall.

'There is no call for anything like that.' Peggy looked astonished at the request.

'Cold milk then,' Watters said, 'and a flask to put it in.' He passed over sixpence.

'Have you signed the pledge?' Peggy asked. 'Cold milk, indeed. That's for suckling children.' Her smile was more motherly than mocking.

Atlantic Street was busier than on the previous day, with the Wild Geese roaring with custom and people standing outside in groups talking and smoking. Watters jammed his tall hat on his head, swung his cane and approached a short man with an excellent set of whiskers.

'I am Sergeant George Watters of Scotland Yard,' he announced and waited for the reaction.

There was immediate silence, with one or two men on the fringes of the group sliding away. A woman gave a high-pitched laugh.

'There was a murder here yesterday,' Watters reminded them, 'and I am looking for witnesses.'

The bewhiskered man shrugged and said something in Gaelic, which caused his companions to laugh.

Watters recognised a face. 'You speak English,' he said. 'You were swearing at me a few days ago.'

The man's grin was disarming. 'I do,' he said, 'I know I do. I can swear at you again today if you wish.' He proved his point with a colourful selection of oaths.

The crowd laughed again. Watters was aware that more were gathering around him, talking excitedly, pulling at long pipes, encouraging each other, raising their courage.

'Did you see anything of the attack?' He felt a hand on his coat and pushed the owner away. 'Stand back!' he ordered.

Space cleared around Watters, as sullen faces withdrew one by one.

'That's better,' he said. 'Now, I am accusing nobody,' he ran his gaze over the assembly, searching for anybody that fitted the descriptions that Elwood had provided. The faces all looked the same, unwashed, suspicious eyed, lank-haired. 'Was anybody here when the assault took place?'

There was a shake of the collective head.

'We don't like the peelers here,' somebody said, 'asking questions as if they had the right.'

Watters tried to identify the voice from the mass of ragged humanity that surrounded him.

'I do have the right,' he said. He felt, rather than saw, the figure of a tall man behind him, and then somebody knocked his hat off his head.

Watters swung backwards with his cane, moving aside at the same time as the cudgel hissed downward. His sidestep saved his head, but he winced at the sudden pain when the heavy stick caught his shoulder.

'Kill the peeler bastard,' somebody said as voices rose around him, shrieking in English and Gaelic.

Watters remembered the words of a veteran Marine sergeant: 'If the enemy ambushes you, boy, don't retreat; they expect that. Don't stand and fight it out; they are ready for that. Go forward and kick their teeth down their throat.'

Watters swung sideways with the weighted end of his cane, felt the satisfying jar of hard contact, saw a tall man staggering, and thrust forward at a pair of gaunt-faced men who flapped wild punches at him. He smacked the end of his cane into the forehead of the nearest man, sending him reeling back as the second landed a weak blow on his shoulder. Ignoring him, Watters pushed on, felt something slide down his right side, kicked out at a yelling man who tried to block his path, ducked a swing from a bottle, and barged into the gap he had made.

'Stop!' he roared as the mob swayed toward him, with the leading men and women recoiling from his swinging cane. 'You are putting yourself in danger of imprisonment.' The words sounded weak in the face of so much anger.

He studied them, trying to identify faces, wishing he had the back-up of experienced uniformed men. 'I am only interested in the people who attacked two soldiers on Christmas Day.' He heard the raggedness of his breathing and knew he was on a knife-edge with a full-scale riot pending, then gave a wide smile. 'Look, ladies and gentlemen, I am not trying to arrest any except the guilty.' Using both hands, Watters brandished his cane above his head, then slowly placed it on the ground. 'You see? I am now unarmed before you.'

He felt a slight relaxation in the tension. He kept his smile, feeling the ache of his jaws and wondered if his face looked more like a death's head skull than a man hoping to appease a volatile crowd.

'We could tear your head off,' somebody said.

'I know that,' Watters replied, 'and then there would be two murders here and no profit to you or anybody else.'

Watters was unsure if the crowd's low murmur signified dissent or agreement. He kept his wolf's-head grin in place.

'I ask you again, did any of you witness the attack here on Christmas Day?'

'Let me through. Let me talk to the policeman!' The voice was shrill as if the owner was very young or very nervous, and Watters saw a woman pushing her way through the crowd. They parted reluctantly, with one man trying to drag her back. She shook him away. 'I want to see the blue devil.'

'Sergeant Watters?' All five foot of the woman was shaking as she stepped forward, with her bare feet making little sound on the greasy cobbles and her head bowed, covered with a shawl of stained tartan.

'Yes. Thank you for coming forward. Do you want to talk here or somewhere more private?'

'Here is grand.' She looked very vulnerable as she stood in front of the hostile crowd. 'I found something on the ground.' She reached into the pocket of her skirt, and as Watters stepped forward, threw a handful of black powder in his face.

The pain was instant and so intense that Watters doubled up, swearing, with his hands to his eyes. He heard the woman screech with laughter.

'How do you like that Mr Policeman?'

There was cruel laughter from the crowd, and another voice sounded. Low but intense, it carried beneath the baying of the mob. The howls died away to a chilling silence. Watters turned away, desperate to ease the burning agony of his eyes. He reached inside his coat as that low voice spoke in a soft Irish brogue.

'Time to teach our policeman a lesson. As true as Christ's holiness, he needs one.'

Watters hauled the flask from his inside pocket, fumbled to open it as he heard the footsteps thumping toward him.

'What's he doing?' That was a man's voice.

'Who cares, kick his teeth out.'

Watters popped the cork, which rolled on the ground out of his reach. Fighting the pain, he forced himself to open his eyes and splashed the milk from the flask in each. The pain receded slightly, sufficiently for him to see a blurred image of his cane lying where he had dropped it. As he reached for it, the first boot crashed into Watters's ribs, followed by a laugh from that small woman. He grabbed at her, with his fingers closing on her shawl and dirty black hair.

'Don't kill him,' that low voice sounded from the back of the crowd, 'by Christ's holiness the police don't like when one of their own is killed but make sure he learns not to come back.'

The small woman's maniacal laugh sounded again as she kicked out, aiming evilly at Watters's groin. He recoiled, lifted his cane, and slashed blindly, hearing the woman's yelp as the blow caught her across the leg.

'You bluebottle bastard!'

Watters poured the last of the milk onto his eyes and gasped as a cudgel crashed against his head. He felt the start of blood and looked out through half-closed eyes. The people who surrounded him were blurred, with irregular features and misshapen bodies, so Watters could not tell who was kicking him. He slashed with his cane, swore as a boot crashed into his knee, punched out and felt only fresh air. A shadowy shape loomed over him, something slipped around his neck, strangling him as a rough hand covered his mouth and nose, pressing hard.

'Burke him! Burke the bluebottle bastard!' That was the small woman shouting, her voice shrill, triumphant.

With the pressure on his throat increasing and a knee against his spine forcing him backwards, Watters kicked out wildly, seeing only dim shapes through his burning eyes and with each breath feeling like red-hot broken glass in his throat. Somebody punched him hard in the stomach, and then a boot crashed into his groin. Unable to yell, Watters sank his teeth into the fingers that closed his mouth, worried for a second and released as the hand's owner jerked it away. He took a whooping breath of air, reversed his cane, and flicked it over his left shoulder, once, twice, and the third time he heard a scream and the pressure on his throat released. He fell backwards, rolled, rode the boot that crashed into his ribs and staggered to his feet.

He fumbled in the fog of demi-blindness, seeing only shapes as he lashed out blindly. Knowing he was outnumbered, gasping in pain, aware that he was at a terrible disadvantage, Watters backed away, step by slow step, striking anyone who came close. He winced as kicks and punches landed on his legs, his ribs, and his head. Jeers and catcalls echoed, mocking laughter, and that low, clear voice ordering them to attack, to hurt, to injure, and to 'teach him a lesson.'

Watters withdrew, trying to control the pain, trying to keep on his feet, for he knew that if he went down again, the mob would surge over him with boots and cudgels and fists. He swung his cane in a figure of eight, occasionally feeling the jar of contact but more often only glad that it might keep his assailants at bay.

He staggered as another kick landed, swore as something crashed into the side of his head, changed his stance, so the cane swung upward, grunted as it made contact and took another step backwards, and then another.

Watters remembered the words of his old sergeant. 'Don't let the enemy see your back.' If he went down, the mob would kick him to a pulp. He withdrew step by step, swinging as the rabble closed around him.

'What's all this?' The new voice was nearly as welcome as the harsh sound of a police rattle. 'Police!'

Watters swore as something hard and heavy crashed onto his head. 'Get me a cab, for God's sake,' he said.

'Stay upright,' the voice said. Watters saw only a tall man in a blue uniform. 'Don't let the bastards see you fall.' A strong arm held his shoulders. 'I've got you.'

Chapter Seven

The hands were gentle on his face, the voice soothing. 'It's all right. Let me help.' Watters felt soft fingers at his eyelids, fought the harsh light that tortured the pupils and strove to keep them closed.

'It's all right. I'm trying to help. Keep your eyes open, please.'

Watters obeyed. Light flooded him, with a shadowy shape moving behind. 'Who's that?'

'It's all right, it's me.' Water scoured his eye, burning, scratching, sending deep shafts of agony into his head. 'That's the way.' Something soft and cool covered his face. He closed his eyes, aware only of pain.

Watters lay still and tried to remember. The confusion of faces and words echoed in his head with that sudden blinding pain and the cloud of black powder. The high grating laugh of the small woman and that low, calm voice giving orders, then the shadowed, dark figures of the mob returned like a nightmare.

'Where am I?' He tried to open his eyes, but pain forced them to shut again.

'At home,' the voice was female, vaguely familiar, and very comforting. 'Rest now; you are safe.'

Sleep came unbidden. Watters allowed it to comfort him away from pain. He lost count of the hours. He only knew that when he woke, gentle hands were there to nurse him, and that caring voice soothed his fears. His pillow was soft, and the covers clean above him. Light came slowly, creeping into the periphery of his vision in a gradual realisation that the world was not all darkness and pain did not exist alone.

'Well, my boy?' The police doctor smiled down at him. 'You are back with us, then?'

'I am here.' Watters looked around. He was in his own bedroom, with grey light seeping through the window and a single candle burning in its brass holder. 'How long have I been here?'

'Three days,' the doctor said. 'You came by cab and fell against the door.'

'Three days?' Watters made to rise until dizziness forced him back down. 'I must go. I have a murder to solve.'

'Not today, Sergeant Watters,' the doctor said.

'Have you been here all the time? There was a woman here.'

The doctor nodded. 'There still is. Your wife saved your sight.' He looked up as the door opened. 'Here she is now.'

Rowena smiled shyly as she looked into the bedroom. 'Hello, Sergeant Watters.'

The doctor stepped back.

'This is Rowena.' Watters stopped. 'I think she is a lodger here.'

'Lodger, wife, or guardian angel, she saved your eyes and cared for you before I came,' the doctor said.

Watters nodded and looked toward Rowena. 'Thank you,' he said, watching her. The words seemed inadequate. Already Rowena looked more relaxed than she had been the past days, and Watters could have sworn she had filled out slightly. He looked away. 'Doctor, do you know what was thrown at me?'

'Black lead,' the doctor said at once. 'There is a spate of that type of injury among some levels of society. I will leave you in this lady's more than capable hands: I have other patients who do not have such a devoted nurse.' He leaned closer, 'hold on to this one, Watters, or Florence Nightingale will recruit her.'

'Thank you,' Watters said again as the doctor left the room.

Rowena inclined her head. 'I hoped you would not mind,' she said. 'You needed help.' She hesitated. 'I am sorry; I had to go into your pocketbook for money to buy bandages and goose grease for all your injuries.'

Watters suddenly realised that he was naked under the covers, with bandages on various parts of his body. 'You did that? You took my clothes off and,' he felt the itch of bandages on his upper thigh and his ribs, 'dressed my hurts?'

'Yes.' She held his gaze. Her eyes were concerned. 'I've seen a man before,' she said. She held his gaze. 'It's all right, Mr Watters. You are safe with me.'

Those were the identical words he had used when he invited her in on Christmas Eve.

'Only two other women have ever seen me unclothed,' Watters told her seriously. 'One was my mother, who I don't remember, and the second I won't talk about.'

'You can tell me about them sometime.' Rowena did not lower her eyes.

'Perhaps.' Watters already regretted that he had said so much. What was there about this woman that made him open up?

'You are much better now,' Rowena bustled to the bed and tucked in the loose covers, 'but you must stay warm and get your strength back.' She stepped back. 'I don't believe you need me anymore.'

The sharp rap on the door interrupted them. 'Could you get that, please?' Watters asked. 'It seems very busy here today.'

'You're looking well.' Silver had Angela at his side. 'You look quite comfortable lying in bed while others do all the work.'

'You never did a day's work in your life,' Watters told him.

Angela laughed. 'You know him so well.' She pressed his arm, smiling. Light from the window gleamed on her wedding ring.

'What happened?'

Watters saw the shadow of concern beneath Silver's cheerful front as he explained the events.

'Hold on.' Silver held up a hand, palm out and fingers outstretched. 'You went into Atlantic Street alone to make enquiries?'

Watters nodded. 'There was nobody else available.'

Silver shook his head, 'I'm sorry to see you in this situation, George, and you know it, but you were a bloody fool to go there alone!'

Acutely aware that Rowena and Angela were watching him, Watters stiffened in the bed. 'Don't forget I am your sergeant, Detective Silver.'

'We're off duty, George, so don't come the old soldier on me.' Silver knelt beside the bed. 'Atlantic Street is known as 'little Donegal' because of all the Irish living there, and you know that police are not welcome in that neighbourhood.'

'There was nobody else available,' Watters repeated.

'I agree with your friend,' Rowena said. 'I know it's not my place to say anything.'

Watters glared at her in anger. 'What do you mean: it's not your place?' It would have taken a sharp knife to cut the sudden silence. He lowered his tone. 'You saved my sight, dammit, woman! Surely that gives you as much right as anybody else!'

It was Angela who asked the direct question that Silver never would. 'Who is this woman who saved your sight, George?'

'I am a lodger here,' Rowena said quickly. 'Except I haven't paid any rent.'

'I didn't know George had a lodger,' Angela smiled to her. 'He can be a bit of a dark horse, can our George.'

Rowena glanced at Watters. 'He took me off the street on Christmas Eve,' she said.

'Oh?' Angela raised her eyebrows, gave Rowena a long stare and took Silver by the crook of his elbow. 'Excuse us, George. There is something that William and I must discuss.'

'Welcome to married life,' Watters said as Angela dragged Silver out of the room.

'They are talking about me,' Rowena told him. 'Your friend Angela is telling him whether he can accept me or not.'

Watters heard the murmur of voices from his living room, and then Angela and William returned.

'You looked after him well,' Angela said at once.

Rowena nodded slowly. 'Thank you.'

'Some women would have taken advantage,' Angela was still smiling, but Watters recognised the edge to her words and struggled to sit up.

'Her name is Rowena, and she looked after me when I came in battered and blinded—'

'It's all right, Mr Watters.' Rowena put a hand on his arm. 'Your friend is making sure that I don't rob you, or worse.'

'And will you?' Silver asked bluntly.

'No,' Rowena was equally direct.

Watters looked from one to the other. William Silver, the friend and colleague he had known for some years and the young Irishwoman who had entered his life a few days ago yet who had made such an impact. *Damn it, man! Say something.*

'I would like you to be my housekeeper, Rowena, if you want the position. Long hours, a bad-tempered master, and little money are all I offer.'

The silence continued for what seemed a long time before Rowena spoke. 'I'll need some money to replenish your pantry,' she said, 'and you have almost no cleaning materials in the house. Your brush drops bristles every time I lift it, and you have not properly washed the windows in years, I warrant.'

'It would appear that you have a housekeeper,' Angela said.

'When are you coming back to duty?' Silver asked.

'As soon as I have peace to get out of this damned bed,' Watters growled.

'You're not fit yet,' Rowena said severely.

'I'm fit enough, madam,' Watters said, 'so if you would all leave the room I am sure my housekeeper can find something drinkable in the house, and maybe a hunk of bread and cheese to go along with it.'

'The bread is stale,' Rowena said.

'Well, do something about it,' Watters growled. 'You're the damned housekeeper after all.'

Chapter Eight

Some came in coaches pulled by four stately horses, some in dog carts. Some rode alone, with the hooves of their horses kicking up clods of mud that spattered the multitudes of pedestrians who walked singly, in pairs, or in small groups to their eventual destination.

Limping to assuage the pain of his many bruises, Watters hunched his shoulders and walked with the others, looking up only to curse when a carriage sprayed him with liquid mud. He blinked to try and clear his vision and winced at the pain.

'Two to one on Lancashire,' somebody sidled up to him. 'Two to one.'

Watters swore at him and lifted his cane. The men slid away to approach a more congenial customer.

'Where are the police?' Watters looked around. With so much traffic across Hampstead Heath, it was apparent that something was happening. Surely, some constable or detective had noticed. He grunted. Obviously the police were not as observant as they should be. He was alone again as the criminal fraternity flouted the law at the very beginning of 1855.

'I wish Peggy had given me more information,' he said, 'but at least it's dry.' After days of near-constant rain, the clouds had cleared, and an unfamiliar sun was sending light, if not warmth, on the masses below.

'Here! You!' Watters poked the tip of his cane into the rump of a smart-looking young man. 'Where is this blessed prize fight being held?'

The man jumped and rubbed at himself. 'Be careful with that thing, can't you? It's on the Mound, don't you know?' He sounded and looked like a clerk with his smoothed down hair and white face.

'No I don't blasted know, I wouldn't ask, else! Which mound would that be?'

'Why Boadicea's Mound of course!' The man shied further away as Watters made to poke at him again.

'That's all I wanted to know.' Watters hurried on. Rather than follow the route of the crowd, he cut across the Heath, not caring that his boots and trousers would become befouled with mud.

Boadicea's Mound was a small hump on the still-wild landscape. It was rumoured to be the burial place of Boadicea, who had fought the Romans in 61 AD but privately Watters doubted that was accurate. Why should the Romans have buried an enemy in such a prominent place and if the Romans had defeated Boadicea, would there have been enough Britons left alive to take the trouble?

There was quite a crowd already at the Mound, with more arriving every minute. Watters leaned against a small mountain ash tree and watched them come, recognising many of the Fancy among the crowd and wondering if they knew him. Not that he cared much. He was not there to break up the prize fight but to try and solve a murder and, if possible, find that damned foreign woman to see what sort of mystery she had behind her.

The first coach to arrive at the Mound was black painted with dark blinds drawn over the windows, while the driver wore a two-penny wide-awake hat drawn low across his face. Watters watched without moving from his chosen spot. He had no real interest in pugilism except to know who the current champion was, and to break up illegal prize fights when ordered.

The crowd was gathering now as men, and a few women, arrived after their journey across the Heath. Some had come prepared with bottles while others wished that they had as much foresight. Watters spotted a couple of pickpockets working the fringes of the crowd, wondered if he should stop them and decided not to. None of these people should have attended this illegal event, so in his mind, they deserved all they got.

A group of men set up a rough ring, with posts thrust into the ground joined by ropes to keep the crowd back. A Clarence rolled up, with its massive wheels churning great gouges in the grass and its bodywork and blinds both green.

Watters nodded; not long now but save for the pickpockets he had not seen anybody who might help him in his investigations. Mind you, he told himself, with his eyes still hazed and smarting, he was lucky to see anybody more than twenty yards away. Watters grunted as the door of the Clarence opened, and two men stepped out. One was white, the other black and he had seen both in the Wild Geese.

'Now we may be getting somewhere,' Watters said to himself.

The door of the black coach also opened, and two equally large men stepped out. They eyed the Geese men across the width of the ring until one stepped cautiously forward to meet his opposite number. They shook hands, spoke briefly and parted. As the crowd gathered thickly at the ropes, Watters shoved himself away from the tree and slipped through the press until he was close enough to get a good view but sufficiently far back to be an anonymous face in the mass.

As the big men patrolled the ropes, pushing back any of the audience who attempted to cross into the ring, the corner-men placed down three-legged stools, and the bottle-men readied their concoctions of water-and-gin for the fighters, who were the last to appear.

Finally, a small, dapper man in a sharp suit with a flowery waistcoat and a mauve topper entered the ring and held up his hands for a silence that was long in coming. Sunlight reflected from the rings on his fingers and the Birmingham jewellery that adorned his suit.

'I am Bill Yellowford and welcome to the ring for the other Championship of All England!' He did not speak loudly, but his East London accent carried across the crowd without any difficulty.

The crowd whooped and cheered, with men throwing hats in the air and catching them again. A couple of dogs began to fight until their owners kicked them apart.

'Are there any Cockneys with the Fancy?' Bill Yellowford asked and clapped his hands in the air at the resulting roar. Watters noted sourly that his hands rattled rather than clapped, they were so festooned with rings.

'Are there any Scotchmen in the crowd?'

There were only a few shouts, and Yellowford moved quickly on.

'Are there any Irishmen with the Fancy?'

The cheer was nearly as loud as it had been for the Cockneys, and Yellowford milked it, throwing his hat in the air, and catching it again. 'Hurrah for old Ireland!'

Watters eyed one vociferous group that stood behind the green carriage and moved closer. There seemed a high number of Irish in London this season.

'Are there any peelers in the Fancy?' Bill Yellowford asked, and men and women looked around at their neighbours.

'If there are any, you can go straight to hell!' Bill Yellowford said, and the crowd cheered again at his wit.

'I said, go to hell!' Bill Yellowford shouted.

The less sober of the crowd chanted the words, 'Go to hell, go to hell,' until Yellowford held up his hands for silence again.

'Now let's get to business before the Devil rejects the peelers and returns them as unwanted.' That brought another cheer.

'Introducing,' Yellowford said, 'from the dark satanic mills of Blake's North Country, the Lancashire Lass, Mighty Mary Ogden!'

As he finished, the door of the black coach opened again, and a figure stepped out, draped in a long tasselled black cloak. It stepped to the centre of the ring, dwarfing Yellowford, and suddenly tossed aside the cloak to stand there, naked from the waist up and wearing only a pair of male drawers beneath. She was undoubtedly the largest and ugliest woman that Watters had ever seen in his life.

Half the crowd cheered while the other half, who presumably had money on Mighty Mary's rival, booed and hissed.

'And now, the Pride of Ireland, from County Cork, Fighting Bridget Flannery!'

The door of the green Clarence opened, and Mother Flannery from the Wild Geese stepped out. Her cloak was green, edged in gold, and she was a full half head shorter than Mary Ogden, but when she dropped her cloak, she looked in better shape. While Ogden carried at least two stones of excess fat and her breasts swung like pendulums, Flannery was broad-shouldered and muscled.

Watters grunted. Was this the spectacle that Peggy had wanted him to see? A prize fight between two women? Or was Peggy merely warning him that Mother Flannery was not a woman with whom it was wise to tangle?

Yellowford held out his hands and ushered both women to the centre of the ring, with the mound behind them and a cold sun highlighting the scene. He shouted for silence and then raised his arms as the hooting and cheering of the mob gradually subsided.

'I want a good, clean fight,' he began and stepped back as Ogden swung a roundhouse right that landed with an audible smack on Flannery's arm.

It was like watching a savage beast oppose a professional. While Ogden telegraphed each assault with a roar and lunged forward, fists swinging and her hair a black mass around her head, Flannery countered with jabs and footwork that could have come from a manual of scientific pugilism.

'Brute force against science,' a man beside Watters murmured. 'If you put your money on the Lancashire Lass it was a bad choice, mister.'

'Bad indeed,' Watters had already lost interest in the fight and was surveying the crowd. They were as he would have expected in such an event; there was nothing to be learned here.

'You're Sergeant Watters,' the man said. 'Peggy told me you would be here.'

Watters looked at the man for the first time. It was the same bald man who had stood beside Peggy's stall but dressed in shabby-genteel clothes that might indicate a petty clerk or shopkeeper. 'And what else did Peggy say?'

'She said you would be probably watching the pugilists rather than Bill Yellowford.'

'She is a clever lady, our Peggy,' Watters agreed. 'You forgot to give me your name.' But the man had already gone, an anonymous face lost in the crowd.

Watters focussed on Bill Yellowford, who stood arms folded, beside the group of Irishmen he had noted earlier. Save for his flash appearance and the profusion of Birmingham jewellery, there was nothing to make Yellowford stand out from the crowd. He was a man of barely average height and build, with a nondescript face that would not be noticed in a group of three. Then Watters blinked. It was the jewellery that mattered; the decoration behind which the owner hid his true personality. The man's fingers were ablaze with rings, and one in particular held Watters's attention as the sun gleamed on the Masonic device.

As Watters moved closer to Yellowford, Ogden launched a fist-swinging charge at Flannery, who sidestepped coolly and landed a single punch to Ogden's jaw. The Lancashire Lass staggered, and Flannery finished her with a combination of blows to body and head. Ogden crumpled to the ground, and Flannery stepped on top of her, grinding the heels of her boots into the Lass's ample stomach to emphasise her triumph.

There were cheers and jeers as men and women sought their winnings; the crowd surged forward, the Irishmen mounted Flannery on their shoulders to parade her around the ring, a few fistfights began, and there was the sound of a police rattle. Watters backed away. He had seen what he came for and had no desire to explain his presence to Inspector Larkin.

* * *

Watters tipped forward his hat as a protection against the near-horizontal sleet that rattled off the windows and bounced from the sides and roofs of the hansom cabs that stood in two long rows outside Scotland Yard.

'Larkin's done wonders here,' Watters grudgingly admitted.

'He was wild that the rabble attacked you' Silver said.

The men filed out of Scotland Yard, boots thumping from the stone pavements, removed their tall hats and entered the cabs in pairs, to sit stolidly side by side, staring straight ahead with their truncheons held upright between their knees.

'He's making certain, our Inspector Larkin, is he not?' Silver pointed to the cutlasses that thoughtful authority had issued to every uniformed man.

Watters tapped his shoulder, where the revolver hung reassuringly heavy in its holster. After his last encounter with the denizens of Atlantic Street, he was taking no chances. 'You know the area better than I do, Silver, what would you do?'

'I'd bring in the Brigade of Guards and two regiments of Highlanders if they were not already busy outside Sevastopol.'

Watters smiled. 'You don't like Atlantic Street, do you?'

'Larkin's called up every available man, doubled the area of beats in quiet locations to garner more and asked for reinforcements from the county police,' Silver murmured. 'Murder, attempted murder, and an attack on a detective in one street within three days is a bit much, even for our man Larkin.'

With yellow light from the gas streetlamps reflecting from their bodies, the ranked hansom cabs occupied all the space in the street in a display of police might Watters had never seen before. He watched as Larkin mounted a black charger and looked back over his men. Larkin rode tall, with a curved sabre hanging on the left side of his saddle and a long staff on the right. He faced his front, kicked in his heels, and walked to the head of the cabs.

'You know what to do,' he shouted, 'I'll not have one of my men attacked,' and led on, with the hansom cabs following, cab after cab rolling over the cobbles, each with its quota of uniformed police.

'Here we go then,' Silver said. 'Are you sure you're fit for this?'

'Fit as a fighting flea.' Watters hid his wince as he swung into the hansom that Larkin had allocated to them. 'Fit to fight the French.'

'I think the Frenchies are on our side this time,' Silver kept his tone neutral, 'I know you are old enough to have seen off Boney, but we have a different enemy now.'

Watters nodded and blinked. He did not admit that his eyes were still giving him some trouble.

'Ready, gents?' The driver peered through the communication hatch in the back of the coach. 'I'm Arthur, but people call me the Duke.' He grinned, 'after the Duke of Wellington, you see.'

'Just drive us,' Watters said.

'That's what I'll do, officer.' When Arthur withdrew, Watters slid the hatch shut.

Only a few early risers watched the convoy roll through the streets of London, hansom after hansom in a long snake of black vehicles. A pair of scavengers lifted curious heads while a gaggle of barefoot boys ran alongside, tumbling for pennies until they saw the dark uniforms inside the cabs.

'Run, it's the bobbies,' one squeaked, and the whole bunch scampered up a side street, with the last boy stopping to throw a defiant stone before his friends hauled him away.

'Don't do that. Them bluebottle bastards will lock you up for sure.'

The convoy split as it approached the Ratcliffe Highway, with one half rolling into the Highway itself and the other rumbling through Whitechapel to block the further entrance to Atlantic Street.

Watters nursed bruised ribs as the cab lurched over a pothole but felt the reassuring bulk of his revolver and tested the weighted end of his cane in the palm of his hand. 'I want these murdering bastards,' he said.

'I know, Sergeant,' Silver said. He produced his pistol, checked the chambers were all loaded and replaced it. 'I thought I'd better come prepared as well.'

They stopped at the entrance of Atlantic Street, with the cabs forming three lines across the street and the police jumping out in pairs, truncheons at the ready and cutlasses swinging awkwardly from their belts.

'Post three men at the entrance of the Wild Geese,' Watters shouted orders, 'and be careful, the porters are hefty and violent.'

Constable Anderson gave a gap-toothed grin. 'I was a guardsman myself, Sergeant. I would not mind a crack at these bastards.' Standing well over six feet tall and with the truncheon in his hand looking like some child's toy, he appeared capable of handling himself and anybody else careless enough to cross his path.

'Watch your language, Constable,' Watters sweetened the reproof with a wink.

'Yes, Sergeant,' Anderson agreed happily. He jerked a thumb at his companion, a saturnine constable with dark whiskers and a scar across the bridge of his nose, 'Williams here was in the 113th,' he said, 'he's an evil bastard when he gets going.'

'Right, Silver, let's clean up this mess.' Watters watched the uniformed police at work. He knew a few of them from his time on the beat and approved of their methods. There was no subtlety in their approach. They worked from one end of the street to the other, with two men banging on each door in turn to wake the occupier, and more men battering the door down if the residents did not immediately respond. The occupants, men, women, and children were unceremoniously hustled into the street in whatever state of dress or undress they happened to be and stood there under the less-than-friendly eyes of cutlass wielding constables.

As the police converged from two sides, resistance stiffened, with a few missiles thrown from the upper storey of the houses and a few doors hastily locked and reinforced. Watters walked behind the main body of police, stepped aside hurriedly as a bottle smashed on the ground at his feet, and pointed upward as a figure stepped back from a window.

'That house there, constable, bring me everybody inside it.' He watched as a squad of police rammed open the door and rushed inside. There were a few moments of furious noise and then they returned with two struggling men. Watters glanced at them without recognition. 'All right, put them with the others.'

'Are you not going to charge them with assaulting a police officer?' Silver asked.

'With all that paperwork? It's hardly worth the trouble. I am after murderers today and the people that attacked me. Not some illiterate rubbish who can't even throw a bottle properly.'

The rising tide of noise came from the middle of the street, where a formidable body of police gathered outside a house.

'What's the trouble here?' Watters asked.

'They've barricaded the door, Sergeant, and they are not going to open for us.'

The upper window opened, and a barrage of missiles hurled down. One chair-leg hit a constable on the shoulder as bottles and stones clattered and bounced from the ground.

'That is what I would expect on this street,' Silver did not flinch as a broken table leg crashed to the ground and skittled toward him. He controlled it with his right foot, deftly flicked it into the air and caught it in his left hand. 'They will make a break for freedom soon.'

No sooner had Silver spoken than the door of the neighbouring house opened, and a press of men and women rushed out, wielding makeshift clubs and broken bottles.

'What the devil?' The uniformed police recoiled before the attack, with one man, bowled over and trampled in the rush.

'Form a line, boys,' Watters ordered, 'draw your truncheons.' He stepped in front of the double blue line that took up the entire width of the street. 'Follow me.'

He moved at a fast pace as the mob decided not to take on the police, and grinned when they scrambled to a sudden halt only twenty yards further down the street. Sitting astride a glossy black stallion, Larkin towered above the crowd, supported by a squad of constables.

'Cutlasses,' Larkin ordered, and the screech of steel rasped at Watters's nerves. The subtly curved blades gleamed, beautifully vicious amidst the filth of the street.

'Keep moving,' Watters ordered, 'herd them in.' He saw a shudder run through the mob at sight of the naked cutlasses. Some screamed defiance while most turned back and saw Watters's men approaching them. Something between a moan and a snarl arose.

'Charge the peelers!' somebody yelled while others roared in Gaelic that Watters did not understand.

Watters shook his head and gave an order he had never thought to give in his life. 'Right men, draw your cutlasses.'

Trapped between two disciplined forces of stalwart men with swords, the bravado of the mob collapsed. Only two tried to escape; one man who dashed toward Larkin's little army and a small woman who ran into the nearest house. Larkin's police pounced on the man with flailing truncheons and flashing cutlasses, but he fought hard and would have struggled through had Larkin not interfered with a sharp kick to the head that knocked him to the ground.

'Have them all rounded up, Silver,' Watters ordered, 'and search each house inch by inch. I want that woman.' Long-striding, he followed into the house the small woman had entered. 'Stop you,' he roared. 'Police!'

Without looking around, the woman banged shut the door behind her. Watters wasted no time but lifted his boot and kicked hard at the lock. The door burst open, and he crashed in, shouting. 'Stop!'

The door opened straight into a dim apartment, scattered with sticks of furniture. Watters had a glimpse of a saffron shawl disappearing into a second room and followed, only to stop. The room was empty; the woman had vanished.

'What the devil?' Watters looked around; it took a few moments to focus his damaged eyes and see that a section of the far wall was moving slightly. He stepped forward, hand outstretched. The wall was of brick, smeared thinly with plaster except in one corner where it gave way under his hand. 'It's only a blanket over a hole, by God.'

The blanket led to the next house in the row. Watters thrust inside. The woman was not in the first room he entered, nor the following, but now Watters knew what to look for and tested the walls for hidden exits. This time there was a painted canvas screen to the next house.

Watters opened the front door and ran into the street. 'Constable Anderson!' he roared.

'Sergeant?' Anderson remained at his post at the Wild Geese.

'Watch out for a little woman with black hair; she might be wearing a saffron shawl! She helped attack the Guardsmen.'

As Anderson lifted a massive hand in acknowledgement, Watters returned inside the house and followed the trail of the woman. 'Stop!' he shouted.

In each house, there was an entrance to the next, until Watters reached the last house of the row. He barged in just as the small woman reached into her pocket. 'That's far enough.' Watters looked around. The walls were of stark brick with no plaster to conceal a hidden exit, the only door led out the back, and he blocked that. 'You've got nowhere to run.'

Watters expected the next move. When the woman tried to throw her handful of black lead in his face, he quickly turned away, closing his eyes. The woman kicked his leg and darted past, her breathing harsh in the cold room. Watters recovered quickly, narrowed his eyes against the floating particles of black lead and followed, to see her darting outside the back.

'Got you!' Anderson's cheerful voice sounded. 'Where did you think you were going, my beauty?'

When Watters emerged, Anderson was holding the woman by the scruff of her neck at full stretch of one arm while her feet kicked and jigged in the air. Anderson clamped his free hand over her mouth to stop her screeches.

'Now watch your gum, my gal. You have got your dander up, haven't you? Is this the one you were looking for, sir?'

'That's the one, constable. Take care of her please and put her under arrest. I have a lot of questions for that woman.'

With all the inhabitants of the street herded into one mass under the falling rain, Watters walked from person to person, examining faces and selecting those he recognised. 'Take these people away,' he ordered, 'I will question them later. Hold the others outside and comb the houses.'

There were six faces that Watters recognised including the woman with the saffron shawl. As he ensured they were handcuffed and taken away in some of the hansom cabs, the uniformed men searched the houses. Silver and Watters followed, poking into every corner, overturning what little furniture there was, lifting and examining anything that might be useful.

'There is a crowd gathering in the Highway,' a stocky uniformed sergeant reported.

'Let them gather,' Watters said. 'Inspector Larkin will deal with any disorder.'

'Sergeant.' A freckle-faced young constable saluted. 'I found this in the hearth of that house over there.' He handed over what looked like a crushed piece of metal. 'It's a Masonic ring, Sergeant.'

'Good man,' Watters said. 'Find out who lives there and round them up. Make sure you know who comes from where.'

As Watters spoke, the door of the Wild Geese opened, and the burly white porter looked outside. 'What's all this noise?' he said as if had only become aware of the sixty policemen and some scores of people congregating outside the premises.

'Police,' Watters shouted and added in a lower tone, 'You stay outside, Anderson, in case of trouble.'

Anderson gave his ubiquitous grin. 'There'll be no trouble, sir.' He sounded quite regretful at the prospect of a quiet morning.

'We are not interested in the public-house, Watters,' Larkin spoke without dismounting from his horse. 'Both the murder and the attack on you happened outside the premises, not inside. Leave the proprietor to conduct her business in her normal and patriotic manner.'

'That's Sergeant Watters, sir, and I suspect—'

'Suspicion is not proof, Watters. Your job is to follow my orders, not to persecute legitimate businesses.'

'Yes, sir.' Watters stepped back from the door.

The porter grinned. 'You look like you've had some rough handling, Sergeant Watters. You'd be better watching where you go in future.'

Watters held the porter's gaze, took out his notebook and scribbled a short note. 'We'll meet again,' he said, 'you can count on it.' He turned away, unable to hide his frustration. He desperately wanted to see inside the Wild Geese, and he had hoped to pick up Billy Yellowford. The woman with the black lead would have to do; he would work on her and see what else might open up.

Chapter Nine

'I had a complaint about you, Watters.' Larkin leaned back in his chair and pressed the fingers of his hands together. 'Mrs Bridget Flannery mentioned that you visited her premises on numerous occasions and tried to break her door down on Christmas Day, disturbing the peace of her establishment.'

'I have already reported to you about the Wild Geese, sir.'

'I am fully aware of your unhealthy interest in that establishment, Watters.'

'That's Sergeant Watters, sir, and there is something very wrong about the Wild Geese.'

'I am taking you off that case, Watters, and away from that area. I need detached and professional detectives, not loose cannon who engage in private feuds.' He tapped his fingers on the desk in a manner strikingly similar to that employed by the departed and much-missed Inspector Field.

'No, Watters, I have no doubts about your ability as a detective, but I do harbour doubts about your professional detachment. I gave you a task to hunt down pickpockets on the omnibuses, and you turned that into a crusade against a perfectly legitimate business. I relented and allowed you to investigate the murder of a soldier, and you charged in like the last survivor of the Light Brigade. You got yourself badly injured and necessitated a full-scale invasion of Atlantic Street that cost over two hundred pounds and no-doubt disturbed the peace of that area for weeks to come, and once again you wanted to terrify poor Mrs Flannery.'

'Hardly terrify, sir, and it's Sergeant Watters.' The thought of anything terrifying that tall, brass-faced woman was slightly amusing.

'I am taking you away from Nixon's murder, Watters, although I will need you as a witness to your own foolish assault. Obviously, you cannot work on that case.' The smile was forced and mirthless as his fingers continued their rhythmic tap-dance on the desk. 'No, I think I will put you somewhere less arduous to your hot temper. I wish you to help Silver lay his ghost.'

'I have unfinished business in the Wild Geese, sir.'

'Wrong, Watters.' Larkin leaned forward in his chair, fingers busy on the desk. 'You have no business at all in the Wild Geese.'

'Sir,' Watters remained at attention, 'I truly believe that there is something amiss in that establishment.'

'And I truly know that your duty is to follow orders, Watters.'

'Sergeant Watters, sir.'

'Your duty is to follow orders, Watters, and my orders to you are to find this ghost that is terrorising the gullible of Hesse Square.' When Larkin looked up, there was no warmth in his eyes. 'Unless you wish to continue your crusade in Atlantic Street as a uniformed constable, or without any official sanction at all, I suggest you say 'yes, sir' and leave my office at once.'

'Yes, sir.' Watters was careful not to bang the door as he left.

* * *

'Larkin was quick off the mark that time,' Silver said. 'He was concerned when the mob attacked you.'

'He was equally concerned to keep us out of the Wild Geese,' Watters said sourly. 'Tell me about this bloody ghost that is so important.'

They sat in the snug of the Admiral Rodney public, a seagull's call from the river. Watters contemplated his pint of half-and-half with his mind whirling between his future career and the mystery of the foreign woman and the Wild Geese.

'I remember when this was nothing more than a dirty pot-house.' Silver took a deep swallow of his London ale. 'It was a dirty pot-house with a dirty old barman with a dirty red nose and a dirty apron. Now we have three smiling women who look pretty for the customers but who don't know beer from a bar stool.' He sighed. 'Progress is not what it was.' He glanced at the new mahogany counter and shook his head.

'Hesse Square,' Watters persisted. 'The ghost.'

Silver finished half his ale at a single swallow. 'No progress at all, George. The residents tell me that they have seen a figure in white drifting over the rooftops and gliding around the doors, but they never catch it. Most are amused at the thought of a ghost and think I am wasting my time. Some of the servant girls are a bit nervous.'

'Is this ghost thing seen every day?' Watters asked.

'No, but quite often.'

'We'll stand watch then until the bloody thing shows up and snare it.' Watters sipped at his half-and-half and put it back down. 'The sooner we get this spooney-sam locked up, the sooner we can get back to real policing.' He lifted his hat and cane. 'Sorry, William, you'd better tell Angela that you might not see much of her for the next few nights.'

'She won't be smiling,' Silver said.

'She'll get used to it.'

Gas lights pooled their yellow light over the impressive Georgian architecture of Hesse Square, showing patches of the paved street and dark railings protecting a central locked garden. Most of the surrounding windows were dark, with only the occasional gleam of light wavering behind panes that were barely visible in the thickening fog.

'We chose the wrong night for this.' Silver pulled up the collar of his coat against the damp chill.

'We did not choose this at all,' Watters grunted. 'Where's the best place to hide so we can watch for this imposter?'

'I sat under a tree in the gardens,' Silver said. 'It gave a little shelter from the rain.'

'We'll find separate trees at opposite ends of the garden,' Watters decided, 'and whistle if we see anything untoward.'

'In this muck, I doubt if we'll see anything at all.' Silver waved a hand in front of his face in a vain attempt to clear away some of the fog.

'It's a good night for a ghost.' Watters climbed over the iron railings that protected the central garden and negotiated the trees and shrubbery to get to the furthest corner of the square. He grinned at Silver's subdued curse as he stumbled into an unseen bush, and prepared for a long, frustrating night.

Policing was very much like soldiering, Watters decided as he shivered under the stark branches of an elm. So much time was spent just waiting for something to happen, and when it did happen, one often wished that it had not. On the beat, one could patrol for hours without incident and then there would be an explosion of trouble as a public disgorged its drunken denizens into the street. Now he was waiting, not expecting to see anybody save the odd late-night reveller reeling past, yet this was part of the policeman's lot. It paid the bills and would provide a pension in about twenty years' time if the good Lord spared him for so long.

The crackle of dry twigs was louder in the fog, followed by sharp male laughter, quickly stilled, then another, female, giggle. Watters swivelled slowly to see the dim shapes of a man and a woman walking hand in hand under the trees. When the pair stopped to kiss, Watters looked away.

The stifled laughter ended; the muffled footsteps passed. Quiet descended, broken only by fog-distorted night sounds: the roar of iron-shod wheels across greasy cobbles, the neigh of a horse, a dog's frantic barking fading into silence, out-of-tune singing as a drunk staggered her way homeward, and a policeman's urgent but distant rattle.

One by one, the lights in Watters's half of the square vanished. He saw the dim shape of a maidservant closing window shutters and heard the muted tinkle of a pianoforte from somewhere behind him. A faint breeze shifted the fog.

Silver's whistle startled him.

'Silver?' Watters crept beside him.

'Over there,' Silver's whisper was so low that Watters strained to hear him.

'The ghost?'

'Might be better than that, Sergeant.' Silver pointed at a lit upper window. 'Watch that window, sir, and see what you think.'

Reluctant to admit that he had still not regained his full vision, Watters squinted upward. At first, he could see only a vague shape, but as the fog shifted, he realised he was looking at a woman sitting at something, presumably the pianoforte he had heard earlier.

'Is that not the woman from the bus?' Silver asked. 'I'm damned sure it is.'

Watters tried to blink away the haze from his eyes. 'I think you could be right,' he said. He felt a mixture of frustration at his damaged eyesight and excitement that they could have found the foreign woman.

'Are we going in?' Silver asked, then sighed, 'what about the ghost?'

'Damn and blast the ghost,' Watters said. 'Come on, Silver.'

'We can't go now, sir.' Silver checked his watch. 'I forgot the time. It's nearly one in the morning!'

'She's awake, and we're here,' Watters said. 'We'll catch her off guard. We might never get another opportunity to speak to her.' He was moving before he finished talking, trusting that Silver would accompany him.

'Which house is it, Silver?' Watters squinted at the doors.

'This one, sir.' Silver led the way to one of the near-identical terraced houses and waited for Watters.

There was a long pause before he heard scuffling footsteps in reply to Watters's knock, and a dishevelled servant answered.

'I wish to speak to the lady of the house,' Watters announced.

The servant was around forty, with a half-shaved face and lugubrious eyes. 'At this time of night?'

'Who is that Hubert?' Watters recognised the voice at once, with its intriguing foreign accent.

'There are two men to see you, Madam. Shall I send them away?

The woman seemed to glide down the interior stairs and arrived at Hubert's side in a wave of satin. She smiled over his shoulder. 'Please introduce yourselves, gentlemen? It is an unusual hour to come calling.'

Watters removed his hat and gave a small bow. 'Good evening Ma'am. I am Detective Sergeant George Watters of Scotland Yard, and this is Detective Constable William Silver.'

The woman inclined her head politely. 'Good evening gentlemen, but I don't understand—' Her hand flew to her mouth, and she said something in her native language. 'Has something happened to Wolfgang? Is my husband hurt?'

'Not at all Ma'am,' Watters hastened to reassure her. 'I apologise for calling at this terrible hour, but I had to ensure you were in.' He gave what he hoped was a warm smile. 'You may remember that you lost a certain item while travelling on an omnibus.'

The woman stepped aside. 'Of course I remember. Please come in Sergeant Watters, and you, Detective Silver.'

The furniture was elegant and light, the décor subtle, and the books in the glass-fronted bookcase a mixture of British and German titles with the novels of Walter Scott and Dickens alongside works by Johann Goethe and plays by Eduard Duller.

'I admire your taste in literature, Ma'am,' Silver said. 'Politics and romanticism. Very catholic in taste if you don't mind the irony.'

'I always appreciate irony,' the woman replied. 'Please take a seat,' She indicated the comfortable armed chairs that surrounded a small table. 'Hubert, lights please, and some refreshment for my guests.'

She was taller than Watters had remembered, with all the poise and charm he expected from one of the aristocracy, for he did not doubt that she was very well connected.

'What shall we call you, Ma'am?' The question sounded clumsy even as he spoke.

The woman gave a little smile. 'Yes, what indeed? "Ma'am" sounds very formal from a British policeman. It is what my servants call me, and I think you are a servant to nobody, Sergeant Watters.' She accepted the tray of drinks from Hubert and dismissed him. 'You may go back to bed, Hubert, and thank you for rising so promptly. I will be perfectly safe with these gentlemen.'

'If you're sure, Ma'am,' Hubert gave Watters a hard stare.

'Quite, thank you.' She waited until he had left the room. 'Hubert is a good man and so very loyal.'

'Good servants are hard to find,' Silver said, 'you are lucky to have one.'

'I have a few,' she said.

Watters saw that small smile light up her eyes for only a moment before it faded into something like anxiety. 'May we know your name, please?'

'I am Karin Stegall,' she announced the name as if it should mean something.

'Is that any relation to Wolfgang Stegall?' Silver asked quietly.

'He is my husband,' she was equally quiet.

Silver glanced at Watters and back. 'Your husband is an important man,' Watters knew that Silver was explaining things for his benefit. 'If I am correct, he is one of the diplomats from the Austrian Empire involved in the meetings about the war in the East.'

'You are precisely correct,' Karin agreed. The anxiety was strong in her eyes. 'Is it about Wolfgang that you have come to see me?' There was a slight but definite pause. 'Is he in some trouble?'

'Not that we are aware of,' Watters said.

'Please call me Karin.'

'As you wish, Karin.' The name was pleasant on Watters's lips. 'We have not come in connection with your husband.' He saw the instant relief flood her eyes. 'We have come in connection with quite another matter. We recovered the purse you had stolen on the omnibus, and you can collect it from Scotland Yard, or, if you wish, we can have a uniformed policeman deliver it here.' He paused for a moment as Karin offered wine. 'There is one thing that confuses me, Karin. In your purse was an address for a public house in the Ratcliffe Highway.' He saw her face stiffen and the anxiety return to her eyes.

'You have looked through my purse?' she broke in. 'You have no right!'

'I was looking for your address,' Watters said, 'so we could return it.' Karin fell silent.

'I know you are a visitor to London, Karin,' Watters continued, 'so you will not know which areas to avoid. However I would strongly advise you not to visit the Wild Geese, or indeed any establishment in that street, and certainly, don't attempt to go there alone.'

Her smile was forced. 'Thank you for your advice, Sergeant.'

Watters nodded as two pieces of the jigsaw clicked together. 'Have you ever been to the Wild Geese, Karin?'

She hesitated, raised her head, and looked him full in the eyes. 'Once only,' she said.

'When we came in here, your first questions were about your husband. You thought he could be in trouble, and you have that unpleasant address in your purse. Tell me, pray, do you suspect that Wolfgang may be in trouble?'

She half rose from her chair, glanced at Silver and back at Watters, then sat down again.

'Come now, Karin, there is nothing to fear from us. We are Scotland Yard; it is our job to help people when they are in trouble. Out with it, now.'

He saw the moisture in her eye and sighed. Silver produced a handkerchief.

'I cannot say.'

'If he is in trouble, the best way you can help him is by telling us,' Watters encouraged.

There were more tears as Karin shook her head. Watters had seen scores of women crying as they were charged with offences from drunkenness to assault or common theft, yet there was something about Karin that moved him. He shifted forward and put an awkward arm around her shoulders. 'Come on now, try and help Wolfgang.'

She shook her head. 'It's not Wolfgang that's in trouble: it's me!' The tears became a flood as she collapsed onto Watters's shoulder. He held her, patting her back. He was aware of Silver scribbling in his notebook and wished that Karin had chosen the constable as a comforter instead.

'You speak English very well.' Watters tried to ease her discomfort.

Her reply was muffled. 'Thank you. I speak German, English, French, and some other languages.' Her voice broke into a paroxysm of sobs.

'Compose yourself and tell us what happened,' Silver asked.

Karin took a deep shuddering breath and pushed herself off Watters's shoulder. She dabbed at her eyes with Silver's handkerchief. 'I do apologise,' she said. 'I should never have acted in such a manner. It is unforgivable.'

'It is quite natural, and you have no reason to apologise,' Watters said.

Karin breathed out slowly. 'Wolfgang was at one of his interminable meetings,' she said, 'and I was searching for diversion in London. Nobody ever considers the women you know. Men attend the meetings and discuss important matters while we are supposed to be content with sewing and painting and other silly accomplishments.'

'I know,' Watters agreed. 'It is not right.'

'Sewing and painting in London are no different from sewing and painting in Vienna or Paris,' Karin said, 'so I decided to visit the sights of the city. When I was in Oxford Street, a tall and very charming lady spoke to me and asked if we could walk together. After a while, she suggested that we visit an establishment she had heard of in another part of town. She told me it was quite delightful, and the London people were enchanting, quite unlike the stolid peasants of rural Austria, she said, or even the sophisticates of Vienna.'

Watters nodded. 'It is always good to have somebody with you when you tour a new city.'

'This lady called herself Mary and called up a cab. She took me around streets I have never seen before, and we ended in the establishment known as Wild Geese.'

'Pray continue,' Watters said.

'I had thought it would be an elegant dance hall perhaps, but it was instead a place where men meet women. There were common soldiers there and women of the worst character. Mary disappeared. She vanished right away.'

'You were gulled,' Watters said quietly, 'duped into going there. It is nothing to be ashamed of.'

'There is worse to come,' Karin said, 'much worse. When I was there, a gentleman came in, and he immediately saw that I was distressed and came to my aid. He bought me a glass of wine and guided me away from the soldiers and upstairs to a small room.'

'You went with him alone to a room?' Watters asked. 'Would it not have been wiser to leave the place entirely?'

'There were two large men at the door.' Karin looked away. 'They would not allow me out. And I was scared.'

'Do you know the name of the man who took you to the room?' Silver asked.

Karin nodded. 'He was called Christopher. A tall, well-made man, Prussian he said, and very handsome with well-shaped whiskers,' she put her hands to her cheeks to illustrate what she meant. 'He had a scar on his forehead, I recall, quite distinguished.'

'I see,' Watters nodded. 'So far Karin you are entirely innocent of any wrongdoing,' *but very naïve*, he thought.

'I do not remember much of what happened next,' Karin said, 'I felt dizzy and sat on the bed, and when I woke up I was alone, and some of my clothes had been taken from me and put on the bed. I dressed and ran out of that place, and the men at the door did not try to stop me. I thought that if I did not tell anybody, I could forget all about it, but two days later an elegant tall man came to this door, here, and showed me a photograph.' Karin stopped and looked away.

'The man had a photograph of you with Christopher,' Watters said.

Karin shook her head. 'No. Somebody must have taken a photograph when I was unconscious. It was not Christopher beside me.'

'Were you dressed?' Watters asked bluntly.

There was a long silence before Karin spoke again. 'I was not dressed at all. The man said that unless I do as he orders he will show the photograph to Wolfgang and the Austrian ambassador to Great Britain. He said he would also have the photograph copied and would distribute it to these horrible men who sell obscene books around the town so everybody would see me.'

'If you tell Wolfgang first, he will understand, surely?' Silver said. 'He is your husband and must know you would never deceive him.'

'You do not understand!' For the first time, Karin showed a flash of temper. 'If the ambassador finds out, Wolfgang's career will be ruined, and my reputation also. His family will disown him, and I will never be able to show my face in Vienna again.'

Watters nodded. 'I have heard the like before. Somebody lured you into a trap. How much are they asking for?'

'Nothing,' Karin said, 'they are not asking for money. Rather, they want me to tell them where Wolfgang is and what he is doing. They want me to get any papers he has and bring them to them.'

'Them?' Watters asked gently. 'Do you know who they are?'

'I only met Christopher, once, and the tall woman, and the elegant man who came to me.' Karin's shrug made her appear like a mischievous schoolgirl rather than a woman in serious trouble. 'There are messages left for me at the door. Once a small man came to me in the street and told me to pass papers onto the Wild Geese, but they were in my purse when it was stolen.'

'We found them,' Watters did not say that the notes were only selections from Gaelic stories. 'Now if you describe Christopher and Mary, we can start our enquiries.'

'No, no, please.' Karin looked terrified. 'If these people find out the police know they will reveal everything.' She looked away. 'I have started to carry a knife now, like the gypsies do, in case these men try and take me away.'

'That is unlikely,' Watters said. 'And you can trust the British police,' Watters promised. 'Detective Silver and I will work unofficially until we uncover something. In the meantime, you do what the criminals tell you. Keep notes of everything and one of us will drop by from time to time. Now, descriptions, please. Mary first?'

* * *

The Admiral Rodney was crowded, with a one-legged sailor regaling a crowd of admirers with his fictitious adventures at sea and a thimble-rigger eyeing Watters as a possible gull. Watters nursed his half-and-half pensively.

'So what do you make of all that, William?'

Silver shrugged and downed a quarter of his ale in a single swallow. 'Forget the big innocent eyes, Sergeant, Karin Stegall alleviated her boredom with a man and got gulled. That is why she did not collect her purse with documents she thought were incriminating. Now she is scared and expects us to pull her out of the mire.'

Watters borrowed Silver's notebook and re-read her descriptions. 'A tall red-haired woman could be anybody, but this Christopher fellow, tall, broad, gentlemanly with neat whiskers and a scar on his forehead? Who does that sound like?'

Silver shook his head. 'I'm sure I don't know.'

'Inspector Larkin,' Watters sat back, 'it fits him to a tee. The same man who prevented us from searching the Wild Geese and who pulled us off the Atlantic Street murder case.'

'What nonsense,' Silver said. 'You are upset because he and you don't see eye to eye. Why would Inspector Larkin do a thing like that?'

'Now that I don't know,' Watters said, 'but I fully intend to find out. Lucy told me that the girls at the Wild Geese have one night off a week. I'm going back there, and I will investigate Larkin until I know more about him than even his mother does.'

'I'll come with you,' Silver volunteered.

'You will not.' Watters put down his glass more forcibly than he had intended. 'You have responsibilities now. If I lose my position, I only have myself to worry about. You have Angela as well.' He saw Silver's internal confusion and added in a softer tone, 'Your wife comes first. Always.'

* * *

Three o'clock in the morning was not Watters's favourite time of day. Carrying a canvas bag of tools and dressed in dark clothing to merge with the night, he followed Constable Anderson at a respectable distance. Watters ensured his feet hit the ground at the same time as Anderson's so the constable could not hear him and slid into doorways when the policeman turned to survey the street behind him. Anderson would be a formidable adversary in any confrontation, but his portentous patrolling was too predictable to catch a wily burglar. Watters resolved to teach him a few tricks on a later occasion.

Atlantic Street was quiet, with a chill rain hosing down the dirt of the day and not a single light in the malign eyes of the windows. Watters knelt at the door of the Wild Geese and examined the padlock. It was reliable and serviceable, but he knew he could pick it open in seconds. He applied gentle pressure to the door; it held at the top and bottom where bolts were drawn on the inside.

Swearing, Watters muttered, 'No entry that way,' and checked the windows.

All had four wooden shutters, with each slotted into place and a padlock over the central two: to move one would mean moving all, an operation that would take time, and with no way of replacing them while he was inside, Constable Anderson would notice their absence on his return in thirty minutes.

'Well secured, Mother Flannery,' Watters gave grudging approval. 'Upwards, then, and try the roof.'

With a last look along Atlantic Street, Watters pulled himself onto the ledge of the window, used the padlock for a foothold and scrambled upward. Not for the first time he blessed his hard upbringing as he ascended the outside of the three-storey building. The roof was slated, with two skylights, the weakest point of entry for most properties and often the least protected. Watters cursed as his feet slipped on the rain-dampened slates, and tried the skylight, to find it secured by a simple catch. Lying prone on the roof to attract as little attention as possible,

Watters peered through the glass. He saw only darkness and hoped he was not above a bedroom. Some poor girl would take it badly if he descended upon her when she was busy entertaining a customer. Taking a small knife from his bag, Watters began to carefully scrape away the putty from the lower pane of the skylight. The sounds he made seemed to resound like the clashing of military cymbals around the deserted street. He stopped, checked for passers-by, and continued, gradually removing the putty so he could ease the lower pane away from the frame.

Lifting the glass, Watters placed it on the slates and again peered into the blackness below. Taking a small coil of rope from his bag, he tied one end around the chimney stacks and dropped the other into the room below before climbing hand over hand into the dark. Within seconds he was on a bare wooden floor inside an attic room.

'That was easy enough,' he said to himself, pulled a bull's eye lantern from his bag, lit the wick and adjusted the shutter, so only a pencil-thin shaft of light probed the gloom; sufficient to light his path but hopefully not enough to attract unwanted attention.

The door was locked from the outside, with the key still in the lock, so Watters withdrew a set of long-nosed pliers from his bag and inserted the business end inside the lock to turn the key. It moved with a satisfying click, and he waited a moment before emerging. His lantern shot its probing beam around the upper landing, showing only one other door. The key was already in the lock, and it opened into a small room, packed with chests. Watters opened the nearest lid: gaudy women's clothing. The second and third were the same. This apartment was used to store the dollymops' working clothes. That was one way that the Wild Geese made money then; they hired out clothes to the women who walked the streets.

The faint murmur came to Watters, and he hurriedly closed the shutter of the lantern, then came a rough male laugh, a female voice raised in protest and silence. A door opened and shut. Silence again. Watters waited on the stairs, counting the passing minutes until he deemed it safe to move. He stepped downward, one step at a time to the floor below. He recognised the corridor with its multitude of doors; Lily was presumably behind one, sleeping the sleep of the innocent.

The majority of these doors would open into the apartments of the girls. Watters had no interest in these rooms. He wanted only to find the administrative records that would presumably be held in Mother Flannery's office. He moved slowly from door to door, angling his lantern, so the light did not probe through the keyhole and waken the people within.

He stopped when he heard the creak and again closed his lantern. The wind was rising, wailing around the roof of the building, knocking one of the shutters against its slides. Watters remained still, listening. One of the girls was quietly sobbing to herself, the sound fading as sleep released her from the torments of life. Silence again so he opened his lantern, and the narrow beam probed the stuffy dark.

At the head of the corridor were two doors, one large and the other narrow and low, presumably a store cupboard. Watters played his light at the lock of the larger. It was more complex than the others in the corridor, so he nodded satisfaction and withdrew his wallet of lock-picks from his bag. Mother Flannery would not spend money on an expensive lock without good reason.

When he had been a beat constable many years before, Watters had arrested a notable cracksman who had passed on some of his knowledge and his tools in return for a few last hours with his wife before years of incarceration. Now Watters knelt at the larger door and inserted a small tension wrench into the bottom of the keyhole to gauge what type of lock this was. He applied slight pressure to find the lock pins and inserted a lockpick, moving it back and forth, setting the pins back to the open position, one by one.

Easing the door slightly ajar, Watters peered inside, ensured that the room was unoccupied, slipped through and closed the door behind him. He shone a low beam across the interior, seeing a very ornate French desk with a high-backed chair, matching drawers, and a luxurious carpet. A glass-fronted bookcase occupied one corner of the room, and a dark green Chubb safe filled another. On one wall was a framed portrait of a serious-looking auburn-haired girl, directly opposite a clock that ticked away the seconds with its pendulum slowly swinging.

Watters probed the room, with the lantern light picking up more pictures on the wall. There were racehorses, the prize fighters John Gully and Henry Pearce, the Irish politician Daniel O'Connor side-by-side with another of Cuchulain, the green-clad warrior whose picture had been in Lily's room. Watters grunted as he saw an array of whips, canes, and other more cheerful implements of the prostitute's trade. Moving quietly to the desk, Watters unlocked the three drawers, one by one.

The top drawer contained pens and ink, together with a penknife and sheets of writing paper. The middle had folders of accounts, neatly tabulated and balanced. The bottom drawer held letters from satisfied clients. Watters flicked through them but did not recognise any of the names. For a moment, he contemplated keeping some, but he was after one specific thing and was about to replace the letters when he noticed a single sheet of paper in the midst. He scanned it and saw it was written in Gaelic so folded it and stuffed it in the large pocket of his tight jacket.

Watters turned to the bookcase. A person's choice of books gave away a great deal of their character and interests. He had expected obscene publications and garish writings, but instead found volumes of business practise and philosophy, a whole shelf dedicated to Irish history, some volumes with Gaelic titles and a section of military manuals. He nodded at this next Irish connection and moved to the safe. Watters was well aware that Chubb's burglar-proof lock had been undefeated until an American named Hobbs had opened one during the Great Exhibition of 1851, and he knew Chubb's safes had levers with false notches to fool the cracksman, curtains around the key pins and key access, and methods to prevent entry by gunpowder. Placing his lantern on the chair, so the light shone on the lock, he knelt beside it and began work.

The lock was like nothing he had ever met before, more complex, with tricks to capture the unwary and deceits that would block any access unless the user had the correct key. Watters shook the perspiration from his face as he worked, easing the pins back one slow movement at a time.

The touch of steel on his temple shocked him. 'What have we here?'

Chapter Ten

Watters moved slowly. His concentration on the safe had been so intense he had not heard the men enter the room. Both wore dark clothes, and while one watched from the right, the other pressed a short-barrelled revolver to his head.

'A cracksman,' the man on Watters's right spoke quietly. 'I don't know him.'

The first man pushed the muzzle of his revolver harder into Watters's head. 'What's your name, friend?' He spoke in educated accents, so he may have been one of the gentlemen thieves who robbed for the thrill of things rather than for financial gain.

'John Temple,' Watters gave the first name that came into his head. He pulled away from the muzzle of the pistol.

'Well John Temple, this crib is not yours to crack.' The first man eased back the hammer of his revolver. 'Keep quiet, or I'll blow your brains all over the wall.'

'We shouldn't kill him,' the second man sounded nervous.

'We may do so, or we may not,' the gunman said coolly. He jerked his gun aside, 'move away from that safe.'

Watters did as the gunman ordered. The second man took his place at the safe. 'Old fashioned equipment,' he gave his opinion. 'If you had carried on you would have closed this lock for good.' He removed Watters's tools very carefully. 'Brummagem rubbish.' There was scorn in his voice. He pulled a small packet from inside his close-fitting jacket. 'Now watch a professional at work.'

Watters watched as the man inserted his tools into the lock of the safe, moving slowly but with confidence. 'If you shoot me the porters will be in here in seconds,' Watters reminded.

'Good,' the gunman said, 'then we will shoot them as well.'

The second man grunted as an audible click came from the safe. He swung the door open and stepped back. 'There you have it.'

'Watch this one,' the gunman handed the pistol to the cracksman and moved to the safe.

The inside of the safe was split horizontally into two compartments, with a strongbox on the top, presumably holding money or other valuables and documents beneath. Ignoring the strongbox, the gunman lifted out the papers. He sifted through them, glancing at the contents quickly but with no sense of urgency.

'You've done this before,' Watters said.

'You shut your teeth.' The second man waved the gun around. He was undoubtedly an expert cracksman but not used to firearms.

'Be careful with that thing, son, or you'll have someone's eye out,' Watters injected enough scorn into his voice to unsettle the cracksman even more.

'You keep your teeth closed,' the gunman said.

Watters sat back and cursed the bad luck that had brought him to this place at the same time as these professionals. He watched the first man look through the documents and noted that there was a selection of photographs pinned to sheets of foolscap paper. The man took out a small notebook and copied details from each file but kept his back turned so Watters could not see what he wrote.

There was a photograph of a plump man with a very young girl, a naked young boy lying beside a well-known politician, an elderly woman with two men and then, with a slight start, Watters recognised Karin's photograph. She lay on her back, naked as a baby, with her face clearly seen and two athletic-looking young men at her side.

It was instinct as much as anything else that propelled Watters forward. He punched the cracksman in the throat, knocked the gun away and grabbed for the photograph. The first man spun around, kicking out backwards and catching Watters on the knee with sufficient force to make him gasp but not enough to stop him.

'You stupid fool!' The first man's voice was low. Watters snatched the photograph away, grabbed his bag and swung it, catching the man full across the face.

Then he ran.

Pulling the door open, he dashed into the corridor. Without his lantern, he could see nothing but remembered where Lily's room was, and her pride in having her name on a brass plate. He burst in, backheeled the door shut, saw Lily sit up in bed, clamped a hand over her mouth and hissed, 'Keep very quiet.' There were soft footsteps in the corridor outside and then silence. He turned the key in the lock of her door.

'I'm going to take my hand off your mouth,' he told her quietly, 'and believe me, I mean you no harm. Will you promise not to scream?'

He felt her nod.

'Good girl.' Watters gently eased his hand away. 'It's George,' he said, 'you might remember me from a few days ago.'

He could feel her trembling. 'It's all right,' he said, 'I don't mean you any harm.'

'What do you want?' There was as much anger in her voice as fear when she swore at him. 'I don't do the rough stuff. Other girls do that sort of thing but not me! What do you mean by coming into my room at this hour?' Her voice was rising. Watters had to block her hard slap. He held her wrist as she extended her fingers and tried to rake his eyes.

She lowered her voice. 'If Mother Flannery finds you here, you'll get me into all sorts of trouble!'

'You'd better keep your voice down, then,' he said.

'What are you doing here?' Lily asked again.

'Hiding from a man with a gun,' Watters said, 'and hoping to escape as soon as possible.'

'A gun?' Lily pulled back.

'He won't hurt you,' Watters said, 'it's only me he wants.'

Lamplight flared in the corridor outside, accompanied by heavy footsteps. A deep voice shouted, 'Are there any men in here?'

'Quick,' Lily said, 'get under the bed!' She poked a finger in his ribs. 'Go on!' She quickly hauled the covers off the bed and piled them in front of him as he squeezed into the narrow space. Watters heard a sustained hammering at the door and Lily's voice.

'What's the matter?'

'Do you have a man in there? Open up!'

Lily opened the door wide, 'Of course I have, Davie. I've got three. Come and look! You know you want to look at me!' A giggle followed her words, and Watters heard the scratch of a Lucifer and the flicker of yellow candlelight. 'Come on in Davie-boy, nobody will know. I have the peep-hole covered.' She ended with a high laugh as the door banged shut. There were more footsteps as the man, presumably Davie, stomped to knock on the next door.

'All right, George.' Her voice was low as she hauled back the bed covers and extended a hand to help him out, 'he's away now. He won't come back here.' She had stripped until she wore nothing but a smile.

'What the devil?' Despite himself, Watters looked her up and down, which broadened her smile.

'I thought you were a lady's man,' she said. 'Davie's not. He prefers young boys. He's scared of women, so he would not come in if I was naked!'

'Oh, you clever, clever lady!' Watters could not help his smile. 'I wondered how the porters could resist the temptation of all these women!'

'Mother Flannery has them well under control,' Lily posed for him, thrusting out her hip. 'Men are easy.'

The heavy footsteps returned to thump past Lily's room and back downstairs. Watters waited, listening at the door. He heard small sounds from the other apartments as the women settled back down, and then silence.

'What did you mean when you said you had the peep-hole covered?'

'Look,' Lily pointed to the rag she had fastened over the face of Cuchulain. 'You know that's how they check up on us when we are busy, but they can't see through a towel.'

Watters nodded. 'Thank you, Lily,' he touched her on the shoulder. 'You're a brick.' Then he was back out in the corridor and heading toward the stairs and escape. He hesitated at the end of the passage; he knew what lay behind the office door, but the storeroom may hold something more interesting than clothing; he had already found a store of that upstairs. Why two rooms for the same commodity?

After wrestling with a burglar-proof Chubb safe, a store-room door posed no problems and Watters had it open in seconds. He eased inside, thankful that Davie had left the lamps burning in the corridor, so sufficient light seeped under the door for him to see.

At first, the equipment was unfamiliar. The tripod leaned against the wall, its use obscure until Watters recalled the photographs, and Watters identified the two bulky cameras that occupied much of the floor. He opened the wooden boxes piled against the wall. They contained clear glass slides and various bottles that he surmised held chemicals for developing photographs. There was also a second door that slid into an aperture in the wall, to reveal a very narrow, dark passage. Taking a deep breath, Watters entered, testing each footstep, and groping his way along what felt like a plaster wall. The surface was smooth until his hand touched a small wooden panel that slid along a groove, leaving a small circular hole that gave visual access to the room beyond.

The first spyhole was blocked: Lily's room, Watters knew. He stepped further along, acutely aware of the dark and the passage of time. He had to be out of this building before it properly awoke. He did not care to think of the consequences if Mother Flannery discovered him here. The second spyhole was also blocked, and the third. Watters grinned. Mother Flannery may be deviously smart, but her girls also had a repertoire of tricks.

He froze as he heard a rustle in the dark corridor behind him and saw the faint glimmer of lamplight. Somebody had entered from the storeroom and was moving toward him. He glanced over his shoulder; with no space to pass, he could not return so must move on and hope for somewhere to hide, or an alternative exit. Watters hurried on, keeping as quiet as he could. The people behind him were silent save for the slight pad of feet on the floorboards and the subdued hiss of breathing.

The passage narrowed, and for a moment, Watters thought it ended in a blank wall. He felt his heart race before his hopeful hands found space; he had reached a sudden turn as the passage negotiated the end of the girls' apartments. Another ten steps and he came to another door, inset into the wall, and securely locked.

He knelt quickly, felt in his bag, and withdrew his tools. The lock was simple, yet he fumbled as he heard a subdued curse behind him: whoever was in the passage had reached the hidden corner. He dropped his pick and shuddered as the faint sound seemed to echo like a clash of cymbals in the dark corridor.

He fumbled for the pick, winced as it rammed up his fingernail, lifted it, and inserted it into the lock. The pins gave a faint click, and he pushed the door open to find himself in a dimly lit corridor. The instant he emerged, a young woman opened the door opposite. She stared at him, too surprised to scream. He stared back for a fraction of a second, lifted a finger to his mouth to keep her silent, shut the door far too noisily and, with no hope of escaping unseen, ran along the corridor past the prostitutes' apartments. He heard doors opening behind him querulous women's voices, and the deep growl of a man. He threw himself up the stairs to the attic level.

'There was a man!' A girl was yelling, 'There was a man in the corridor!'

This place is a brothel, Watters thought, *why all the blasted fuss about a man?*

Other women joined in, creating an uproar of noise and confusion. Watters ran up the final flight of stairs and into the attic storeroom.

He breathed his relief that his rope still hung from the skylight, scrambled up and rolled onto the slates as the volume of sound from within increased. He heard men shouting, a roar and a high-pitched female screaming as he lifted the discarded pane of glass and tried to fit it back into place. The rain had made it slippery; it slid through his fingers and fell, agonisingly slowly, to shatter into a thousand shards on the attic floor.

Watters swore, turned, and fled across the ridge of the roof, feeling his feet slither and slide on the wet slates as lights appeared in the windows of Atlantic Street and the Highway. He heard a deep-throated challenge, saw Constable Anderson staring up at him and ducked onto the Highway side of the roof. He knew Anderson was not the sort of man to give up easily, so he slid down the roof, grabbed at the guttering and swung quickly around. The bag slipped from his fingers and tumbled end over end, to land with a tremendous clatter. Watters swore again.

With a good forty feet to the ground, Watters had no desire to drop. He swung his feet onto the ledge of the top floor window. He balanced there, hearing the harsh gasp of his nervous breathing, and knowing he could not stop, for Anderson would pound around the corner any second, so he crouched and swung to the next window ledge. He glanced inside the window and saw the two dark-clad cracksmen staring out; their eyes met for a moment, and then Watters swivelled and dropped to the next window; he scrabbled for purchase, slipped, slowed his descent a fortuitous second and slipped down to the ground. He landed with a thump, rolled, rose, staggered, grabbed his bag and ran down the Highway. He heard Anderson spring his rattle a long way behind him and kept running, gritting his teeth against the recurring pain of his recent injuries.

Peggy was setting up her stand as Watters approached. He stopped at her side and slid his bag under the trestles of her table. 'Coffee please, Peggy, as soon as you are ready.'

'You've been running, Sergeant,' Peggy said, 'is there some trouble?'

'There's always some trouble,' Watters took the mug of coffee, controlled his breathing with an effort and sipped. It was too hot to drink, so he took a deep breath and blew on the surface.

'You are puffed, Sergeant,' Peggy sounded amused. 'You're out of condition; too much time spent in the Admiral I'd say.'

Aware of the sweat trickling down his face and his ragged breathing, Watters tried to look casually curious when Anderson and another constable pounded up to him.

'Is everything all right, Anderson?' Watters asked.

'I was chasing a man dressed in dark clothing,' Anderson eyed Watters's dark coat and soft shoes. 'You didn't see anyone like that did you, Sergeant?'

'Nobody has come this way except me,' Watters said truthfully. 'Did you see anybody suspicious, Peggy?"

Peggy busied herself with cups and saucers. 'Only yourself, Sergeant Watters.'

Watters forced a laugh. 'Well, I am suspicious enough for any three people, the things I have to do. Sorry I can't be more help, Anderson.'

'That's all right, Sergeant,' Anderson touched the brim of his hat. 'He must have taken a different turn somewhere.'

Watters waited until Anderson had returned to his beat area before he handed back the cup. 'Thank you, Peggy, that's one I owe you.'

'I won't forget it,' Peggy said, 'and it's two pence for the coffee.'

Chapter Eleven

'Are you all right, Sergeant?' Silver looked up from the pile of documents with which he shared his desk.

'I've been better,' Watters admitted as he slumped in his chair. 'Our commander in chief is miffed that we have not yet captured his ghost.' He produced his pipe and stuffed tobacco into the bowl. 'The country is at war, we have murders and assaults in the Highway, we have what could be a major case involving Karin Stegall, and we are wasting our time chasing after a non-existent ghost that only nervous maids and bottle-headed little boys can see.'

'We failed in our duty,' Silver reminded quietly, 'Larkin is right in that, at least.'

'Larkin can go to hell,' Watters voiced his frustration.

'He will,' Silver said, 'but not today.' He leaned back, puffing at his pipe. 'So while I was failing to catch the ghost, what did you find at Mother Flannery's?'

'Quite a lot,' Watters swallowed his pride, 'and I don't understand a blessed thing.'

'Tell me,' Silver invited.

'I found this,' Watters produced the papers written in Gaelic, 'and this.' He showed the photograph of Karin Stegall. 'You know a few screevers don't you?'

Silver nodded, 'Oh, I know the best screevers in London. Why?' He studied the picture for a long minute. 'Very nice.'

'I want you to find the most trustworthy of your screevers and get him to copy these two beauties,' Watters indicated the naked men on either side of Karin. 'Cover up Karin and tell him to concentrate on their faces. I want a few copies, and I want them circulated through the town.'

Silver continued to study the photograph. 'Nice looking woman,' he said.

Watters put his hand over Karin. 'You're married,' he reminded.

'I can still look,' Silver protested. 'There is something queer about that picture,' he nodded. 'Of course, look at the men … are they men? They are very smooth.'

'Smooth?' Watters did not catch on.

Silver lowered his voice, 'Sergeant, they have no body hair,' he spoke in a whisper as though afraid to shock the desk, 'anywhere!'

Watters raised his eyebrows. 'Good God, you are right. Now there's a strange thing.' He shook his head. 'Do you recall how I wondered how the Wild Geese made any money? Well, they have a safe stuffed full of photographs.'

'Of whom?' Silver asked.

'That I could not tell you,' Watters said, 'I had a gun pointed at my head when I saw them.' He explained what had happened.

'A cracksman and a man with a gun? Do you have any ideas?' Silver asked.

'Not just any cracksman,' Watters said. 'This man was a diamond-squad man, an expert. He opened a Chubb safe in minutes. Only a handful of people in the world could do that, perhaps less than a handful. Why would a man with that level of skill wish to break into a brothel in the Highway?'

'Money?'

'Not so' Watters shook his head. 'They ignored the strongbox completely and rather than steal the photographs, one of them copied something from the attached documents.' Watters blew smoke into the room. 'They were good, very good. They caught me cold, and I'm no novice.'

Silver raised his eyebrows. 'That is outside my experience, Sergeant. Most of the people I pick up are drunken wife-beaters, pugnacious brawlers, or petty thieves.'

Watters nodded. 'I have not seen anything like these two either, William. They were different from anyone I have met before.'

'Two mysteries then. Who they were and what they were doing,' Silver said.

'Three mysteries,' Watters said quietly. 'Peggy pointed me in the direction of a prize fight between Mother Flannery and some woman from the North. It was pretty brutal stuff, and I had thought Peggy was showing me how dangerous Flannery was with her mauleys, but it was the fellow who introduced the pugilists that mattered.'

'Why?'

'Because he wore a Masonic ring,' Watters said. 'I did not notice at first; he was a pippin and smothered in Birmingham jewellery, and then I saw the Masonic ring plain on his pinkie.'

Silver sucked at his pipe. 'We found one battered ring in Atlantic Street,' he reminded.

'Now we might have both,' Watters said, 'and I have yet to interview the fellows we apprehended and that woman with the black lead.'

'Anything else?' Silver asked.

'Yes,' Watters said slowly. 'Mother Flannery had books in Gaelic. If I had thought properly, I would have copied the titles to see if they match the stories Rowena translated for me. With them, and a picture of Dan O'Connell the politician and some fellow called Cuchulain, the connection to Ireland is powerful.'

Silver shrugged. 'Well, Bridget Flannery is Irish, so I suppose that's natural.'

'Do you think it is only that, Silver?'

'It is never *only that* in this job, Sergeant, is it?' Silver gave a small smile. 'Was there anything else?'

'Yes. The girls take notes from their clients, yet I did not find any such notes in Flannery's office.'

'So they are elsewhere,' Silver said at once. 'That is interesting. Flannery may be working for somebody else.'

'I will bear that in mind,' Watters said. 'I had thought she was the spider at the centre of the web.'

Silver grunted. 'Maybe she likes to think she is the spider, but a larger spider is tugging at her web.'

Watters took a deep breath. 'You're a clever man, Silver.'

'Anything else, Sergeant?'

'A portrait,' Watters said. 'A young girl.'

'How young?'

Watters pondered. 'About twenty perhaps.'

'A favoured prostitute?' Silver shook his head. 'That's unlikely. Maybe it's a portrait of Flannery as a youngster?'

'Maybe,' Watters said. 'That's something else I have to think about.'

Silver nodded. 'It looks like we have work to do.'

'It looks like *I* have work to do,' Watters corrected quietly. 'You have a wife to think of now, William. You can't afford to jeopardise your position helping me.'

Silver looked away. 'Did you tell Larkin all you found out?'

'I told him nothing,' Watters said. 'By the time he had finished ranting at me, I was more inclined to break his head than anything else.'

'That's not like you, George,' Silver was very direct. 'Maybe you'd better lay off this case and follow orders for a while. How are you going to explain finding the photograph?'

'I'm not,' Watters said flatly. 'I'm going to hand it over to Karin.'

Silver's look was sharp. 'Is that wise? It is important evidence.'

Watters nodded. 'I know. I am breaking every rule in the book, but what would you have me do? Allow her to suffer?'

'You'll be the one suffering if Larkin finds out,' Silver said. 'You'll end up selling bootlaces on London Bridge.'

Watters glanced out of the window at the grey London day. 'I won't be doing that,' he said. He thought of his previous life in the Royal Marines and wondered what he could do if he lost his position. What could he do but policing? He was not suited for anything else.

'Sergeant.' Silver nodded to the door. 'You're wanted.'

'Sergeant Watters,' Constable Williams stood rigidly at attention and threw a salute so precise that his hand made a red mark on his forehead.

'That's me,' Watters agreed. 'Williams, isn't it? You were with Anderson guarding the Wild Geese during the raid on Atlantic Street.'

'That's right, Sergeant, and it's about that raid I want to see you.'

'All right, Williams, stand at ease for God's sake, man! I'm only a bloody sergeant!'

'Yes, sir.' Williams banged down his boots as if on parade. 'I want to report, Sergeant, that one of the prisoners we apprehended in the Atlantic Street raid is a deserter from the army.'

'Thank you, Williams, I think you had better relate that information to Inspector Larkin. I am no longer involved in that case.' Watters stored the information in his head for later use.

'I have told him, Sergeant. I thought you had better know as well.'

Watters hid his smile. 'Thank you. How do you know he is a deserter? What's his name anyway?'

'Costello, Sergeant, although he told us that his name is John Smith.'

'And how do you know he deserted?'

'We were both in the 113th Foot in India, sir. I was there when he and some others ran back in '48 or '49. We were fighting the Sikhs.'

Watters nodded. 'I see Williams. Take me to this Costello fellow, if you please.'

'Careful, Sergeant.' Silver had been listening. 'Remember that Inspector Larkin took you off the case.'

'I remember,' Watters said. *But I'm damned if I will take any notice of Inspector bloody Larkin.*

Chapter Twelve

Nine feet long by four wide, the cell had only a high, grated window for light and a metal bucket for sanitary purposes. Costello lay supine on his wooden bed with his hands folded behind his head and his ankles crossed. He looked up when Watters opened the door, frowned, and edged slightly back on the bed. Watters recognised him as the man who had tried to break through Larkin's cordon.

'I'm Sergeant George Watters of Scotland Yard, come to ask you a few questions.'

'I'm here if you need me,' the warden reminded over his shoulder, 'Smith's a troublesome blackguard so be on your guard.' He closed the door with a bang that echoed through the station.

'What the devil do you want, peeler?' Swollen lips thickened Costello's voice as he peered at Watters through bruised eyes. 'I remember you.' He sat up and lifted his fists in a gesture of defiance.

'I only want to talk,' Watters leaned against the door. 'Have they been treating you well?'

'What do you think?' Costello indicated his bruised face. He winced as he swung round to sit on the bed.

'I think it would be a lot worse if the Army knew you were a deserter, Costello.'

'My name's Smith.'

'If you help me, Costello, your name will remain as Smith. If you don't, you will be Costello once more, a welcome gift for the Provost

Marshal. I wonder what they do to deserters nowadays. Is it the cat? Or years in a military prison?'

Costello shrugged, 'I'm sure I don't know.'

'I'm sure it is something supremely unpleasant,' Watters took out his pipe and began to stuff tobacco in the bowl. 'You deserted during the Sikh Wars I believe?'

'Who says I deserted at all? My name is Smith, and I'm a porter.'

'The 113th is in the Crimea, Costello, where you should be.' Watters applied a match to the tobacco and sucked dull life into it. 'I heard you survived the great famine in Ireland?' He held Costello's gaze, hoping for exactly the reaction that he got.

'You bastard English caused that!'

'How did England cause that?' Watters blew smoke into the cell. 'Did England poison the potatoes and cause the rain to fall?' He forced a laugh. 'You must think England has great powers.'

Costello glowered at him from his bruised eyes. He spoke in a torrent of Gaelic, then lay back on his cot. 'There is too much grief in Ireland,' he said slowly, 'and we can lay much of it at England's door.' His eyes, wild and accusing only a second ago, were calculating, even contemptuous, Watters thought.

'The guardsman you murdered was Irish,' Watters said quietly. 'You killed one of your own.'

'His death was stupid,' Costello's voice was solemn. 'I did not kill him.'

'Were you involved in his murder?'

Costello shook his head. 'No.'

'I believe you,' Watters said. 'You and Mother Flannery are deeply involved in something much bigger, aren't you?'

His smile was slow. 'There is a storm coming, Sergeant, and when it comes, it will blow you all away.' Costello grinned as if he had said something very clever. 'There's a storm from the West and the East, and it will blow your world upside down.'

Watters puffed more smoke into the cell and stepped closer. 'I don't like Ireland,' he said, 'and I don't like the Irish. You are a moaning set of work-shy Papists that don't know what's good for them when we hand it to them on a plate.' He leaned over Costello and poked him with his cane. 'Good for nothing Pope loving bastards, the lot of you!'

Watters had hoped that Costello would react, but his kick nearly caught him unawares. He had to suck in his middle to avoid the boot.

'You English bastard!' Costello followed up his kick with a tirade of words, 'we're going to destroy your country, you'll see. There won't be an inch of England safe from us. Mark my words, there's a storm coming from west and east.'

Watters stepped back. 'Thank you, Private Costello, you have been most helpful. I will make sure that your co-operation is known. Mother Flannery will be pleased to hear that, with her intense patriotism.' He saw Costello's expression alter. 'I have another question for you.'

'You're a bastard, Watters.'

'I know,' Watters agreed. 'Who else is in your little group? I know about you and Mother Flannery. Who is the tall chap with the scar on his forehead? And the pippin with the love of gaudy Birmingham gold?'

Costello held his gaze unblinking. 'Who would you like it to be?'

Watters nodded. He could try persuasion or violence, but he knew neither would work. He tapped his cane against the door of the cell. 'Thank you, warden, I have found out all I need to know.' He held Costello's eye. 'I have others to visit.'

* * *

'What's her name?' Watters asked.

The turnkey glanced at the name chalked on the door of the cell. 'Maureen O'Halloran.'

'Thank you. Open the door so she can see me.'

O'Halloran sat on her bed and glared up as Watters stood in the doorway. 'Well? Are you having a good look? I should have blinded you as I did to the lobster.'

Watters tapped his cane on the ground. 'They will try you for assault and murder,' he said quietly. 'You were involved in the death of a guardsman. The court will find you guilty, and you will hang.'

'I never killed the redcoat,' the woman said.

'You made it possible for others to murder him.' Watters kept his voice quiet. 'I am going to watch you hang.' He withdrew. The warden closed and locked the door. 'Let her stew a while,' Watters said. 'Let her contemplate the noose tightening around her neck.' He thought of Guardsman Nixon lying cold and stark. 'Let her suffer and keep a note if anybody visits her. I want names and addresses.'

* * *

'You look tired.' Rowena placed a cup of hot tea at Watters's elbow as he slumped at the table. 'You'd benefit from a few hours in bed.'

'Too much to do.' Watters produced the documents he had taken from Mother Flannery's office and placed them in front of him. 'I have far too much to do.'

Rowena frowned, 'you'll do yourself a mischief if you work all the time. That's what happened to my husband. He worked until he could hardly stand and then bang! Dead! And there was nothing to show for all his work.'

'Except happy memories,' Watters said.

'I have them,' Rowena said. 'Now drink your tea while I find you something to eat, and it won't be bread-and-cheese either. A man needs more than that when he works all the hours God sends. You'll have to start to look after yourself better, Mr Watters, you're all covered in scars and bruises.' She stopped as if afraid she had said too much.

'I might need your interpretation skills,' Watters filled the silence.

'Just ask,' Rowena sounded relieved. 'More Irish stories, are they?'

'I think so,' Watters pored over the Gaelic words.

'Let me see,' Rowena lifted the first foolscap sheet, leaving the rest for Watters. 'I'll read this in the kitchen.'

Watters felt waves of exhaustion sweeping across him as he pored over the unfamiliar words. He searched for repetitive terms as his eyelids became heavier by the minute. When he woke, his tea was cold, and Rowena had placed a pillow under his head and a blanket across his back.

'Welcome back, sleepyhead,' she said cheerfully. 'I'll make fresh tea and re-heat the soup.'

'Thank you,' Watters groaned as he tried to straighten up. 'I'm all stiff.'

'You should have gone to bed when I told you,' Rowena scolded. 'You have to take better care of yourself if you run around chasing criminals. You're no longer twenty years old, you know.'

Watters sat up. 'I know that only too well.'

'Now,' Rowena bustled around with hot tea and hot soup, 'eat something, and you'll feel better. These papers are just nonsense.'

'Nonsense? In what way?'

'They are not passages from any Irish literature that I know,' Rowena said, 'they just seem to be random sentences with the names of heroes and heroines from Irish mythology and history thrown in for no reason.'

'Which names?' Watters looked over Rowena's shoulder as she leaned over the text.

'Well, this one here,' she said. 'Princes Aifa. She is named as the 'evil queen' here,' she pointed out the passage, 'and the 'leader of the foreigners' here, so if these are parts of a story, she is undoubtedly the villain. And here,' she pointed to another, 'that is Manannan mac Lir, the sea God.'

'Do these names mean anything to Irish people now?' Watters asked.

'They mean less than they used to,' Rowena said. 'People are forgetting the old stories.'

'You obviously know them,' Watters said, 'so others will as well.'

'My father taught us—' Rowena lapsed into silence. Her face coloured.

Watters forced a smile. 'Don't stop there. Carry on. Who is your father? He is a clever man to pass on his knowledge to his children.'

Rowena looked away. 'You are my landlord; you don't want to know.'

'I am also your friend, and I do want to know.' Watters put a hand on her shoulder. 'I am interested to hear about your father, and not in a professional way.'

She took a deep breath. 'My father was the gardener at Trinity College in Dublin.' She looked away again.

Watters's smile took on a life of its own. 'I wondered about the plant name: Rowena from the rowan tree.'

'I grew up in and around the College,' Rowena relaxed a little, 'with free rein in the library, and my father encouraged learning and education.'

'That must have been a wonderful childhood,' Watters said.

'It was,' Rowena agreed, 'and look at the mess I made of my life! If it were not for you, I would be wandering the streets, living off crusts and charity.'

'But you are not!' Watters hardened his voice. 'You are warm and dry and using your knowledge to help an uneducated detective sergeant unravel a case that has him completely bewildered.' He gestured to the papers. 'I envy your education. It is a precious attribute.'

Rowena's nod was not convincing as she returned to the documents. 'There are other names from Irish mythology here,' she said. 'There is Cuchulain again, and the Morrigan. I have already told you that Cuchulain is a warrior hero, but the Morrigan is different. She is the Great Queen, a war goddess who lusted after men.' There was guilt or embarrassment in the glance she threw to Watters.

'So three strong characters then,' Watters eased over the awkward pause. 'I don't think they were chosen at random.'

'They are two characters who were heroes of a kind, Cuchulain and the Morrigan, and one villain, Aifa, all from Irish mythology.'

Watters stood up and paced the room, three steps in one direction, a tight turn and three steps back. 'I have a question for you, Rowena. How do you feel about the terrible famine in Ireland in the forties?'

A mixture of emotions crossed Rowena's face, and it was a few seconds before she replied. 'It was horrible,' she said. 'In Dublin, we missed the worst; the West was affected far more, but I heard the stories. There were thousands and thousands of dead and as many emigrated to Great Britain or the United States.'

'Who was to blame?' Watters asked bluntly.

Rowena stepped back. 'I am not sure what you mean. The potato crop rotted.'

'There are some who blame Britain for that,' he said.

'I know,' Rowena said, 'and I do think there could have been more help for the people in the west of Ireland. Did you know there was grain being exported from the east of the island while people only a few score miles away were dying in their thousands?'

'I did hear that,' Watters said.

Rowena stood very upright. 'I think that was wrong.' Her tone was defiant. 'I don't think that farmers or landowners should make a profit while others starve.' She lifted her chin. 'And you may agree or disagree, Sergeant Watters, but that is what I believe.'

'I think it was wrong, too,' Watters told her. 'I don't agree with the rich thriving while the less fortunate suffer. And don't worry, I am sure we can disagree about things without falling out.' Although there was a large part of him that wished he had not started this conversation, he knew he needed her opinion as an intelligent Irishwoman. He knew sufficient about the Irish famine to realise that falsehoods and prejudice probably coloured his ideas.

She studied him for a long minute, her eyes unreadable. 'Why did you ask?'

'I wondered if you blamed Britain for Ireland's suffering.'

'Britain is not blameless.' There was still heat in Rowena's eyes. 'The government's policies to Ireland made a bad situation worse.'

Watters nodded. 'That could be correct,' he said, 'is there a solution?'

'I hope so,' Rowena said, 'otherwise there is going to be a lot more misery.'

'Is the solution to bring bloodshed to Great Britain?' Watters pressed.

'Killing one set of people never made things better for anybody,' Rowena's answer surprised him. 'We are all meant to be Christian, after all.'

He nodded. 'We are,' he agreed. He changed the subject, having discovered all he wished to know. 'This Morrigan woman. You said she was powerful and lusty. Did you mean lusty with men?'

'She was man-hungry,' Rowena was surprisingly blunt. 'Like a man lusting for women – she used men like men use prostitutes.'

Watters felt something slip into place. 'That was an interesting simile,' he said. 'What if this Morrigan was more like a woman who ran a brothel to trap men? Would that make some sense?'

'It is not in the literature,' Rowena said.

'You said yourself that these passages,' Watters tapped the papers on the table, 'are not from any book you know, and you grew up in a library. Perhaps they are about something that is happening today?' The ideas flowed as he spoke. 'I wonder if these names refer to people who are walking the streets as we talk, not people from thousands of years ago.'

Rowena frowned. 'Why? Why change their names?'

'To hide their identities,' Watters said. 'You gave me the idea with your comments about the Morrigan, but that sounds exactly like—' He glanced at her, unsure how much he should reveal.

'It sounds exactly like a brothel-keeper that you know,' Rowena finished the sentence for him.

'Just that,' Watters agreed.

'And the other names? Cuchulain and Aifa?' She widened her eyes. 'Are there people to fit these names?'

Watters shook his head. 'If there are, I have not yet found them.'

Rowena perched on the edge of the table. 'You need more chairs, George, or should I call you Sergeant when you are working?' There was mischief in her eyes.

'George is best,' he said.

'Cuchulain was a warrior then, so maybe a soldier would fit his name, and Aifa would be a queen.' There was enthusiasm in her voice. 'Who is the current head of the British Army? Raglan?'

'I believe so,' Watters enjoyed her spirit.

'Cuchulain could be Raglan then, and Aifa might be Queen Victoria.' Rowena was smiling as her reserve dropped away. 'Or maybe not, George, because in these stories, Aifa is evil and Cuchulain is good; he is on the opposite side, an enemy of Aifa.'

Watters nodded. 'I see. What else do they talk about?'

'They talk about an attack on a meeting at Da Derga's hostel. That part is from the old tales, but they've altered it as Cuchulain was never in the original story.' She reread the documents with her head puckering in concentration. 'Yes, I think I understand. They have used Da Derga's hostel to talk about some meeting between warring factions, or maybe only different tribes or people, with Cuchulain organising an attack on Aifa and her friends.'

Watters closed his eyes as the pieces began to click together. 'That's it, Rowena! You've cracked it!'

'Have I?' Rowena looked pleased. 'What have I cracked?'

'Quite a lot.' He fought his sudden desire to hug her. 'Thank you.'

'You are welcome,' Rowena smiled through her confusion.

* * *

There was no rain that night, only a threatening sky above the smoke of ten thousand chimneys and no breeze to stir the stark branches of the trees in Hesse Square.

'We have made some progress,' Watters said. 'There is a definite Irish connection here, with Mother Flannery being in some way involved. I don't know how yet. 'He explained about the Gaelic names and his tentative linking with the mythical Morrigan and Flannery.

'That's a bit thin to go on,' Silver said. He had borrowed a small telescope and scanned the rooftops for a sight of the ghost.

'True, but it's all we have.'

'That meeting you spoke of at the hostel of Da Derga,' Silver focussed on a chimney pot. 'Do you think there could be a connection with the diplomatic meetings in London?'

'That would tie in with blackmailing Karin,' Watters said. 'I'll give her the photograph back this evening and find out the dates of any peace talks.'

'Why would a bunch of Irish want to know about talks between the Allied powers and Austria anyway?' Silver asked. 'Austria is a great power with a huge empire and Ireland is part of the United Kingdom.'

Watters shrugged. 'I have no idea,' he said. 'International politics does not interest me in the slightest.'

'Maybe it should, Sergeant,' Silver suggested and looked away quickly at the expression on Watters's face.

'Let's get this over with,' Watters said. 'I've had enough of searching for a blasted ghost. I'm going to see Karin.'

Karin opened the door in person. 'Constable Anderson informed me that you might be coming,' she said. 'Have you had any luck?' She ducked in a graceful curtsey, which also allowed the light to reflect from the diamonds around her neck.

'Indeed yes,' Watters allowed Karin to usher him into the drawing-room, where a silver tray held a silver teapot and two bone-china cups. He inhaled her perfume, unconsciously at first, and then with intent. 'I have something for you.' He handed over the photograph.

'Oh ... ' Karin looked at Watters with her mouth open and a look of comical amazement on her face. 'Oh, Sergeant Watters. How did you manage to get this?'

'Do you recognise either of the two men?' Watters thought it best not to answer her question.

She looked at the picture. 'No, no, I don't know them.' Suddenly the colour rushed to her face. 'You must have studied this photograph!'

'I had to see if the men were known to the police,' Watters admitted.

'You saw ...' She withdrew a step and ran both hands down her front.

'I did not look,' Watters immediately wondered if Karin might take that as an insult.

'Oh,' Karin looked away.

'I think it best to burn that picture now,' Watters suggested. 'Don't you?'

The fire was little more than red embers on the grate, so Watters used the bellows to puff some life into it before Karin placed the photograph on top. They watched as it curled up at the edges before brown spots appeared and then slender flames. Karin's image was last to be burned, with the thick paper curling around her naked body before the picture blackened and burst into flames.

'And that is that,' she said. 'How wonderful.' She looked at him. 'I don't know how I feel. I don't know how to thank you.'

'Your feelings I can do nothing about,' Watters said, 'but you can thank me by telling everything you know about your husband's future meetings. Have you told anybody else?'

She took a deep breath. 'You mean, have I responded to the blackmail?'

'That is what I mean.'

'Yes,' Karin looked away.

Watters quelled his sympathy. 'How did you contact him?'

'He came here. I could not get away.' Karin bowed her head. 'I had no choice.'

Watters nodded. 'What is done cannot be undone, but we may be able to mitigate the effects. Is he coming back?'

'I don't know. The blackmailer arrived dressed as a tradesman. It was the same man that I met in the Wild Geese.'

Watters nodded. 'The handsome Christopher fellow with the scar on his head? What did you tell him?'

The tears were free flowing when Karin looked up.

'I told him the time and place of the next diplomatic meeting and who will be there, as far as I know.'

Watters frowned. 'Would we not find that in the newspapers? These things are normally quite well known.'

'Not this one,' Karin shook her head. 'It is a secret meeting to decide if the Austrian Empire will join the allies against Russia or try to negotiate peace.'

'Tell me,' Watters invited, 'tell me everything.' He sipped at the tea in the delicate china cup and listened as Karin spoke.

Chapter Thirteen

'When did this happen?' Watters stood inside the door of the cell, looking down at the twisted body. O'Halloran had been bitter in life; in death, she seemed small and insignificant, curled on the bed with her black hair a tangle across her face.

'This morning, Sergeant.' The turnkey sounded indifferent to the death of one of his charges.

Watters bent over the body. There were bruises on O'Halloran's neck and throat; her eyes were wide, and her tongue protruding from her mouth. 'Somebody has strangled her,' he said. 'How did it happen?'

'Her husband came to see her, Sergeant. You said to take note of any visitors, so I did.' The turnkey seemed pleased that he had managed to do something right. 'Here's his address.'

Watters read the scribbled note. 'Johnathan Wild, 1 Peel Street, London.' He grunted. 'Could you describe Mr Wild?'

The turnkey screwed up his face. 'Not very well, Sergeant. He was English though, London born and bred I'd say with a charming manner about him.'

'He is also dead,' Watters said bluntly.

'What?'

'Jonathan Wild was a master criminal who did the Tyburn jig over a hundred years ago,' Watters said. 'You've been duped, man.' He held the paper under the turnkey's nose. 'This is as false as a leather guinea!' Crumpling it up, Watters threw the note onto the floor. 'God, man! What in creation were you thinking? You let some yahoo dance in here, murder this woman, and prance out again.'

'He never danced, sir.' The turnkey seemed hurt by the suggestion. 'He just walked like anybody else. Save for his boots. They were raised. They were higher than they should be.'

Watters took a deep breath. 'Was he a tall man, then?'

'Lord, no, Sergeant. He was only the same size as me.'

'So his boots made him taller?'

'No, bless you, Sergeant. That's what I'm a-telling you. He was only a little fellow, so his boots made him bigger, the same size as what we are.'

'I see.' The murderer had not been the tall and elegant Christopher then. He had a last look at O'Halloran. That was the second murder. He hoped there would be no more.

* * *

Watters had not known of the existence of the Stationers Hall, tucked away in Ave Angela Lane a long stone's throw from St Paul's, but as he waited for the carriages to drop off the delegates one by one, he had time to admire the classical lines of the building.

'Not quite the same as Atlantic Street,' he said quietly as another carriage rolled up, turned in the courtyard and a very elegantly dressed man stepped out. Watters watched him make minor adjustments to his collar and brush some imaginary dust from his tall hat before looking behind him. His gaze passed over Watters as if he was not there; ordinary people were obviously beneath this gentleman's attention.

A footman dressed in beautiful red and white livery aided a woman from the carriage. Watters could not help his quick draw of breath. Dressed from plunging neck to ankles in shimmering silk, the woman looked more elegant than anybody he had ever seen in his life. If he were superstitious, he would have said that she looked more like a goddess than a human. Her hair was immaculate, and the diamonds around her neck would have cost more than he earned in ten lifetimes, he calculated.

'Karin Stegall,' Watters said softly, 'what sort of life do you live?'

The two burly doormen moved to intercept Watters.

'Detective Sergeant Watters,' he said, 'Scotland Yard. I am providing extra security for the meeting.'

'It's a private meeting,' the elder of the two had a neatly trimmed beard and eyes of flint.

'I am aware of that,' Watters said, 'Scotland Yard knows everything.' He eased past the doormen into the splendours of the building. Karin had informed him that the meeting was inside, with the wives invited to the reception but not the conference itself.

'We are only to provide a blind,' she had said, 'so the people of London believe it is merely a ball of some sort.'

The interior of Stationers' Hall matched the exterior splendour, with each room more striking than the last and impressively deep doorways that led to the Livery Hall where the conference was being held. Watters's mention of 'Scotland Yard' ensured him access to the reception room. He stepped in, trying not to look awed by the ornately carved oak panels that stretched to half the height of each wall, an array of beautiful stained glass windows that coloured the grey London light and ceilings whose plasterwork would have graced any royal palace. Flags and banners moved slowly in the draught of the array of liveried servants who smoothed the passage of delegates and their women. There was soft music from behind a carved screen as the delegates introduced each other in quiet, cultured tones.

A man of medium height, immaculately dressed but with granite eyes, stepped closer to Watters and held out his hand. 'I don't think we have met.'

'I don't think we have,' Watters countered. There was something about this man's suave, smooth look that hid all the charming menace of a waiting tiger. Watters guessed he was an official hard case. 'I am Sergeant George Watters of Scotland Yard.' The man's grip was firm, with the ring on his pinkie an unexpected accessory.

'Frank Walsingham. I did not know Scotland Yard would be here.' The man did not appear surprised.

'Extra security,' Watters said.

'Does Scotland Yard expect trouble, Sergeant Watters?'

'We are here to ensure that everything runs smoothly,' Watters said.

'I am sure everything will go according to plan.' Walsingham nodded and moved away.

Watters positioned himself beside the screen, from where he could survey all that was happening. There were fewer people than he expected, with delegates from Great Britain, France, Turkey, and the Austrian Empire, but none from Russia or Prussia.

Watters checked the delegates as they moved around, talking to one another in what he took to be French, smiling, occasionally laughing. They all walked with grace and poise, none more so than Karin. He found himself concentrating on Karin rather than on the others, noting the austere line of her jaw and cheekbone, the subtle curve of her hips, the gleam of her smile. He was aware of her perfume, even amidst the confusion of scents and heard her light laughter through the babble of sound. She seemed to float on the luxurious carpet.

Watters tore his gaze away. Dammit! He was not here to look at some foreign woman. Her husband was tall, well over six feet, and slender, with manicured side-whiskers, eyes as blue as Karin's but bitter-cold and a mouth like the slash of a sabre. He wore dark clothing with a diagonal sash in Austrian colours, while only the Turkish delegate was distinctive with his red fez, ornate coat, and a curved sword at his side. *Should that sword be permitted at such an august gathering?*

Servants eased between the delegates, nearly invisible as they served drinks and removed glasses with silent skill. Watters studied them, looking for anything suspicious, any tiny hint that a man was out of his place.

Walsingham, or whatever his real name was, had vanished. Watters had not seen him leave. He knew that the two muscular doormen were scrutinising him as much as he was watching them. He slid around the walls, avoiding the delegates, hoping to catch Karin's eye while trying to keep out of her husband's line of sight.

Watters whirled around at the crash of breaking glass and a sharp scream. He half-crouched, one hand on the butt of his revolver, and then straightened up as he saw the cause. One of the footmen had dropped a tray, with shards of crystal glittering and red wine already soaking into the carpet. The French and British delegates had stepped away from the chaos, with the Turk looking on with a smile. Watters nodded as Karin slipped free from Wolfgang and stepped forward to help the distressed footman. Wolfgang motioned her back with a disapproving shake of his head.

Watters glanced around the room. One of the security men had moved for a better look while the other remained immobile. The music had momentarily stopped, and a violin player peeped into the chamber, his bow tie askew, to be violently hissed back by the grey-haired conductor. Within a minute the orchestra began to play a soothing waltz, the security men resumed their positions, and an elderly servant was supervising the cleaning-up process.

Wolfgang chided Karin for helping, smiling to hide his evident anger, and Watters resumed his inspection of the room. Servants cleared away the broken crystal, the musicians changed the music, and a tall man ushered the delegates into the Court Hall next door, leaving the women to their own devices. Watters followed, nodding to the sole doorman who followed. Taking his stance at the far side of the room, Watters ensured he was out of the diplomat's hearing but close enough to offer assistance if required. Karin eased her gloved hand into the crook of Wolfgang's closed elbow; both smiled as they spoke, giving no hint of the tension between them.

A group of men entered the room, dressed in smart dark suits and white shirts with high collars and black ties. They positioned themselves behind their respective delegates. Moving silently, the dark-suited men readied pads of paper and pens, with inkwells already placed on the long oval table. The delegates spoke to them with the ease of long familiarity.

The security man closed the door and stood facing inwards as Watters scrutinised each window in turn. He checked his watch. Once again, Silver was covering for him.

Once again, he was disregarding his duty to follow a hunch. Watters knew that if Larkin found out, he may lose his position, but if he neglected to follow these leads, there could be loss of life. It was a gamble. Basing his suspicions on a chance reading of a two-thousand-year-old Irish story would not impress Larkin.

As a burst of noise came from the corridor outside, Watters took a deep breath; he was not sure for what he was looking. Perhaps some angry Irishman who had lost his family in the Great Famine, or a latter-day O'Connell or Parnell choosing the path of violence rather than politics? Watters sighed. He had not even heard an Irish accent in this building.

The delegates had a map unfolded on the table and were rooted in earnest discussion. Their voices rose and fell as they pointed out national boundaries and various towns. Watters frowned. Something was wrong. He was not sure what. Something was niggling him, something he had forgotten or neglected, some detail he had omitted.

The music floated from the adjoining room, light, frothy even, not loud enough to disturb the concentration of the delegates. Watters found his feet were tapping to the rhythm and stopped. That was what bothered him: the music, or rather the musicians. He recognised that tune; it was the Irish Washerwoman's Jig, hardly suitable for such a gathering, and it was growing louder.

'Let me through!' Watters said to the security man. 'Something is not right.'

The man stepped aside just as the first shot ran out, and the first scream.

'What the devil?' The British delegate spoke first as Watters and the security man tried to rush through the door together. Watters thrust the man aside and powered through, hauling out his revolver.

The interior of the Livery Hall had descended from a place of grace and elegance to one of chaos. One woman lay on the ground, writhing, as the others crowded around the door on the far side of the room. The conductor of the orchestra pointed a short, double-barrelled pistol toward the women while a violinist levelled another at the cowering musicians.

Watters's aimed but did not fire in case his shot hit one of the women. 'Scotland Yard! Put the gun down!'

In reply, the violinist swivelled toward Watters and fired. Watters dodged, aimed, and squeezed the trigger of his revolver. His shot missed, but the report was sufficient to make both gunmen duck, so Watters fired a second shot, catching the conductor in the lower leg. His roar of pain joined the high screams from the gathered women, and Watters fired again, just as the violinist squeezed the trigger of his pistol.

Watters felt the violinist's bullet hiss past his left ear. He fired again, saw the violinist stagger, and moved forward. Stamping on the conductor's wrist to make him drop his pistol, he skiffed the weapon away and lunged at the violinist before he could take a second shot. By that time, both security men were in the room, and Watters could relax slightly.

'Sergeant Watters!' He had to ignore the light behind Karin's eyes as he knelt to the wounded woman.

'She's still alive!' Watters shouted. 'Somebody fetch a doctor!'

The bullet had hit her on the left thigh so, uncaring of her dignity, Watters raised her gown to check. The blood flowed from a wound two inches above the knee, painful but not dangerous. Without thinking, Watters ripped off his hired tie and fastened it above the injury to act as a tourniquet, then shouted for two chairs from the Court Room. It was the French delegate who dragged them in and helped Watters sit the wounded woman on one chair with her leg raised and balanced on the other.

'It's not dangerous,' Watters hoped she could understand English, 'the doctor will soon have you dancing around like a two-year-old.'

'Who the devil are you?' The British delegate stood a good three feet away as he spoke.

'Sergeant George Watters. Scotland Yard.'

'A common policeman and only a sergeant.' The delegate looked away. 'Good Lord.'

'My wife,' The French delegate delicately lowered the woman's skirt.

'You saved her life, Sergeant Watters,' Karin said.

'I hope so Ma'am,' Watters gave a low bow. He noticed that most of the wives comforted each other as the delegates stood in a clump with Wolfgang a few steps apart, brushing at the shoulder of his coat. He did not try to read the expression in Karin's eyes.

Chapter Fourteen

'You look pleased with yourself,' Larkin said, 'Irish plot to disrupt the peace conference foiled, French diplomat's life saved, and case solved.' He looked at Watters across the width of the desk. 'Is that what you are thinking?'

'I am glad that nobody was killed,' Watters said.

'Are you also glad that the French diplomat's wife was wounded, that you broke my orders to withdraw from this case, and you failed to stop the attack despite your lack of discipline?' Larkin's expression did not alter.

'I am never glad when an innocent person is hurt.' Watters thought it best not to mention his break-in at Mother Flannery's or the return of Karin's photograph.

'You speak with caution, I see, Watters,' Larkin said.

'I am speaking only the truth, and it is Sergeant Watters, sir.'

'Perhaps you won't be "sergeant" for much longer, Watters.' Larkin looked up when there was a knock at the door. 'Come in!'

Watters did not turn around at the approach of the footsteps.

'Is this the man you saw, Mr Alba?' Larkin addressed the newcomer.

'This is the man,' the voice was familiar. 'He claimed to be John Temple.'

Watters swivelled and looked into the face of the gunman from Mother Flannery's house.

'His name is George Watters,' Larkin said. 'At present, he is a detective sergeant here.'

'Sergeant Watters,' the man extended a hand. 'Raymond Alba.'

'Should I arrest you for burglary?' Watters hid his surprise.

'Only if I should arrest you for the same thing,' Alba said.

'I tried to keep him away from your operations,' Larkin said. 'He has a reputation for interfering.'

'I thought it was a strange sort of burglar who ignored the valuables,' Watters kept all emotion from his voice.

'Secret service,' Alba said without hesitation. 'I am sure you had worked that out.'

'I did not think that Mother Flannery was so important,' Watters said evenly.

'Your blundering could have cost us dearly,' Larkin broke in.

'Your refusal to allow me to pursue a legitimate police operation was unprofessional.' Watters was determined to go down fighting if he was to lose his position.

Alba held up a hand. 'I am sure that Sergeant Watters acted with the best possible motives. I also heard that you prevented a nasty incident at a diplomatic meeting talks yesterday.'

'I was not successful,' Watters said. 'Somebody shot and wounded the wife of the French delegate, and one of your fellow secret service men was conspicuous by his absence.'

'You may have saved her life and others,' Alba said, 'but I am intrigued by your mention of a secret service man. To my knowledge, we had nobody there.'

Watters frowned. 'He called himself Walsingham. Frederick, no, Frank Walsingham.'

Alba smiled. 'Francis Walsingham was the name of Queen Elizabeth's spymaster. The fellow you saw was not one of ours, Watters.'

'Then who the devil—' Watters stopped himself. The fellow who called himself Walsingham was a small man with granite eyes who just happened to be present when there was an attack on the diplomats. Add the ring on his little finger and—

Alba nodded. 'It appears that you have met one of the opposition, Watters. You can tell me about him later. In the meantime, tell me how you knew to go there.'

Watters explained about the Gaelic phrases and the use of code words that his housekeeper had guessed indicated significant individuals.

'That was a deuce of a gamble, Watters,' Alba said.

'It was,' Watters glanced at Larkin. 'I don't believe that any senior officer would have concurred with my conclusion, but I could not take the chance of people being killed.'

Alba nodded. 'This type of operation is like that,' he said. 'Sometimes one must hang one's coat on the most slender of pegs.'

When Larkin did not indicate assent or dissent, Watters asked: 'How did you know about the Wild Geese?'

'We have been watching Flannery for some time,' Alba said, 'a lot longer than you have.' He looked around the room. 'I think we should continue this conversation somewhere more comfortable. I am sure Inspector Larkin will not mind.'

Larkin took a deep breath and shook his head.

'Splendid. Take me to some suitable public house, Sergeant Watters.' Alba gave Larkin a grin. 'I am absconding with your best man, Larkin. I hope you can cope without him.'

Larkin's glare was as warm as an Arctic iceberg.

* * *

'You are a strange man, Watters.' Alba slid into the seat at the Admiral Rodney with as much aplomb as if he was in his gentleman's club. 'Who was in the photograph? The one that you broke into Mother Flannery's to steal?'

Watters shook his head. 'I am sworn not to say.'

'Come, come, man, I am an agent of Her Majesty. There can be no secrets from such as me.'

'I am sworn not to say,' Watters repeated. 'What were you doing in the Wild Geese?'

'I am sworn not to say.' Alba's grin was so youthful that Watters wondered how old he was. He looked around forty, but his attitude was as flippant as any schoolboy.

'I think we were both after the same thing,' Watters said. 'I was looking for a photograph of one particular individual while you were listing the people of whom photographs were taken.'

Alba's smile did not slip. 'I presume you have worked out the Irish connection then.' His tone continued to be light, nearly banal, but his eyes were shrewd.

'I did,' Watters admitted, 'although you know far more than I do. I think it is time to stop playing silly playground games and put our cards on the table. You must want something from me, otherwise you would not allow me to know who and what you are, despite the obviously false name.'

'Indeed, Mr Temple,' the grin remained.

'Touché' Watters acknowledged.

'How much about the Irish connection do you know, and how much have you guessed?' Alba asked.

'Most of it is guesswork with hopeful deductions.' Watters put his glass of half-and-half on the table. 'There is an Irish soldier named Costello who was involved in the murder in Atlantic Street and an attack on me. When I interviewed him, he was very bitter about the late Famine of a few years ago and blamed it on Britain.'

'Costello,' Alba repeated. 'I did not know about him.'

'He threatened me with a storm from the west and the east.'

'A storm from the west and east? Were those his exact words?' Alba leaned closer as Watters nodded. 'Here is what we gather. The Wild Geese is only one part of this organisation. We know that it is Irish, and we know they recruit Irishmen and probably Irishwomen who are bitter about the Famine, but we are not yet sure why.'

'The girls in the Wild Geese ask soldiers and sailors about their military experience and the morale in their regiments,' Watters said quietly. 'Perhaps they are looking for more desertions from the Irish soldiers.'

'That could be true,' Alba said, 'but why? Some desertions might weaken the British Army slightly, but how would that benefit Ireland?' He shook his head. 'There is more to it than that, Sergeant Watters. You are thinking like a policeman. I want you to think like a politician.'

Watters shook his head. 'I am probably the least political person in London,' he said. 'I don't even know the name of the cabinet, or what party is in power.'

'I don't mean party politics,' Alba said. 'I mean international politics. What would Irish deserters from the army want with such information? And what would the Madame of a back-street brothel want with photographs of naked men and women?'

'Blackmail,' Watters said quickly. 'I know one of the people and blackmail was involved.'

'That would be the photograph of Karin Stegall that you removed,' Alba smiled again. 'Yes, of course, I knew all the time, Sergeant. I merely wished to test your loyalty.' He finished his drink and signalled for another. 'It is this blackmail that intrigues me. What did the blackmailer want? Money to boost the organisation's funds? Or information?'

'Information,' Watters said.

Alba nodded. 'As were the others. The photographs included two politicians, a lawyer, and a police officer far above your rank, three men of the cloth and four high-ranking army officers.'

'A fine collection of the great and the good,' Watters said. 'To whom does the information go? I know the girls took notes of what was said, and we both know they were watched or could be watched, yet when I looked through Flannery's room, there were no notes.'

'That I do not know,' Alba said. 'We are trying to find that out, and that is the main reason I did not welcome your intrusion into the Wild Geese. Your presence warned them that we were aware of their actions.'

'There was a murder right beside the pub,' Watters pointed out. 'A mob killed a guardsman and badly injured another. I already knew things at the Duck were queer, but that meant I had to check it out.'

'I know,' Alba said. 'We had to use a lot of influence to make Larkin back away from the Wild Geese.'

'I can think of no reason why disgruntled Irishmen should want the sort of knowledge these people possess,' Alba continued, 'but I can think of other people who would want that conference destroyed.'

Watters nodded. 'It would benefit Russia if Britain was unable to guarantee the security of her ally's diplomats in London.'

Alba leaned back in his chair. 'Imagine if the French, Turkish, and Austrian diplomats had all been murdered by British subjects in London. Or worse, imagine the furore if the diplomats' wives had been murdered. What would that do to the alliance? What would be the chance then of the Austrian Empire with its hundreds of thousands of soldiers joining the allies against Russia?'

'It would not have helped,' Watters said slowly.

'Indeed not. Do you think that would have been an act of fitting revenge for the Irish Famine?' Alba leaned back in his chair but held Watters's gaze. 'Now consider this. You spoke to this Costello fellow: he was a soldier. The conductor and violinist of that orchestra were Dubliners with no history of political life. They were pawns, puppets, nothings. You dealt with them very well, Sergeant Watters, but who pulled their strings?'

'The man I thought was one of yours, perhaps?'

'That is a possibility,' Alba agreed.

'Perhaps Mother Flannery would know?' Watters said. 'If you brought her in,' he paused.

'We have her in hand,' Alba assured him.

'There was another Irishwoman I hoped to interview, one who tried to blind me.' Watters remembered the pain of his eyes. 'But she was murdered in a police cell. Her name was O'Halloran.' He sipped at his tankard. 'A small man with raised heels and a local accent murdered her.'

'She was only another pawn,' Alba said quietly. 'Women like her, and men like Guardsman Nixon, or you, or me,' he rolled his tankard in his hand, 'we don't matter in the big game, Watters. We are unimportant, even our bosses, Larkin, regimental colonels, and such like, they are small fish in a pond they don't even understand. If the enemy, of whatever persuasion, eliminates one of us, there are scores more to take our place.'

Watters nodded. 'I see that, Alba, and quite frankly, I don't care. I can't do anything about it. I do know Flannery was involved in a murder.'

'The government has asked Inspector Larkin not to pursue that case for the time being.' Alba spoke quietly.

'Then the government can hang its head in shame, Alba, if it chooses to ignore the death of a good man.' Watters felt his temper rising.

Alba's smile was as jovial as ever. 'I think we can compromise, Sergeant Watters. If you share all your information with me, I shall apply persuasion to Inspector Larkin, and you will be able to find your murderer.'

'I'll find him anyway, with or without Larkin's permission,' Watters sipped his half-and-half without dropping his gaze from that of Alba.

'Do you know, Sergeant Watters, I rather think you will.' Alba ordered another round of drinks. 'Now, tell me all you know about this small man, and the fellow who seduced Mrs Stegall.'

Watters took another drink to give himself time to think. 'I don't know much about the small man, Alba, and what I do know is confusing. I don't even know if I am right. He seems to appear at all the crucial places, but he never looks the same.' He shook his head. 'I am not even sure if it is the same man.'

'Tell me what you can.'

Watters described Yellowford and Walsingham, emphasising that both were under medium height, and then mentioned the man who claimed to be O'Halloran's husband. 'He was about the same height as well.'

'There are many small men in London,' Alba said. 'This fellow, whatever his name may be, seems to be able to adopt different personalities. That makes him difficult to trace. Now,' he signalled to the barman to fill up their tankards, 'the other fellow? The seducer called Christopher?'

He listened to Watters's description and drew in his breath sharply. 'You say he was tall and handsome, with whiskers and a scar. I may know that man, Watters, and if I do, then we are in deep trouble.'

'Who do you think it could be?' Watters asked.

'A Russian fellow named Markovic,' Alba said. 'He's one of their top agents and we've had our eye on him for some time.'

'So Russia comes up again?'

'It is only a possibility.' Alba waited until the next round of drinks arrived before he continued. 'Now tell me about these old Gaelic names.'

'We have three names that occur frequently.' Watters looked around the room in case they were overheard and then wondered if this small man was making him neurotic. 'They are Princes Aifa, Cuchulain, and the Morrigan – I might have the pronunciations wrong there. We guess that the Morrigan is Mother Flannery, but the other two continue to elude us.' Watters pulled the papers from his inside pocket. 'They are in Gaelic,' he said, 'And Princes Aifa seems to be an enemy of the others.'

'So the Morrigan is Flannery, you think.' Alba looked around. 'I am familiar with Irish mythology, Sergeant. One picks up strange things in this job. So Cuchulain may be the male of the species, the counterpart to Flannery?'

'I think so,' Watters said. 'I wondered if it might be the man who first enticed Karin Stegall into the bedroom of the Wild Geese, and who had her drugged.' He did not mention his momentary suspicion of Larkin. 'Or it might even be Yellowford.'

'I have your description,' Alba said. 'Cuchulain was an Irish warrior, a hero. The tall man with the scar—Markovic or Christopher—might be better suited than the smaller Yellowford.' He looked at the portraits of the two men who had been in the photograph with Karin. 'I don't recognise either of these beauties.' He glanced at the documents Watters handed over. 'I will have the experts look at these,' he said. 'Now, if Morrigan and Cuchulain are on the same side, then presumably Aifa is their enemy, and therefore on our side. A female?'

'It is a female's name,' Watters confirmed.

'Her Majesty?' Alba said the name in a tone of hushed reverence.

Watters pondered for a minute. 'I don't know,' he said, 'but if that was the case, can you imagine anything more likely to make the British people angry than an attempt at the Queen? There would be a mad rush to join the army to get at the Russians if it is them.' He shook his head. 'Or the Irish if we can prove they were the attackers. It might strike a major blow at the country, but it would do the opposite than the murderers wanted.'

'There is no other prominent woman worth attacking,' Alba said. 'We do have a plethora of duchesses and such like, and we have Florence Nightingale.'

'Attacking Florence Nightingale would be like attacking a saint,' Watters said.

'We will have to think about that one,' Alba said. 'In the meantime, Sergeant, I will have experts examine these documents.'

Chapter Fifteen

It was good to get home and slide off his boots, to sit in front of a ready-made fire and have a mug of sweet tea brought to him. It was good to hear Rowena bustling around in the kitchen, clattering dishes, and singing some strange Gaelic song. Watters stretched out on the chair, wondering why he barely regretted his loss of privacy.

'Things have changed this last day,' he thought out loud. 'I am no longer out in the cold battling a case I do not understand.'

'Who are you talking to?' Rowena's rich voice sounded a second before she poked her head through the adjoining doors. 'The fire can't reply to you.'

'I was just talking to myself,' Watters said.

'That's the first sign of madness, they say,' Rowena told him, 'and the second sign is answering back.'

Watters smiled, 'I will try not to answer myself then.'

Rowena dusted flour from her hands. 'You look cheerful this evening, George. Is your case making progress?'

'We have ups and downs,' Watters told her, 'with the ups in no small measure due to your help in translating the Gaelic documents.' He turned around to smile at her. 'I think I should get you a position as the translator in chief to Scotland Yard.' He stretched out his hand, touched her arm. 'Thank you, Rowena.'

She pushed into him and then pulled away. 'Oh nonsense,' she said. For a second, she stood still with her blonde head to one side, bright alive and nervous, with the lines of suffering already easing from around her eyes and mouth.

Rowena started at the sudden hammering. Watters sighed. 'That will be another crisis of one sort or another,' he said. He put out his hand as Rowena moved toward the door, 'it's all right, Rowena, I'll get it. It will be some uniformed constable with critical information about a broken window, or a case of furious driving, or a child who has lost her glove or some such.'

Watters was wrong. When he opened the door, Karin staggered in with her face swollen with tears and a newspaper in her hand.

'Sergeant Watters,' she sobbed. 'They must have had a copy of my picture. They sent it to the ambassador and told the newspapers,' she brandished the paper as if it was a weapon, 'and now the whole world knows. You must help me!'

'Come in,' Watters put an arm around her shaking shoulders, 'Rowena! Make some tea, please.' He helped Karin to his seat by the fire. 'Now, calm down and tell me what has happened.'

'Look!' Karin handed over the newspaper. 'There!' She stabbed downward with her forefinger. 'You told me that I was safe now! You told me you had taken the photograph away, but they must have had another and sent it to Wolfgang!'

Watters took the newspaper.

'*Scandal in diplomatic society*' it read, '*today it has been revealed that Karin Stegall, the wife of the Austrian diplomat Wolfgang Stegall, has been exposed in the most outrageous manner. Mrs Stegall has been discovered in the company of some of the most obnoxious characters in a low place of public entertainment in London. This newspaper is in possession of pictures of the most terrible nature that should never be revealed to the public and which show Mrs Stegall in the most unpleasant situation.*

Mr Wolfgang Stegall is presently in London on a diplomatic mission for the Austrian government. He is an attaché to the Austrian ambassador, and it is rumoured that his position is of the most delicate nature. He was present at the recent meeting in the Stationers' Hall which, as readers will remember, some Irish assassins disrupted.

Although we must sympathise with Mrs Stegall in her trying week, we think it is our duty to bring notice of these facts to our readers. It is our belief that despite this terrible event, Mr Stegall will continue with his diplomatic venture. We can only praise his dedication to duty, although we think it likely that these events will have an untoward effect on his future career.'

Rowena pushed a mug of tea into Karin's hand. 'We need more cups if you are going to get as many visitors, George,' she said quietly.

'Wolfgang ordered me out of the house,' Karin spoke through her tears. 'He slapped me,' she showed the side of her face, where there was a fading red mark, 'and threw me out.' Her hands were shaking as she held the mug. 'I have no money, Sergeant Watters, and nowhere to go. No hotel will have me with my name in the newspapers, and Wolfgang must hate me.'

Rowena glanced at Watters before she spoke. 'He won't hate you, Ma'am. He will be angry with you for a spate, but he will not hate you.' She touched Watters lightly on the arm. 'May I speak to you alone, George?'

Leaving Karin by the fire, Rowena took Watters into the kitchen. 'Is this the Austrian woman, George?' Her voice was a low hiss.

'Yes,' he said, 'it looks like the Irish had a copy of the photograph.'

Rowena's accent thickened as she spoke. 'And what good would exposing the poor woman do to Ireland?'

Watters felt her concealed anger. 'Carry on, Rowena.'

'This is not about Ireland, George, this is about something else.'

Watters put a finger to his lips. 'Keep it quiet, please. Karin is upset enough as it is.'

Rowena gave him a look that would melt glass but lowered her voice to a vicious hiss. 'Don't blame Ireland for this, George. These are evil people intent on causing trouble.'

Watters nodded. 'I know that already, Rowena.' He was slightly surprised by her intensity.

'You said they are bitter about the Famine,' she did not stop her verbal assault, 'so I presume they were affected by it?'

'I would presume so,' Watters agreed.

'So they were near starvation,' Rowena said, 'yet now they are already able to organise something that touches on people like that unhappy woman there?' She jerked her head toward Karin.

Watters nodded. 'I have already worked that out,' he told her.

'And have you worked out that she can't stay with us?'

'With *us*?'

'She can't stay here,' Rowena quickly amended. 'She is already in a great deal of trouble. Can you imagine the scandal when the newspapers learn that she ran to another man? Can you imagine how it would affect you?' She lowered her voice, speaking urgently, 'Your name will be linked with a scandalous woman, George, and that will tarnish both your reputations forever. You must take her elsewhere.'

'It is too late for that tonight.' Watters looked through the window at the darkness outside. 'Tomorrow I will sort things out.' He ignored Rowena's glare.

* * *

'I have put her in the Adelaide Hotel, sir,' Watters said, 'although I cannot afford more than a few days of her keep there.'

Larkin snorted as Alba gave his usual grin, 'I am sure she would prefer Fenton's or the Clarendon to the Adelaide, but beggars can't be choosers, can they?' He lounged back in his chair in Larkin's office. 'Send the tab to me, Watters. I'm sure Her Majesty's government can afford a few more shillings. So Karin Stegall came a-running to you, did she? You seem to have a way with women, what with that prostitute in Mother Flannery's, the old mother herself, your housekeeper … yes, I know about her, and now Mrs Stegall.'

Watters grunted and decided to ignore that remark. He knew he was not good with women. 'We could use Mrs Stegall's knowledge to help crack this case,' he said. 'Detective Silver knows an excellent artist. He could draw pictures of the man who enticed Mrs Stegall to the Wild Geese, and we could distribute them across London.'

'We could,' Alba acknowledged with a wave of his cheroot, 'and then we must decide what to do with the unfortunate Mrs Stegall. Her husband is continuing with the negotiations despite the scandal,' he shrugged, 'but that is not our concern. The fate of one Austrian woman is neither here nor there compared to keeping the country secure. By all means bring her in, Sergeant Watters, so we can milk all the information out of her.'

'Watters,' Larkin had been a silent and mostly impotent witness as he sat at his desk, 'I will take Silver away from his ghost hunting duties and appoint him to assist you. It seems that the two of you work well enough together.'

'Thank you, sir,' Watters sensed the influence of Alba in that decision, 'and it is Sergeant Watters, sir.'

* * *

It was hard to believe that the country was in the throes of its most bitter European war since the defeat of Bonaparte. The Thames was busy with shipping; the streets were crowded with people bustling to business or perambulating for pleasure, the shop windows were bright with promise. London life had not altered in the slightest. As Watters loped along the street, a one-legged soldier limped past, a reminder that only a couple of thousand miles away, the cream of the British army was starving and freezing to death in the trenches outside Sebastopol.

Peggy had his coffee ready for him. 'Here you are, Sergeant. What are you asking today?'

'Oh, Peggy, that is cruel, I don't only come here to ask you questions you know.'

'Not always,' Peggy stopped to serve the mate of a Tyneside collier, 'not always Sergeant, but usually.'

'Well since you ask,' Watters produced the sketched images of the men Karin had described. 'Do you know any of these beauties?'

'Handsome looking fellows these,' Peggy looked at the two younger men. 'I would not kick them out of my bed to let you in, Sergeant!' Her cackle sounded around the street. 'That older man? He is familiar, but I don't know him. I'm sure he passes here sometimes, but he never buys anything from me, the hog-grunting bugger.' She looked again. 'I definitely know that one though.' Her long-nailed finger jabbed at one of the younger men. 'Oh I do know him.'

'Do you know his name?'

Peggy shook her head. 'Not a bit of it. He does not come here, but he is a regular over at the Tap,' she pointed to a public-house across the street. She lowered her voice. 'There are some strange men in there, Sergeant Watters.' Her laugh cackled across the street and attracted the attention of passers-by. 'You better take care of yourself in there.'

'I can take care of myself,' Watters said.

'Not very well, Sergeant Watters, I heard somebody beat you up not long ago!'

'You hear too much, Peggy,' Watters said.

'Don't go in alone,' Peggy seemed to find something very amusing. 'You had better have somebody guard your arse!' Her laughter increased as if she had said something incredibly smart.

Watters surveyed the public house, the Tap of the Thames. It seemed no different from any of the hundreds of places of refreshment in London, and probably no more dangerous than the hole-in-the-wall dives and backstreet hovels that sold kill-me-deadly spirits and watered beer. All the same, he knew that Peggy was not prone to exaggerate and decided to take her advice.

* * *

'All ready?' Watters asked.

Silver tapped the inside of his coat. 'As ready as I can be.' He surveyed the Tap from the outside. 'It doesn't look too bad, and we don't have any records of any incidents in here.'

'I trust Peggy,' Watters said. 'She's never let me down yet.'

They pushed in through the single door and looked around. There was an oval bar of polished wood with the usual array of taps, a score of chairs and tables and groups of men drinking and murmuring in twos and small groups. They all looked up when Watters and Silver entered, a few nodded, and one of the two barmen hurried to greet them.

Silver showed the barman the drawing. 'I am looking for this man,' he said. 'I know he comes in here.'

The barman nodded, 'Why do you want him?' His glance at the door in the far wall was momentary but significant.

'Oh, we just want to talk to him,' Silver said.

'Just talk?' the barman said.

'Talk is free,' Silver told him.

'Not always.' The barman evidently delighted in cryptic conversation.

Watters had moved toward the door in the end wall. He tried the handle and pushed. It was locked. 'Is he through here?' he asked.

'You can't go up there without permission.' The second barman stepped toward him. He was broad with the cauliflower ears, and broken nose of an ex-pug, the sort of man Watters had seen employed in brothels and troublesome clubs. He did not quite seem to fit in this seemingly respectable establishment.

'Oh, that's all right,' Watters said pleasantly. 'He won't mind; I know him by sight.' He put pressure on the door as the pug advanced.

'Come away from there before I make you.' The pug stood two feet back. 'We don't want any trouble in here.'

Watters was surprised to see some of the customers edging away, with a few drifting out of the room. 'If you let us see this gentleman, there will be no trouble, I promise. But if you try and stop us, we will give you more than you can handle.' He tapped the weighted end of his cane against the wall to emphasise his point.

The pug glanced at the other barman, who eyed up Silver, shifted his gaze to Watters and nodded. He threw a key to Watters.

'Thank you,' Watters opened the door quietly and pocketed the key. 'I'll keep this to stop you having any silly notions of locking us in here.' He pushed through, with Silver following him. 'Well, that was easy enough.'

'Did you see these men when tapped your cane on the wall?' Silver asked. 'They looked like rabbits caught in gig-lamps. I've never seen anything like that in my life.' He grinned. 'They must have heard your reputation.'

The door opened to a single flight of steps lit by a small skylight. Watters led Silver up, with their feet echoing on bare wooden floorboards and their elbows rubbing on whitewashed plaster. There was a square landing at the top, from which three doors opened.

'Listen,' Watters said. There were slight sounds from the central door. 'I think he has a woman in there.'

'It would be cruel to spoil his pleasure,' Silver said.

'And more cruel to blackmail Karin,' Watters tested the door. It was locked from the inside. Stepping back, he lifted his boot and kicked hard just below the lock. The door crashed open, to the accompaniment of loud shrieks from within. Silver plunged through with Watters one step behind.

Watters kicked the door shut behind him. 'Right you,' he said, reached forward, and stopped. The two faces that stared up at him were both males. One belonged to the man in the photograph, a golden-haired, smooth-faced youth, while the other was an elderly man with greying whiskers and a pop-eyed expression in his watery blue eyes.

'Oh, dear God in heaven,' Watters took a step back.

'Oh, God!' The elderly man pulled back into the bed and hauled the covers over his face until Watters pulled them completely off the bed. Both men were naked.

'Oh, my hat,' Silver breathed. 'What in the devil's own name?'

'Pederasts,' Watters did not need to explain further. 'I am Sergeant George Watters, and this is Detective William Silver of Scotland Yard.'

'It's you I want,' Watters pointed to the younger man. 'You,' he jabbed the older with a hard finger, 'I do not.' He stepped back. 'Take their names, Silver, and we'll interview them in the office.'

'No!' The older man covered himself as best he could. 'You can't do that! It would ruin me! My position, my family—'

'You should have thought of that,' Silver was barely able to contain his disgust.

'No, wait!' Watters thought quickly, 'Take this man's pocketbook, Silver,' he nodded to the older man, 'I want his real name and address. The other creature is coming with us.'

'I'm not, I can't.' There was genuine panic in the young man's eyes as Watters threw his clothes to him.

'Get dressed.'

There were tears in the older man's eyes as Silver searched through his pockets. 'Here we are, Sergeant,' Silver said, 'we have his card.'

'That will do,' Watters said. 'Are you sure it's his?'

'Yes, there are six of them, all the same, and another in the pocket of his vest.'

'Right, you,' Watters jerked a thumb at the older man. 'You can go. We might come for you later. Go on, get out!' He watched as the man fled, struggling to dress as he opened the door. 'Right, handcuff that fellow, Silver, and let's get out of here.'

* * *

'Name?' Alone in a small room with Watters and Silver staring at him, the man looked terrified. Watters fought his sympathy. 'What's your name?'

The man tried to wipe his tears away with a handcuffed hand. 'Peter Travis,' he said.

'And your real name?' Silver stood behind him with both hands pressing his shoulders.

'That is my real name,' the man nearly screamed. 'Ask anybody.'

'Oh, we will,' Watters said, 'you can depend on it.'

'All right, Travis,' Silver spoke softly, 'I will believe that you have given your real name. Now we want all you can tell us about the Wild Geese, what goes on there, who runs it and why, and who this man is.' He produced the sketch of the man who had seduced Karin.

'I don't know,' Travis was sobbing.

'Do you know that you are accessory to giving a woman a drugged drink, blackmail, assault and probably murder,' Watters said. 'That might mean the rope, or it might mean ten- or twenty-years' transportation. Do you know what happens to men like you when the Law transports them?'

Travis tried to cover his ears with manacled hands.

'Well, I'll allow you to imagine,' Watters said, 'but I can assure you that it is worse than anything you can picture. Men commit murder so they will be hanged just to escape the horrors of daily life there.'

'Oh, God, help me.'

'He won't' Silver said happily. 'You disgusted Him with your behaviour. But we can help you.'

'But only if you help us,' Watters added.

'What will you do?'

'That depends on how much you help us,' Silver said. 'If you help us a little bit, then we can ask the nice judge to reduce the sentence to maybe ten years. If you help us a bit more, he might make it eight years. If you help us a lot, why, we may even convince him not to transport you but to imprison you here instead, so all your little friends can visit you.'

'Or we could have you sent to Norfolk Island,' Watters wondered if Travis knew that transportation to Norfolk had ended the previous year. 'That is the most brutal of all the convict settlements. A life sentence there under the lash...'

'I'll help you!' Travis nearly screamed the words. 'For God's sake, I'll help you!'

'Good man!' Silver patted him on the shoulder. 'Off you go then, and I'll write down all you say, every blessed word.'

When Travis looked up, his face was wet with tears. 'You bastards,' he sobbed, 'you'll regret this, you'll see!'

'No,' Watters shook his head. 'We won't regret this, but you will. Your actions have broken at least one marriage and may have endangered the lives of thousands of others. Just think of that, and all for what? What were you paid?'

'A golden boy,' Travis said.

'And look where it's got you,' Watters said. 'A golden boy for a golden boy.'

* * *

Alba read through Silver's notes. 'We'll have this all analysed,' he said.

'Most of it is mundane, routine material,' Watters said. 'Travis told us the name of his partner in sin, so I sent a couple of bluebottles to pick him up. He did not know the name of anybody else, or who they might be.'

Alba scanned the notes. 'As you say, it's mostly mundane, but I see Travis spoke about a storm coming from the west and east, and a pending attack on the woman called Aifa.'

'Costello spoke about a storm as well,' Watters remembered. 'It is strange that both used the same phrase.'

'Typical rhetoric by that sort of person,' Alba sounded casual. 'The Danish and Prussian Nationalists used the same sort of tactics. It helps build up their opinion of themselves, so they sound important to their ears. They use stirring words, helped by stories of a mythical past, half-forgotten heroes who probably never existed and so-called patriotic songs to appeal to the romantic nationalism of the impressionable.'

'The Wild Geese public had pictures of warriors dressed in green and with Gaelic words beneath.'

'I know,' Alba said quietly. 'As I said, we have had our eye on that place for some time.'

Watters thought it best to change direction. 'The attack on Aifa may have been the one in Stationers Hall.'

'It might be' Alba said. 'But we have already decided that Aifa was either Her Majesty or Florence Nightingale.' He gave his characteristic grin. 'Somehow I don't think that Karin what's-her-name is sufficiently important to be Aifa.'

Watters shook his head. 'I thought we had already decided that attacking the Queen would not help anybody. That leaves Miss Nightingale, and as she is in Scutari, she's nothing to do with us.'

'I know we said that Watters, but I don't believe in taking chances, so we have increased security around the queen,' Alba said quietly. 'I have surrounded Her Majesty in a ring of steel,' Alba allowed his grin to return, 'and to make sure, I have also appointed a guards captain and permitted him to retain some of his best men.'

'Would that be Captain Fletcher, Alba?' Watters asked innocently.

'It would,' Alba briefly held his eyes. 'We have given him carte-blanche to do all he needs to protect the queen with however many men he needs.'

'It might not be the best job for the Guards,' Watters mused.

'Carte-blanche,' Alba repeated, 'Fletcher is a good man; he knows what to do.'

'Apart from her Majesty, what other woman might be in danger?' Alba wondered. 'Your man Travis said, and I quote from Silver's notes: "they're going to blow up Aifa." '

'Blow up,' Watters said, 'not attack, not kill, but blow up.'

Alba grunted. 'They're planning to assassinate her with a bomb.'

'Why?' Watters asked, 'it is far easier to shoot somebody. A bomb is unstable. You can throw it if you get close enough. You use a bomb if you want to kill more than one person, or you can leave a bomb to explode on a fuse.'

'Or both,' Alba said. 'One can plant a bomb to explode in a place where more than one person gathers or meets.'

Watters took a deep breath. 'Who would unhappy Irishmen wish to blow up?' He closed his eyes. 'Who do they blame for the Famine: the government? There are no women there, not one, so no individual woman as a target.' He waited for Alba to nod to show he was following. 'Now we come to the nub. Where do these governmental men meet?

'In the House of Commons,' Alba caught on immediately. 'The Mother of Parliaments.'

Watters nodded. 'An elderly woman that is even more important than the queen.'

Alba shook his head. 'Not so,' he said quietly, 'politicians are replaceable. Her Majesty is not.' He held Watters's gaze, 'I trust you will remember that Sergeant Watters. We are all subjects of Her Majesty, while the government is elected to serve us, not for us to serve them. That is something all politicians would do well to remember.'

Watters grunted. 'I have never claimed to know anything about politics, Mr Alba, but it would seem that parliament could be the target.'

Alba nodded. 'You had better do something about that then, Sergeant Watters.' He grinned again. 'Not that the country would not benefit by having fewer politicians.'

Chapter Sixteen

'Is there a law that says the weather must always be foul when we are watching for something?' Silver pulled up his collar and huddled deeper into his coat for warmth.

'It's the same law that states that nine-tenths of a policeman's life is spent waiting for something to happen and the other tenth wishing that it hadn't.' Watters jammed down his hat and swore as collected rainwater cascaded over his face. 'There must be an easier way to make a living.'

Silver's laugh was sardonic. 'You would miss this,' he said, tried to stuff tobacco into the bowl of his pipe, cursed as his cold hands refused to work and his wad of tobacco dropped to the ground. 'Who would be a policeman on a night like this? Is this our fifth night on or our sixth?'

'I've lost count,' Watters said. He glanced up at the sky. 'It's getting lighter. Time for the patrol.' Turning away, he strolled across Westminster Bridge, grateful for any movement to ease some of the stiffness from his legs.

There was the usual traffic on the river and roads as the early morning workers trudged to their day's labour and the late-night grafters slogged to the cramped hovels they called home.

Watters watched a coal-cart rumble across the bridge, followed by a bakery van and a brewer's dray. Heat, food and drink, all the necessities of London life. He stopped, leaned against the parapet, and looked back at the Palace of Westminster.

Even set against the dull light of an early December morning, it was impressive. The Mother of Parliaments, the hub of Empire, and a guiding light to drag other nations and peoples of the world toward a better way of government. Light glimmered from a few upstairs windows as clerks toiled at the business of running the country. The uniformed policeman on duty looked bored as he paced back and forward on his solitary beat.

Watters reached the south side of the river, turned, and walked back, watching as a Thames Barge battled upstream and a coasting brig lowered her sails and steered for safe anchorage.

Silver had managed to light his pipe and stood with his back to the wind. 'This city could be quite beautiful if it wasn't for the poverty.'

'And the crime,' Watters said.

'That too,' Silver exhaled a mouthful of smoke.

Watters faced the opposite direction, finding it hard to express his feelings. 'I am sorry to keep you from Angela at this time of year. You've hardly seen her since your marriage.'

'Can't be helped,' Silver said. 'It is the way of the service.' He tapped his pipe on the parapet. 'At least the rain has died down.'

A couple of seamen lounged across the bridge in near silence with their seabags balanced over their shoulders. They gave Watters and Silver a long stare, glanced at Westminster as they passed, then slowed down. The uniformed duty policeman ignored them as he began his perambulation of the outside of the building.

'Turn your back,' Watters said quietly. 'Look away from Westminster.'

Too experienced to argue, Silver did as Watters ordered. 'What's to do?'

'These sailor lads,' Watters said. 'They look as if they have just come ashore, but they smell of scented soap.'

'Time to act?' Silver asked.

'I think so.'

Silver raised his eyebrows, gave a wild laugh, and began singing loudly.

'Stow your noise, you drunken fool!' Watters shouted. 'You'll have the bloody bluebottles buzzing around us else.'

'Bugger the blues,' Silver yelled, 'I'm not scared of the law.' He affected a stagger, recovered, and slipped to the ground, rolling onto his back as Watters crouched to help him up. 'They're at the door of Westminster,' he said urgently.

Watters turned around. Now empty-handed, the two seamen were walking quickly away from the parliament building. 'Come on, Silver!'

The second that Watters and Silver moved, both the seamen broke into a run.

'Stop!' Watters knew his shout would be ignored but hoped it would attract attention. The beat constable joined them. 'Spring your rattle!' Watters pointed to the running men. 'Stop these two!'

He glanced at the door of Westminster. The seamen had left their bags, one on either side of the door. Similar to ten thousand other carpet bags used by seamen and travellers throughout the country, only their positioning made them sinister. Watters hesitated for only a moment. Although he desperately wished to pursue and catch the two men himself, he knew that Silver was younger, fitter and very capable when it came to a resisted arrest.

'Get after them, Silver,' Watters ordered, 'I'll deal with the bags.'

He did not need to say more as Silver loped after the fugitives.

Watters took a deep breath as he saw a thin trickle of smoke ooze from one corner of each bag, to dissipate quickly in the stiff breeze. The bags looked ordinary, with the expected leather bottom and a fold-over catch fastened with a lock. Watters wondered if he had time to unpick the lock, decided he had not and swore, knowing that if the smoke indicated a lit fuse, then he had to act fast. Lifting the first bag, he ran to the parapet and was about to throw it into the Thames when he heard voices.

'Halloa!' he yelled as he saw half a dozen mudlarks on the riverbank. 'Get out of the way!' He blinked as smoke seeped into his still imperfectly healed eyes.

The mudlarks looked up at him. One swore at him, fluently and with great imagination.

'This is a bomb!' Watters said.

'So is my arse,' the vocal boy said, bending over to give Watters a better view.

'Get out of the way!' The smoke was thickening as Watters stood there. Thinking quickly, he pulled a handful of change from his pocket and threw it as far away from the river as he could, so the boys could chase after it, then hurtled the carpetbag into the water. Without waiting to see the result, Watters dashed back to the doorway for the second bag. He heard the explosion behind him even as he realised that there was no longer smoke coming from the second bag. Either the fuse had failed, or it had reached the explosives, and he had only a second to live.

There was no explosion.

'What's all the fuss?' The doorman had evidently just awakened as he blinked at Watters. 'What's the to do?'

'Do you have a knife? A knife? Quickly man!'

'Yes, I can get one!' The doorman dashed away, to return with a small penknife.

Lifting the carpetbag carefully, Watters slit it open and saw a simple mechanism inside. There was a length of lead piping with a fuse, black and dead at the end. Reaching inside the bag, Watters plucked out the fuse and threw it away. 'Look after that,' he handed the bag to the doorman, 'I'll be back for it,' and ran to the railings overlooking the river. The water was still disturbed where the explosion had taken place.

'Are you lads all right? Is anybody hurt?'

There were no impudent remarks this time as the boys stared at him. 'No, mister,' the tallest one said.

'Keep out of trouble,' Watters advised and ran in the direction the two bombers had gone. He heard the distinctive sound of a police rattle in the distance and headed toward it.

A group of weary dock porters saw him coming and moved aside. 'Police!' Watters roared to clear a path through streets that were already busy. He pushed past two arguing coal-heavers, ignored the resulting curses and strode on. The rattling was louder now, more distinct as Watters threaded through the streets of Whitehall and northward.

'Police!' Watters yelled as a group of gossiping maidservants blocked his path. He swerved to avoid one middle-aged woman who refused to move for him and ducked the slap of a thin-faced harridan who was apparently more used to giving orders than obeying them. He stopped as he saw a portly policeman puffing against the pole of a hansom cab.

'What's to do?' Watters shouted. 'Where are the fugitives?'

'That way.' The constable was bent double, red-faced with exertion. 'They've gone toward the park.'

The park? Watters swore. There was plenty of cover there. Where was Silver?

The roads were already heavy with traffic, hansom cabs and drays, tradesmen's vans and dog carts grinding over Tothill Street and York Street. When the rattle sounded again, Watters heard Silver's hoarse shout, somewhere ahead.

'Silver!' he roared. 'Where are you?'

There was no reply, so Watters ran on. The dull greenery of St George Park loomed ahead, an oasis in the middle of the most extensive urban sprawl in Europe.

'Silver!'

'I'm in the park!' Silver's voice sounded as Watters pounded through the gates.

Away from even the dim lights of the streets, St George Park was as dark as any country field, with only a faint gleam showing where St George Lake bisected the greenery, a peaceful place for Sunday promenading or a trap for hunted men.

Watters stopped. 'Keep still,' he shouted, 'and we'll hear them move.'

An unwelcome wind rustled the stark branches of winter trees, while the unearthly call of exotic birds disturbed the silence. Thin beams from police lanterns probed the dark like fingers of an uncertain God.

'I hear something,' a flat Midlands voice sounded, 'over by the lake!'

'Keep still!' Watters ordered as he heard the echoing thunder of heavy boots thumping over the grass. He swore, knowing that the fugitives could vanish in the confusion. 'Silver. How many men do you have?'

'Not sure, Sergeant! At least three.'

'Shout your names!' Watters ordered. 'Say who you are!'

'Constable Mercer!' that was the Midlands voice, over by the lake.

'Constable Anderson!' Watters nodded at the resounding roar from the ex-guardsman.

'Constable McKeefe,' music in the Irish accent.

'Right! Use lanterns to sweep the ground.' Watters shifted forward as his eyes grew accustomed to the dark and individual trees and bushes took shape. 'There is a dirty great lake in the way so they can only go right or left: Anderson and McKeefe take the left, Silver and Mercer the right. Move.' He heard the thump of feet as lantern light ghosted across the grass, highlighting the tracery of tree branches and glinting from the water like triple bars of moonlight.

Watters stepped toward the lake. The growl of traffic faded into the distance; it was such a constant in London that the citizens could ignore it. The grinding of wheels and clopping of horses was a backdrop to every conversation and every thought. Watters heard Anderson's loud voice call a challenge, followed by a deep laugh as a bird flapped away.

Watters searched left and right, aware that the strengthening light was a powerful ally. Men who could hide by lying prone in the dark would be vulnerable as daylight increased.

'Keep alert!' Watters shouted and slowly moved forward, looking to the right and left. If the fugitives doubled back, they could easily get lost in the maze of alleys and byways around Orchard Street. He stopped at a hint of movement, realised it was only the shadow of a bush caught in the light of a police lantern, and stepped on.

'I see you!' that was Silver's voice, clear and sharp to the left. 'Stop there!'

There was a sudden flurry of movement and the hard crack of a pistol shot, with the muzzle flare momentarily lighting up the park.

'God! He's got a gun!' Mercer yelled. 'Get bloody back!'

Pulling out his revolver, Watters ran forward, 'Drop the gun!'

Four beams of lantern light flickered across the grass, searching for the gunman. One focussed on Watters, temporarily blinding him.

'There he is!' McKeefe's voice. 'Get him, boys!'

'That's the sergeant, you stupid bastard,' Anderson rebuked, and the light shifted away quickly.

'Sorry, Sergeant!'

Watters blinked. His eyes had not yet fully recovered from the black lead, and now his vision was again starred. 'Don't let them get away.' He had the horrible thought that the fugitives could get past him when he was blinded. 'Anderson! Make sure they don't double back!'

There was the sharp crack of another shot, and Watters threw himself down. It was better to look foolish but alive lying on the ground than remain upright and be a dead hero. Thankfully, the old army adage of 'don't bob' did not apply to the police. He heard a splash, and somebody cursed.

Watters looked up with his vision slowly clearing. The light was strengthening so he could distinctly see the lake now, a silver-grey gleam beyond the trees. Silver was moving forward, seemingly in slow motion, with Mercer nowhere in sight. Had he been hit? On the right, Anderson and McKeefe were advancing in long, confident strides. Anderson had his truncheon in his hand, ready to fight two gunmen with nothing more lethal than a length of wood, while McKeefe flicked his lantern light along the bank of the lake.

Watters stood up. There was no sign of the fugitives.

'Where are they?'

'One jumped in the lake,' Anderson said, 'and the other's gone to ground.'

'Who fired the shot?'

'The man who went to ground,' Silver said.

'Anderson, you help me hunt for the shooter. Silver, Mercer and McKeefe,' he hoped that he chose the younger and more agile of the police, 'run around the lake and get the other man. Move!'

Taking a deep breath, Watters stepped forward, searching to his left and right. 'Up you get, son, there's nowhere to run and better for you to give yourself up quietly. Nobody has been hurt so it won't be the rope, but if you do shoot somebody all that will change.'

A few moments previously, Watters was glad of the growing light. Now that he stood in the open in front of a gunman, he would have welcomed night's protection. He breathed out slowly. 'Up you get!'

Less bright in the greying dawn, Anderson's lantern ghosted light across the ground.

'There he is!' Anderson roared as if he was standing on Inkerman Ridge with the Russian Army approaching through the sleet.

At the sound of his voice, a figure leapt up, fired a single shot in the direction of Watters and ran westward. Anderson shouted and ran after him with long, lumbering strides as Watters followed, limping heavily as his injuries began to take effect.

The man was fast; much faster than Anderson, who was soon left in the rear, shouting noisily and promising terrible things if the fugitive did not surrender. Watters was about fifteen yards behind and saved his breath as the man put his head down and raced for the exit.

Watters remembered the threat to Aifa and hoped he had been right that it was the Parliament. He realised that they were heading toward Buckingham Palace, where the queen was in residence. 'Stop!' As he ran, Watters reached inside his coat and loosened the pistol from its shoulder holster. He saw the man scramble over the top of the palace railings, halt momentarily, and leap down again.

'Jesus,' Watters raced after him, ignored the renewed pain from his recent injuries as he threw himself up the iron railings, cursed as his coat became entangled in the spikes, hauled it free with the sound of tearing fabric, and leapt down the other side. Knowing that the guards were on duty, he raised his voice again. 'Guards! A gunman is coming toward the palace!'

He saw the fugitive falter and turn, saw the flash of his pistol an instant before he heard the crack of the shot, ducked instinctively, recovered, and carried on.

Watters became aware of the line of red-coated men advancing from the palace gates, with the tall, loping figure of an officer in front. 'That man! Stop!' Watters ordered. 'Surrender while you can!'

But the fugitive either did not hear or did not heed; he altered his angle and ran diagonally past the palace gates, with Watters falling further behind.

Captain Fletcher gave crisp orders. 'Stop that man!'

Watters saw the fugitive stop, desperately trying to reload his pistol.

'Don't shoot him!' Watters ordered, but when the fugitive lifted his pistol and fired a single shot in the direction of the palace, Fletcher ordered his men to fire.

Watters stopped dead as the guardsmen knelt on one knee and a volley of shots sounded. The gunman staggered, looked down at himself, and lifted his pistol.

'Bayonets!' Fletcher ordered, and the guardsmen advanced. Watters watched as two bayonets plunged in and out, and the gunman crumpled to the ground, then one of the guardsmen thrust again.

'He's dead, sir,' the guardsman reported.

'Very good, Jackson.'

Watters hesitated only a second. 'Pray inform Inspector Larkin at Scotland Yard,' he said and waved on a panting Anderson. 'Come on, Anderson, we have the other one to catch.'

Back in Green Park, early morning strollers had stopped in astonishment at the sound of gunfire.

'We're involved in manoeuvres,' Watters shouted, 'best keep out of the way.'

A blue-coated policeman moved to intercept them. 'And where are you going?' he said until Anderson grabbed hold of his arm.

'He's from Scotland Yard, you bloody flat! Come along with us, and you might be some use.'

Following the gaze of astonished civilians, Watters passed through Green Park and into Hyde Park, where there were more police and a large crowd of civilians.

'It should not be allowed,' a stern-faced matron complained, 'having all these police in the park.'

'Who's guarding the streets, that's what I want to know!' an upright man with white whiskers and a face the colour and texture of leather asked.

'What's to do?' a sharp-looking man asked Watters, who ignored him and ran on.

The gunfire was staccato, echoing around the park. Watters swore and pointed to a policeman: 'I'm Sergeant Watters of Scotland Yard. What's your name?'

The constable stared at him. 'Hayes 276, Sergeant.'

'Right, Hayes 276, gather as many uniformed officers as you can and keep the civilians out of the park. I don't want any more casualties.'

Watters moved on, with Anderson at his heels.

'Sergeant,' Silver appeared from behind a tree. 'He's over there, hiding at the back of that elm.'

Watters nodded. 'How many men do we have?'

'Five, sir, including the lads from St George Park, but there are a lot of men around the entrance that are not with us. That fellow has not moved for a few moments.' He looked around. 'Where is the other bomber?'

'Dead,' Watters said flatly. 'Where are our men placed?'

'All around,' Silver pointed, 'there and there and there. But that fellow has a gun and our lads have only their staffs.'

'It's up to you and me then,' Watters decided. 'I don't want any more deaths.' He took a deep breath. 'I'll talk to this man and see if I can get him to see sense.'

'Be careful, Sergeant.'

Watters knew his smile was more like a death's head grin. 'I will be.' Taking a deep breath to ease his racing heart, he listened to winter birds calling and wondered if this were the last time he would ever hear such a sound.

'Halloa there,' he shouted. 'I am Sergeant George Watters of Scotland Yard. Your companion is dead.' He stepped forward, keeping in the open so the fugitive could see he was alone. 'Unless you give yourself up, you will also be shot.'

He stopped ten yards from the tree behind which the man was sheltering. 'I know you are here. If you had wanted to shoot me, you have had plenty of opportunities. If you wanted to kill people with your bomb, you would have planted it when Parliament was in session. You are no killer, whoever you are.'

Watters glanced right and left. Uniformed police were hiding in the bushes and behind the trees, watching him. He was acutely aware of how easy it would be for the gunman to shoot him as he stood there alone and exposed.

'There is no escape,' he said quietly.

'Stop there, or I'll blow your head clean off.' It was the first time the man had spoken. Watters was not surprised to hear the Irish accent.

'I've stopped,' Watters said. 'If you give yourself up now, you have not committed a capital crime, but if you shoot me, or anybody else, you will not have improved your situation and you will either be shot here and now or hanged to death after a long trial.'

'Did you shoot Cormac?'

'If Cormac was your friend, no, I did not shoot him. A guard at Buckingham Palace shot him.'

A voice sounded behind Watters, distorted by the metal of a speaking horn. 'This is Inspector Larkin. Give yourself up now.'

'Quickly, man,' Watters urged, 'before it's too late!'

He was only vaguely aware of the movement behind the tree, and then there was a loud thump and Alba stepped forward. 'Give me a hand with this fellow will you Watters? He's a dead weight.'

* * *

The man sat casually in his chair with a bandage over his head and wearing rough grey prison clothes. 'The name's Doyle' he said.

Watters passed over a mug of tea. 'You have had quite a day, Doyle,' he said, 'planting a bomb at the Houses of Parliament, swimming the St George Lake, having a gunfight with Her Majesty's constabulary.' He shook his head, 'whatever next?'

Doyle shrugged. 'Now you will hang me.' He did not appear concerned.

'Not yet,' Alba said. 'Not until you have told us who you are and for whom you work.'

'I'm Dermot Doyle, as I've already said.' He leaned back in his chair, placed his handcuffed hands on the table and grinned across to Watters. 'I work for Ireland.'

'Then God help Ireland,' Alba was equally cheerful, 'if you are an example of what she produces: attempted murder, running away, and surrendering when things get tough. Thank the Lord that I have met many Irishmen who are intelligent, brave, and resourceful, the very opposite of you indeed.'

'There are fewer of us now,' Doyle said, 'since your Famine in our country.' He tapped the handcuffs on the table. 'It will be England's turn to weep blood soon, and there will be great lamenting across Blake's green and pleasant land.'

'I don't think you will be able to do much where you are headed,' Alba told him.

'I will be a martyr for the cause,' Doyle was quite complacent, 'and thousands will visit my grave.'

'You will languish for many years in Van Diemen's Land, and nobody will remember you,' Alba said cheerfully. 'Your masters have used you, and they will abandon you.'

Doyle laughed. 'England has tried to control Ireland for centuries, yet you understand nothing about us. They will remember us in songs and poetry as the new Fenian heroes of the age.' Raising his head, he shouted, 'Up the Green!' and began to sing in utter defiance.

Alba did not lose his smile. 'I don't think that two failed bombs and five pistol shots that missed their target will put you with fables like the Fenians,' he walked to the door as Doyle stopped his song in mid-stanza.

'We are only the vanguard,' Doyle said, 'there are more coming in a storm from east and west that will blow Britain away.'

Watters spoke softly. 'I wonder how often I have heard these sentiments from bitter peoples and petty states. If Ireland is so poor, how can you possibly blow England away, let alone all of Britain? You tried, and your little bombs did not even raise a puff of wind, let alone a storm.'

'You will see,' Doyle shouted. 'Ireland is not alone. This time we have powerful friends.' He shut his mouth with a snap as if he had said more than he intended.

Signalling to Watters, Alba stepped out of the room and ordered two uniformed officers to take Doyle to his cell.

'As we thought, there is more to this than a few disgruntled men,' Alba reported to Larkin. 'That is another who quotes the same phrase. He said a storm from East and West. It what he says is correct, then it seems that there is indeed another country backing the Irish.'

'Which other country?' Larkin wondered.

'We have mentioned Russia before,' Watters said, 'but how the devil could a handful of Irishmen get into contact with Russia?'

'Maybe Russia got in contact with them,' Alba said. 'God knows the world learned of the suffering of the Famine. Hundreds of thousands of the poor souls died then.'

'And most of the rest are over here,' Larkin said.

Watters caught Alba's eye but said nothing during the next few tense seconds. Watters broke the silence. 'If the Russians are involved, it could be bad.'

'It could be worse than bad,' Alba agreed. 'That fellow Costello and this one Doyle were both deserters from the Army. How many Irish are there in the British Army?'

'Thousands,' Watters said at once, 'maybe tens of thousands.'

'In 1830, before the Famine, 42.2 % of the army was Irish.' Alba had the figures at his fingertips. 'We have fifteen officially Irish regiments, and tens of thousands of Irishmen in regiments nominally from Scotland, Wales and England.'

'The Russians can't make them all desert, surely,' Larkin sounded alarmed.

'They don't have to,' Alba said. 'All they have to do is spread discontent among them and lower their morale so they cannot fight like British soldiers.' He took a deep breath. 'If the reports we are getting from outside Sevastopol are correct, then things are bad enough with disease and the weather.'

'When I was in the Wild Geese,' Watters said, 'Lily asked me how the British soldiers felt about going to war,'

'It is high time we closed that place down,' Alba decided. 'Inspector Larkin, I want you to take your men and clean it up.'

Larkin frowned. 'It was you who wanted it left well alone,' he reminded.

'I know,' Alba said, 'but at that time we were gathering information. Now we know there is a threat to the country, we should show strength.'

Larkin nodded to Watters, 'I think you would be the best man for that duty, Watters,' his smile was slight, 'that is, Sergeant Watters.'

'My pleasure, sir.'

'In the meantime, Sergeant,' Alba said, 'I will have the experts at the Royal Arsenal look at that bomb you defused.'

Chapter Seventeen

Watters watched as the uniformed police gathered a few doors from the Atlantic Street entrance to the Wild Geese. He shone his lantern down the solid blue line, with the light reflecting on brass buckles and gleaming from tall hats and leather belts. Anderson stood in front, leaning on a felling axe sufficiently large to do credit to any Norse warrior.

'There might be resistance,' Watters reminded. 'There are at least two hefty porters and maybe others that I don't know about.' He allowed the words to sink in. 'Mother Flannery is also inside, we think. You have all seen our artist's impression of her, and I want her treated gently.' He remembered the prize fight. 'Now, she will undoubtedly resist, and she is as strong as any two men. Don't try to arrest her alone.'

'She's only a woman,' a saturnine constable said.

'I'll remind you of that when we visit you in the hospital,' Anderson said with his usual grin.

'My wife's a woman too, and she is worth three of you, Peter,' another constable said.

'I've met your wife, Edmund. Are you sure she's a woman?'

The laughter and bickering helped relieve the tension of waiting, although the men looked pleased with the prospect of resistance. Watters ran his gaze over them, nodded to Anderson and Williams, and checked that his revolver was secure.

'Lastly, watch for a small man. He may call himself Yellowford or some other name. If you see him, hold him secure.'

'Is that every man smaller than me, Sergeant?' Anderson looked down from his six feet four inches.

'No,' Watters did not hide his bitterness, 'just an evil little bastard that might be responsible for the murder of Guardsman Nixon and the O'Halloran woman.'

Anderson's grin faded. 'Right, Sergeant.'

Watters continued: 'I want all the documents removed from every room, and all the people, men and women, taken in for questioning.' There were grunts of understanding as Watters emphasised every point by tapping his cane on his left hand. 'To remind you once more. Be very careful of Mother Flannery. She is important to this investigation and try and apprehend this small man.'

He checked his watch and counted down as the hand crept slowly toward three o'clock. He knew that around the corner, Silver was doing precisely the same thing at the Ratcliffe Highway entrance.

'Sergeant Watters!' Anderson spoke in a hoarse whisper that carried half the length of the street. 'Somebody is coming.'

Watters was already aware of the steady clip of the horse's hooves and the rumble of wheels on the ground. He turned around as the hansom cab ground to a halt at his side and Karin stepped out.

'Hello, Sergeant Watters, Mr Alba told me you were here.' Her eyes were wide and very bright in the gleam of the carriage lamps.

Watters shook his head. 'He should have known better. This situation could be hazardous.'

Three minutes to three.

'Mr Alba said I might be useful.' Karin looked over the assembled constables. 'You have many police here to protect me. He said I would be best placed to recognise Christopher.'

Watters opened his mouth to protest but closed it again as he realised the logic of her words. 'Try and keep at the back,' he said, 'out of the way of any trouble.'

'Mr Alba said that I was to keep close to you,' Karin widened her eyes to him, deliberately provocative.

'Then Mr Alba is a damned fool.' Watters knew his nerves were showing. He never liked the final few moments before any operation. 'It could be dangerous.'

'It could be dangerous for you too,' Karin said. 'Or for any of these men.' Her touch thrilled his arm. 'I have more at stake here than any of you.'

'Keep in the rear, then,' Watters said.

One minute to three. Watters lifted his hand to warn his men, just as Silver shouted from around the corner and crashed into the Ratcliffe Highway door.

'In we go, boys!' Watters shouted and allowed Anderson to attack the door with his axe. The ex-guardsman grinned as he swung the weapon behind his head before bringing it down with a resounding crash on the central bar. The door shook without opening. Anderson stepped back a pace, aimed again and threw himself at the door. The axe hurtled down, sheering the door in two as Anderson staggered with the force of his blow. The bolts at the top and bottom held until Anderson smashed them with two deft strokes and Watters led the rush forward, booting in the remnants of the shattered wood.

Most of the police followed, with three men remaining outside to ensure that neither resident nor customer managed to sneak out. Passing through the spacious saloon, Watters ordered Anderson to stay there as he kicked open the door that led upstairs.

'What the hell?' The black porter appeared from behind the bar, took one look at the press of police and attacked, swinging his blackjack. Leaving him to the uniformed officers, Watters pushed on. He heard the sounds of combat behind him and wondered briefly how long the porter's aggression would last against the experience and muscles of Anderson. Thundering upstairs with a dozen constables behind him, Watters heard noises in the upper levels of the building. That would be Silver. He stopped on the first floor as they had planned.

'Light these gas lamps, open every door, and arrest whoever is inside the rooms.'

A press of police powered past him, beams from their lanterns dancing along the walls until somebody put a Lucifer to the lights and the slightly sinister hiss of gas sent its softer glow along the corridor. The guests began to complain.

'Halloa. What's the to-do?'

'What's happening?'

'I thought this was a quiet establishment!'

'What the devil?'

Most of the doors had opened with white, nervous faces of girls and women peering out, with men behind them, angry or worried depending on their natures. Men's voices sounded, rough and impatient, turning to quick anger as the police barged into the tiny cubicles where the guests had sought an hour's pleasure or a night's comfort.

'Handcuff them and take them outside,' Watters ordered, 'and watch out for the second porter.' He opened the storeroom door, 'I want all this photographic equipment taken outside as well,' he watched as the police hauled out the first of their customers, a naked man with the tattoos of a sailor and the herculean biceps and chest of a ship's fireman.

Karin looked, widened her eyes, and turned her head away quickly. 'That's the room I was in,' she pointed to a door halfway along the corridor.

Watters had forgotten she was there. 'See if you recognise anybody. You!' He pointed to the nearest policeman. 'Take care of this woman.' He was about to run up the stairs to the next floor when he heard the sound of a body falling behind him.

'What the deuce?' He turned around, holding his cane like a club.

The second porter bowled over a policeman and charged toward the exit with a blackjack in his hand. By sheer bad luck, he had emerged from one of the rooms just when Karin was the only person in his way. She stood there with both hands over her mouth and her eyes wide with fear.

The giant put one hand on Karin's throat and roared something incoherent.

'Halloa!' Watters lunged forward, swinging his cane. The lead-weighted end caught the huge porter on the top of his head. The man grunted, staggered, and turned around. A head taller than Watters and broader in the shoulder and chest, his punch landed above Watters's heart and knocked him gasping to the floor. Watters looked up to see the porter standing over him with his boot raised to crunch down on his groin.

'Sergeant!' The scream came from Karin as Watters rolled aside. The metal-shod boot crashed down, scraping the side of his Watters's hip in its shuddering descent. Watters struck upward with the weighted end of his cane, catching the giant in the groin, saw him stiffen in sudden agony, rolled aside again, and jumped to his feet.

Lifting his cane, Watters smashed it down on the giant's head, again and again. The man continued to step toward him, grunting as the blood began to flow but determined to fight on.

'Sergeant Watters!' Karin was backed against the wall of the corridor, watching as Watters faced the giant.

'Leave him to me, sir!' Anderson's intervention was welcome as the ex-guardsman thumped along the corridor. 'Here, you! I want you.'

The giant had hardly turned when Anderson's truncheon smashed down on his head, a giant in blue facing a giant in anger. The porter staggered, and Anderson hit him again, breaking his nose, so bright blood gushed. Before the porter recovered, Anderson grabbed his hands and snapped on a pair of handcuffs. 'Now you come quietly, you big blackguard, or I'll have to get rough with you.' Sporting a fresh black eye, Anderson gave Watters a big grin. 'There we go, Sergeant. Easy as pie. I'll take him downstairs with the others, shall I?'

'Yes please, Anderson,' Watters did not like to admit that the encounter with the porter had left him shaking. He noticed Karin smiling at him and turned away. 'Has anybody seen Mother Flannery? We need her!'

'No sign of her up the stairs,' Silver reported. 'We've bagged all the documents Sergeant, but we can't get into the safe.'

'Get Anderson and some other men with muscles,' Watters decided, 'throw the blessed thing out the window, and we'll get a cart to take it to the Yard. We'll work on it there; we've no time to waste here.' He raised his voice. 'Find that bloody woman! Search every room, every nook and cranny.' He heard a familiar female voice and saw the saturnine constable wrestling Lily to the ground with her hands twisted behind her back.

'Hoy! Go easy there! Don't hurt that woman!'

Lily looked up, her face twisted in pain and tears in her eyes. 'I wasn't doing anything wrong, sir, I was just with a sojer.'

'It's all right, Lily, we're not after you. We'll straighten it all up down at the Yard.' Watters loosened the handcuffs on her slender wrists and eased her upright. 'You'll be free by tonight, and if not, you ask for me, George Watters. It's Mother Flannery we want. Do you know where she is?'

There was a sudden silence in the corridor as police and prostitutes and the blood-streaked porter all seemed to listen for Lily's answer.

'You give her away, and it's bad for you,' the porter said until Anderson clamped a hand over his mouth.

'You threaten that girl, and I'll have you my bucko, just you and me in a nice quiet cell, and we'll see how tough you really are.'

'Enough, Anderson,' Watters said. 'On you go, Lily, this man won't be hurting anybody for quite some time.'

Lily shook her head. 'I don't know,' she said, but she blinked to Watters, darted her eyes toward the stairs for a fraction of a second and gave a tiny inclination of her head.

Watters nodded. 'Take them downstairs,' he shouted, 'and get them all to the Yard. Be gentle with the women! If any of them are hurt, I'll have your uniform, and you'll spend the rest of your life collecting pure!' He touched Lily on the arm and stepped away.

'What's pure?' Karin's eyes were bright.

'Dog waste,' Watters moved for the stairs.

'I'm coming too!' Karin was at his back, 'I want to find the woman more than you do.' She lowered her voice slightly, 'do you genuinely like that woman, Sergeant Watters?'

'Do I like her?' Watters asked, 'Do I like Mother Flannery?'

'No,' Karin shook her head. 'Do you like that girl, the prostitute?'

'Oh, Lily,' Watters stopped halfway up the steps, 'I had not thought about it. I don't dislike her if that's what you mean.'

'That is not what I mean,' Karin took hold of his sleeve. 'I mean, do you like her? I suppose you have slept with her? I know men do that with that sort of woman, but do you like her as well?'

'What?' Watters stared at her. 'Oh for God's sake, Karin, I haven't the time to talk about that now.' He turned away, trying to clear his head. Lily had hinted that Mother Flannery may be still upstairs, but Silver had already checked the upper rooms. He remembered the store cupboard and how that had led to a secondary corridor used for spying on the girls; perhaps there was something similar.

Silver greeted him with a smile. 'No trouble up here, Sergeant.'

'Nothing down there either,' Watters said. 'The porters were a bit unruly but nothing unexpected.' He nodded to Anderson, who had followed him quicker than he had expected. 'Constable Muscles there was on hand.'

'The name's Anderson, Sergeant,' Anderson said seriously.

'Indeed it is,' Watters agreed. 'Can you move that safe?'

The safe was four foot by five foot of solid iron. Anderson put his shoulder to it. 'No, Sergeant. Not an inch.' He looked closer to the safe. 'It's bolted to the floor, sir.'

'Get it unbolted,' Watters ordered, 'and get it out. I don't care how you do it.'

'Wait!' Silver was on his knees beside the safe. 'There's something queer here.' He looked up. 'I was an apprentice plumber, Sergeant, before I joined the Force. We did all sorts of things besides pipes and taps. There's a hinge here, look.' He pointed to a large brass hinge half-hidden behind the safe. 'This thing must be on a pivot.' He shoved at the angle, 'see?'

The safe swung around, to reveal a dark opening that seemed to suck Watters in. He stared at it for a long minute, feeling the hidden menace.

'Well done, Silver,' Watters said. 'I wager that's where Mother Flannery is.'

'Shall I go, Sergeant?' Anderson said eagerly.

'We need your strength with the safe,' Watters decided. 'This is my job.' He hefted his cane. 'You get that safe onto a cart and over to the Yard, Silver,' he said, lifted a discarded lantern, and stooped into the dark cavity. 'And look after the Austrian lady,' he shouted over his shoulder.

The lantern light arrowed along a brick-lined corridor to show an unpainted deal door. 'This place is a blasted rabbit warren,' he muttered. He started as Karin spoke behind him. 'Go through the door, Sergeant.'

'Good Lord woman!' Watters hissed. 'What the devil are you doing here? I told Silver to look after you! You could be in danger here!'

'We've been through that,' Karin said. 'Go on, Sergeant, try the door!'

Watters turned the handle and pushed. There was a faint creak from rusted hinges as the door opened into a low room with a dirty, multi-paned window and another unpainted door. He flicked the lantern around the room and saw Mother Flannery inside. She glowered at him through eyes like a sullen cat, and suddenly Watters wished he had Anderson to back him up. A cornered Flannery would be a match for any ordinary man.

'That's her,' Karin yelled excitedly, 'that's the woman that took me.'

At the words, Mother Flannery hurled a bottle. It missed, breaking into a hundred shards against the wall, but Watters's instinctive flinch gave Flannery sufficient time to turn and run out a door behind her.

Watters followed, with Karin, giggling nervously, at his back.

The door opened onto a flight of stairs that led straight down a second narrow brick-lined passageway to yet another door that banged shut a few seconds before Watters reached it. He heard the screech as Mother Flannery tried to draw a bolt across, raised his boot and kicked hard to prevent her. The door crashed open, and for a fraction of a second, he looked right into her eyes. Wide and green, they stared at him as she faced him, fists raised, and Watters was aware of other people in the room behind her.

'Leave me be!' she yelled, 'I never done nothing. As true as Christ's holiness, I never.'

Watters recognised the words. 'You're under arrest, Flannery.'

She lunged at him, shoved him against Karin and ran as he regained his balance.

'Sergeant Watters's,' Karin shouted, 'she's getting away.'

'I know,' Watters said. A woman and three children sat on a pile of rags staring at these people who had entered their lives. Ignoring them, Watters ran after Mother Flannery, down steep wooden stairs and out into the Highway.

They emerged a few doors down from the Wild Geese, where the police were marshalling those they had arrested. Without hesitation, Mother Flannery turned in the opposite direction, lifted her skirts above her knees and ran. A lone man in a green waistcoat stood in her path, but Mother Flannery landed a single punch that knocked him spinning to the ground.

'Police!' Watters roared, 'Stop that woman!'

'You bloody stop her!' somebody said as the man in the waistcoat knelt on the ground, spitting blood.

Despite the din of the prisoners, a handful of police heard the shouts and two loped after Mother Flannery. A tall policeman appeared in front of her, arms wide to catch her. Mother Flannery stopped dead and held her hands out, wrists together. As the policeman reached in his pocket for his cuffs, Flannery altered her stance to that of a prize fighter, feinted with her left and landed a right-handed punch that knocked the policeman clean off his feet. A second constable came from the side, springing his rattle. Flannery closed with him, wrapped her arms around him and tossed him to the ground.

'Come on then, peelers!' She followed her challenge by a wild yell that sounded as if a banshee was loose on the Highway.

'Get that woman!' Watters roared as the police around him either flinched or drew their truncheons, depending on their natures.

One eager young constable dashed in front of Watters, stumbled over an uneven paving stone, and clutched at him for support. The sudden weight took Watters by surprise, and he also faltered, so Karin raced ahead.

'Karin!' Watters yelled. 'Be careful!'

Either Mother Flannery heard his shout, or she had some instinct for vulnerability for she turned, saw Karin a few steps in front, and pounced. As Watters rose, Mother Flannery grabbed Karin, twisted her hair in her hands and dragged her against the wall.

'Take one step, Peeler, and I blow her head off.'

Only then did Watters see the small pocket pistol that Mother Flannery pressed behind Karin's ear. He stopped. Karin's eyes were wild, and she was no longer laughing. He heard her gasp in fear.

Watters felt the weight of his revolver in his shoulder holster, wondered if he could draw and fire in the time it took Mother Flannery to squeeze the trigger, knew he could not and waited until a couple of uniformed police pounded up beside him.

Mother Flannery cocked her pistol and pressed it harder. 'Back off, Peelers.'

'Step back, lads,' Watters said. 'She's serious.'

'I'll blow this woman's bloody head off,' Mother Flannery warned.

Watters nodded. 'I know you would,' he said and shrugged. 'But why?' he asked. 'She is only some woman of the streets. Ten a penny.'

Mother Flannery pulled back Karin's head and inserted the pistol into her mouth. 'That's a lie, peeler. This woman is Karin Stegall. Her name's all over the newspapers.'

Karin was making small mewing noises, like a new-born kitten. Her eyes were wide, terrified.

'Ah,' Watters thought quickly. He motioned for the police to stand clear. Silver was there, looking from Watters to Karin and Flannery and back, desperate to help but unsure what to do.

'If you shoot her,' Watters spoke slowly, 'you will surely hang. Murdering the wife of a foreign diplomat will make you a great many enemies.' He forced a grin, aiming to unsettle her. 'After all, you are not in the least important, you're merely the keeper of a cheap whore house.' He knew by the expression on her face that the insult had gone home.

'You bastard!' The word was ugly in Flannery's mouth.

'So I've been told,' Watters said. He took a single step forward and squared his shoulders. 'Karin must be about the same age as your daughter.' He saw Flannery's eyes narrow. 'That is your daughter's picture hanging on the wall of your room, isn't it? The good-looking young woman with your eyes and the beautiful red hair.'

'That's right,' Silver said. 'She's a lovely looking girl. Could you imagine a bullet going through her mouth, smashing her teeth, ripping out her tongue, crashing through to her brain?'

'Stop!' Jerking the pistol from Karin's mouth, Flannery pointed it directly at Watters. It was an old-fashioned single-barrelled affair, Watters noted, with a wide bore that at this range would blow his head clean off.

'Get back from me, lads,' Watters motioned with his hands to clear a space around him. He stood foursquare in front of Flannery, too stubborn to withdraw.

'You have only one shot with that Mother Flannery. Here I am!' He folded his arms, holding her gaze. If he distracted her long enough, Karin might be able to wriggle free. 'Or you could give yourself up and face a fair trial.'

Watters realised that Flannery had a firm grasp of Karin's hair. 'What crimes have you committed? Running a disorderly house? That will be three months at most. Resisting arrest? Another three months, perhaps, and pointing a gun at a police officer. That will be maybe six months more for that.' He spoke on, searching for words that might buy him time; another few moments was suddenly very precious.

'That will be a year at most. Or you could shoot me and be hanged within the month. Think of it. The crowd watching, the touch of rope rough around your throat, and then the white hood over your head and face, the drop, the choking, kicking death as everybody you know watches, if anybody cares for you, that is!'

The final words were enough. Flannery released her grip on Karin's hair, shoved her aside and took a single step forward. 'You bluebottle bastard. You think you're so clever! You'll know when the storm comes and blows your world upside down!'

When Karin screamed, staggered, and fell, Silver scooped her up and hurried her behind the police lines. Watters spared her a single glance and returned his attention to Flannery.

'Drop the gun now, Bridget.' He used her first name to try and create a bond. 'You voluntarily gave up your hostage; that will help you in court.' He took a single step forward and held out his hand. 'I'll take your gun now.'

'You'll get the contents!' Flannery pointed the pistol. For a second the muzzle was directly in line with his eyes, seemingly as broad and dark as a twelve-pounder cannon. Watters saw the concentration in Flannery's face, the hardening of her eyes and the slight whitening of her knuckles as she increased pressure on the trigger before she fired.

For the first time in years, Watters experienced a shadow of regret, as if he was leaving something behind if he died.

The sound of the shot was like the crack of Armageddon, and the intensity of the powder flash nearly blinded him. Watters stiffened, expecting the agony of the lead ball. Instead, he saw Flannery's face change, elongate, and then shatter into a welter of blood, bones, and brains. He breathed out slowly.

'Damned shame. A brothel-keeper would have been a useful source of intelligence.' Alba replaced the revolver in his pocket. 'You did well.' He glanced over Watters's shoulder. 'Her shot broke a window. I do hope nobody was standing behind it!' His grin was as wide as ever.

'I'm glad you didn't miss,' Watters said.

Alba stepped over Flannery's body. 'It was a lucky shot,' he said.

'You saved my life.' Karin rushed forward and took hold of Watters's arm. 'You could have sacrificed your life for me.'

Watters felt himself shaking in reaction. 'It was my duty.' He badly wanted to sit down away from everybody else. He had not wanted to die. That realisation ran over him like cold water. He suddenly felt very vulnerable as somebody had lifted a shield from him. Since he was a child, life had not mattered to him, but right at that minute, he was glad he was still alive. He badly wanted a drink.

'Wolfgang would never have done that.' Karin squeezed his arm.

'I am sure he would,' Watters said, and added, 'he would be a fool not to,' and wished he had kept these words to himself.

'You would make a better husband than he does.'

Watters looked away from the warmth of her eyes. He did not remove her hand from his arm.

Chapter Eighteen

'It is a great pity we had to kill Flannery,' Alba sorted through the pile of photographs they had retrieved from the safe. 'She could have told us who financed this operation and to whom she handed her notes. I presume that is the same person.' He looked up. 'I am afraid I cannot agree to your request to free one of the prostitutes, however. We must treat her like the others.'

'Lily has proved a great help to me in the past,' Watters said.

'That is irrelevant compared to the greater picture.' Alba smiled. 'I am sure that you understand that, as a policeman, you cannot allow a criminal to evade justice.'

Watters took a deep breath. 'I am well aware of that, Alba. I am also aware that her crimes are small compared to those of others, and I think it is unfair that the Law should punish her while others walk free.'

Alba shrugged. 'That is the way of the world, I am afraid.' He held one of the pictures at arm's length and narrowed his eyes. 'Good God! I did not know that was possible! And a Tory politician too! Well, I never. I was at Eton with his son, don't you know?' He shook his head. 'Well, we always did call the son Piggy, so I suppose it runs in the family.'

Watters glanced at the picture and away again. 'I have no interest in politics,' he said, 'but once we return all these photographs, we will ease a great deal of heartache and worry.'

'Return them?' Alba pursed his lips, 'I am not so sure about that. Sometimes it's no bad thing to have information on men of power. It prevents them from doing something completely against the good of the nation.'

Watters put his hand out. 'It is our job to uphold the law, not twist it to our own ends. Maybe I had better take care of these.'

Alba smiled. 'Upholding the law is your concern, Sergeant Watters, making sure the country is secure is mine. The two do not always co-exist.'

Watters did not withdraw his hand. 'We are all under the law. It is the security of the land. I had better take care of these.' He held Alba's gaze, well aware that he was dealing with a man with power which far exceeded his own.

'You are a straightforward man, Sergeant Watters,' Alba's smile did not waver, 'but we live in a world that is far from straightforward.' He selected one of the photographs and placed it face-up on the desk. 'This man is a government minister. As you see, he appears a very willing participant in his, eh, amorous exercises. As you also see, his activities are neither legal nor moral, yet this man has the power to decide legal matters that affect us all. Now, Sergeant Watters, what would you say if this so-called gentleman decided to introduce a bill that made this activity, with children of that age, legal?'

Watters looked again at the photograph. The politician was about fifty, while the little boy he was with could not have been above eight years of age. He handed the picture back. 'I would not be happy to support that law,' he agreed.

'As I said, Sergeant, you are a sincere man while politics is a murky business and politicians hide behind their power to do exactly as they damn well please.' For the first time, Watters heard anger in Alba's voice. 'You try to keep this country safe from blackguards, thieves, and scoundrels, Watters, while I try to repel threats from outside. And all the time we are working, rubbish like this,' he tossed the photograph across the desk, 'are exploiting both of us so they can indulge in their filthy habits, protected by their status as gentlemen.'

Watters understood. 'Aye, and it's always the people at the bottom who suffer, like the poor in Ireland or the Scottish Highlands during the Famine, or those who dwell in the worst city slums or filthy country cottages. What do these people care which party is in control at Westminster, or who wins the war in the East—' He stopped, suddenly aware that what he was saying could be construed as treason in time of war.

Alba was watching him with a curious smile on his face as if listening to a child spouting nonsense, or the rantings of an inmate of Bedlam. He shook his head slowly and passed the photographs across the table. 'We'll decide which of these are innocent, which we can keep, and which we might return,' he said, 'and who it is best to keep under control.'

Watters took a deep breath. He was sworn to uphold the law, but when the law protected supposed gentlemen who were damaging the lives of very vulnerable people, surely it could, or should be bypassed? 'That would help,' he agreed. 'And it would be even better if you could see your way to releasing Lily. As I said, she has proved useful to me on more than one occasion.'

Alba's smile broadened. 'It sounds as if you are bargaining with me, Sergeant.'

'Does it?' Watters did not back down.

'You are learning. I will allow Lily Maguire to go free. Now all we need to do is find this Cuchulain fellow,' Alba said, 'and we will have this case cracked.'

Watters nodded. 'It is a great pity that we killed Mother Flannery,' he said.

* * *

'Bring in the next one,' Watters stifled his yawn. 'How many is that now, Silver?'

'This is the fourteenth so far.' As always, Silver's notes were impeccable. 'Seven prostitutes and six of their overnight customers, four soldiers, one seaman, and one very embarrassed banker who begged us to let him go.'

'We'll let him go when we have finished our enquiries,' Watters said, 'and then he can explain all to his loving wife. Who is next?'

'Next is another sailor, Sergeant, Brian Lord.'

Watters glanced through Silver's notes. 'So far, we have found nothing of interest, and we've been doing this for how long?'

'Eight hours, Sergeant.'

'Eight wasted hours,' Watters sighed again. 'All right, bring him in.'

Fair-haired, stocky, and freckled, Brian Lord appeared unperturbed as two uniformed constables marched him into the room. He sat opposite Watters and looked around with some interest. 'Well, this is a rum do. One minute there I am sleeping happily with a little peach and the next here I am staring across a table at two ugly peelers.'

'Perhaps this is not the best time to be insulting,' Silver suggested.

'Pray could you tell me what it is I am supposed to have done?' Lord said, 'then when I have proved my innocence, I can leave.'

'The quicker and more truthfully you answer our questions, the sooner that may happen,' Watters told him. 'Tell us why you were in the Wild Geese and what you and your lady friend talked about.'

Lord shook his head. 'That is hardly police business,' he said. 'I was in the Duck for a woman, and she was friendly enough.'

'She spoke to you then?' Silver asked.

'Of course, she spoke to me!' Lord shook his head. 'Have you peelers never been with a woman before? Do you prefer to bullyrag sailormen instead?'

'What did she talk about?' Silver asked.

'Lord shrugged. 'The usual sort of thing. What I liked, where I was from, just talking.'

'Anything else?' As he spoke, Silver wrote in his impeccably neat script.

'Well yes,' Lord said. 'She was a nosey little flashtail that one. Nice udders though. Bouncy. She asked where my ship was from, our cargo, and if we sailed to the army out East.'

Watters allowed Silver time to take notes. 'She could have found that out in the shipping notes column of the newspapers,' he said. 'All except the dealings with the army. That is a strange thing to interest the Irish.'

'She also asked how I wanted her.' Lord went into some intimate details until Watters raised his hand.

'We are not concerned with your personal dealings with her,' he said.

Lord looked disappointed. 'That's the only interesting part,' he said. 'Who the devil wants to know about *Northern Storm?'*

'*Northern Storm?*' Watters asked.

'My ship,' Lord explained patiently. '*Northern Storm.*' He shook his head. 'She's one of Jack Storm's Storm Line vessels ... *Northern Storm, Southern Storm, Baltic Storm, Western Storm...*'

'*Eastern Storm,*' Watters finished. 'Of course. It is a ship!'

'Of course it's a blasted ship!' Lord shook his head at the obtuseness of the police. 'How else would I get across the sea? D'ye think I would bloody swim?' He looked at Watters. 'Well, can I get free now? I'm wild to get another baggage before old Stormy sails again.'

* * *

'It's the name of a ship,' Watters said, '*Eastern Storm* is a ship.'

Alba raised his eyebrows. 'Now, that is something that I had not considered.' He passed two small metal tubes over the desk to Watters, 'and here is something for you to consider. I had your bomb taken to pieces while you were playing chase-me-Charlie with Mother Flannery's girls. It was quite a simple construction, a tube split into two sections, with a hole bored through one section. The bomb maker fills the interior with gunpowder and inserts a fuse into the hole. When the lit fuse makes contact with the powder, it explodes, and the tube makes splinters into deadly fragments that spray the surrounding area.'

Watters lifted the tube. 'Very simple,' he said.

'And very deadly if the bombers place it in the right place. But the right place is not outside the door of a near-empty building. Your man

Doyle was a fool. Hatred controlled him so he did not wait until he could use the bomb properly.'

'Perhaps,' Watters examined the tube, 'either that or these bombs were merely a trial to see if they worked.'

'Look inside,' Alba invited.

Watters inspected the tube. 'Why?' he asked, 'Oh, I see, there is a maker. Reilly of New York.' He looked up. 'That's a long way to go to get a metal pipe,' he said, 'would it not have been easier to get one made in London or Birmingham?'

'Where did tens of thousands of Irish emigrate after the Famine?' Alba's voice was flat.

'The United States,' Watters said softly.

'The pieces are clicking into place,' Alba said. 'We have angry Irishmen, mass emigration, bombs from America, and now your ship.'

'The only thing I don't understand,' Watters said, 'is why the Irish want to know about the Army,' he paused, 'unless they plan an attack on it, or we were right with the mutiny and desertion theory.' He pulled out his pipe and began to stuff tobacco into the bowl.

'They would not need bombs for that,' Alba pointed out. 'No, there is more to this yet. We must concentrate on the bombs just now.'

'Doyle spoke about a storm from the East,' Watters quoted, 'and he said they were going to blow England away.'

'Quite literally too,' Alba agreed. 'The storm part could either be the name of the ships, or a reference to the bombs. It looks as if they planned to blow up parliament with bombs from America.'

'Storm from East and West,' Watters reminded, 'and Flannery hinted there was more to come.'

'Putting everything together, I would guess that the ship *Eastern Storm* may be connected,' Watters said, 'perhaps bringing more bombs from America or more bombers.'

'Except the United States is in the West,' Alba pointed out.

'The ship sails east to get here,' Watters reminded. 'And the Irish said a storm from the East and West.'

'That might mean they're using both ships. We'll check the shipping lists,' Alba said.

'I have them here.' Watters passed them across the desk. 'Silver got them, and he circled *Eastern Storm* in case we could not understand the big words.'

Alba studied the lists. '*Eastern Storm* is bound to London from Boston, no less.' He looked up, 'Many of the emigrant Irish settled in Boston.'

'And others in New York.' Watters held up the tube. 'Do you have any people over there?'

'That's in hand,' Alba said. 'I'll leave you to think about this ship, and we will concentrate on the American connection for now.'

* * *

'Show me that cargo manifest again,' Silver leaned back in his chair in the Customs office, sipped from his deep mug of coffee and studied the paper. 'It's a bit of a mixed bag,' he said. 'Timber, cement for God's sake, rum and sugar. There is nothing suspicious there.'

'What did you expect the manifest to say?' Watters asked across the width of the desk. 'Bombs and explosives for the Irishmen?'

Silver nodded. 'Something like that maybe. Have we checked out this Jack Storm fellow?'

'Of course,' Watters said. 'He's a true blue, as British as you can get, member of the Methodist Church, a Whig, and a staunch supporter of half a dozen Christian charities.'

'That does not necessarily preclude him from turning a profit by importing explosives,' Silver murmured. 'Whigs are notoriously business-minded.'

'All the Irish we have interviewed are Roman Catholic,' Watters reminded. 'Storm is a Methodist.'

'Or he says he is,' Silver said. 'Anyway, that is just two sides of the same religion; only the administration is different.' He continued to peruse the manifold. 'I can't see anything sinister here.' He looked up.

'Where is the cargo headed? Not the Roman Catholic Irish centre for Political Reform or anywhere is it?'

Watters shook his head and passed across more documents. 'Here are the loading and destination documents, the invoices and all the ship's papers. I've checked and re-checked it, but I am blessed if I can see anything wrong.'

Silver pulled the invoices to him and studied them, one by one. 'Timber for a timber yard, as it should be. Who owns the yard? Hubertson and Smith. They are reputable. Cement for a builder's merchant although I can't see why he does not get it in Britain. He is worth watching. If it's cheaper to import it could be poor quality, so anything built with that stuff could fall to bits.' He looked up. 'That's something to bear in mind, Sergeant.'

'I can't see anything to worry about,' Watters said. 'Use your superior education, Silver.'

'Yes, Sergeant. There is rum for a spirit merchant, as it should be, and sugar destined for six different addresses …' He ticked off each on his fingers, one by one until he came to the last: 'and the Tobago Warehouse.' He raised his head. 'Now that is very queer, as the Tobago Warehouse has been abandoned for years.'

'I should have seen that,' Watters said.

'You've been out of London a lot, Sergeant, while I've been here all the time.' Silver grinned again. 'Either that or you're just getting old and past it.' He lost his smile at the expression on Watters's face. 'Sorry, Sergeant.'

Watters tapped his fingers on the desk. 'Sugar from Boston to an abandoned warehouse has possibilities. We will investigate that further.'

'Aye, maybe the Irish are going to sweeten their next bomb,' Silver said.

Before Watters could reply, the door opened, and a uniformed customs official looked in. '*Eastern Storm* is sailing up the River,' he said quietly. 'She is expected to dock in about an hour.'

'Time to go,' Watters lifted his hat. 'We must act like gaugers.' He nodded to the uniformed constable who had stood a silent spectator. 'Run along to the Yard, Thomson, and inform Inspector Larkin that *Eastern Storm* is in the River.' He waited until Thomson had left. 'Larkin will get word to Alba.'

* * *

When the police dragged back the hatch cover, Watters peered down into the hold. The sugar was packed in jute sacks, each one crudely marked with a company name: Southern State Sugar. 'We'll check that company later and see if it is real.'

Alba wandered across the deck of the ship, hands in his pockets and face as cheerful as ever. 'Morning, gents, are you ready to do some detecting?'

'Something like that,' Watters said.

Silver looked at the mountain of sacks that filled the hold of the ship. 'How much sugar does this bloody country need for God's sake?'

Watters shone his lantern into the gloomy hold. 'Too much,' he said, 'luckily we don't have to test every sack. It has been pre-divided into destinations by number, see?' He indicated the thin wooden partitions between different batches of sacks. Waiting until a seaman dropped a rope into the hold, Watters climbed down, with Alba following and Silver at the rear. 'How many were for the Tobago warehouse?'

Silver checked his notes. 'Eight bags,' he said.

Watters counted the bags. 'Here we are,' he said. 'This consignment has eight bags.'

Alba produced a stiletto and slit open one bag. A thin trickle of sugar eased out. 'That looks innocent enough.' He lifted a handful to his mouth and tasted it. 'Sugar. I wondered if it might be gunpowder or some such, but they could have bought that in this country with perfect legality.'

'And better quality too,' Watters said, patriotically.

'There could be something hidden inside the bags,' the customs officer advised from the deck above. 'These smugglers are up to all the dodges. You would not believe the things they do.' He produced a long, slender brass instrument. 'Probe it with this. If you touch anything solid, you will know.' He grunted. 'I wish there were a way to see inside the sack without opening it.'

'I wish I were born a belted earl,' Watters said softly as he caught the probe the officer dropped.

They moved from sack to sack, pushing in the probe hopefully. The first two sacks seemed innocuous, with no contact, but when he tried the third Silver stiffened. 'There's something hidden in here,' he said.

'Let me see,' the customs officer joined them and inserted the probe at an angle. 'Oh yes, undoubtedly.' He tried again, and again. 'There is more than one object hidden in here,' he confirmed. He lifted the head of the sack. 'Did you see this?' He pointed to a tiny blue cross below the company name. 'This sack has been marked.' He looked at the others. 'Somebody has labelled three like that. I would wager that these hold the contraband.'

'Get these sacks away from the others,' Alba said, 'and let me see.' He pushed with the probe. 'There is undoubtedly something inside here. You know your job,' he approved.

'When is it due to be delivered?' Watters asked.

'As soon as we have completed our checks,' the official said, 'the dockers will unload the ship, and it will be stored in warehouses here until carters take it to its destination.' He glanced at a sheaf of papers. 'This load is due to be carted away as soon as it's cleared customs.'

'Could you release it later today?' Watters asked. 'That will give us time. We will be at the Tobago Warehouse before the sugar arrives, and we will wait for somebody to collect it.'

'And when they come to collect it, we scoop them all up?' Silver asked.

'No,' Watters shook his head. 'We follow them to wherever they take it, and then we arrest them. This case has gone on long enough. I don't want the delivery men. I want this Cuchulain fellow. I want the head of the whole thing.' *I want Markovic*, he thought. *It makes sense for a Russian to seek news of British troop movements and soldiers' morale.*

'It could be innocent,' Silver said, 'or rather, it might be something worth smuggling but not connected to the bombers.'

'We'll take that chance,' Watters decided. 'It would be too much of a coincidence for there to be no connection.'

'I will make sure that Larkin provides sufficient uniformed men,' Alba said.

'No,' Watters shook his head. 'I will go alone. The more men there, the more probable it is that somebody will make a noise, or drop something, or sneeze. The fewer people, the better.'

'You should not go alone,' Alba said.

'I'll be there,' Silver said quietly. He did not drop his gaze when Watters looked at him.

Chapter Nineteen

'You are quiet tonight,' Rowena said. She dragged the chair from its position in front of the fire and sat opposite Watters at the table. 'There is something on your mind.'

Watters looked up from the map and pushed his case of lockpicks to one side. 'Nothing particular.'

Rowena placed her arms on the table. 'Then why have you been staring at that map of London for the past fifteen minutes?' She smiled across at him. 'It might help to talk about it.'

'It's only this case I am working on.' Watters sat back. 'It's not straightforward.' He seldom mentioned his cases to anybody outside the police force.

'It is worrying you,' Rowena said. 'Come on, out with it.' She raised her eyebrows and Watters felt something shift inside him. This woman disturbed him for some reason that he did not understand.

Watters looked away. 'There are aspects of it I do not like.' He found himself explaining about the politicians with the very young girls, wondered why he was doing that and continued anyway. He looked up a couple of times and realised she was genuinely listening to him.

'You are between the deep sea and the blue devil,' Rowena said when he finished. 'No wonder you are concerned, but George, there is nothing that you can do. This Mr Alba seems to be very powerful. You must do your duty as best you can; you can't carry all the world's problems on your shoulders.' She leaned across the table as if to touch him, thought better of it, and withdrew.

Watters stirred, uncomfortable to have said too much. She was still watching him.

'You are going after him.' It was a statement rather than a question.

'I am,' Watters said. 'I am going after the man who organises the blackmailing.'

Rowena's gaze did not leave his face. 'Take care,' she said.

'It is a simple arrest,' Watters told her. He could not explain the new tension that racked him or the dryness of his mouth.

'You think it will be dangerous.' Again Rowena spoke the words as a fact, rather than a question.

'No more than many other cases in which I have been involved,' he smiled to her. 'In fact, I don't anticipate any trouble at all.'

'Is that why you have checked your gun twice and put spare bullets in your pocket?' Rowena asked sweetly. 'You left gun oil over the kitchen table, and the bullet box is on the floor beside your chair.'

'You should be a detective,' Watters said sourly. 'Anyway, that is just routine.'

'Then it is a routine you have not followed since I have known you,' Rowena said tartly. This time she did touch his arm. 'You take care, George.'

'I will' he promised.

* * *

There was still that unfamiliar feeling of unease as he stepped to the cab, that twisting tension in his stomach and that new fear of the finality of death.

'Is that you again, Sergeant Watters?' Arthur touched a finger to the brim of his hat. 'Where to this time, sir?'

'Wapping,' Watters said.

Silver was already in the cab, thumbing tobacco into the bowl of his pipe with an air of intense concentration. 'Why do we have to do these things in the dark?' he asked. 'Just once I would like to work in daylight, with the sun shining.' The lamp-light glimmer showed dark rings around his eyes.

Watters gave a wry smile. 'Let me know when that day comes,' he said, removing his hat and placing his cane at his side. He sighed and tapped the ceiling to instruct the driver to start and leaned back.

'It's only a couple of miles,' Silver said, 'I don't know why we are taking a cab.'

'Inspector Larkin must be feeling generous in his pocket,' Watters looked out of the window at the damp, dark streets. He tried to fight his discomfort, wondering why he should suddenly feel like this. *I've been involved in many cases more dangerous than this one, yet without this feeling of inner dread.* He must be getting old, and that thought worried him.

After ten minutes, the cabby tapped on the back of the cab with his heel and slowed down. Watters opened the door and thrust his head outside.

'Are you expecting company?' Arthur asked quietly.

'Not at all.'

'You'd best be prepared for some then, Sergeant. Somebody is following us.'

Watters controlled nausea that rose in his throat. He looked behind him, but the street was empty, with the gaslighting reflecting from damp cobbles. 'Who and where?'

'A hansom cab. It just pulled into that side street, but it's been with us since we left the Yard.' Arthur glanced behind him. 'I was in the force once, Sergeant. I know when somebody's dogging me.'

'All right. Go back into the centre of the road and drive slow, as if the horse is lame, then if the cab's still there, turn into a side street, let me out and stop further up.'

'Right you are, sir,' Arthur touched his hat. 'I've got a life-preserver by my seat if you need me.'

'I might do,' Watters was thankful for the offer. He had no desire to get injured or killed. He withdrew his head and felt the slight jerk as the cab moved off again. 'Keep your gun handy,' he told Silver, 'we might have trouble.'

'When do we not have trouble?' Silver pulled his Colt revolver from his pocket, checked the chambers, and replaced it. 'Angela nearly had a fit when she saw me with this thing.'

Watters nodded. 'Best keep it away from her,' he said, 'and the children.'

'We don't have children,' Silver sounded pained, 'unless you know something that I don't.'

'Give it time,' Watters felt the tilt as they turned a corner. 'Here we go.' When the cab eased to a halt, he released the door catch and jumped out, shut the door quietly and ran to the shadow of a doorway to hide.

He watched as Arthur started to drive again, the wheels growling slowly over the cobbles, keeping to the centre of the road. A few moments later, another cab appeared, with the driver muffled against the morning chill and the window blinds drawn so the passenger was concealed. Watters waited until the cab passed before he stepped from the doorway and followed.

'Halloa!' he hailed. 'Cabbie!"

The cabbie looked around, apparently surprised that somebody in this quiet street would hail him.

'I've already got a fare.'

'That's all right,' Watters said. 'Now, you have two. Can you take me to Scotland Yard?' Opening the door, he barged in, holding his cane, and ignoring the driver's protestations. 'My fare would not like it one little bit, sir, no, not one little bit.'

The woman passenger's initial smile turned to a gasp of shock when the cab's opposite door opened and Silver thrust in, pistol in hand.

'Karin!' Watters allowed his cane to slide down his hand. 'What the devil are you doing here?'

'I heard that you were looking for the Cuchulain man. I am the only person who has seen the man who brought me to the Wild Geese.'

'How did you hear that?' Silver had not responded to Karin's smile. 'We told nobody and—'

When Karin's smile widened, she looked even more appealing. 'Mr Alba returned a horrible photograph to the Prussian ambassador and told him that he had men on the case.'

'And?' Silver's face could have been set in granite. He was evidently immune to Karin's charms.

'Oh,' Karin's smile faded. 'The ambassador told his manservant, who told the valet of the Austrian ambassador, who told me. I knew that my Sergeant Watters would be involved, so I waited outside Scotland Yard until I saw him get a cab and had my man follow.'

'And that is how secrets leak out,' Silver said. 'Tell nobody anything, I say.'

Remembering how he had spoken to Rowena, Watters pressed his lips together. 'All right, Karin; you know that I am working, please turn around and go home.'

'I won't,' Karin said happily, 'and you have no power at all to order me. I am breaking no law, and I still have the protection of my government.'

'You are interfering with the police in the pursuit of their duties,' Watters said.

'Oh, how pompous!' Karin repeated his words in as deep a voice as she could. 'You're interfering with the police in the pursuit of their duties. I prefer to think of it as helping a friend catch a man who did me wrong.'

'Go back to the hotel, please.'

'No!' Karin smiled again. 'I'm coming with you unless you want to carry me back to the hotel.'

'We haven't the time to argue,' Watters said.

'I know,' Karin said happily. 'If you send me away, I will follow anyway.'

Watters took a deep breath. 'You are the most troublesome woman I have ever known.'

She nodded. 'Yes. If there is only one carriage, it will be easier, George.'

Silver glanced meaningfully at his watch.

'I could call a constable to carry you back,' Watters said.

'Then I would scream and scream and lodge an official protest at my undignified treatment at the hands of Sergeant Watters of Scotland Yard,' Karin said sweetly.

'Sergeant,' Silver tapped his watch.

Watters took a deep breath. 'Come with us then, Karin,' he said reluctantly, 'and keep out of trouble.' He could feel Silver's disapproval.

'I knew you wanted me here,' Karin said.

'She's trouble, Sergeant,' Silver warned.

Watters grunted. He agreed but short of tying her up or having her sent back to her hotel in the care of a uniformed constable, there was little he could do. It was a squeeze with all three of them in the hansom, but luckily only a short distance to their destination.

Watters opened the hatch and spoke to the driver. 'Stay close but out of sight.' He pointed to a nearby street. 'Park there and wait. It could be some time.'

'I'll lose money,' Arthur complained.

'You'll be paid,' Silver promised. 'You've got a good number here, Arthur, with definite fares with Scotland Yard. If you go wrong on me, I'll make sure your licence is revoked, and you'll never drive a London cab again.'

'In my country, a cab driver would never speak to an official like that,' Karin said as she followed Watters.

'In this country, we are glad if they speak to us at all,' Silver murmured.

* * *

Watters said nothing as he surveyed the warehouse. Two storeys high of ochre brick, it occupied half of Tobago Lane. When it was built, sometime in the mid-eighteenth century, it had been ornately decorated with a frieze showing life on a sugar plantation, but time, grime, and the London weather had blurred the images to little more than faint shadows of themselves. High-arched windows stared like black eyes up the lane, while the door to the courtyard hung open on a single remaining hinge.

'We'll wait inside the courtyard,' Watters decided. 'You may wish you had not joined us,' he said to Karin. 'And if there is any likelihood of danger, I want you to keep well out of the way.'

She smiled brightly, white teeth gleaming in the night. 'You will protect me.'

They tripped over a ground of broken bricks and weed-infested cobbles, ignored the scurrying rats, and followed the probing beam of Silver's lamp to what appeared the driest and most sheltered corner.

'This will do,' Watters ushered Karin underneath an archway that had once proclaimed the owner's name, but which was now bare and crumbling brick.

'Can you get us inside the warehouse, Sergeant?' Silver indicated a tall wooden door. He checked his watch. 'It's coming up for six now. We may have a long wait, and it's a bit exposed out here for the lady.'

'According to Mr Alba, the delivery is to be here at 6:30,' Watters said.

'Who's the carrier?' Silver asked, 'have we questioned him?'

'I interviewed him myself,' Watters said. 'He was paid cash in advance by an agent who did not know the man who made the arrangements. Whoever has organised this delivery knows his stuff.' He glanced over to Karin, 'if nature calls, you better find somewhere sheltered. Be very careful.'

'As long as you don't look,' Karin did not look embarrassed.

'We won't,' Silver said bluntly.

The door to the interior of the warehouse was broken, and it opened to a push. Watters entered cautiously, preceded by the beam of Silver's lantern. There was a vast space on the ground floor, with the rotting remains of a wooden staircase to the upper storey whose floorboards now sagged dangerously and from which plaster and lathes hung down like flesh from a ripped body.

'There's not much here,' Karin said.

'It's no place for a woman,' Silver said.

'Or a man,' Karin added.

They found an alcove with a view of the courtyard and settled down to wait. Silver produced a pewter flask. 'Coffee,' he said with a smile. 'It's a bit cold now, though.'

'Angela spoils you,' Watters said.

Strengthening morning light only enhanced their sordid surroundings as rain wept from heavy skies. They slumped against the brickwork, watching, thinking their private thoughts, waiting. Karin spoke, her words without meaning, only serving to pass the time. Water droplets gathered on broken guttering above, to drip in occasional splashes on the weed-infested ground. Outside the walls, London awoke in an increasing murmur of sound.

'Something's happening,' Silver gave the warning. They watched as a cart trundled through the broken courtyard door. The driver and his mate climbed down and unloaded six sacks of sugar.

'Here will do,' the driver said. 'Give us a hand, Bill.'

The delivery men piled the bags in an untidy heap in one corner, clambered back on board the cart and drove away, leaving the gate yawning open. A flight of pigeons fluttered from above to investigate. One sat on top of the sacks.

'I am king of the castle,' Silver intoned.

'You are a king?' Karin's eyes widened with interest.

'I was referring to that pigeon,' Silver said.

'Oh,' Karin gave a half-smile, not understanding.

As time passed, the noise from the surrounding area increased, and a group of street–Arabs sidled into the courtyard. One lit a pipe, and another grabbed it from him and ran. The others followed, swearing mightily. The pigeons returned. After another half hour, a closed brougham entered the courtyard, with two matching black horses.

'Fancy equipage to pick up sacks of sugar,' Watters muttered.

'Not quite what a sugar merchant would have,' Silver was writing in his notebook. 'These horses are bloodstock, I reckon.'

'They look it,' Karin spoke louder than Watters liked. 'Pedigree I would say, and the carriage is quality, mahogany wood.'

Watters nodded. 'There is money backing this operation, whatever it is for.'

'I think you have your ideas,' Karin said.

'I am open-minded,' Watters said cautiously. He watched as two burly men left the brougham. They did not waste time as they lifted the sacks, selected four and bundled them inside. The driver flicked the reins, and the brougham creaked in a circle until the horses' heads pointed toward the gate.

'We can take them now.' Silver fingered his revolver.

'I want the head of this operation,' Watters said, 'not the hirelings. We follow them.'

The brougham pulled out slowly, as if the driver was afraid of scratching its glossy paintwork on the gate, and then rolled along Tobago Lane before turning into Wapping High Street.

'Right, Silver, follow on foot, keep it in sight. Karin, you and I get the cab.'

They picked up Silver a few minutes later, and he pointed them in the direction the carriage had gone.

'Don't get too close,' Watters instructed the driver. 'We don't want him to see us.'

'I know what I'm doing, Sergeant,' Arthur said. 'Nobody notices a cab in London.'

Again Watters felt that new anxiety, so removed from the natural tension inherent to any police operation. He saw Silver touch the butt of his pistol, saw the bright hunger in Karin's eyes and wondered if he was just getting old. No, he shook his head, there was something else.

'We're moving steadily west,' Silver reported.

'So I see,' Watters said.

'We are in Belgravia,' Silver said, 'Eaton Square.'

'We don't need a geography lesson,' Watters said. He realised he had allowed his thoughts to divert him from the matter at hand. Karin was smiling to him, obviously expecting a reply to some remark she had made. He looked out of the window. Terraces of white stucco houses, winter-stark branches of trees contained within the iron railings of city squares, the town palaces of those who could use their fabulous wealth to ride out any political storm. The owners of these houses were as far above policemen on the social scale as police were above rats.

'We're still moving,' Silver reported.

'I can see that!' Watters's sharp reply revealed the state of his nerves. Karin's putting a small hand on his arm did not help his temper in the slightest. He peered out the window, finding it hard to concentrate, as thoughts and emotions jumbled in his mind. What the devil was wrong with him?

'Still heading west.' Silver continued his running commentary despite Watters's glower. 'I wish I could see the coach in front.'

'Trust the driver,' Watters said. 'He's ex-police.'

'Why did he leave?' Silver asked. 'Did he fall from grace, or was he pushed? I don't trust anybody that leaves the force.'

Watters grunted. 'You can be too cynical Silver.'

'We're pulling up,' Silver said at last.

A moment later, the door opened, and Arthur poked in his head. 'The carriage stopped at a house around the corner,' he reported. 'I drove past, so he would not know we were following him.'

'Good man,' Watters threw Silver a sour look to emphasise his trust in the driver. 'Show us the house.'

'Follow me, gents,' Arthur seemed glad to help.

Broken glass set in concrete augmented the downward-curving spikes that surmounted the tall brick walls concealing the house and its grounds. Watters watched as one of the burly men closed wrought iron gates and fastened a padlock before returning inside the brougham. It withdrew up a tree-shaded path toward the house. Watters allowed the brougham two minutes to get clear before cautiously approaching to peer through the gate.

The bare trees failed to conceal the gentle curve of the path or the impressive winged house that stood at its head. Three storeys high, an array of windows stared back at them.

'That's some place,' Silver muttered. 'Those destitute Irish certainly know how to live.'

Karin gave a small smile. 'It is a cottage compared to Schönbrunn,' she said.

'But a palace compared to anywhere else,' Silver said.

'I am about to break the law,' Watters said quietly, 'and it will not be good for your career if you are with me, Silver.'

'Stop wasting time,' Silver said.

Watters nodded. 'You might wish to go home now,' he said to Karin. 'Silver and I are breaking into the house.'

'I am coming with you.' Karin looked her defiance.

Watters raised his eyebrows to Silver. 'What do you think?'

'I think she will be trouble,' Silver was brutally frank, 'but I also think she is the only person who will recognise this Christopher cove who brought her to the Wild Geese.'

Watters nodded. 'You'll get your clothes dirty,' he warned as he walked carefully around the walls. He stopped her laugh with a quick hand. 'At least try to keep quiet, for God's sake!'

'As if clothes were my main concern!' Karin said.

Whoever told him that Austrians were stuffy and stiff had never met Karin Stegall, Watters thought.

As he had expected, there was a gate inset into the wall at the rear. 'Nobody checks their back gate,' Watters said, kneeling on the ground. 'They lock it and leave it from one week to the next, hoping the gardener or some other servant takes care of things.' Somebody had wrapped a chain around the gate and gatepost, clicked on a padlock and left it to rust. Watters took his case of lockpicks from his pocket and started work. 'Yet the back gate is an easy entry into the garden of any house.' Rather than a satisfying click, there was a tired creak as the padlock opened; Watters waited for a second and eased it off, unwound the chain and pushed the gate open.

'Let's hope they haven't got a dog,' Silver said sourly. 'I don't like dogs.'

The gardens were planned but not extensive, an acre or so of groomed lawns with isolated trees and small groups of shrubs that provided cover as Watters led them toward the walls of the house, where they were less likely to be seen. The brougham stood outside an outbuilding that a long, slope-roofed extension linked to the main house. 'That will be the stable block—' he stopped at a sudden murmur of voices.

Karin stifled a giggle. 'I do apologise,' she said.

'We've no idea what is inside here,' Watters spoke softly. 'It is daylight, all the advantages are with the criminals, we don't know how many there are, who they are, or what they may do. We only know they have connections to bombs.'

Silver nodded. 'You'd be best elsewhere, Karin.'

In response, she stepped away and spoke over her shoulder. 'We'd best get inside then. We are likely to be seen out here.'

'We have to see where that sugar goes.' Watters moved toward the stable block, with the others following. He heard Karin stifle another nervous giggle and Silver roughly shush her to silence.

Watters did not see from which door the smallish man emerged to supervise as the two burly men threw the sugar sacks onto the ground outside the stable block.

'That's Yellowford,' Watters said quietly. 'Do either of you recognise him?'

'No,' Silver said at once. 'I don't know him.'

'Nor I,' Karin said.

Yellowford pulled a knife from his pocket and slit the bags open, allowing the burly men to take out long wooden boxes from inside.

'The bombs,' Karin said, dramatically. 'Isn't this exciting?'

Watters put a hand over her mouth and shook his head when she pushed against him. It was not an unpleasant feeling.

When the burly men closed the stable door and carried the boxes inside the house, Yellowford followed slowly, shutting the front door. Watters heard him draw the bolts.

'Did you recognise any of these men?'

Karin pushed Watters's hand from her mouth and shook her head. 'No, I do not know them.'

Watters pondered. He could fetch a body of uniformed police and round up everybody in this house. That would take time and the man he wanted, the one they knew only as Cuchulain, may escape. The fellow may not even be in this house. There was no choice. He had to find out more before he contacted anybody.

'We're going inside,' Watters decided. 'Karin, pray try and control your tongue. Silence is essential.'

'I'll be as silent as a church on a Sunday morning.' The sparkle in her eyes made Watters distrust her words.

'We'll find an empty room and get inside,' Watters said.

It took him a few moments to remove a pane of glass from a back window, unfasten the catch, and slide it open so they could all slip inside what was obviously a servant's room. There were three simple beds and three deal chests, while the picture of Jesus Christ on the wall was in a style Watters had never seen before.

Karin wrinkled her nose. 'I've never been in a servant's quarters before. They are rather small.'

'These are better than most,' Watters said. He opened the door cautiously and peered out into a dark corridor, smelling of dust. 'Nobody here, thank God.'

'Where are we going now?' Karin appeared to be enjoying herself.

'To find out what Yellowford is doing here, who your seducer is, and what these bombs are for,' Watters said.

He winced as his feet clicked on wooden floorboards, then softly cursed when he heard Silver's sharper tread and the quick patter of Karin's boots. 'Keep quiet for God's sake,' he hissed. Light seeped in from stained-glass windows, painting the stark corridor in multi-coloured hues.

'Listen for voices,' Watters whispered.

The corridor led to a steep staircase with that same eerie light filtering in and each footstep seeming to echo like the beat of a military drum. At the head of the stairs was a door-lined passage so long it must have stretched the full width of the house. Watters heard the low rumble of male voices coming from one room, and instinctively tried the handle to the room next door. It opened to his touch, and the room was thankfully empty, so Watters jerked his head to Silver to step in first, ushered Karin in next and made up the rear. The room was in darkness, with shutters closed against the outside world.

'Now what?' Karin's whisper reverberated through the gloom.

'Now we keep quiet and try to listen,' Watters said.

'Isn't this exciting?' Karin said again.

The sudden slam of the door opening took Watters by surprise.

He started up and stared straight into the intense glare that shone in his still-weak eyes, blinding him again. He closed his eyes, swore, and reached for his revolver. Karin's scream was deafening, echoing around the room.

'No, Sergeant Watters!' The voice was close to his ears as a hard hand closed on his. 'You will not need your pistol.' Something hard and heavy cracked against his head, sending him reeling to the ground as expert hands slipped inside his coat, removing his pistol. Karin screamed again until there was the sound of a hard slap, and she subsided into sobbing.

Chapter Twenty

'Put them against the wall.' The words were immaculate English, but the modulation was foreign, as though the speaker had learned from a non-native speaker.

Watters blinked and held up a hand to shield his eyes from the searing glare. Sickened by the blow to the head, the punch he threw was weak and failed to make contact as two men dragged him across the floorboards and tossed him against the wall. He heard Silver swearing and the solid thump and grunt as somebody either kicked or punched him.

'I'll not forget you,' Silver grunted.

The lights withdrew for a moment then four circles of brightness brought intense pain to his eyes as lanterns shone in his face.

'Open the shutters,' that same foreign voice sounded. There was movement and a sudden flood of softer light. Watters blinked and looked away, unable to focus.

'You bastard,' Silver was not a man to hide his feelings. 'You back-stabbing dirty bastard.'

Watters looked up. When his starred vision cleared, he saw Arthur standing beside four other men. 'What the devil?'

The cab driver smiled and showed a slim wad of banknotes. 'Money, Sergeant Watters, money. Oh, you made your promises, "You'll get paid," you said, but police promises are easily made and often broken.' He held up the notes and flicked through them.

'No wonder the police kicked you out, you bastard,' Silver said.

Watters switched his attention to the other men. One was Yellow-ford, standing with a bowler hat on his head, his hands hooked into the waistband of his trousers and a crooked little smile on his mouth. On either side of him stood one of the stocky men who had collected the sacks of sugar. Watters allowed his gaze to drift across them. They were large, muscular men with dull eyes. Second class pugs, maybe failed prize fighters, hired for half a guinea a week for their potential for targeted violence. The larger had only one eye, the smaller a smashed nose. Watters knew he could discount them as being unimportant. The remaining two were far more interesting and potentially extremely dangerous. The closest wore a morning suit. He was slender and saturnine with a pistol in his hand and mobile eyes. That would be the messenger who called at Karin's house. The last was a tall man, immaculate, broad-shouldered and with a small but distinctive scar above his left eye.

'Sergeant Watters,' the scarred man said, 'Detective Silver and—'

'I think she is a police spy,' Arthur broke in. 'She joined them later, and I thought you would like her as well.'

'We have already met,' the scarred man said quietly. 'Karin Stegall, discredited wife of the Austrian delegation to the negotiations between the Austrian Empire, the Ottoman Empire, Great Britain and France.'

'And you are a devious lying swine,' Karin replied with a spirit that Watters could only admire.

'Thank you,' the scarred man gave a crisp little bow. 'The insults of an enemy are praise to a warrior.'

'You pretended to be a gentleman named Christopher,' Karin continued, and Watters could have sworn she was about to spit on him.

'And you were prepared to cheat on your husband with such a gentleman,' the scarred man said. 'We are a well-suited pair of blackguards, I think.'

Karin relapsed into silence, looking hatred at the man.

'You'll be the Russian fellow, Markovic,' Watters decided to shake the scarred man's composure a little.

Markovic's eyebrows rose. 'I am he,' he agreed softly. 'Search them,' he ordered, and Yellowford and the two pugs dived forward, removing Watters and Silver's pistols and police batons, landing a few punches in the process. The elegant man collected Watters's revolver, checked the chamber with professional expertise and said nothing.

'My country will exact vengeance for this,' Karin said.

'That is unlikely,' Markovic said to Karin. 'Now I advise you to behave, or I'll hand you to my friend.' He nodded to the elegant man.

'You are no gentleman,' Karin retaliated with the most cutting phrase she knew.

'And if you are what the Austrians think of as a lady,' Markovic retaliated, 'then it is not surprising your country is fading as a great power.'

'But now you have us,' Watters gave the driver a look he hoped would chill his blood, 'what are you going to do with us, Mr Markovic?'

Markovic raised his eyebrows again. 'I will kill you, of course. You will all quietly disappear, never to be seen again.'

'This is London, not the back boglands of bloody Donegal,' Silver tried to rise until Arthur kicked him full in the face, sending him crashing back, holding his mouth. Blood seeped between his fingers.

'You'll pay for that,' Watters promised.

'That is unlikely,' Markovic turned aside.

'The police will be most unhappy to lose two of their own. Inspector Larkin knows where we are.' Watters tried to sound calm, but once more he felt that desperate desire to live.

Markovic shook his head. 'Nobody knows where you are. You will vanish as completely as if you had never been.' He turned away and spoke to the slender man in a language Watters did not understand.

'Can you not talk English rather than that gibberish,' Silver spoke thickly through his damaged mouth. He wiped away more blood. 'Blasted Irish heathen.'

Watters leaned his head against the wall. Whatever language Markovic had used, it had not been Gaelic. He had heard Rowena translating enough of that to recognise it.

Arthur's laugh was cutting. 'You think that is Gaelic?'

Silver's reply was succinctly Anglo-Saxon, short, and not sweet.

'That man knows where we are,' Watters nodded toward Arthur. 'Do you honestly think he won't tell anybody? A man who betrays his trust once will likely betray it again.'

'I am not telling anybody,' Arthur said quickly.

'You're right,' Markovic agreed, you're not.' He nodded to the two pugs. 'Put him with the others.'

'What? But I helped you!' The driver made a lunge for the door, only to find Yellowford standing in his way. 'Let me out!'

'I won't be doing that,' Yellowford spoke softly, with an accent as pure Dublin as Watters had ever heard.

'No—' Arthur tried to sidestep until Yellowford dropped a short leather cosh from his sleeve and cracked him over the side of the head. As Arthur reeled, Yellowford pushed him beside Silver.

'And then there were four,' Watters said. 'You are gathering quite a collection of bodies. Imagine the fun when the police find us and trace our deaths to you.' He lifted his head to meet Markovic's bright blue eyes. 'Which will happen, of course. The hansom cab will be found only a few streets away, and the police will search this entire area house by house.'

'They will find nothing,' Markovic said.

'They will find you and hang you like a dog,' Karin said. 'You will kick and squirm at the end of a rope with your face turning blue and your tongue protruding, and I will be there to watch!' She twisted her face to show how Markovic would look at the wrong end of the hangman's noose.

Markovic shook his head. 'Get some rope and tie these men up until I decide how to dispose of them. Tie the woman too.' The one-eyed pug left the room. Markovic nodded to the elegant man and spoke in that harsh language again. The man nodded, wordless and looked up as the pug returned with a coil of rope looped around his arm.

'I'd better do that,' Yellowford took the rope. 'I want to make sure it's nice and tight.'

'You're a bit of a chameleon, Yellowford, are you not?' Watters asked. 'You change your accent as much as you change your underwear. Probably more.'

'You can go to hell, Sergeant Watters,' Yellowford said. He slashed Watters over the face with the rope and bent down to tie his ankles. Watters waited for a second and then lashed out with his boots. With two pistols pointing towards him, he had no hope of escaping but had no intention of giving up quietly. He felt a surge of satisfaction as his boot made crunching contact with Yellowford's mouth. Yellowford reeled back, cursing in Gaelic.

Watters rose to his feet, followed up his attack with a short jab, and then the nearest pug cracked him across the head with his blackjack. As Watters staggered back, both pugs jumped on him, their combined weight crashing him to the ground.

'Stay still!' Markovic rammed his pistol into Silver's chest.

With two heavy men on him, Watters could not move as Yellowford rose, kicked him in the ribs and tied him hand and foot.

'Gag them,' Markovic ordered. 'And leave them here just now.' He pointed to Yellowford. 'You get the cab into our stable. You,' he pointed to the broken-nosed pug, 'close the shutters.' He waited until darkness once again shielded the room, ushered them out, had a last look at his prisoners and slammed the door shut. The key turned smoothly in the lock.

There were only a few seconds of silence before Watters heard the scuffling noises as the others struggled to free themselves. He tried to unpick the knots around his wrists and ankles and grunted in frustration when his fingers failed to make an impression. Yellowford had ensured they were tight and hard. He peered through the gloom, seeing the vague shape of bodies and little else.

'That was not the result I had hoped for,' Karin's voice was very distinct. 'That Christopher man, or whatever you call him, is even worse than I remembered. He is undoubtedly not a gentleman.'

'His name is Markovic,' Watters said. 'He's a Russian agent.'

'That must be why they were speaking Russian,' Karin said. 'Turn sideways, George, if you please.'

Watters felt small fingers at his wrists and felt something tugging at the cords. A few seconds later, he felt the tension release, and pulled his arms apart. Even those few moments had been uncomfortable, and he rubbed his wrists before tearing off his gag.

Light eased in as Karen pulled one of the shutters slightly open. Karin smiled at him. 'I told you I was going to carry a knife as the gypsies did,' she said. Her eyes seemed even more wondrous than ever. 'They did not even search me, after all, I am only a woman.'

'And some woman you are,' Watters praised her. He pulled the gag from Silver's mouth and helped release him.

'What about him?' Silver indicated Arthur.

'Leave him,' Watters said.

'They will murder him, sure as death,' Silver pointed out.

'Let them,' Karin said carelessly, 'he deserves no less.'

Watters swore softly. 'Give me the knife,' he said and cut the driver free. 'Stay with us,' he hissed, 'and keep your mouth shut. If you say one single word, I will cut your throat myself.'

The driver nodded his head violently. 'Yes, sir. It was the money, sir. I've got three girls to support—' He stopped as Silver cuffed the back of his head.

'I would leave you to die,' Karin said.

Watters knelt at the door and looked into the keyhole. The key was still in the lock. 'We'll be out of this room in five minutes,' he said. 'Listen for people outside in the corridor.' Using Karin's knife, he probed gently into the keyhole, turning the end of the key a fraction at a time.

'There will be a small clink,' he said. 'Wait.' He unfolded the handkerchief that Rowena had been careful to put in his pocket and slowly pushed it through the gap under the door.

'What are you doing?' Karin's breath was hot in his ear.

'I'll push the key through,' he explained, 'catch it on the handkerchief, and pull it under the door.'

'Oh, isn't this exciting!' Karin leaned on his back with her hair drifting onto his face.

'Sergeant!' Silver put a hand on his shoulder. 'Somebody's coming.'

Watters nodded. Would he be better to leave the handkerchief where it was, or should he replace it? Deciding to let it lie, he whispered: 'Get back from the door.'

Heavy footsteps sounded in the corridor and halted outside the room. Watters took a deep breath to control his racing heart and held the knife ready in case someone should enter. Karin started a nervous giggle that Silver ended by quickly clamping his hand over her mouth.

'Shush now.'

The footsteps started again and pounded past. A door opened and closed, followed by the deep murmur of voices in that same harsh language. Watters guessed that it was Russian.

'They're next door,' Silver said.

'We'll be quiet,' Karin said brightly.

Watters waved her to silence. 'If we can hear them, they will hear us,' he whispered. 'I wish I knew what they were saying.'

'Oh,' Karin did not lower her voice. 'They are talking about somebody or something called Mannie. Something like that, but I do not know the name.'

'You speak Russian?' Watters forced himself to whisper.

'Of course. I already told you that I speak languages. French and German and English ...' Karin looked surprised as if she expected everybody to have mastered more than one language.

'All right ... shh!' Watters put two fingers over Karin's mouth to keep her quiet. 'Listen to what they are saying.'

Watters blinked as his eyes began to pain him. He knew he was a police sergeant, not a government agent such as Alba, and was out of his depth with Russian agents. For an instant, Watters was tempted to gather Silver and Karin and leave as quickly as he could, but then he realised that they were in a position that could be useful. He had to stay here, whatever the danger, and find out all he could.

'Are you all right, Sergeant?' Silver looked concerned.

'Thinking things through,' Watters said.

Karin had her ear to the wall. 'I can hear them talking,' she said, 'but I can't make out the words.'

'Here,' Watters carefully opened a wall cupboard. 'The walls in these old houses are thick,' he said, 'but the cupboards in the rooms are placed back-to-back, with only a thin wooden partition between them.'

Nodding her understanding, Karin stepped inside the shallow cupboard and pressed her ear to the dividing wall. When Watters came closer, she waved him away, frowning in concentration. Watters felt his tension rise. Without weapons and under threat of death, he knew that getting as far as possible from this house was the only sensible option, yet Karin might hear something that helped finally solve this case.

That new, yet already familiar, fear surged within him. He fought to control it and sought the cause. Ever since he was a child, he had been nearly numb to fear. Each time he had faced dangerous men and women or had been close to death, he had welcomed the prospect. Life had never been more than a burden, so he had no fear of death. So what had altered? Why this new feeling?

The answer stunned Watters with its simplicity. He cared for somebody else.

'Dear Heavens,' Watters breathed. 'That's it!'

'Sergeant?' Silver looked at him.

Again, Karin waved him to silence. She turned around with those wondrous eyes bright. 'It's not Mannie, it's Manann. They're going to blow up a place called Manann.'

Watters pushed aside his more personal feelings. 'What the devil does that mean?'

'I've never heard of it,' Silver said. 'Are you sure you got the correct name? Was it not Manchester?' He looked at Watters. 'Mind you if they blew up Manchester nobody would notice much, it's an uncommonly queer place.'

'I would not say that along the banks of the Irwell,' Watters murmured. 'They will cut your head off and thrust it down your throat.'

'That's impossible,' Karin said, frowning. 'You could not do that.'

'Repeat the name,' Watters said. 'I'm sure I've heard it before.'

'Manann I think,' there was more doubt in Karin's voice. 'It might have been Manchester as Constable Silver said, but I am sure it was Manann.'

'I do know that name,' Watters whispered as the memory returned. 'It was in the papers that Rowena translated for me.' He stepped away from the wall, wishing to walk to stimulate his mind but very aware of their dangerous position.

'I remember,' he said, 'it was Manann mac something. He was the Celtic God of the sea.'

'Is there a place named after this Manann fellow?' Silver asked. 'Is there a building such as the Mother of Parliaments?'

'I can't think of one,' Watters frowned, 'or perhaps I can. The last two Gaelic names were obscure: there was the Morrigan, who we took for a heroine and was Mother Flannery and the wicked Princess Aifa for the Mother of Parliaments, yes? And we think that Cuchulain is this Russian fellow, Markovic.'

Silver nodded. 'Yes, that's so. What's in your mind, Sergeant?'

'This Manann fellow was an old sea god, Watters spoke as he thought. 'Or that's what Rowena told me,' Watters said cautiously. 'I think that these Russian fellows mean to blow up the current sea god.'

'We don't believe in such things anymore,' Karin told him solemnly. 'They can't blow up a god that does not exist.'

'We certainly don't believe in the supernatural Celtic gods,' Silver caught Watters's drift, 'but if that other Celtic goddess could be the Mother of Parliaments, then Manann could be the present most powerful ruler of the sea.'

'That must be Admiral Sir George Dundas,' Watters said. 'He is the most powerful man in the most powerful navy in the world.'

'He is also sailing in the Black Sea,' Silver said. 'He bombarded Se-bastopol did he not?'

'Yes, Silver,' Watters agreed, 'he *was* in the Black Sea, but if you'll recall, he is also coming to London this month.'

'When?' Silver asked.

'You told me he was coming, a few weeks ago,' Watters reminded. 'You read it in the papers and wrote it down.'

'Did I?' Silver produced his notebook, 'lucky the Russians didn't take this.' With agonising slowness, he pored over his past entries. 'Oh, here we are. Admiral Dundas is viewing HMS *Royal Albert*, the latest ship in the Royal Navy, together with admirals of the French and Austrian navies.'

'That's it! You've got it,' Watters said. 'Could you think of a more splendid target? Hit the head of the Royal Navy when he is showing off the latest addition to the fleet to our allies and friends.'

'Well, Sergeant,' Silver glanced back at his notes, 'we'd better hurry because the Admiral is on *Royal Albert* tomorrow.'

'Tomorrow!' Karin's eyes were wide and blue as they met Watters's. 'Oh, George, we have to stop them.'

We? You're not coming, woman, Watters thought. *It's far too bloody dangerous.*

'We do have to stop them,' Watters said. 'Get out of here!' Realising that the handkerchief had been on display outside the room for far too long, he used the blade of Karin's knife to push the key out of the lock. The clatter of it landing seemed as loud as the peal of church bells, so he waited an interminable twenty seconds before dragging the handkerchief under the door. He retrieved the key and breathed slowly out.

'You did it,' Karin told him.

With his hand shaking, it took Watters three attempts to slide the key back into the lock and slowly turn it, with the eventual sharp click of the door opening making him start. He moved the handle slowly and peered into the corridor. The one-eyed pug stood outside the room next door, puffing on a stubby clay pipe, and looking very bored. Watters knew he could subdue him, but the noise would alert the others. He closed the door as quietly as he could.

'There is one ugly bruiser outside,' he whispered.

'We can kill him,' Karin pointed to the knife. 'Cut his throat!'

'You are a bloodthirsty little beggar, aren't you?' Watters said. 'Try the window.'

Opening the shutters wider created even more noise than retrieving the key with Watters wincing with every creak. The resulting light flooded the room.

They were one floor up, overlooking the side of the house. Watters slid the catch, pushed up the lower half of the window and looked down. There were few hand or footholds, but a broad architrave surmounted the window directly beneath them, which would provide a stable platform for their feet.

'It's about eighteen feet to the ground,' he whispered. 'With a foothold about five feet down. I'll go first, and then you, Karin, and Silver last. I'll help Karin.' He glanced at Arthur. 'We'll leave you to take your chances.' He knew he should arrest the driver but taking him with them might jeopardise their chances of success.

Arthur shook his head. 'Please … they'll kill me!'

'Good!' Karin nodded. 'I hope they do.'

Watters pressed his forehead hard against the bridge of Arthur's nose. 'If you live and help them in any way,' he said, 'you will wish that they had killed you because, so help me God, I will hunt you down and chop you into a thousand pieces.'

Leaving the driver shaking, Watters eased himself outside, hoping that nobody was in the grounds as he faced the room and felt with his feet for a hold. The brickwork was newly pointed, with crisp joints that he could slide his toes in, and he scrabbled downward until he felt the architrave of the window immediately below. He rested briefly and glanced downward. It was a simple drop to a gravel path.

'Right, Karin,' he said softly. 'Out you come.' Balancing on the architrave, he held out his hand. Expecting Karin to hesitate, he was surprised when she immediately backed out of the window with a whisking of petticoats and lowered herself quickly beside him.

'Well done,' he breathed. For a second Karin pressed against him and then he crouched, hoped the room below was empty, and lowered himself onto the windowsill. The interior shutters were shut, and he looked down, checked the path beneath was clear, and allowed himself to drop. He landed with a painful crunch on the gravel, rolled and recovered. 'Come on!'

He looked directly upward, had a tantalisingly shocking glimpse of her ankles and calves as her petticoats ballooned outward when she fell toward him. Her arms were outstretched and her hair flying free, a blonde bird floating down with her head thrown back as he moved to catch her. For a second, he wrapped his arms around her, but her momentum knocked them both down to roll in gasping unity on the gravel.

'Are you all right, Sergeant?' Karin looked down at him through her bright blue eyes.

'I am,' Watters said. 'You have bottom, haven't you?'

She looked perplexed. 'I have a bottom?'

'You're spunky … game … you are a brave girl to jump like that with no hesitation.' He saw Silver drop, roll, and recover. 'Never mind, let's get away from here.'

'It was fun,' Karin said.

'Wait for me!' Arthur fell heavily to the gravel, groaned, and dragged himself to his feet 'Please take me, sir. Don't let them kill me.'

Watters swore; he had hoped the driver would have remained behind. 'Stay with us then, keep up, and keep quiet, man.'

'The main gate's open,' Silver pointed out.

'They must have opened it to bring in the cab,' Watters said. 'Come on!' He led the way, putting out his hand for Karin. After the noise, they had made he was not surprised to see an upper window open, and the debonair man's face thrust out. He shouted something in Russian and withdrew.

'They've seen us,' Watters said. 'Run!' He pushed Karin in front of him, heard a door open behind him, tensed his muscles in anticipation of a pistol shot, and swore as Silver shouted:

'Watch for the bruisers!'

Watters saw the two pugs lumber to the gate. The one-eyed man carried a shotgun, the other held a heavy chain. 'Get over the wall!' He saw Silver launch himself at the enclosing brick wall, mount it in a second and lie on the top with an arm outstretched to help Karin up.

Watters heard the pistol crack behind him and saw the bullet raise a small spurt of red dust beside Silver's head. He jerked back and pushed Karin ahead of him. 'Take Karin,' He saw her stumble, heard her cry as her ankle twisted. Silver stretched to reach her, but his despairing fingers were a few inches short.

'Karin!' Watters crouched beneath her, placed his shoulder under her and heaved upward. This was no time for delicacy. She gave a little cry, clutched for Silver's hand, and missed as the pistol fired again. The shot hissed past Watters's ear, cracked against the wall, and ricocheted away. He turned around. The broken-nosed pug was lumbering toward him, with Yellowford at his side and the dapper Russian emerging from the front door. Markovic stood against the wall, aiming his revolver.

'Silver!' Watters said urgently. 'Leave us! Get to Scotland Yard and warn Alba.' Markovic fired his pistol again, and Watters distinctly saw the bullet pass him, a streak of black against the red brickwork, and the spurt of blood as it entered Silver's chest.

'William!' Watters reached up as Silver's eyes and mouth widened in shock, and then the pistol cracked again. Silver's head jerked back in a cloud of blood, and he tumbled down the far side of the wall.

'Silver! William!' Watters ran forward, just as the pistol fired yet again. Karin screamed, once, and fell on the inside of the wall.

Chapter Twenty-One

Watters swore: 'Karin!'

Karin hauled herself upright, holding onto her arm. She shouted something in German, said, 'I'm all right!' and moved, half running, half hopping, toward the back of the house.

'Sergeant Watters!' Watters had forgotten about Arthur, who now ran diagonally past him and tried to clamber up the garden wall. The dapper Russian stepped forward and hauled him down.

Watters hesitated, torn between checking on Silver and ensuring that Karin was safe, between friendship and duty, between his old companion and a woman in need. He swore, glanced back at Markovic who was sauntering toward him casually reloading his revolver as the dapper Russian and Yellowford moved behind Karin.

'Your companion Silver is dead,' Markovic said as he clicked shut the revolver. 'I put one through his lungs and one in his head. You are next and then the woman.'

The pug gave a low laugh and moved forward, shoulders hunched, and arms extended like a gorilla. If Watters had his cane, he would have no hesitation in facing the pug, but unarmed and shaken by the death of Silver, he knew the pug would destroy him.

Karin screamed again as Yellowford reached out to her, with the light gleaming from the rings on each finger. Watters ignored the crack of the pistol as he slammed his full weight into Yellowford just as the Irishman's fingers closed around Karin's arm. All three of them sprawled on the ground with Watters on top and quickest to rise. He planted a hard kick in Yellowford's groin before dragging Karin to her feet.

'Come on.' Watters pushed Karin in front, saw her stagger and favour her left leg, ducked at the bang of the pistol, and ran on. He heard a high-pitched yell and glanced over his shoulder in time to see the dapper Russian break Arthur's neck between his hands. 'Run, Karin, run.'

The pug was panting in his effort to intercept them while the dapper Russian dropped Arthur's body and ran smoothly along the inside of the garden wall to the back gate. Behind them both, Markovic stood with his right arm fully outstretched, aiming his revolver. Yellowford was lying on the ground clutching at himself and whimpering.

'We're trapped,' Karin said. 'There's no way out.'

'Get back to the house!' Watters waited for an interminable two seconds until the pug closed, scooped a handful of gravel, and threw it in the man's face. As the pug flinched, Watters landed a solid kick on the man's muscular thigh and then turned abruptly and pulled Karin toward the house.

'There's no door here,' Karin yelled. Without hesitating, Watters smashed his elbow through the nearest window and slid his hand inside to unfasten the catch. He threw up the sash, flinched as a bullet crashed against the brickwork, then stooped, lifted Karin bodily and nearly threw her inside. 'Run!'

Watters followed, rolling through the open window, and lunging for the door at the far side of the room. 'Keep moving!'

'Where are we going?' Karin was gasping, limping on her left leg.

'Right through the house and out the other side,' Watters told her. The door was locked, so he booted it, swore when it held, drew back, and kicked again, harder. The door flew open, crashed against the casing, and bounced back, but he thrust through, taking hold of Karin's hand to drag her behind him. A flight of stairs ascended before them, with plastered walls painted a hideous green and rat droppings thick on the ground. 'They'll come in to head us off.'

Taking the stairs two at a time, Watters ignored Karin's brave little squeaks of pain and ran upstairs to another corridor. Thankful for the daylight that seeped through a row of round-headed windows and hoping he was moving in the right direction, he hurried on. Twice he winced as the image of the bullet hitting Silver came, fresh and painful to his mind.

The corridor ran the full width of the house, with doors on either side. Watters pulled open each door behind him to obstruct any pursuers. Most rooms were empty of either furniture or servants.

'Where now?' Karin stopped as the corridor ended in a dead-end.

'In here!' Watters pulled her into the nearest room and looked out of a window onto a roof that sloped to a small parapet wall, with a single dormer window breaking the monotony of blue-grey slates. 'Out there,' he said. 'It's less of a drop than you did a few moments ago.'

Karin hardly hesitated as she threw open the window, had a single look outside and lowered herself as far as she could. She gave a nervous smile and let go, dropping for a few seconds before she landed with a scrambling thud and a small yelp on the slates. Watters followed even before the parapet stopped her rolling.

'In there.' He scrambled crabwise toward the dormer window and held out a hand for her.

'There they are!' Yellowford's voice sounded from below. 'They're on the roof!' Watters tried the window and swore. The shutters were locked from the inside. With his boots sliding on the slates, he held the frame with both hands and kicked at the shutters until one of the slats gave in, and then, ignoring the splinters that ripped into his palm, wrenched it free.

'Hurry, George,' Karin pleaded, 'they've seen us.'

Watters felt a splinter rake up his wrist as he thrust his hand inside the window to haul back the bolt. It was stiff, so he jerked it sideways, back and forth until it loosened, and he could draw it open. He threw the shutters wide and pushed in, nearly overbalancing as he realised there was only a foot-wide ledge behind the glass-less window. The pleasant smell of damp hay and horses rose towards him.

'We're in the stable block,' Watters helped Karin inside and side-footed along the ledge to where a ladder descended to the ground.

'There will be horses,' Karin said.

'Maybe!' Watters looked down. There were two vehicles inside the stable. One was the brougham that had carried the sugar while the second was a hansom cab, with the horse still between the shafts.

Watters checked the number. 'That's our cab,' he said. 'Arthur must have come straight here. That's our way out.'

Karin widened her eyes. 'Can you drive a cab?'

'We'll find out in a few moments,' Watters slid down the ladder and held out his arms, taking hold of her around the waist to swing her down. She was firm under his hands, lighter than he expected, and her hair was pleasantly scented as it brushed against his face. Watters placed her carefully on the straw-strewn floor. 'Come on, Karin, it's time to leave.'

The cab stood in the middle of the stables, with room to turn. Watters hauled opened the stable door. Light and air flooded in.

'Get inside,' he ordered, pulled the lever to open the door, and pushed Karin inside before mounting the driver's seat at the rear. He lifted the reins, cracked them on the rump of the horse, and rode the jerk as the cab moved forward.

The stable doors were on light hinges and were already swinging shut as he pushed forward, so the horse had to shoulder them open as Watters guided the carriage onto the drive.

The one-eyed guard at the gate looked up as the cab burst out of the stable. He raised his shotgun, hesitated, and lowered the barrel, obviously unsure who may be driving.

'Good lads,' Watters said softly, 'give a gun to a man with one eye and a punch-addled brain!' He cracked the reins as Yellowford shouted hoarsely:

'That's Watters the peeler!'

The one-eyed pug lifted his shotgun again.

Karin slammed open the communication hatch. 'George! The gate is open!'

Watters looked over; the pug was holding the shotgun as if he was scared of it, with the butt an inch away from his shoulder. Watters yelled and cracked the reins again. The horse dashed forward so violently that Watters slipped backwards on his seat, just as the pug fired his shotgun. The recoil sent the pug staggering back, and where the pellets went Watters neither knew nor cared as he flicked the reins again, driving the horse through the gateway. The body of the cab crashed into the wrought-iron gates, sending them battering back with a sound that must have wakened the neighbourhood if the gunfire had not done that already. He heard Karin give a whoop that could have been fear or delight, eased the horse in a tight right-hand turn, and flicked the reins on its rump again. Although he disliked hurting the animal, he needed as much speed as possible.

Watters guided the horse around the front of the building, saw the broken-nosed pug chasing after him, lifted the whip at the side of the driver's seat and aimed a vicious lash. Unfortunately, the lash missed, to coil around the iron spikes on top of the wall. Watters swore, dropped the handle of the whip, and steered the cab right again, around the side of the house.

'Where are you going?' Karin's voice sounded plaintively through the communication hatch.

'To pick up Silver,' Watters shouted. 'I'm not leaving him behind!'

'But he's dead! Markovic shot him!'

'All the more reason to rescue him,' Watters yelled. He did not explain more. He remembered how various enemies had mutilated the bodies of British servicemen and had no intention of allowing that to happen to a man he thought of more as a friend than a colleague.

'That's not logical!' Karin said.

Watters clamped shut his mouth and concentrated on negotiating the narrow passage between this house and its neighbour. He heard the scream of wood on brick as the wheel of the cab scraped along the wall, felt the shudder as friction delayed him and again cracked the reins on the rump of the horse. Red dust clouded behind them.

Silver's body lay where it had fallen, face down in a drying pool of dark blood. Pulling the reins to stop the cab, Watters leapt off the seat. He crouched at Silver's side. 'Open the door, Karin,' he ordered.

Luckily, Silver was wiry rather than muscular, and the corpse had not had time to stiffen. Moving quickly, Watters lifted the body, bundled it inside the cab, and frowned at the blood seeping from the ugly wound at the side of Silver's head. 'Sorry, William.'

'You can't put him here,' Karin moved away from the body.

'He won't bite! He died trying to help you,' Watters slammed shut the door and hurried back to the driver's seat, aware that the Russians were already on the street behind him. He once more rapped the reins, absorbed the jerk as the cab moved forward, and then swore as the broken-nosed pug clambered onto the back of the vehicle beside him. Watters punched sideways, but the pug absorbed the blow as if it was nothing. Watters staggered as the horse sensed his sudden weakness and broke into something close to a gallop. The pug swayed and tried to stabilise himself, with the increase of weight slowing the cab down.

Yellowford was limping in the rear, shouting something as Karin screamed, either in excitement or fear, Watters did not know which. Wrapping the reins around his wrist, he saw the pug lift his fist, but with most of his attention on driving the cab, Watters had little to spare for the bruiser at his side. He inched away, knowing that if an experienced bare-knuckle fighter landed a single mighty blow, the contest would be over before it had properly begun. He would have to act quickly.

Unable to leave his seat, Watters pulled the horse to the right, so the carriage swung to swing left and smash against the brick wall they were passing. He heard the pug gasp and saw him grab the roof of the cab for balance. Judging his time, Watters lunged to the side and barged into the man, forcing him to release the roof.

Twisting the reins harder around his wrist, Watters slammed the cab sideways, so it scraped the pug along the wall, leaving a broad blood smear. The pug yelled and fell to the ground, rolling over and over in the wake of the cab. With the weight reduced, the vehicle leapt forward as they passed the wall and into a small open area. Despite the loss of weight, the cab did not steer correctly, and Watters knew it was damaged; he hoped it would hold together until they were safe. After that, the welfare of the vehicle was supremely unimportant. He hauled at the reins as the hansom slewed from side to side, seemingly of its own violation.

The brief open area terminated in Chiswick High Road. Watters heard the buzz and spin of wheels and saw the glimmer of gas lamps; the short winter day had nearly ended, and the long darkness of night was already creeping in.

The sudden attack took him by surprise as Yellowford jumped on him from behind. Watters staggered under the weight and grunted when Yellowford's punch slammed him against the back of the cab. He had a glimpse of gritted teeth and tawdry gold jewellery as Yellowford drew back his fist, saw knuckles covered in massive rings and ducked. Shaken by the assault, Watters's retaliatory punch lacked conviction and merely bounced from Yellowford's forehead. Completely undirected, the cab slewed into the street, causing a butcher's dog cart to swerve out of its way and the butcher to rise in his seat, shaking a mighty fist.

'Bloody furious drivers!' the butcher's voice faded as Watters faced Yellowford. He heard Karin's voice raised in a scream for help, quickly stilled. Watters kicked out, catching Yellowford a sharp blow on the thigh, then glimpsed the driver's blackjack behind the seat. Lifting it, he jabbed it underhand into Yellowford's already-tender groin, then kicked out again as the man doubled over. Roaring in pain, Yellowford fell off the seat to land face-first on the road.

Grabbing at the loose reins in an attempt to control the now galloping horse, Watters looked around, flinching as an omnibus rattled past with the cad glaring at him and shouting a mouthful of foul abuse. The horse had pulled the cab into the centre of the road, so that traffic swerved aside or stopped altogether. Watters pulled hard at the reins, trying all he could to halt the cab's erratic progress.

'Whoa there! Slow down, boy!'

Perhaps recognising the voice of authority, or more likely tired after its long day, the horse slowed. Watters took a deep breath. 'Thank God.' He spoke through the communication hatch.

'We're safe now, Karin,' he said. 'We'll get along to Scotland Yard and drop you off.' He saw Silver's body there, and the tragedy hit him anew. What would Angela do now?

'They're following!' Karin yelled.

'What?' Watters glanced behind.

The Russians' brougham was thirty yards behind, with the driver cracking his whip to clear a route.

Watters swore and lashed the reins on the horse. With any luck, the police would interfere when they saw him racing through the streets.

'George!' Karin screamed.

Watters felt the wind of the whip as the elegant man lashed at him from the brougham. He put his head down and forced speed from the horse.

'Hold on, Karin!' He cracked the reins on the rump of his unfortunate horse and pushed on.

As they approached the centre of town, traffic increased, slowing them down. Watters used the superior manoeuvrability of the cab to ease ahead, overtaking a lumbering brewer's dray and moving fast, keeping a lookout for any police, who seemed to have vanished.

Every time he glanced behind him, the brougham was there with that elegant man driving and Markovic staring at him, expressionless except for the intense hate in his eyes. As traffic increased, Watters slowed further, searching desperately for the friendly blue of a police uniform. A coal waggon lurched across the road in front of him, forcing him to stop, just as the brougham slammed into him in a tangle of reins, a splinter of shattered wood and the high neighing of frightened horses. The impact threw Watters backwards off the cab, so he struck his head on the ground and lay there, dazed, as the vehicle tottered and crashed onto its side.

'You blasted idiot!' the waggon driver shouted. 'You shouldn't be on the road!'

Watters looked up to see Markovic rushing at him from the body of the brougham, while the elegant man opened the door of his cab.

'Fortunately, I am a police detective,' Markovic spoke loudly for the benefit of the watchers. He displayed Watters's baton as a badge of office as he reached down and dragged Watters to his feet. 'Up you get, fellow. We'll take care of you.'

Watters saw the elegant man haul Karin from the body of the cab.

Markovic spoke again. 'Come along, Miss. We'll soon have you safe from this driver. He'll lose his badge, never you fear.'

Karin shook the elegant man off and began to shout, but in her agitation, she spoke in her native German.

'Here,' somebody in the gathering crowd said, 'she's a foreigner. Bloody Russian or something.'

The word quickly spread through the crowd.

'Bloody Russians causing trouble in the street,' somebody said, and within minutes the curious watchers turned hostile. There were calls to 'string them up' and 'kick their teeth out' as the mob edged closer to Watters and Karin. Watters looked around: where were the police? There was never a policeman when he wanted one.

'Look!' Somebody peered into the cab, 'there's a dead body in there. Murder!'

That cry quickly spread around the crowd, so the anger increased. 'They're bloody Russian murderers!'

Watters ducked his head as a bottle spiralled past him. He knew that persuading a crowd against its beliefs was next to impossible, and convincing an angry crowd was worse. They had no option but to run and hope the mob prevented the Russians from shooting them. He hated to leave Silver behind, but there was no help for it, and the police must be here soon; they would treat Silver with respect.

As soon as Karin was free of the cab, Watters grabbed her and pushed Markovic away. 'Run!' he said. 'And keep on running!'

Karin was still nursing her left leg, she had lost a shoe in the crash, and her hair was a tangled mess over her head and face, but she understood the urgency and obeyed without question. The debonair man put a hand on Watters's shoulder.

Glad of the opportunity, Watters swung with the cabbie's blackjack, catching the man a blow on the face that was powerful enough to send him reeling back. For a second Watters was tempted to stay and finish the job until he heard the rising howl of the mob and decided that explanations would have to wait. Karin scrambled back, grabbed his arm, and pulled him away.

'Run, George!'

'After them!' Watters heard somebody yelled, and there was the sound of charging feet.

'Cabbie!' Watters hailed a cab, whose driver took one look at the howling mob, decided that elsewhere was better than here and cracked his whip.

'Run, George!' Karin dragged him away, 'run!'

In London, the most elite areas co-existed within a few hundred yards of some of the poorest, so within a few moments, Watters was in an area of narrow lanes with one central, reasonably wide street that he recognised.

'This is Rosemary Lane,' he gasped to Karin and added, 'they tried to change its name but ...' The details did not matter.

Despite the evening dim, old-clothes dealers packed the street. Some looked up as Watters grabbed Karin's hand and ran past.

'You need a shoe on both feet, dearie' a woman called hopefully to Karin, while others looked fearfully at the oncoming mob and began to gather their stock together preparatory to a quick retreat. Watters glanced behind him, wondered if a call for help would work, decided it would not and read the name of the side streets that he passed. 'Glasshouse Street, Russel Court, Parson's Court ... none of these.'

'What are you looking for?' Limping gamely, her hair a blonde explosion and her face streaked with grime, Karin had never looked better. Watters grunted: Wolfgang and his ilk would be hard-pressed to recognise her now.

'Blue-Anchor yard,' Watters said quickly, 'the mob won't enter there.'

The sound of the crowd had attracted men, women, and the ubiquitous children, who gathered at the side street entrances in menacing groups of coal-whippers, dredgers, and sundry hangers-on. The accents were a mixture of Irish, Jewish, Eastern European, and native London, but there was no disguising the tones of menace.

'Blue Anchor Yard is where the pure sellers congregate,' Watters said. He glanced over his shoulder. Most of the mob had halted before the sinister shouts of the locals, but one of the pugs and the two Russians continued, ignored by everybody. Markovic had a hand in his pocket, presumably holding his revolver.

'Can't we call for help?' Karin was limping badly, with blood oozing from her left foot. She kicked off her remaining shoe to make moving easier. The quick hand of an urchin grabbed it.

'Round here? They would watch a murder and gamble on the amount of blood,' Watters said.

'Is there not a policeman?'

'We'd be dead before he got here. This way.' Watters hauled her into an alleyway. He heard Markovic shouting and saw him pointing in their direction. 'Quickly.'

'My foot's bleeding,' Karin was drooping with tiredness.

The houses closed in above them, blocking out the darkening sky as Watters saw a lane of closed doors and piles of refuse. The group of boys seethed toward them. Ragged of clothes, they were tousle-headed and barefoot, with tired eyes that stared from filthy faces. Most held a stout stick or another weapon.

'George,' Karin stepped behind him. Sensing that she was close to tears, he put a steadying hand on her arm.

'Halloa,' the tallest of the boys was about fifteen and carried a long stick tipped with a sharp metal spike, like a medieval pike. He pointed the weapon at Watters as his companions spread out. 'I know you,' he looked closer; 'you're that peeler cove.'

Watters felt the atmosphere worsen as the other boys lifted their sticks. The words, 'He's a peeler,' passed through them like a breeze through a field of grass.

The other youths crowded around, swearing, pointing, and urging each other to violence or theft.

'You were at the bomb,' their leader raised his voice. 'This is the cove that gave us money!'

'You're the mudlarks,' Watters pretended to recognise them, although their faces were indistinguishable from the thousands of other filthy, mat-haired ragamuffins that filled the streets.

'Who're you running from?' the tall one asked.

'Men with guns,' Watters kept it simple. 'You'd best hook it.'

'This is our street,' the tallest boy said. 'Follow us.' He led the way along a passage so narrow Watters's shoulders rubbed the worn brick walls on either side. It opened into a filthy court where a dog scratched its fleas, and a black-faced woman sat in a bundle of dirty rags. The boy kicked open the nearest door. The stench of dog waste nearly made Watters gag, and he held onto Karin's hand as she pulled away.

'Pure collectors,' Watters explained, 'for the tanning industry.'

She nodded, with her face screwed into an expression of disgust that Watters shared. It was a long way from the elegant palaces of Vienna.

The boys guided Watters around a monumental pile of dog waste in the centre of the room and showed a small, wooden sided apartment little more substantial than a dog kennel that hugged the wall. 'In there,' the tall boy said. 'This is where we hide when the peelers are after us.'

'I won't tell anybody,' Watters promised. He pulled Karin toward him. 'In you go,' he said and pushed her in first. Watters followed, squeezing together into the tiny, filthy space. The boys laughed as Karin gagged at the stink.

'Stay here,' the tall boy said, 'and I'll tell you when it's safe to come out.'

'I will die with this smell,' Karin said.

'You'll likely die if you don't hide here.' Watters produced his handkerchief. 'Put this on your face. It might help.'

'Thank you.' Karin did as Watters suggested.

Watters was acutely aware of the pressure of Karin's body against his as they waited. He tried to shift aside, but there was no room. She glanced at him, screwed up her nose and smiled. 'I will not tell of this to the ladies in Vienna,' she whispered.

'Better not.' Watters tried not to gag at the smell. His head was still spinning with the effects of the fall from the cab.

The voices were harsh and Gaelic as a group of men thundered into the room. They spoke for a few seconds and withdrew quickly.

'The smell chased them away,' Watters said.

'No wonder.' Karin gagged again. 'We can't stay here long.' Her voice was hoarse.

After a few more minutes, Watters eased out of the box, only to hear a Gaelic voice. He peered through the open door, to see Yellowford outside, talking to a group of men and women.

'It appears that the Russians have mobilised all the local Irish against us.'

'Why do they hate England?'

'That would take a long time to explain,' Watters said.

Watters guessed that two hours passed before the tall youth reported that the street was clear. 'The Paddies are all gone now,' he said.

'I won't forget this,' Watters said as he ushered Karin past. 'What's your name?'

The youth hesitated before he spoke. 'Liam Murphy.'

'Well, Liam Murphy, you probably know as much about shipping on the river as anybody else. Do you know about Admiral Dundas?'

'Oh yes,' Liam's grin showed discoloured teeth in his permanently dirty face. 'We know everything that's happening on the River. He's coming to *Royal Albert* tomorrow with half the admirals of Europe.'

'Thank you.' Watters wondered if he should ask Liam to take a message to Scotland Yard, decided that the police would undoubtedly arrest him as a vagrant rather than listen to anything he said, and shook his hand instead. 'I won't forget your help.' He took hold of Karin's arm and hurried back into Rosemary Lane. He looked around, hoping to see a blue uniform. 'There is never a policeman when you want one,' he said and moved on with Karin limping at his side and looking every inch a vagabond of the street.

He took hold of Karin's shoulder. 'I want you to get to Scotland Yard,' he told her. 'Find Inspector Larkin and tell him everything. Tell him that the Russians are behind this, not the Irish, and they plan an attack on Admiral Dundas.'

'And what will you do, George?'

'I am going to find *Royal Albert*,' Watters said. 'There might not be time for Larkin or Alba to arrange anything.'

'You're just getting me out of the way,' Karin said.

'I'm keeping you safe,' Watters told her frankly, 'and ensuring that the police know about the Russian threat if I fail.'

'No,' Karin shook her head. 'I am staying with you.'

'I work better alone,' Watters said.

'Is that why you are so angry that Silver was killed?'

'Silver was a friend.'

'Am I not a friend now?' Karin pressed closer. With her feet bare, her hair as tangled as any mudlark and her face smudged with sweat and dirt, she did not look like the sophisticated women who had greeted him in Hesse Square.

'Yes, Karin, yes, indeed, you are a friend now.'

'Then you can work with me.'

Watters consulted his watch. It was nearly midnight. The Russian attack was due the next day, presumably with the bombs they had imported from the United States. Even as he wasted time arguing with this strong-willed woman, somebody could be on the ship planting bombs, murdering seamen or even assassinating Admiral Dundas himself. Which would be quicker: warning the Royal Navy himself, or sending Karin to Scotland Yard, from where the message would go through tedious official channels to the Admiralty and then to the ship that Dundas was on?

But what right did he have to put her life in danger? Watters took a deep breath. He had no time to argue with such a stubborn woman. She had made up her mind, and they would both have to live with the consequences.

'Come on then if you are sure.'

Karin's smile was a mixture of triumph and excitement.

Chapter Twenty-Two

Even at this late hour, the river was busy, with lights of ships reflecting on the dark water and the nearly unnoticed shush of the current pressing against the bridges and banks. Watters heard the bark of a dog and the low throbbing of an engine, and then the distinct ring of a ship's bell. The regulated lights of the Royal Navy were distinctive amidst the less disciplined merchant shipping.

'Over there,' Watters said quietly. 'That's our ship.'

HMS *Royal Albert* was impressive by anybody's standards. With 121 guns standing in pugnacious ranks, she had been launched in May 1854 and completed in November, only two months previously. Now she lay at the furthest point up-river her draught would allow, with Captain William Mends probably cursing the impending visit of a clutch of dignitaries as he tried to prepare his vessel for the voyage to the Mediterranean and the war with Russia.

'She is huge,' Karin commented as they surveyed the three-decked, 220-foot long battleship as she swung to her anchor with her masts soaring to the dark sky and her watch padding over the scrubbed deck. Her riding lights reflected on the water, pretty in the night, hiding the potential destructive power of her guns. 'How do we get out there?'

There was a small rowing boat beside the bank, tied securely and with its oars removed for security. Watters found a sprung plank on a battered barque and carried it into the boat. 'Are you sure you want to come on board?'

'I am the wife of a diplomat,' Karin said grandly. 'They will listen to me.'

'They might,' Watters did not tell her that she looked more like the wife of a coal-whipper; some things were better left unsaid. 'Come on then, I am certainly not leaving you at the riverside at this time of night.'

With Karin bundled in the bows, Watters unfastened the boat and sculled across the Thames with his plank. He saw *Royal Albert* looming ahead, with her lights casting shadows across the deck and the figures of the watch distinct on the quarterdeck.

'Boat ahoy!' The challenge was welcome. 'Where away?'

'Detective Sergeant George Watters of Scotland Yard,' Watters announced himself. 'I want to speak to the officer of the watch!'

'Do you indeed?' The voice was crisp, professional, and uncomfortably cynical. 'Stand clear of this ship.'

'It is urgent!' Watters said, 'I have to come on board!' He looked around at the sound of quiet orders as a guard boat rowed up to him with a smartly dressed young midshipman in the stern and a dozen Royal Navy seamen at the oars.

'I am Sergeant George Watters of Scotland Yard, and this is Mrs Karen Stegall of the Austrian delegation to Great Britain.'

The midshipman gave a short order, and a whiskered sailor caught hold of the dinghy with a boarding hook and hauled it toward him.

'Of course, you are, mate, and I'm the emperor of France while Joe here is the queen of China.'

'China doesn't have a queen.' Karin's sentence altered to an indignant protest as a bearded able seaman hustled her into the guard boat.

'In you come dearie, and you too, Sergeant.' The man's grin was evident even through his beard. 'You must be the most raggedy arsed sergeant I ever have seen.' He grabbed hold of Watters's shoulder. 'The master-at-arms will have words to say to you tomorrow.'

'I must speak to the officer of the watch,' Watters said, 'your ship is in danger!'

'Of course, it is, mate,' the able seaman said cheerfully, 'the Ruski fleet is sailing up the Thames right now, and nobody noticed except you.'

'Unhand me!' Karin pulled away from the seamen. 'I am with the diplomatic party!'

'Diplomat my arse,' another seaman said crudely. 'You stink like a badger's bum!'

'Quiet!' The midshipman could not have been more than eighteen yet spoke with crisp authority. 'Get these people into the brig. The master-at-arms will deal with them tomorrow.'

'I am Mrs Karin Stegall, wife of Wolfgang Stegall—' Karin began.

'Shut that woman up, somebody,' the midshipman ordered, and a sailor clapped a hard hand over Karin's mouth.

'I must speak to the officer of the watch! There might be a bomb on board this ship.'

'Tell the master-at-arms tomorrow,' the midshipman said. 'Somebody shut that man up as well!'

'Stow your gab, mate,' the bearded seaman ordered, and thrust a wad into Watters's mouth and tied it around his face. 'You'll disturb the captain else, and he doesn't like that, see?'

Watters's struggles were useless as a burly seaman grabbed hold of each arm and held him secure. Hustled on board *Royal Albert*, Watters and Karin were manhandled down a series of ever steeper companionways until they were buried in the interior of the ship and pushed into a small cabin. 'I'm sorry I can't get you separate accommodation,' a cheerful ship's corporal said, 'so you'll have to share. You two stay here until the master-at-arms has seen you. And no making any noise or I'll come and put you both in irons.'

Watters's parting glare did not affect the sailor.

Left alone in the dark, it was the work of a moment for Watters to remove the gags and explore the cell. As he would expect of the Navy, it was stark, clean, and efficient, with a minuscule port hole firmly screwed shut, two solid shelves for beds and a locked door.

'I don't like your navy,' Karin said.

'I don't care for it much myself,' Watters agreed. He pushed at the door. It was very securely locked.

'If you pick the lock we can go and see the captain directly,' Karin suggested.

'My lockpicks have gone,' Watters said. 'The Russians took them.'

'Then what must we do?' Karin looked at him. 'You got us out of the last place.'

Watters nodded. He fought his tiredness. They were trapped inside the brig of a Royal Naval warship moored in the Thames in the belief that some organisation that was either Russian or Irish or both intended to blow it up when Admiral Dundas was on board. Exactly how they could do that he did not know.

'We must attract the attention of an officer,' Watters said, 'the seamen have no power or inclination to help.'

'How do we do that?'

'Make enough noise to be noticed and tell whoever appears that they are in danger,' Watters said. 'I can't think of any other way.'

'They might gag us again.'

'That's why we have to get our message in quickly,' Watters said. 'Ready?' He raised his voice in a shout, at the same time kicking at the door of the brig.

'Help! Help! There is a bomb on the ship! Help us!'

Karin joined in, yelling so loudly she made Watters wince.

It was not long before the same ship's corporal arrived, unlocking the door, and barging in with a smile on his face and a short rattan cane in his hand. 'Now then; what's all the noise? You be good little prisoners and keep quiet, or I'll have to do something about you!'

'There's a bomb on board,' Watters shouted. 'The Russians have planted a bomb!'

'Of course, they have,' the corporal pressed his broken nose against Watters's and lowered his voice to a menacing hiss. 'They sailed up the Thames this afternoon, planted a bomb and sailed away.'

'I am Sergeant Watters of Scotland Yard,' Watters began until the corporal pushed him against the wall of the brig and gripped his throat. The smile vanished.

'Any more of your nonsense and I will put you in irons with a metal gag in your mouth,' the corporal said.

Watters curbed his anger. 'Could you fetch the officer on watch please, corporal. I need to talk to him urgently.'

The corporal withdrew a pace. 'You recognise my rank then. What are you, a deserter from the service?'

'No, I am Sergeant—'

'I heard all that,' the corporal said, 'and I no more believe it now than I did a few moments ago.'

As Watters and the corporal traded insults, Karin quietly lifted the hem of her skirt, slipped out of the door, and fled.

'Hey, you! Stop!' The corporal made a lunge at her and swore as Watters barged into him. Both men collapsed onto the deck in a confusion of arms and legs.

'Officer!' Karin shouted. 'I need an officer!'

'You little minx!' The corporal roared. Pushing himself to his feet, he made a fist and lunged at Watters, who sidestepped and landed a punch of his own before following Karin into the corridor, kicking the door shut as he did so. He heard the corporal roar with anger and hoped he could outdistance him. Carrying so many bruises, he was certainly not at his best.

'What's all the noise?' The lieutenant was about thirty with sharp eyes and a uniform so pristine Watters wondered how he could do anything nautical at all. He had to bend to fit his six-foot-plus into the low headroom below deck. 'What the devil is that woman doing on the ship?'

'I am Mrs Karin Stegall, wife of Wolfgang Stegall of the Austrian delegation to the diplomatic talks,' Karin adopted her most lofty tones while still using all the power of her wondrous eyes, 'and I demand an audience with the captain.'

'To the devil with your demands,' the lieutenant looked her up and down. 'No blasted foreign woman is demanding anything on a British ship, by God.' He stopped. 'Austrian you say?'

Karin had the sense to be polite. 'That is correct. I am the wife of an Austrian diplomat.'

'Good God.' The lieutenant shook his head. 'You look more like a guttersnipe from the sewers. So you're Austrian, are you?' He changed language and asked her a question in German, to which Karin responded, straightening her back and singing a few bars of a song.

The lieutenant nodded, spoke again in German and looked at Watters, 'and who are you, the blasted king of Prussia?'

'No, sir. I am Sergeant George Watters of Scotland Yard, and I am here to inform you that there we think there is at least one bomb planted on board this ship.'

The lieutenant frowned. 'Wait now, I've heard about you. Your name was in the *Thunderer* the other day. Did you not defuse a bomb that was outside the Houses of Parliament?'

'I did, sir,' Watters agreed.

The lieutenant nodded. 'Smart work, Sergeant.' His eyes inspected Watters up and down. 'You've had some rough times, I'd say. And you think there is a bomb aboard *Royal Albert*?'

'I believe so, sir. There are a couple of Russians loose in London with half a shipload of bombs. They shot my colleague, Detective Silver.'

The lieutenant frowned. 'We can't have that, can we?' His eyes narrowed. 'I thought that it was an Irishman that tried to bomb parliament.'

'It was, sir, but now we know that the Russians were behind it.'

'I see. We can deal with the Russians later. Let's find this bomb first.' He turned on his heel. 'I am Lieutenant Fisher.' He looked up as the broken-nosed corporal pounded along the corridor. 'Corporal Adams! Rouse your men, I want all hands alert.'

'Yes, sir,' Adams glanced at Watters. 'Sorry, sir, my prisoners escaped.'

'This is Sergeant Watters of the Yard,' Fisher announced, 'you will call him sir. The lady is Mrs Stegall, a very important personage from Austria. You will call her ma'am.' He looked at Karin. 'They have been through some rough times trying to save our ship.'

'I see, sir,' Adams said.

'By God!' Fisher said as a sudden thought struck him. 'It would be a bad thing if the bomb went off while the Admiral was on board. Admiral Dundas is coming here at seven in the morning, with a host of foreign dignitaries and what-nots,' he smiled at Karin, 'including a delegation from the Imperial Austrian navy as it happens.'

'Yes, sir,' Watters said. 'We believe that Admiral Dundas may be the intended target of the bombers.'

'Is that so? I'll have no foreigners playing silly games on my ship.' He looked at Karin. 'I mean no offence to Austria of course.'

Karin smiled back and dropped in a curtsey. 'Of course not, Lieutenant.'

'Up to the quarterdeck, Sergeant, and we'll speak to the captain.'

Within a few moments of Fisher's shout, the ship was alive with men and officers. Despite the hour, Captain Mends wore a full dress uniform that augmented his frown and his broad shoulders.

'Scotland Yard?'

'Yes, sir,' Watters was aware he looked nothing like a respectable Scotland Yard detective.

'You have one hour to prove this bomb exists, Watters.' Mends did not look impressed. 'After that, my men will prepare for my visitors, and we will have other things in mind apart from your ramblings.' He shook his grey head. 'I can't imagine how the Russians could have placed a bomb on board a Royal Naval ship.'

'Nor can I, sir,' Watters said. 'Unless one of the seamen did it.'

'Not my men,' Mends said flatly.

'Sir,' Watters began, 'I can think of no other way. We have already discovered that this organisation includes some Irish deserters.'

'Not my men,' Mends repeated. 'And not on my ship. I have Irish seamen who are as loyal to Her Majesty as any Englishman born.' Turning aside, he called his officers together. 'We have work to do!' He nodded to Watters. 'You will wait on the quarterdeck with me, Watters, until we resolve this situation.'

The next hour saw the crew search every quarter of the vessel from the topmasts to the lowest deck. Watters could only watch, aware of the cold dislike from officers and crew as one by one the officers reported to Mends, saluted, and informed him that there were no bombs in their area. At ten minutes before six, Mends approached Watters.

'Nothing, Watters, and my men know every possible hiding place on this ship.'

'Yes, sir, yet I am certain that I am right. We are dealing with the same group, the same people that planted the bombs at the Houses of Parliament. If I am right—'

'If is the word, Sergeant Watters. If is the word.'

'With respect, sir, I suggest that you cancel the visit of Admiral Dundas and the dignitaries. Their lives are not safe.'

Captain Mends' frown must have terrified his underlings. 'My men have wasted an hour searching my ship when they should have been making ready for the Admiral. You have one last chance, Watters. What made you think there was a bomb on my ship?'

As Watters explained the sequence that had led to his deduction, Mends' face closed further. 'This is utter speculative nonsense, Watters, based on what?' He answered his own question. 'It is all based on the possibility that a name from Irish mythology may refer to Admiral Dundas?' He shook his head. 'Do you expect me to tell the Admiral that he cannot come aboard and that dignitaries from the allied powers and hopeful allied powers cannot visit the pride of the Royal Navy because of a possible threat based on a name from an ancient Irish story?'

Watters took a deep breath. 'Yes, sir, I do. It is better than having them killed on a Royal Navy ship, which would do more damage to the alliance than a mere cancelled appointment. You can't take the risk, sir.'

Mends' face tautened even further. 'Don't presume to tell me what to do on a vessel under my command, Watters.' He turned to Fisher. 'There is no blame attached to you, Fisher. You did your duty. Now forget this nonsense and return the men to their duties. I want a full ceremonial reception for the Admiral. And you, sir,' he faced Watters, 'keep yourself and that woman out of view. I don't want you disgracing the ship. Fisher, put them both back in the brig. We will be safe from their nonsense there.'

'Yes, sir.' Fisher nodded to Watters. 'Come with me, Sergeant. You know the way.'

'You must not let the ceremony continue,' Karin said. 'There will be deaths!'

'Take them away, Fisher.'

With a body of scarlet-coated marines ready and perhaps eager to intervene, Watters knew there was no point in resisting. He led the way back below decks.

'You must find that bomb,' Watters said as he entered the brig.

'I have my orders to put you in the brig,' Fisher said, 'and that is what I will do.' He joined them inside. 'Was it a powerful bomb at parliament? Did it have sufficient explosive to sink the ship?'

Watters shook his head. 'No, sir. It was a pipe about two feet long packed with gunpowder ignited with a simple fuse. The powder would explode and burst the pipe, spreading fragments of metal. It would not be sufficiently powerful to damage the structure of a ship, but I do not know how many of these bombs were delivered here yesterday.'

'Nobody except you and members of the crew has entered this ship since yesterday,' Fisher said. 'And nobody has boarded with any package or bundle.'

'Perhaps one of the crew has planted one or two of these weapons,' Watters said.

Fisher had a disconcertingly direct stare. 'If I had a weapon such as you describe,' he said, 'I would do one of two things. Either place it in the powder magazine to blow the ship apart or use it to cause mayhem with the Admiral and the dignitaries.'

'You must continue to search!' Watters insisted.

'Please, Lieutenant Fisher.' Karin put both hands on his shoulders.

'I am under orders,' Fisher said. 'You heard the captain.' He stepped outside and shut the door. The sound of the key turning in the lock was deafening in the cell.

'We're going to die here,' Karin said.

'Perhaps,' Watters said. 'Do you have anything that I could use to pick the lock? Some feminine knick-knack, a hairpin or something?'

Karin shook her head. 'Even if you get us out, what will we do?'

'I'll speak to the blasted Admiral if I have to, and you can speak to the Austrian fellow. By God, I'll not let these bastards win. They killed William Silver!'

'Oh!' Karin put a hand to her mouth. 'Somebody's coming.'

The key scraped in the lock, and the door opened again. Fisher stood there. 'Still here? I thought you would have wriggled your way out of here by now, Sergeant. Look.' He put a neatly folded bundle of what looked like cloth on the deck. 'There are over a thousand men on this ship, most of whom do not yet know each other as they have arrived in dribs and drabs over the last two weeks. The captain only took over a few days ago, and even he is not officially in command of the vessel until next month.' Fisher grunted. 'As you see, nobody will recognise a strange face.' He pointed to the bundle. 'These are seaman's uniforms. I took the liberty of finding a boy's uniform for you, Mrs Stegall, it's the best I could do.' He hesitated a little. 'I am sorry it is not more ladylike.'

Karin glanced down at her ragged and stained clothing. 'I am hardly dressed like a lady,' she said.

'You will get into trouble if we are not in the brig,' Watters warned.

'My orders were to put you in the brig, and that is what I have done,' Fisher said. 'What you do now is up to you. You know where best to look.' He placed a key on top of the bundle and closed the door behind him. He did not lock it.

Watters glanced at Karin, who gave a small smile. Her eyes were bright.

'Shall we?' She indicated the piles of clothing.

Neither mentioned decorum as they turned their backs, discarded their sadly battered clothing, and scrambled into the stiff uniforms. Despite Watters's resolve to maintain a decent distance, he glanced over at Karin, met her gaze as she did the same to him, and both hurriedly looked away.

'You look very dashing,' she said when they emerged, awkward and uncomfortable, in their stiff new attire. 'I do like a man in uniform.'

'You look very fetching yourself.' He kept his gaze firmly on Karin's face as she wriggled her hips and turned around.

'These are very tight,' Karin whispered as if afraid the walls would hear. 'I had better be careful not to bend too far.'

'Indeed,' Watters glanced down. She was positively indecent but also utterly enchanting. When he looked up again, Karin was watching him over her shoulder, eyebrows raised and eyes bright.

'On you go,' Watters said.

They left the brig quietly with Watters thankful that the crew were busy on ceremonial duties so only an occasional sailor hurried past. Lanterns provided dim illumination to the interior of the ship as Watters led the way down companionways and through narrow passageways that took them into the depths.

'Where are we going?' Karin asked, 'we'll soon be out of the bottom of the ship!'

'The powder magazine is below the water line so the crew can flood it in an emergency,' Watters said.

'If the bomb goes off when we are down here,' Karin looked over her shoulder, 'it's a very long way back.'

'Don't think about it.' Watters thought it best not to say that if the bomb exploded in the magazine, there would be nothing left of them except a memory.

As Watters expected, the magazine was securely locked. He indicated the rack of felt slippers that stood by the door. 'Put these on,' Watters said. 'They are to ensure you don't make sparks with your feet.' He took the key Fisher had left and inserted it into the lock. It turned smoothly, and he pushed the door open.

The magazine was empty.

Watters looked around, not sure if he was relieved or disappointed. 'There is not a single barrel of gunpowder in here,' he said, 'so there is no point in the Russians planting a bomb.'

'That's a good thing, isn't it?' Karin asked. 'It means that the Russians can't blow us up.'

'It also means that they must be going for the admiral and the dignitaries,' Watters said. 'It will be much more difficult to find a bomb amongst the crowd that will be on deck than it would be down here.'

By the time Watters and Karin emerged onto the upper deck, most of the crew had formed into orderly ranks. The men were arrayed in dark blue jackets, while a body of scarlet-coated marines guarded the quarterdeck. As they clattered onto the main deck, Watters and Karin nearly barged into Fisher.

'Blasted foreigners!' Fisher swore under his breath, 'always disorganised and wanting to change things at the last moment!' He tugged at his collar in frustration. He glanced at Watters and allowed his eyes to rest far longer on Karin, 'I don't mean you, Madam.'

'Of course not, Lieutenant Fisher.'

'You two better stay near me. You may be dressed like seamen, but you'll be found out in seconds if the Admiral gives any orders. Did you have any luck below decks?'

'Nothing in the powder magazine,' Watters reported. 'Not even any powder. What's happening here?' He indicated a scene of confusion on deck as a group of smart seamen broke off from the main formation and clustered around two officers.

'Oh, first a blasted marine was sent to us at the last minute, and then a couple of Prussians wanted to join the fun. They say they've been attached to the visiting delegation and demanded a tour of the ship. Now they're off on some personal inspection tour. 'Bloody lobsters and bloody, bloody foreigners!' He looked again at Karin and cleared his throat. 'I did not mean you, Madam.'

'Of course not, Lieutenant,' Karin's eyes were laughing.

'You are always welcome on this ship,' Fisher tried to make amends.

'Thank you, Lieutenant,' Karin gave a small curtsey.

'Here comes the main body now,' Fisher said as a bosun's pipe trilled. He looked along the deck as the erect ranks stood to attention to receive the visitors, with other seamen standing in the rigging with the wind flapping their trousers around their legs.

Admiral Sir George Whitley Deans Dundas was a balding, pouchy-faced officer of about seventy. He looked around him at the assembled seamen, acknowledged the captain's salute with grace and led the entourage of black-suited dignitaries onto the deck.

'Where have those blasted Prussians got to, I want to know,' Fisher said under his breath.

'Oh!' Karin took a deep breath and slid behind Watters. 'Hide me, please.'

'What the devil?' Watters asked.

'That's Wolfgang, my husband.'

'God, so it is.' Watters recognised him from the Stationer's Hall.

'He's an ugly looking brute,' Fisher muttered, and added, 'I do apologise, miss, I meant no offence.'

'The truth should never be offensive, Lieutenant Fisher,' Karin said graciously.

Wolfgang Stegall stepped on board with his face set and his eyes seemingly critical of everything that he saw. He said little and barely acknowledged the salutes from the sailors. For a moment, Watters wondered how a lively, vivacious woman such as Karin could end up with a bloodless creature, and then pushed the thought away to concentrate on the matter in hand. Admiral Dundas led the visitors forward, halted briefly in the bows with Mends pointing out the intricacies of the ship's rigging and the figurehead of *Prince Albert*, then began to walk to the stern.

If I were to plant a bomb, where would I put it? Watters glanced along the deck, where the seamen lined the route Admiral Dundas and the diplomats would take. *What would the bomber's object be? It would be to kill or injure the admiral and as many of the visitors as possible, to create friction between allies, end any possibility of Austria joining in the war on Britain's side and embarrass the Royal Navy and Great Britain as much as possible.*

In that case, Watters thought desperately, *the bomb, or bombs, would not be placed where there were many Royal Naval seamen. Their bodies would take the impact, and the powers-that-be would not consider their lives as valuable as those of high-ranking officials.*

'Lieutenant Fisher, is there anywhere that the Admiral and the diplomats are alone, without many sailors around them?'

Fisher frowned, obviously walking his mind through Dundas's intended route. 'There are only half a dozen seamen and a couple of marines on the quarterdeck. All the senior officers will be there, and Captain Mends will explain the workings of the ship to the Admiral and Johnny Foreigner.'

'And after that?' Watters saw Wolfgang looking in his direction and shifted slightly to shield Karin.

'They leave.' Fisher had perfected the knack of speaking without seeming to move his mouth.

'Then Markovic will strike on the quarterdeck,' Watters decided. 'That is where I would plant the bomb.' He watched as the admiral approached with the dignitaries at his heels. He kept his face immobile as first the admiral, and then Captain Mends glanced at his dirty face. Mends frowned but did not linger, then they were past and walking toward the stern. A sudden movement caught his attention as Fisher looked aft.

'There are the blasted Prussians now, damn them.'

Watters followed the direction of Fisher's eyes. Ignoring the admiral's party, the pair of Prussians marched to the portside ladder that led to the quarterdeck. He flinched.

'Jesus,' Watters said, 'that's the Russians!'

'What?' Fisher stared aft.

'The Prussians,' Watters explained quickly. 'They're not Prussian, they're Russian.' He was moving even as he spoke.

Standing in disciplined lines, only the eyes of the crew swivelled as Watters rushed past with Karin, her femininity only enhanced by her boy's uniform, two steps behind him.

'That's a woman,' he heard somebody mutter. 'Look at her arse.'

'Where d'you think I'm looking?'

'Eyes front,' an officer ordered and added, 'Good God in heaven.'

'Here. Get back in formation, you!' Corporal Adams challenged them. 'Oh it's you two again. Where the hell are you going?'

'It's all right, Adams, they're with me,' Fisher said. 'Stand by for fireworks, man.'

'Aye, aye, sir,' Adams saluted smartly while simultaneously managing to look bewildered.

Two short flights of stairs led to the quarterdeck, one on the port side and one on the starboard. The supposed Prussian officers mounted the port side stairs and vanished on the quarterdeck as the Admiral led his party aft. Watters saw Captain Mends frown at this unheralded invasion of his ship, with the Admiral apparently not willing to admit his confusion about this second group of dignitaries on his tour.

'Don't give them time to plant any bombs,' Watters tried to dive forward, but Fisher restrained him.

'You can't jump in front of an admiral!'

'I'm trying to save his life, Fisher!'

'We don't do certain things in the Navy,' Fisher said. 'Tradition demands it.'

The second that Admiral Dundas passed, the Russians stepped toward the port side stairs. The Admiral put his hands on the starboard stairs that climbed to the quarterdeck, turned to speak to Captain Mends and pulled himself up the first few steps.

The Russians did not appear to hurry as both parties passed each other, moving in opposite directions and with polite, if slightly perfunctory salutes.

What is best to do? Warn the Admiral or challenge the Russians? Watters debated for only a moment before he opened his mouth in a shout that shattered the orderly peace of the Navy.

'Master at Arms! Arrest these men, they are Russians.' He pointed to the two intruders. As the Admiral turned to see what the fuss was, Watters shouted again, 'Admiral Dundas! There is a bomb on the quarterdeck!'

Captain Mends stiffened with anger as Admiral Dundas glared at Watters as if he was a circus freak. Watters saw Wolfgang's expression become even more unpleasant as he stared at his wife in the dress of a common seaman. One by one, the diplomats turned to face Watters, and he saw their mouths move as they registered their anger or surprise at his words.

The Russians immediately broke into a run with Markovic in the lead and the silent, debonair man a couple of steps behind. A young seaman stepped forward to challenge, but Markovic easily thrust him aside, knocking him to the deck. The Master-at-Arms and Adams appeared, both burly, whiskered men with years of salt-water experience and no fear of Russians, devils, or anything else. Markovic evidently recognised they would be sterner opposition, altered direction and ran directly for the rail until Watters plunged forward to head him off.

'Markovic!' Watters shouted. The scar on the Russian's forehead seemed to throb as Watters felt the hatred mount within him.

'You murdered Silver, you bastard,' Watters feinted for Markovic's eyes with his left fist and threw a full-force right-hander that would have knocked the Russian down if it had connected. Markovic anticipated the blow, blocked, and retaliated with a straight fingered chop to Watters's throat. Watters jerked his head back, so the Russian made only marginal contact, enough to slow Watters down while not robbing him of the power to breathe.

Without a word, Markovic leapt into the murky waters of the Thames. Watters put a hand on the rail to vault over and follow, just as the elegant Russian barged into him, knocking him against a gun mounting. Watters sprawled there, swearing, as the Russian pulled a pistol from inside his uniform and pointed it at the Master-at-arms.

'Threaten me on my own ship, would you?' The Master-at-Arms face altered from professional interest to outright anger. He did not

falter in his advance. In a working lifetime of dealing with unruly seamen, he would have faced a hundred threats, so a firearm was only a
different weapon.

The sound of the shot made many of the assembled seamen flinch
while Captain Meads roared an order.

'Subdue that murdering Russian!'

Watters could only spare a single glance for the drama on deck. He
saw the Master-at-Arms falling, with bright blood bubbling from his
shoulder and a knot of seamen jumping on the Russian, fists pumping.
He saw Lieutenant Fisher leading a section of cutlass men, and Karin
watching, yelling encouragement, and then other matters demanded
his attention.

Markovic hit the water in a knife-edged dive that split the water
clean and hardly raised a ripple. Watters saw him surface a few yards
away, glanced behind him at the confusion on deck and decided that
Markovic would have to wait.

'There's a bomb on the quarterdeck,' he said.

'So I heard.' Ignoring the Admiral, Corporal Adams beat him up the
companionway by a good yard. He looked around. 'That'll be it over
there, then? The thing that's having a little smoke to itself.'

'That'll be it,' Watters tried to sound as nonchalant as the corporal.
At first, he could not see any smoke until he followed the direction of
Adams' gaze. The bomb was placed at waist height behind the wheel so
that wicked wooden splinters would have joined the fragmented casing and spread out around the entire quarterdeck. Two marine sentries
stared stolidly ahead, waiting for orders.

Without seeming to hurry, Adams reached the bomb first and tossed
it over the side as casually as if it had been a chicken leg. It landed
with a small splash and sunk under the water leaving only ripples and
a small plume of smoke.

'That's that, then,' Adams said. 'Better if you washed your face before you wear that uniform, Sergeant Watters.'

The cry was nearly incoherent as the nearer of the marines lowered his musket and charged straight at Watters, bayonet fixed and mouth and eyes wide.

'Yellowford!' Watters had an instant of recognition as the man lunged at him, and then he sidestepped frantically to avoid the wickedly sharp bayonet.

Yellowford's shout was a mixture of frustration, grief, and hatred as he slashed at Watters. 'You bastard, you ugly peeler bastard!'

That was how long it took for Adams and the second marine to reach them. The ship's corporal parried the blow as the marine felled Yellowford with his clubbed musket.

'You're not a popular man today, are you?' Adams was still smiling. 'Who is this beauty?'

Watters gasped. 'I do not know. I honestly do not know.' He looked up as Alba joined them, smiling softly.

* * *

'Yellowford's real name is Private Patrick Gallagher,' Alba passed over a glass of rum as they sat in the wardroom with the ships' officers gathered around them. 'Late of the 113th Foot. His colleagues knew him as The Mimic because he could impersonate them.' He gave his usual smile. 'He'll spend the rest of his life in penal servitude.'

'It's a pity Markovic got away,' Watters said.

'Got away?' Alba grinned. 'You underestimate the Royal Navy, Watters.' He glanced out of the nearest porthole. 'Indeed, here he is now. Look over the side.'

Watters looked. Sitting in the centre of a six-oared longboat, Markovic had his hands tied behind his back. He looked up at Watters, held his eyes for a second, and looked away again.

'I hope they hang him.' Watters had never said that about anybody in his life. 'He murdered William Silver.'

Alba glanced at his watch. 'At this precise moment,' he said. 'Detective Silver is in a nice warm bed in hospital, being attended to by a trained doctor while his wife waits at his bedside.'

'Silver is alive?' Watters asked.

'Very much alive and will be for many years to come unless you lead him astray.' Alba's smile broadened into a grin. 'It was Silver who told us about the attack on Admiral Dundas, while Gallagher will tell you exactly who murdered Guardsman Nixon, Watters.'

'Sergeant Watters,' Watters said automatically.

'Indeed,' Alba said. He sighed. I doubt that we're heard the last of this Irish business though, Watters. There is a great deal of bitterness about the Famine, much of it justified.'

Watters nodded. 'We'll just have to cope with whatever occurs. So was Markovic the man we knew as Cuchulain?'

'He was,' Alba said. 'He was an important man in the Russian espionage network, and cleverly used the discontent among some Irish to gather information that might be of use to the Russian army.'

'I doubt that ordinary soldiers and sailors could provide much useful intelligence,' Watters said. 'The *Thunderer* gives as much information as the Czar will ever need.'

Alba sipped at his rum. 'I agree. Russell of the *Times* is Russia's most prolific source of intelligence. We'll have to curb that freedom in future wars.'

'That other Russian fellow, the handsome one who blackmailed Karin Stegall,' Watters said. 'Did you ever find out who he was?'

'He was Markovic's personal assassin, a Cossack trained to do what Markovic ordered.' Alba looked up. 'Talking of Mrs Stegall, I think that lady wishes to speak to you.'

Karin slid beside Watters, as much as ease in the ship's wardroom as she had been at the diplomatic meeting at Stationer's Hall. 'Good day, gentlemen,' she said. 'Mr Alba, may I borrow Sergeant Watters for a short time? There is something I wish to discuss with him.'

Chapter Twenty-Three

'That's one way to get out of your duty!' Watters sat at the side of Silver's bed.

'He could have been killed.' Angela sounded accusing.

'I wasn't, though. That Russian fellow missed.' Silver looked very pale as he lay under the sheets.

Angela touched the bandage on his shoulder. 'That wasn't a miss.'

'He missed anything that mattered,' Silver amended.

'Except your head,' Watters said, 'and that's too dense to hurt.'

'Oh it hurts all right,' Silver said.

Angela squeezed his hand.

'I thought you were dead,' Watters broke an extended silence.

Angela looked away. There was the sharp clicking of a nurse's feet on the floor.

'Is the case all solved now, George?' It was Silver's turn to break the silence. 'Were we right?'

'It was as we worked out,' Watters said. 'With a few differences. The Russians were at the back of it. The fellow we knew as Yellowford was Gallagher, another deserter from the 113th Foot at Chillianwalla. Three of them slipped away, hoping the officers would think they had been killed in the battle. The Sikhs welcomed them as deserters but did not need ordinary infantrymen, so they were passed on from person to person until a Russian agent found them in some godforsaken place on the Afghan border.'

Angela shook her head. 'Poor men. What they must have suffered, in Ireland, in the Army, and now in India. Everybody used them.'

'We are all pawns,' Silver said. 'How did they get back to Britain, George?'

'It seems they already hated us, so it was not hard for the Russians to persuade them to join their organisation. Mother Flannery was the head of the group in London and passed on any information she gathered to Markovic. That elegant looking man was just a Russian killer. We never did learn his name.'

'These poor men,' Angela said. 'The famine in Ireland was terrible.'

'I know,' Watters said softly. 'I don't know how many people suffered and died. I don't know who was to blame if anybody was. I do know that bombs don't choose who they maim or kill, they are indiscriminate.'

'George ... Sergeant,' Silver tried to sit up. 'What about my case, my ghost?'

Watters nodded. 'Oh, yes, the famous ghost. The local beat bobby found him. I was wrong though, it wasn't an apprentice having a lark, it was a middle-aged man trying to scare people into selling their homes so the prices dipped, and he could afford to buy one.'

'That's different,' Angela said brightly as she gently pushed Silver's head back onto the pillow. 'How was he caught?'

'Hesse Square has central gardens with a metal rail around them,' Watters said. 'And our ghost slipped as he climbed them.' He winked at Silver as Angela winced. 'I'll leave the rest to your imaginations.' He leaned closer and whispered in her ear. 'The spikes of the rail caught in his trousers, Angela, he was not damaged.'

'George ...' Angela nodded to Silver, who was looking very weak.

'Of course.' Watters lifted his new hat. 'I'll leave you two in peace.'

Angela accompanied him to the door. 'Will he be all right?' For the first time since Watters had met her, Angela was not smiling.

'He should be,' Watters said truthfully. 'He's a strong man.' He gave a rare smile. 'And he's too good not to recover. Scotland Yard needs men such as him.'

'So do I,' Angela said softly.

'He will get better for you,' Watters said. 'He's one of the best,' he lowered his voice, 'but for God's sake, don't tell him I said that.'

Putting on his hat, Watters winked, stepped outside, and allowed the rain to ease the smile from his face. He had some important news to break to Rowena and was not sure how to tell her.

* * *

'Well, Rowena,' Watters removed his hat and sat on the chair beside the fire. He patted the chair opposite. 'Please join me. You have been here for a month now.'

'Yes, George,' Rowena sat opposite, her face suddenly grave.

Watters took a deep breath and poked at the fire, gathering his nerve. 'You may not like what I have to say next.' He tried to show no emotion at the expression of dread that crossed Rowena's face. 'I've been thinking this for a couple of weeks,' he said, 'and I've decided that I have no real need for a housekeeper.'

Rowena closed her eyes and slowly opened them again. Watters saw her shoulders droop. When she spoke, her voice was flat.

'I will pack up and leave,' Rowena said quietly.

'I have fixed my eye on a certain lady,' Watters continued. 'I have not asked for her hand yet, and she may not agree. If she does or does not, my domestic arrangements will alter.'

'I saw the way that Austrian lady looked at you,' Rowena's quiet voice could not hide the quiver. 'I knew what she wanted.'

'It is not her I wish to ask, Rowena,' Watters said softly. 'She told me that she is reconciled with her husband once more.' He altered his gaze from the flames to Rowena's face. 'It is you. Would you do me the honour of becoming my wife?'

Watters heard the hiss of the fire as he waited for her answer. 'We'll need more cups in our house,' Rowena said, 'and another chair or two. I'm not keeping a house like a barn.'

'Does that mean you accept?'

'Of course I'll accept,' Rowena said. 'On one condition.'

'What is that?'

'You call me by my middle name. Marie. I much prefer it.'

Watters could not control his smile. 'I can do that, Marie.' Standing up, he took her in his arms.

After a lifetime of not caring about his future, now he had somebody who mattered. Life would never be the same again, and in the best possible way.

Dear reader,

We hope you enjoyed reading *The Atlantic Street Murder*. Please take a moment to leave a review, even if it's a short one. Your opinion is important to us.

Discover more books by Malcolm Archibald at https://www.nextchapter.pub/authors/malcolm-archibald

Want to know when one of our books is free or discounted? Join the newsletter at http://eepurl.com/bqqB3H

Best regards,

Malcolm Archibald and the Next Chapter Team

The story continues in:

Murdered on the 13th

To read the first chapter for free, please head to:
https://www.nextchapter.pub/books/murdered-on-the-13th

About the Author

Brought up in Edinburgh, educated in Dundee, Malcolm Archibald has a master's degree in History. Married to Cathy for nearly forty years, he is a prize-winning author, whose interests include nautical, military, and social history.

The Atlantic Street Murder
ISBN: 978-4-86747-435-8

Published by
Next Chapter
1-60-20 Minami-Otsuka
170-0005 Toshima-Ku, Tokyo
+818035793528
28th May 2021

Lightning Source UK Ltd.
Milton Keynes UK
UKHW010208300922
409676UK00001B/22